Laurie Y. Elrod

Blackridge

Book One of the So'ladiun

A LEXOGAN PUBLICATION

Blackridge
A Lexogan Book

Published by
Lexogan Publishing

Cover Art, Map, and Design
Laurie Y. Elrod

Library of Congress Control Number: 2013909367

ISBN 978-0615809588

www.laurieyelrod.com

First, as always, all glory to God.
And for my beautiful family, who I love more than life itself.

Dragon
Isle

ANDERAN

Barren Flats

North
Province

Trapper's Way
Lakeshore Glen

Salidair Lake Wilderness

Laurel Grove

Northreach

Salidair

Bald Mountain
Quarry

Abideen

Veihl
Ocean

Fort Denmar

Greystones

Cowethe Forest

Isle of
Boathen

Glimmerdale

Boathen

Agadar

Midland
Province

Kit

Chance's Hearth

Green River
Hollow

Tuhnichi

Jungepointe Hills

West Province

Il Kaffa

Straithe Wood

Rheine

Southern
Province

Hemonstead

Marmuht

Marmuht Bay

Murango

Desert Stone

Brackenwood
Cove

Traphyt

Chyrzah

Village of Xyphra

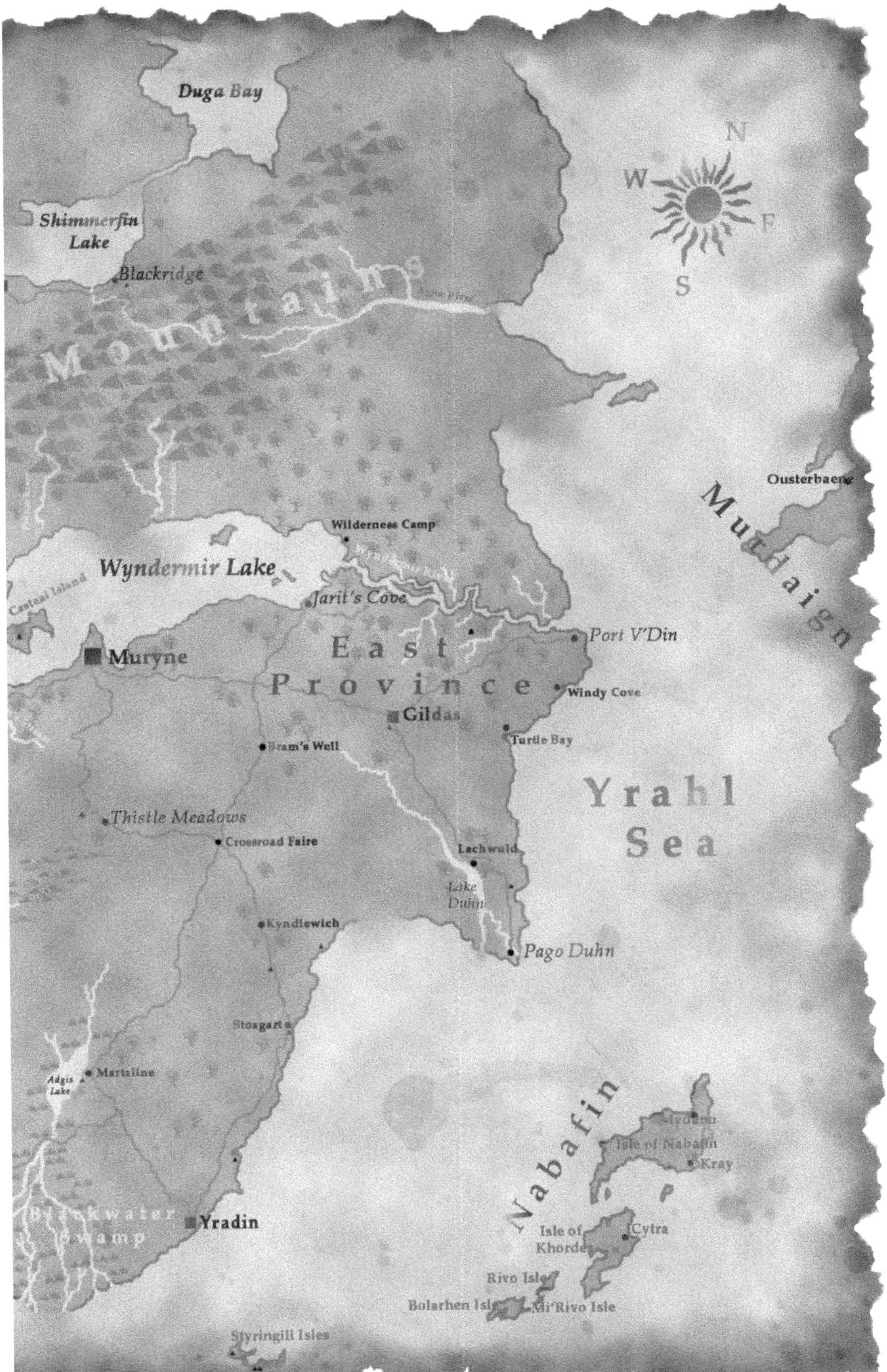

Duga Bay
Shimmerfin Lake
Blackridge
Mountains
N
W
E
S
Ousterbaene
Wilderness Camp
Wyndermir Lake
Casteal Island
Jarit's Cove
Muryne
East Province
Port V'Din
Windy Cove
Gildas
Turtle Bay
Bram's Well
Yrahl Sea
Thistle Meadows
Crossroad Faire
Lachwuld
Lake Duhn
Kyndlewich
Pago Duhn
Stoagart
Adgis Lake
Martaline
Nabafin
Isle of Nabafin
Kray
Blackwater Swamp
Yradin
Isle of Khorde
Cytra
Rivo Isle
Bolarhen Isle
Mi'Rivo Isle
Styringill Isles

Obsudius, God of Do'athra, strode to the parapet of his keep and observed the valley cove spread out before him. The entire dismal landscape from one mountain range to the other was filled with his creations—his Do'athrim. Soon all would be ready, and he would open the Rift and allow his children to leave his realm of the dead and enter the plane of the living.

He allowed his lips to spread upward into a smile, an unnatural and rare formation that felt strange to his face.

His twin brother, Solisius, would see and recognize the threat to his people, but would not know the true scope of the plan. Little by little, everything Solisius held dear would start to disappear, and the noble God of Ts'aura would send his beloved So'ladiun warriors running to try and stem the series of events Obsudius had put in motion—but Solisius would be too late. His weak and far too few children of power would not be able to withstand the tide that was already in motion to carry Solisius' beloved human race into oblivion, thus ensuring the God of Light's own reason for existence to come to a complete and irrevocable end.

Obsudius turned his back on the valley and with a flick of his fingers transported himself thousands of leagues away to a new destination, an island far out in the ocean region, immersed in a supernatural blanket of mist.

Again, he smiled to himself, pleased with what he saw as he looked beyond the veil of his realm and through the mists of his own design.

Yes, he would have this world his father, The Creator, failed to give him in the beginning for his own.

Prologue

"Elhrin, I want you to center yourself and concentrate, seeing in your mind what you want to happen," Master Gryph said, pulling a dark red apple out of his coat pocket. Tall and lean, he stood at ease next to a moss-covered boulder lying at the edge of the river.

Elhrin nodded at her mentor, Gryphon Idwyr, who was a master of the art of magic and had been teaching her how to use and control her special abilities since she was eight years old. Always seeking any excuse to be near any body of water that held fish, he had decided to conduct their lesson for the day beside the Green River situated on the outskirts of their village.

She wondered if he had an ulterior motive for picking one of his favorite fishing holes other than to have her practice her magic, but thought, maybe not, since he did not bring his fishing gear. But then again, thinking back to the times she had seen him use magic to scoop a large trout or catfish out of the water, she knew the lack of fishing gear would not stop him if he wanted fish for supper.

A stiff breeze blew across the river, and a flurry of red and gold leaves detached from their summer long perches to swirl and spiral along its unseen currents. They dropped silently onto the surface of the water and floated downstream like a flotilla of tiny colorful ships. Fall was here, and that meant winter would soon be on its heels.

"Ouch," she heard Bayle grumble. She looked over her shoulder at her brother. He was suckling on his forefinger and jerked it out when he saw her looking at him.

"The hook got me," Bayle said, producing a sloppy wet finger.

She didn't see anything wrong. "Trying to work here," she said annoyed, thinking maybe she should have left home without mentioning to her mother that Master Gryph had planned for them to practice at the river today within Bayle's hearing. Her mentor's passion for fishing had rubbed off on her younger brother, and he had insisted on coming along. "Could you go somewhere else?"

"Elhrin, are you paying attention?" Master Gryph asked. He held up the apple and waved it dramatically back and forth in the air for her to see. "Don't worry about what Bayle is doing. See the apple?"

"Yes, sir," she rolled her eyes at his dramatic waving. Sometimes, he treated her as if she were still eight instead of seventeen.

"Good. I know you already know how to do this, but remember we are working on control and precision. Magical instinct without thought," he said, and started to place the apple on the rock, but then decided to take a huge bite out of it before he put it down.

"Why did you do that?" Elhrin asked.

He wiped the apple's sticky juices from his mustache and beard with his sleeve. "No sense in wasting a good apple altogether," he grinned, chewing noisily. He trod back across the soft sand with a slight limp—the result of an injury he received long ago.

She watched him check to make sure Bayle was out of the way before he glanced down at her. "I want you to throw the apple to me," he said, raising his left arm and opening his hand to give her a target. "I will allow you to take your time this first try, but it will go quick after that. As soon as I catch the apple I will then toss it back into the air and tell you the next destination for it to go. You will grab it and move it to the target. The goal is to hit it dead on. Do you understand?"

"Yes, sir," Elhrin wiped her palms on her trousers and took a deep breath, feeling the brisk air fill her lungs. She centered herself as he had taught her, raised her right hand toward the apple and let the energy of her magic flow through her, willing it out of her fingertips and projecting it toward the apple. She wrapped the magical strands of energy around the apple tightly, and then recalled the flow back a little more forcefully than she had intended. As a result, she lost her magical grip on the apple and it shot off the rock toward them in a high arc, but flew well over Master Gryph's hand to hit Bayle precisely on the side of his head.

"Ow!" he yelled, clapping a hand to his head. His fingers disappeared beneath the thick waves of sandy hair, rubbing the bruise that was now sure to be there. The apple had hit him quite hard. "What did you do that for, Elhrin?"

Elhrin hid a smile behind her hands. She was trying not to laugh because it probably did hurt, but she had to admit it was funny that out of all the places it could have landed, it had been his head.

Master Gryph lowered his hand to scratch the neatly trimmed salt and pepper beard that lined his jaw and studied Elhrin's face. She gave him the most innocent face she could muster.

"Don't bat those big green eyes at me, my young apprentice. Did you mean to hit him on purpose?" he asked.

"No, sir, I truly did not," she denied, knowing he probably thought back to last week when she had locked Bayle in the privy so he wouldn't follow her.

She loved Bayle, but he tended to be a distraction. "But I thought the end result wasn't all that bad."

"Yes, but I believe I said to hit a target I chose dead on, not Bayle's head dead on," he stared at her unsmiling, but his eyes were crinkled around the edges. He was trying not to laugh.

She grinned wide and that was all it took. He burst out laughing, reaching out to muss her untamed, dark curls.

"Go ahead, you two. Laugh all you want. That really hurt," Bayle grumbled, smoothing his hair back away from his eyes.

"Sorry, Bayle," she apologized.

He frowned as if he didn't believe her, then knelt on one knee and leaned out over the water to untangle his line from a spindly bramble bush.

She looked back to her teacher, remembering there was something she wanted to ask him. "So, why did you delay your trip to Muryne?"

Officially, he was the Minister of Specialized State Defense for the country of Anderan, and a council session was set to begin later in the week, which he was required to attend, but he had said he could wait a couple of days before he had to travel to Anderan's capital city where the council met.

"I have a few matters to attend to before I go." He used his magic to retrieve the apple that had rolled into the river after hitting Bayle. It hit his hand with a wet smack. "Toome and I promised the boys we would round up a team to play a game of Harpaball tomorrow. I regret that we will have to punish them severely, but they do need to see how the game's played properly."

"Punish us? The only way you over the hill men will beat us," Bayle gave him a sidelong look as he whipped his line across the surface of the river, "is if you cheat to put the ball in the basket. Especially you, your creaky bones aren't going to let you keep up. I'll be running rings around you and all you will see is a cloud of dust."

"Boy, you are asking for a cold dunk in the river," Master Gryph threatened. "I may not be as young as I used to be, but I can still outrun your scrawny self from here to Doogan's barn and back in spite of my bad leg. You just wait until tomorrow, young man. The only cloud of dust I'll see will be from your teenage tail hitting the dirt."

Bayle snorted, "Oh no, old man . . . ."

"Bayle, fish," Elhrin ordered, realizing she better cut him off. He had become increasingly mouthier the older he got, and it had a tendency to land the two of them in the thralls of a competition. Just the day before, they competed to see who could burp the loudest before Master Gryph's wife Marguerite came into the cottage and called them down. Bayle still insists he won.

Elhrin leveled her gaze on the overly tall middle-aged child. "Master Gryph, do you think we could get back to work before you two get side-tracked? I'm just lucky you didn't bring your fishing pole."

"I have to admit, I did think about it," he grinned. "But you are right. The days are short, and we don't have too much longer before the sun sets, so let's move along. I want you to work on this a bit before I show you how to build a shield."

"A shield?" she asked, puzzled. "Can't we just get one from Master Toome?"

"A magical shield, Elhrin," he replied, patiently. "There may be times you will find that you need . . . ."

A distant roar resonated through the trees on the other side of the river cutting off his words. The surrounding forest froze as if time had stopped. Nothing made a sound.

"What was that?" Bayle broke the silence, just as they heard something crashing through the undergrowth of the forest on the other side of the river.

"It's today," Master Gryph whispered. "Elhrin, Bayle, run!" he ordered.

"What?" Elhrin didn't understand what was happening, then a horde of creatures materialized out of the shadows of the forest, zigzagging through the trees, running straight for them. She had never seen anything like them before. From the shoulders down, the creatures had all the features of human soldiers, clad in black leather armor, and armed with an array of swords, bows, and spears. But from the neck up, the creatures' heads looked like the gray and black wolves that roamed the forests of Anderan.

Master Gryph fired a blazing ball of energy across the river. It exploded into the lead monster, ripping its head completely off its body. The horde did not slow at the loss. Some ran headlong into the waist deep river while others ground to a halt at the river's edge and loaded their bows with arrows.

"Do'athrim!" Master Gryph growled. He flung another deadly ball of sizzling energy at those crossing. This one was larger and more powerful. It exploded with a tremendous boom, sending a geyser of water spraying across the far riverbank. The creatures along the bank ducked under the drenching wave of water. The beasts in the river that had been in the lead were gone. A pool of crimson and chunks of flesh swirled around the rest of the creatures in the water. They looked confused, unsure of whether or not to continue to cross, but a forceful yip from one of the larger beasts on the riverbank compelled them to move again.

"You two, go!" Master Gryph commanded.

Elhrin could not move—couldn't take her eyes off of the snarling beasts.

He grabbed her arm and painfully jerked her behind him. "Run!" he ordered. The fury on his face was terrifying. "Go get Toome!"

"Come on!" Bayle grabbed her hand and dragged her with him.

The sound of dozens of bow strings twanged and the rush of arrows penetrated the air. Elhrin instinctively ducked and covered her head as she and Bayle clawed their way up the slippery bank. Arrows fell like rain on either side of them, thumping into the sandbar or thudding into the trunks of trees lining the riverbank. Strangely, none of the arrows came near enough to harm them. She stopped to look back just as they topped the short, but steep incline.

Master Gryph had his arms raised before him—arrows were colliding into an unseen force and bouncing harmlessly into the river. He was protecting them so they could get away.

"What are you stopping for?" Bayle grasped her arm, almost jerking her off her feet. They started into Doogan Phisk's newly harvested corn field, but their way was blocked by a dry irrigation canal he used to water the fields during the dry spells of summer. She and Bayle didn't take the time to run down to the small bridge Doogan had built over the ditch, they jumped into the dusty, hard-packed bottom and started up the other side.

Another explosion echoed across the field.

I can't do this! she thought and slid back to the bottom of the canal.

"Elhrin, what are you doing? Come on!" Bayle yelled.

"I can't leave him!" She whipped around, barely able to see Master Gryph at the river's edge, facing the creatures that were slogging their way through the currents of the river. Arrows thudded all around him and he jerked to the side as if he had been hit, but he did not fall. Getting a grip on her fear, she ran back across the ditch and started to crawl out. Bayle grabbed her arm and whirled her around to face him.

"We need to go get Master Toome," he yelled.

"You go! I have to help. There are too many."

She heard a hideous blood-freezing howl. The beasts were now midway across the river and Master Gryph faced them silently with outstretched arms. A round iridescent sphere flashed into existence above the water in front of him. Pulsing with raw energy, the sphere rapidly expanded to a size as high as the treetops that grew along the water's edge. Even from a distance Elhrin could feel the power contained in the sphere.

The creatures on the far side released another volley of arrows. Elhrin and Bayle watched, transfixed, as the bolts soared over the water like an ocean wave about to break on shore.

BOOM!

Elhrin forced a painful breathe into her lungs. She was lying on her back staring at the sky, not understanding how she came to be on the ground or why her lungs burned.

Faintly, she heard kittens crying. No, that's not right. Trying to clear her mind and focus, she realized she was hearing screams. Awful, howling screams and they were coming from the river. She sat up with a groan, and Bayle struggled to his knees beside her. A few arrows were embedded in the ground around them, but luckily, neither of them had been hit.

"What happened?" Bayle asked, sitting back on his knees and wiping dirt from his face.

"Master Gryph's sphere exploded," she replied, amazed that she could hear anything over the loud ringing in her ears. She struggled to her feet and had to keep herself from falling back down when she saw the level of destruction that lay before her.

"Son of a . . . ," Bayle whispered.

Most of the creatures had been obliterated, and the lazy green waters of the river had turned a sickly deep crimson as blood and body parts floated slowly downstream. The trees along the far side of the river and those that were closest to where Master Gryph had stood were decimated. All that was left was shredded and blackened stumps, sticking haphazardly out of the ground like weathered tombstones in an old graveyard.

The few remaining creatures that had managed to escape the explosion unharmed were in a state of confusion along the far riverbank. They growled and barked in their dog-like language at each other. It was clear they did not know what to do. One large black beast used his bow to point across the river and barked a command the others were willing to follow. They all turned and ran back into the woods.

Elhrin glanced at Bayle, noticing that Master Toome and a group of men from the village were running across the field in their direction. That was why the beasts ran.

"Bayle! Where is Master Gryph? I don't see him," she asked, fear once again pierced through her body.

Bayle scanned the area. "I don't know. Let's go."

They scrambled out of the ditch and ran towards the river.

"There," Bayle pointed to a large rock along the water's edge. Master Gryph was lying in the sand on the other side.

"Oh no! No. No. No," Elhrin cried.

They half-jumped, half-slid down the riverbank and ran to the rock. Master Gryph, pale as death, had half of a shattered arrow embedded in his chest—a dark stain of crimson saturated his shirt around its splintered shaft.

"No!" she screamed, dropping to her knees beside him.

He stirred at her cry. "Elhrin," he said. His deep voice was hoarse with the effort it took for him to speak. He opened his blue eyes that had just moments before sparkled with humor, but were now clouded not with pain like she expected, but with something else—almost like regret.

"Master Gryph, hang on, help is coming. We'll get Marguerite," Elhrin said, as tears began to spill down her face.

Weakly, he lifted a corner of his mouth. Even in this state, he tried to reassure her with a smile. "It is . . . too late," he breathed.

"Don't say that," she said, her heart pounding with fear.

"Elhrin, listen . . . carefully . . . take the pendant . . . around my neck . . . keep it safe." He could hardly speak, having to gasp for air to continue, and she could hear something liquid rattle in his chest every time he paused.

"No, I won't. It is yours," she protested.

"It is . . . yours now . . . do . . . as I say . . . quickly," he ordered, and began to cough. Groaning, his face contorted in pain and a stream of blood poured out of his mouth and flowed into his beard. She reached with shaking hands into the top of his shirt to pull out a luminescent green crystal attached to a gold chain. She opened the clasp and removed the pendant from his neck.

"Put it on . . . never take it off," he gasped, his voice was barely audible and she noticed that his breaths were slowing down.

"Please, Master Gryph, hold on," she sobbed, wiping the blood from his mouth with her sleeve. "Please."

"I'm sorry . . . sweetheart . . . needed . . . tell you . . . not . . . enough time . . .

tell Marguerite I . . . love her . . .'' he closed his eyes tightly, his body convulsed and he stopped breathing. His face slowly relaxed into a peaceful state of eternal slumber.

"Nooooo!" she moaned, her heart breaking into a million pieces. She laid her head on his chest. "Don't go!"

Crying, Bayle sank to his knees and put his arms around her. The men from the village poured down the embankment. Master Blacksmith Lee Toome tore across the sand towards them while the others jumped into the river to go after the retreating creatures on the other side.

"What happened? We heard the explosions and came as fast as we could." He stopped short at the sight of Master Gryph lying on the ground. "Damn," he breathed.

Minister Gryphon Idwyr's funeral was held two days later on a cloudy afternoon that promised rain. The graveyard, situated on a hill above the village of Glimmerdale with a grand view of the distant peaks of the Northreach Mountains, was filled with hundreds of people who knew and loved, and maybe even hated the renowned Minister of Specialized State Defense.

Through the haze of her grief, Elhrin registered the fact that King Goruth and an entourage of councilmen and women from the other Provinces of the Kingdom of Anderan were standing on the other side of the grave from where she and her family stood by Master Gryph's wife, Marguerite. They were the reason his funeral had to wait for two days, so that they could be in attendance. Master Gryph had been a close friend of the king's, the two basically grew up together as young men, and the king had trusted him like no other individual within his close circle. Master Gryph had also held an advisory position on Anderan's High Council and was well respected by most of its members.

Elhrin glanced at the olive-skinned, senior council member from the Southern Province. She was a rare beauty with her sleek black hair and doe eyes. The woman was obviously having a hard time with Master Gryph's death, and Elhrin thought it was strange for the reaction of a colleague to be so different than that of Master Gryph's own wife. Councilor Idora Shulftar looked to be on the verge of a hysterical breakdown while Marguerite stood rigidly by Elhrin's side, allowing no tears to fall down her pale cheeks. But that was who Marguerite was, strong and tough in times of hardship, and not prone to show drastic emotions in public. She would only allow her true grief, her true emotions to flow in the solitude of a time and place of her own choosing.

Elhrin tore her gaze away from Councilor Shulftar as Anderan's Honor Guard, reserved only for the highest members of Anderan's government or military, began to lower the casket into the grave while Father Jerome brought the ceremony to a close. When the casket disappeared, Elhrin closed her eyes, trying to stem the out-of-control emotions that threatened to bring her to her knees and create a scene. Taking a deep, steadying breath, she opened her eyes and found that King Goruth was staring directly at her. His face was set in a mask of hard stone as if he was displeased with her personally. Slowly, he shifted his steely gaze to Marguerite and Elhrin felt a profound sense of relief that the weight of his stare was no longer on her. He knew she had been with Master Gryph on that fateful day. She wondered if he found fault with her for not helping him in some way.

As the service came to an end, the sky darkened noticeably, and a light drizzle began to dampen the hillside. A distant rumble of thunder rolled across the sky. Marguerite put her arm around Elhrin's shoulder and squeezed. Elhrin looked up at the grief-stricken lady she loved like a second mother and felt guilty for being such an emotional catastrophe and unable to give her the support she needed. The woman may appear to be strong to those surrounding the grave, but Elhrin knew the real Marguerite—the woman who had insisted on cleaning and dressing her dead husband's body alone—the woman who had not yet shed a tear—the woman who was waiting for everyone to return to their own lives and leave her to hers. Only then, when she was truly alone, would Marguerite allow herself to fall apart.

Before Elhrin could voice the words she wanted to say to Marguerite, King Goruth walked around the open grave and held out his hand. "Marguerite, would you allow me to escort you back home?" he asked. His gruff voice did not shield the sadness he felt at losing his friend.

Wordlessly, Marguerite nodded and with one last brief squeeze of Elhrin's shoulders, let the king lead her to one of the waiting carriages, followed closely by the rest of Anderan's government officials.

Elhrin stared at the open grave and wanted to scream at the unfairness of the situation. How could they be heading home when he had to remain in the cold unfeeling earth? She allowed the tears to come for what seemed like the thousandth time since he was killed and felt someone clasp her hand. She looked at her mother, "How can he be dead?"

"I know, it does seem impossible," her mother embraced her. "But as Father Jerome said, there is no doubt that he is at peace in the Realm of Light with Solisius. It will be hard for awhile because we will miss him, but you more than anyone knew how he always talked about one day walking with the God of Light in his domain."

Elhrin wiped the tears from her eyes and nodded. He had been a dedicated follower of the teachings of Solisius, the God of Light. She had no doubt he was happily sitting on a riverbank in Solisius' realm of Ts'aura, fishing.

"It will take time for the pain to lessen, but one day it will," Xarah kissed her cheek. "Let's go home."

As they followed the crowd of mourners down the dirt road to the village, a flash of light illuminated the sky in the distance, followed by deep growls of thunder. A storm was coming.

After all mourners left the damp hillside, Nute and Graem pushed away from the large oak tree where they had been waiting and approached the gravesite. Without a word spoken, they stuck their shovels in the nearby mound of dirt and began to fill the grave while the storm that had threatened the nearby countryside finally rolled over the village. Lightning flashed spidery strands across the surface of the ironclad clouds, followed by booming claps of thunder that shook the ground. Occasionally, Nute would glance at the dark, ominous clouds when the thunder felt like it was going to pound them into the earth. He hated storms, but he did not stop his efforts to fill the grave even when the soft pattering of rain turned into a blinding downpour.

Without warning, a flash of light exploded into the oak tree behind Graem.

Both men instinctively dove for cover beside the grave as chunks of bark flew across the graveyard, pelting the tombstones all around them.

"That was too close. What do you think about finishing this when the storm lets up?" Graem said, wiping rivers of water from his eyes with a muddy hand.

"I don't know," Nute said, peering over the edge of the grave. "Do you think there's enough dirt in the hole to protect the casket?"

"It should be okay. It's sealed tight. Let's go."

Graem scrambled to his feet and Nute followed him as he ran down the hill toward the village. By mutual agreement, they decided a few pints were in order while they waited out the storm. The grave was forgotten as soon as the door to the Glimmerdale Inn slammed shut behind them.

Early the next morning the two men returned to fill in the grave, their steps slow and a little unsteady.

"Let's get this over with," Nute said as he ran a hand across his eyes. His head felt two sizes bigger than normal and it pounded as if someone was beating his temples with hammers. "I really need to go home."

"Home is the last place I want to be," Graem said with a grimace as he picked up a shovel off the ground. "My wife . . . what the . . . ?"

"What is it?" Nute asked.

"The lid's up here," Graem pointed at the casket lid lying shattered in the tall grass. He peered down in the hole. "Damn, what happened?"

Nute joined him at the grave. The casket was empty. Its insides were charred and blackened and full of water from the previous night's storm.

"Do you think the storm did this?" Nute asked.

"How should I know?"

"Should I go get the mayor?"

"The man's body is gone, lunkhead, probably dragged off by animals. Do you want to tell Mayor Toome we left this grave without filling it in? He'll cut you down before you can take two steps, and if he doesn't do that, I guarantee he will have us arrested or hanged for leaving it open all night long," Graem growled. "Let's fill it in, and you'd better swear to keep your mouth shut."

"But, Graem, this is important. I really do think we should tell someone."

"NO!" Graem yelled, shoveling a thick chunk of wet mud into the hole. It hit the bottom of the casket with a splashing thump. "Get the damn lid."

Nute watched Graem chunk several shovels full of mud into the hole before he trudged across the grass to pick up the scattered pieces of lid. He knew they weren't the brightest of fellows in the village, but he did know that what they were doing wasn't right. Yet what was he to do? Graem was the only friend he had, and he looked up to him. Going against anything Graem said was unnatural to his way of thinking and, frankly, it just wasn't in him.

Chapter One

Gryzzl made his way down the darkened tunnel and came to a stop when he encountered a new passageway branching off to the left of the one he had just been following. For the past hour, he had been traveling through the caves underneath Casteal Island, a large, densely forested clump of land far out in the sea-like waters of Wyndermir Lake. Twisting and turning, the damp caves were a maze of tunnels and passageways that could disorient the best of experienced explorers. But that didn't bother Gryzzl. He was not afraid of getting lost because he was a Do'athrim wolven, a creation of Obsudius, God of Do'athra, the Realm of Darkness. He was half-human, half-wolf, and Obsudius had enhanced his natural senses, giving him a heightened sense of smell and the ability to see clearly in the dark. Even with the solid blanket of blackness inside the caves, he did not need to carry a light source of any kind.

He contemplated the new passageway and could faintly make out the scent of the one he had killed last fall. The human had not been here recently. The scent was old and almost non-existent as the moisture in the cave had partially washed it away, but it was enough to guide him, and he followed it as it led off into the new passageway. Around him water drops fell from above, ringing loud in the dead silence of the caves as they plopped onto the solid surface of the cave floor. Occasionally, he would stop to listen, fairly certain he was alone, but careful, nonetheless, because he was in dangerous territory. He did not think with the magician dead that he would be alone in this search and the sound of his footsteps and the clanking of his weapons would certainly draw attention if anyone was in the caves.

The roaring of fast moving water reached his pointed ears, and after rounding a sharp bend in the tunnel, he exited the passageway into a large cavern where a waterfall surged out of a black hole high above where he stood to fall into an underground stream that split the length of the cavern. Crouching low, he tested the area for the scent and found it followed a steep path down to the cave floor by the stream.

When he reached the bottom, he stopped. He had lost the scent. Moving up and down the stream, he sniffed repeatedly, looking into the many openings along the cave wall and even the fissure where the stream emptied out of the cavern, but he did not pick up the scent. He decided to cross the stream.

Jumping across rocks jutting out of the water, he made his way to the far side and continued his hunt, searching the openings that dotted this side of the cave, but still could not pick up the scent. Growling with frustration, he turned and noticed that he had overlooked a narrow ledge leading upward along the far wall. He crossed to the path and climbed up. Halfway to the top, he picked up the scent again and followed the path until he reached an opening in the cave wall near the top of the waterfall.

He reminded himself to be wary. The magician had been powerful and would not have left what Gryzzl was after unprotected. His Master, the favorite of Obsudius, told Gryzzl he must not fail. If he did he would be sent to The Void, a place, if you could call it a place, where nothing existed. That terrified Gryzzl, and he did not scare easily.

"I will not fail," he growled low, pushing aside the possibility of no longer existing.

He cautiously entered the passageway and found that it was different from the rest of the caves. The walls didn't seem to be formed naturally, they were almost too smooth—too symmetrical, and they gradually started to narrow, causing him to turn his large body sideways. As he made his way through, light from a strange glow pierced the darkness ahead almost blinding him until his eyesight adjusted.

Finally slipping out of the narrow crevice, Gryzzl found himself in a human-made room. The soft eerie light he had noticed in the passageway came from glowing blue crystals embedded in four stone pillars supporting the ceiling near the center of the room. In the middle of the pillars was a chest-like marble coffer placed upon a stone table.

He surveyed the room, looking for anything that might suggest a trap. Finding nothing, he slowly walked around the perimeter of the room, cautiously inspecting all sides until he reached the passageway opening again without incident.

He took a step toward the table then stopped. Nothing moved in the room, nor did he hear anything except the distant roar of the waterfall. Taking his time, he made his way to the table and froze . . . waiting . . . listening . . . sniffing to test the air. Nothing was out of the ordinary. In the soft blue-hued glow coming from the crystals he could see ages of dust stirred by his passing, wafting along unseen currents, mingling with the damp musky air of the cave.

Deciding that he was safe for the moment, he studied the coffer on the table. Rectangular in shape, it had no markings with the one exception of a burning sun carved into the heavy lid. Gryzzl curled his lip in distaste. The sun was the sign of Solisius, the God of Light, Obsudius' twin brother and eternal enemy. He slid a hand around the entire seam of the lid. There was no handle or hinges attached. Slowly, he slid the heavy cover of the coffer to the side, flinching as it made a loud echoing thud when it slipped from his hand and hit the tabletop. Daring not to breath, he waited. Again, nothing happened. This made him very nervous. His Master had warned him to expect a trap, yet nothing was happening. He had made it here easily—too easy—yet, easy or not, he had to move forward. He peered into the darkened recess of the coffer and let out a howl of frustration. It was empty!

No! This cannot be! Frustrated, he pounded the tabletop with both fists.

CLICK!

Gryzzl froze. For the first time, he noticed the tabletop had been carved with whorls and flowers with dark blue gems embedded in their centers. One of the flowers was pressed down into its surface beneath his fist. Slowly, the coffer on the table began to move to the side with a grinding sound, revealing an opening in the table. Inside was a dark, leather-bound book.

This is the object the Master wanted? A book?

Cautiously, he pulled the book out of its resting place.

SNICK!

All of the blue gems on the table burst to life. Fine rays of light sprayed outward and connected with the crystals on the pillars. The crystals changed from their soft blue hue to an angry red. Two red beams shot from the crystals out of the room through the tunnel. A low rumble sounded from the cavern with the waterfall. The floor began to vibrate and dust sifted down from the ceiling. A solid slab of rock appeared from a hidden crevice at the tunnel's entrance, sliding slowly across the opening to seal off his escape.

Damn! He had set off the trap he had been expecting.

He ran for the tunnel and squeezed into the shrinking gap. Heedless of snaps and buckles being ripped away from his armor, he managed to struggle through before being crushed by the stone seal. But the danger did not end there. All around him rock and dust fell from the ceiling. The tunnel was caving in. He scrambled down the narrow passageway. Hair and skin ripped from exposed flesh as rocks pelted him from above. The passageway started to crumble around him and he thought he wasn't going to make it through, but then he caught sight of the entrance to the grotto with the waterfall. With all the strength from his muscular legs, he launched himself out of the passageway, diving for the safety of the ledge. He landed hard, catching himself in time before falling over the side. The tunnel behind him collapsed. Rock and debris spewed out of the black hole, painfully bashing his body as the chunks of stone covered him and rolled off the ledge to the cavern floor far below. Huffing in a lungful of dusty air, he pushed the debris off of him and staggered to his feet. Below him the entire cave floor was covered in water, and it was rising fast. The hole where the river had exited the cave before was now blocked with fallen rock as were the other openings that lined the cave wall.

Desperately, he looked across the cavern and was relieved to see that the passageway he had come through earlier was only partially blocked with fallen rock. The magician's trap had failed. He skidded down the ledge, nearly falling when his foot slipped over the edge. He regained his balance and scrambled down the rest of the way. When he reached the floor of the cave, he stumbled into waist high water. He held the book over his head, struggling against the strong current threatening to bash him against the far wall. He was only partway across when the water level rose over his head and he had to swim weighted heavily by his broken armor and cumbersome weapons. When he managed to reach the other side without drowning, he pulled himself out of the water and crawled up the steep slope, frantically trying to reach the passageway ahead of the rising water. He had almost made it to the top when he stopped short. He smelled something new—something human. He drew his sword just as a light filtered through the opening, shortly followed by a slight figure carrying a lantern. He growled deep in his throat.

"What an unpleasant surprise," the human said, calmly placing the lantern on a rock. "You have made a mistake in coming here, filthy beast." The human slid a long blade from a leather scabbard.

Gryzzl was surprised to sense no fear from the measly figure. "No, human, you have," he growled, raising his sword, ready for a fight.

"Well, well, the dog can talk," the human said, and pointed at the book. "I will take that."

Gryzzl laughed at the puny human's confidence, an ugly guttural sound.

Without warning the human attacked, slicing downward toward his head. Gryzzl met the attack and was surprised at the human's strength and stamina as he blocked a cunning series of maneuvers. Not the quick, easy kill he was expecting. He sliced to his left and growled in satisfaction when the human had to jump backwards as Gryzzl's sword tip ripped into a shoulder.

"Damn you," the human said angrily, reaching up to touch the wound.

Gryzzl started to swing again, but was caught off guard when the human twisted and kicked him square in the chest, knocking him off his feet and sending him sliding on his back down the path. The book fell out of his hand, landing among a pile of rocks as he came to a halt with a splash into the edge of the rising water. Rolling over, he scrambled to his feet, stepping ankle deep into the water. The human slid down the slope, and attacked. Gryzzl ducked as the sword swept harmlessly over his head, and he started to retaliate, but an intense pain exploded on the side of his head. He howled and dropped to his knees, clutching his eye where the human's sword hilt had slammed into his face. As blood streamed through his fingers, he felt something sharp penetrate the thick fur on his neck and froze, knowing his life was at an end and his master would not be pleased that he had failed.

"This is for Gryph," the human whispered hoarsely, and drove the sword through Gryzzl's neck.

Gryzzl's world went black.

Chapter Two

Elhrin opened the door of her bedroom and spied her mother in the kitchen busily mixing something in a large bowl.

Xarah, alerted by the ever-present squeal of the door's faulty hinge looked up and smiled at her. "Good morning, birthday girl. Did you sleep well?"

"Yes, I did," Elhrin replied, as she crossed the room and peered over her mother's shoulder to see what was in the bowl.

"Yum, butternut," she said, and dipped her finger in the batter then kissed the soft skin of her mother's cheek. She placed the finger in her mouth, delighting in the nutty sweetness of the batter.

"Your favorite cake. We will have it tonight after dinner. If you are hungry now, there are flatcakes and sausage on the sideboard."

"Where is Bayle?" Elhrin asked while she filled her plate and sat down at the table across from her mother.

"Your brother has already left for Toome's. He had to be there early to make a delivery to Krynn Yrwin's farm," replied Xarah, reaching up to slip behind her ear a tendril of her dark hair. The tight bun she wore on the back of her head had loosened and her hair comb was askew. "He didn't take the time to eat, just rushed through here saying he would be coming home late today because Master Toome is going to give him another lesson after work." Xarah sighed heavily, "Bayle is determined to learn how to use that sword of your father's."

"You know, he's not doing too badly. I stopped by yesterday while they were training, and he managed to tag Master Toome," she popped a piece of sausage in her mouth, then snickered. "Of course Master Toome came back and whacked him in the side before he had a chance to move. When I left, Master Toome was yelling at him for leaving himself open."

"Still, it worries me. Bayle is only sixteen, and he is talking about joining the King's Army. I am not sure he understands what being in the army really means. I think he thinks being a soldier would just be one big adventure," Xarah said.

"Don't worry, mother, spending time with Master Toome should change his mind. He doesn't make things easy for Bayle over there and treats him like one of his former recruits," Elhrin said, as she rose to clean her plate in the wash basin. "But Bayle does want to learn how to fight. Being the only man of the house he feels like it is up to him to protect us and what happened with Master Gryph last fall scared him. He didn't like feeling helpless when those creatures came at us by the river. I didn't, either. If it hadn't been for Master Gryph," her voice cracked a little and she had to clear it, "I don't think we would have made it back to the village."

"I can't even think about what might have happened, Elhrin. It was so hard when I lost your father. If something ever happened to either of you I couldn't go on," Xarah said. "What will we do if those creatures come back?"

"No one has seen any signs of them all winter," Elhrin said, giving her mother a hug from behind. "The king has soldiers patrolling the roads and searching for them, and Master Toome still has some of the men of the village going out into the countryside on a regular basis. If they come back, Master Toome has everyone ready for them."

"I hope so. It's hard to think that such creatures even exist. I wonder where they came from," Xarah lifted her bowl and poured the batter into a round pan.

"Nobody knows," Elhrin said. "But Master Toome said the king is determined to find out."

"I hope he does," Xarah said, as she wiped her hands on a small towel. "Would you go get some water? The pail is empty."

Elhrin picked up the pail sitting next to the sideboard and started for the back door.

"Oh, I almost forgot," her mother said, stopping Elhrin before she went out. "Bayle said to tell you that Marguerite wants you to stop by her place today."

"She's back?" Elhrin asked, surprised. "I thought she was planning to stay a few weeks in Muryne. When did Bayle see her?"

"Yesterday evening. She was returning her horse to Toome's stables before she headed home."

"Why didn't he tell me last night?"

"Elhrin Caddoch, if my memory serves me right, you two started arguing over some nonsense nearly the minute he walked in the door. Then you proceeded to not speak to each other the rest of the night," Xarah said, as she put her cake in the oven built into the fireplace.

"Well, he started it," Elhrin mumbled, and slipped out the door.

It was near midday when Elhrin finished her chores and was finally able to leave the cottage and make her way to the shops in Glimmerdale. Her mother wanted her to run a few errands while she started her day of sewing. A single mother, Xarah worked tirelessly to provide for the three of them, sewing for others nearly every day until dusk and earning very little just so the family could have something to eat and clothes on their backs. Elhrin knew it had to be tough on her mother raising two children on her own, especially when one was accident prone and the other had extraordinary abilities and was forever doing something with magic to scare her. Her mother always said that she didn't know which one of her children was going to be the death of her someday, but it was going to be one of them for certain.

Elhrin thought back to the day when she was only eight years old and found out for the first time that she had magical abilities. Bayle had managed to run head-long into the corner of the dining table and cried loud enough for the neighbors to hear. Her mother, who had been trying to get a fire started, had asked Elhrin to take over while she tended to Bayle. Elhrin had just been playing make-believe in her mind, mimicking Master Gryph who she had seen light fires many times with just a wave of his hand, and had waved her hand in the direction of the fireplace. Something inside her stirred and she felt a force move through her and out of her hand as a fire roared to life among the logs. She yelped and jumped back at the same time as her mother screamed in shock and plopped Bayle heavily onto the tabletop. When Master Gryph found out about the incident, he had asked her mother to let him teach her how to control her magic, and her mother had readily agreed, afraid that Elhrin might harm herself or someone else.

Sighing, she tilted her head back to scan the cloud-free sky. It was a beautiful day. Clear and cool, but not freezing as it had been just a few weeks earlier, and she was glad that spring had finally arrived. Already, the snows that had covered the ground all winter were nearly gone, and the tips of early blooming flowers could be seen peeking out of the ground.

Walking out of the narrow lane that ran in front of her cottage to the South Road, she found the main section of the village alive with activity. Glimmerdale might be just a small village in the Midland Province of Anderan, but it was growing at a steady pace, and being only a day's ride from the capital city, Muryne, it was a popular stopping point for road weary travelers.

Elhrin kept to the side of the road to avoid the steady stream of travelers that were coming out of the village, heading for the city. She had to admit that, if given the opportunity, she wouldn't think twice about hopping on the back of a wagon to travel to the far reaches of Anderan and see the sights she had only heard of in stories, but she didn't think she would ever want to leave permanently like her friend Haleigh had last summer. She loved it here. Yes, it was small. Yes, there was the tiny drawback of people knowing all your business. Yes, it sometimes got boring, which usually resulted in the young people getting into all manners of mischief like letting nearby farmers cows out and herding them into the village proper.

She smiled at the thought.

Glimmerdale might be small, but it would always be home—a peaceful community filled with people who were willing to help one another when times became tough, and with the exception of a few closed-minded citizens, a place where no one made her feel out of the ordinary or different because of her magical abilities. She guessed for the most part, Master Gryph had something to do with their ready acceptance of magic. His magic and the feats that he had accomplished over his lifetime had made him legendary among the people of Anderan, and her mother had told her once that the citizens of Glimmerdale were surprised when he had chosen their village to make his permanent home instead of Muryne.

She had never thought of him as someone famous or important. She never saw that side of him. To her, he had just been a teacher, a friend, and if truth be told, the father figure she never had. Still, one day not too long before his death she had asked him why he didn't choose to live in Muryne, since he spent more time there than in Glimmerdale. He had been preparing to leave yet again on one of the innumerable occasions his job needed him in the city and he had told her he didn't like living in the city. Too noisy, he had said. Not to mention that he couldn't move without someone constantly badgering him for one reason or another, and he just wanted a little peace and quiet when he could manage it and had found it in Glimmerdale.

She breathed deeply and let out a long sigh. Today was her eighteenth birthday. He was supposed to be here, and it made her feel frustrated and, surprisingly, angry at the monsters for taking him from her. It had been seven months since he had been killed, but the memory still made her stomach clench and tears spring to her eyes.

He had told her he had something special for her when this day came, and she needed him—she didn't know what to do anymore.

For almost ten years he had been instructing her in the ways of magic, but it wasn't just his instruction that she missed. She desperately missed just being able to talk to him like a daughter would. She had never known her own father. He had been killed when she was three and Bayle was just a baby. Her mother rarely spoke of him, finding it too hard. About the only thing that she knew was that her father had transported goods for a living, that he loved her and Bayle very much, and that Bayle looked just like him with his sandy-blonde hair and moss-colored eyes. So, never knowing her real father, Master Gryph became a father figure to her, and Elhrin wondered if her mother had ever had a problem with the close relationship that she and Bayle had not only with him, but with Marguerite, as well.

Elhrin shook her head.

No, she knew her mother didn't, or she wouldn't have allowed the amount of time they had spent with him and Marguerite. Elhrin fondly remembered that as soon as she and Bayle had been able to get their chores finished and school work out of the way, they had run straight to Master Gryph's home. If his work wasn't demanding his attention he spent time with them doing things any parent would do—taking them fishing, playing silly child games with them, splashing in Harper's Stream behind his cottage, teaching them how to ride a horse, the list of memories went on and on, but her fondest memories were those spent just the two of them working on magic. And now all that would never be again. He was gone, and she found her confidence in herself and her magic was shaken. How was she supposed to learn anything new? She wished there was a school of magic she could attend, but the gift of magic was extremely rare. She had never met anyone else who had the gift except Master Gryph, yet he had told her there were others like them. Briefly, she contemplated leaving Glimmerdale in search of anyone with magical abilities, but quickly discarded the idea. She couldn't leave. Her mother needed her here.

She shook herself out of her thoughts. She was not going to think about this on her birthday.

She stepped up onto the rock-paved sidewalk that ran the length of the shops and was hit with the pleasant aroma of fresh baked bread coming from the bakery next to the Glimmerdale Inn. Grateful that the bakery's smell diminished the stink emanating from the throngs of unwashed working people that filled the sidewalks and horse dung littering the street, Elhrin pushed her way through the crowd, saying hello to those she knew, until she reached the entrance to Marguerite's Apothecary Shoppe. It had been closed since Master Gryph's death. Losing her husband of twenty years had been extremely hard for Marguerite. She rarely came into the village, preferring to stay at home. Elhrin and Bayle visited her often, and she knew Master Toome's wife, Maye, also visited her, all trying to help as best they could to ease Marguerite's sorrow and loneliness. Staring at the dusty display of medicinal bottles and home healthcare pamphlets in the shop's window, Elhrin wondered just how long it would take before the pain of losing one's soul-mate became manageable. It was hard enough to lose someone that was close, but she couldn't imagine having to endure losing the one you meant to spend your entire life with.

She turned away from the window, walked two shops down and entered the open doorway of Triva's Dry Goods Shoppe. Her mother had asked her to stop and see if Triva had received a salt shipment specifically from the city of Marmuht. Built overlooking a bay on the south coast of Anderan, Marmuht was famous for its various salts and fine glassworks, and her mother wanted a sack of their smoked salt to flavor a roast for dinner.

Elhrin found Triva, a short, plump lady with curly red hair that had a mind of its own, busy stacking large sacks of flour against one wall of the shop.

"Good afternoon, Triva," Elhrin said, perusing the various foodstuffs in jars, boxes and sacks that adorned shelves and tables inside the narrow shop.

Triva yelped and dropped the sack she was holding, turning to see who had entered the shop.

"Elhrin, I didn't hear you come in. How are you, dear?" she breathed with a rosy smile.

"I'm fine. I'm sorry if I startled you."

"Never you mind. I was just in my own little world and not paying attention. What can I do for you today?" Triva asked, as she picked up the sack she had dropped and stacked it on top of the others.

"Mother wanted to know if the smoked salt from Marmuht had arrived."

"Not yet. Usually they have come by now, but we haven't seen any shipments from the west for the past week, and some of my supplies are running low. I can't imagine what must be keeping them."

"Maybe the snow melt is making the roads difficult along the South road."

"That's possible," Triva said, dusting her hands off on her skirt. "I am looking forward to when all of this snow finally goes away. If the weather continues to warm like it is, the snow and ice will be gone in no time. But you are right, the melt is making the roads a mess. Jeremy Chalmers came by earlier and said the road to Muryne is like a bog in places. Wagons are getting stuck constantly, making it difficult to get through."

"That reminds me. Did you know that Marguerite is back from Muryne?" Elhrin asked, picking up a small sack of flour.

"Maye mentioned it this morning. I hope it has helped to get out of that cottage of hers. I know losing Gryphon was hard on her, but everyone in the village misses her. She is the closest thing we have to a doctor, since we can't seem to get one to move here from the cities. Poor Father Jerome tries the best he can, but he just doesn't have the knowledge that Marguerite has."

"I know. Maye and I have tried talking to her about coming back, but she just cuts us off and says she's not ready," Elhrin said, gathering a few items she thought Marguerite could use and placing them into a sack. "Triva, I think I will get these for her."

"Maybe she'll come around soon. Here, give her this for me," Triva said, placing a jar of berry preserves into Elhrin's sack. "A little gift from me, no charge," she added, as Elhrin paid her for her purchase.

"Thank you, I'm sure she will enjoy it."

"Tell your mother I will let her know as soon as the salt comes in."

"I will," she said, stepping out the door onto the walkway.

"Elhrin," a young girl called from across the street. Elhrin waved at her friends, Nolina and Sib, twin sisters who lived down the road from her cottage. "Do you want to go with us to Trish's?"

"I can't right now. I might catch up with you later."

"Okay," Sib said, raising a hand to wave, and the two girls quickly disappeared in the crowd.

Anxious to see Marguerite, Elhrin hurried past the last shop and followed the road out of the village, stepping over the deep ruts wagons had made in the soft muck created from the snow melt. As she approached a small wood, the ring of a hammer hitting steel filtered through the trees from Master Toome's blacksmith forge.

Master Toome had at one time been a swords master in the King's Army and Master Gryph's partner whenever he had to conduct missions across the country. When Master Toome retired from the king's service, he had made the decision to make Glimmerdale his home, returning to the trade that had been his father's, he set up a forge and now had a thriving business that was not limited to the village's borders.

She reached the entrance to Master Toome's place and peered into the yard just as Bayle was pushing a cartload of hay towards a horse paddock. She still found it hard to believe that her little brother had grown taller than she into a handsome, lanky figure the young girls of the village loved to moon over. Bayle enjoyed every minute of his popularity and used it to his advantage, never spending time with any one particular girl for long.

Bayle broke out into a raunchy taproom song, and she let out a little snort of laughter. Her mother would kill him if she ever found out he sang those types of songs, and as if he needed to be punished for it, his cart hit something on the ground and came to an abrupt halt. He lost his grip on the cart and it flipped up and over. He tried to catch the handles, but tripped over something and fell forward. His body did a complete roll across the cart and he landed on his back in the pile of hay that had spilled out onto the ground. Elhrin couldn't help herself and laughed. Bayle rose up on his elbows and looked her way.

"Are you hurt?" she asked, laughing.

He smiled at her, and then observed the overturned cart. "No, but I think I broke the cart."

"You're lucky you didn't break your neck," she laughed.

"Well, Master Toome may do that for me when he sees what I did to his cart," he stood up and rubbed his back. "Did mother tell you Marguerite was home?"

"Yes, I'm on my way to her place now. Do you want me to help you fix it?" she pointed at the cart.

"No, I've got it," he said, bending over to examine the damage. "Actually, it's not that bad. One of the supports snapped. Easily fixed."

"Okay then, I'll see you later," she said, and started down the road.

"Hey, Elhrin!"

She looked over her shoulder, "Yes?"

"Happy birthday," he smiled.

"Thanks," she grinned.

Marguerite's cottage was down a little lane that ran from the South Road to a farm owned by Doogan Phisk. To her left was a split rail fence that contained Doogan's cows in a rolling pasture. Across the other side of the pasture was the plowed farmland beside the Green River where Master Gryph lost his life.

Deciding not to dwell on thoughts of him any longer, she busied herself with picking up stones and tossing them down the road with her magic until she reached the gate in the low stone wall in front of Marguerite's cottage. She followed a rock-paved pathway to the cottage's front door and knocked, then opened the door and stuck her head inside.

"Marguerite?" she called. No answer.

Thinking Marguerite was somewhere outside, she sat the sack of goods from Triva's just inside the door, and followed the path that led around the front of the cottage, noticing that Marguerite had cleared away some of the snow and had been working in her herb and flowerbeds, getting them ready for the new season. She hoped this was a sign that Marguerite would be returning to her shop soon because a good portion of her stock was supplied from her own garden.

She searched the small barn off to the side of the cottage but it was dark and silent. The sight made her sad. Marguerite had sold all of her animals except one milk cow and the chickens, and they were out in the pasture behind the barn.

She turned around and studied the expansive back lawn. A flash of color could be seen through a stand of trees next to the small stream that bordered the back of her property.

Elhrin crunched through the snow-encrusted grass and was slightly shocked by the woman's appearance when she drew close. It had only been a week since she had seen Marguerite last, but for the first time she noticed traces of gray mixed in with the long blond hair braided down Marguerite's back and that she had lost weight.

"Marguerite," she called.

Marguerite looked over her shoulder and gave Elhrin a weak smile. "Hello, dear," she said, as Elhrin leaned down to give her a hug and a kiss on the cheek. Marguerite winced.

"What's wrong?" Elhrin asked. "Are you hurt?"

"It's nothing," Marguerite replied. "I just hurt my shoulder a bit."

"How? Is there anything I can do?" asked Elhrin. She used her magic to whisk away snow from the top of a nearby rock and sat down.

"No. It's nothing. Don't worry," Marguerite said, leaning over to fill a bucket with water from the stream. She pulled it back out and sat it on the ground with a grunt.

"How was your trip to Muryne?" Elhrin asked. "I thought you were going to stay longer."

"My trip was fine, I suppose," Marguerite sighed. "I finished with what I wanted to do faster than I expected. There was no need for me to stay any longer."

"What did you do?"

"Oh, I had a little business to take care of."

"What kind of business?"

"Just things that I had put off and needed to finish," Marguerite drifted into silence which was something that she did far too often, nothing like the Marguerite before Master Gryph's death.

Elhrin plucked a leaf from a nearby bush and threw it into the stream. Watching as it floated and twirled with the current, she wondered why Marguerite was being so vague about her trip to the city. She looked across the stream at the shadowy stretch of woods on the other side. It was quiet. Only the rushing water of the stream and the occasional call of a red bird broke the silence.

"It is so peaceful here by the stream," Elhrin observed.

"Yes, it is," Marguerite agreed. "I come down here often to sit and think."

"Bayle and I loved to swim here in the summer," she glanced at the low rock dam that Master Gryph had helped them build one year to create a small, sandy pool.

Marguerite gave her a small smile. "Those were some of my favorite summer days. You two grew up much too fast."

Elhrin laughed. "I didn't grow up far. I'm still the shortest girl over the age of twelve in the village."

Marguerite chuckled. "But you are the prettiest of them all."

Elhrin was glad to hear her laugh, even if it was a small one. "You are just being nice. By the way, I brought you some things from Triva's. I put them inside the front door."

"I appreciate that. I also have something for you. Let's go in," Marguerite said, as she stood and reached for her bucket.

"I'll get that for you," Elhrin said. She took the bucket from Marguerite and followed her to the cottage.

They entered through a back door into a dimly lit hallway that led to the front of the cottage. There were two doors on each side of the hall. The one on the right was partially open, revealing Marguerite's bedroom. The one on the left was firmly closed, and usually remained that way. It was Master Gryph's study, and Marguerite did not go in there unless she had no choice. The entire front of the cottage was one big room. One side was the kitchen, a simple set up that most people in the village had with a brick oven built inside a fireplace, tables and cupboards along the wall for food storage and preparation, and a dining table situated near the front window. The other side of the room was the sitting area. Here is where the owner's true status belied the simplicity of the rest of the cottage. Two padded rockers sat on either side of a rock fireplace, a cushioned settee large enough for three persons faced the warmth of the fire. A shin-high mahogany table sat on a thick, Chyrzinian hand-made rug in the middle of the seating arrangement. Porcelain and colored glass vases, candlesticks, and bowls sat on its top—purchases over the years from their extensive travels. Marguerite had spared no expense on the comfortable furniture and beautiful decorations, nor did she have to. Master Gryph was far from being a pauper—he just preferred to live simply, and Marguerite was fine with it, but said at the end of a hard work day she wanted something comfortable to rest in and something pretty to look at, and if she ever said she wanted something, Master Gryph was more than happy to provide it for her.

Elhrin followed Marguerite into the kitchen area. She placed the bucket onto the cutting table as Marguerite added wood to a low burning fire below the oven and put a kettle of water on a hanger over it to boil. She turned and pointed at something wrapped in a blue cloth sitting on the dining table.

"That is for you," she smiled. "Happy birthday."

"Marguerite, you didn't have to get me a gift," Elhrin said, and sat down at the table. The blue cloth turned out to be a silk shawl, far finer than anything she owned. "Oh my," she breathed, fingering the smooth texture of the hem. "This is too much."

"No, it isn't. A girl only turns eighteen once," she nodded at the present. "The shawl is from me. What's wrapped inside it is from Gryph."

Elhrin was confused. "From Master Gryph?" She pulled back the cloth. Inside was an old book. Its dark leather cover was aged and slightly worn around the edges. It had a hand-carved symbol of a burning sun on the front. She started to open the book, but when she touched the cover, she felt a strange tingle run through her arm and something seemed to click into place in her mind, but she didn't know what. The sun emblem on the cover turned a fiery red and tiny flames shot upward from its rays but then quickly disappeared as if nothing had happened.

Shocked, Elhrin looked at Marguerite. "What is this?" she whispered.

Marguerite sat down opposite her. "That is the *Book of Tolman*. Gryph told me it was to be yours on your eighteenth birthday."

"Why did it do that when I touched it?" Elhrin said, staring in awe at the book. "It felt like it recognized me."

"It wouldn't surprise me if it could recognize you," Marguerite said, and stood up to retrieve the kettle that had started to blow steam out of its spout. "Gryph did not tell me much about what the book is, but did tell me that it was special and has passed down through many centuries from one magician to another."

Elhrin reached out again and touched the book, but this time all she felt was the supple leather of the cover. She flipped open the front cover. On the inside of the cover were two rows of signatures. It appeared that whoever owned the book had signed it. She scanned down the list and saw that the last signature belonged to Gryphon Idwyr. Skimming through the pages, she noticed that written in the book were histories and stories along with instructions of magic. Excitedly, she turned the pages, and began to realize that each magician that had possessed the book had actually written the chapters. She quickly turned to the end and found empty pages. She frowned, flipping backwards until she found the last entries in the book, and stared at the familiar left-handed scrawl of Master Gryph's writing.

"I don't understand how this book is so thin," Elhrin said, as Marguerite placed a steaming cup of tea beside the book for Elhrin and sat down. "Each magician who owned it has written something in here and it has hundreds of pages. Yet, look at it. It should be twice the size that it is."

"It is a magician's book. Who knows what qualities it possesses," Marguerite said unimpressed, as if it were any ordinary book found on the shelf of any house in the village. She took a sip of her tea.

Elhrin shook her head and began to read, quickly becoming engrossed in its pages, and leaving her tea untouched. She didn't notice when Marguerite rose from the table and began working in the kitchen. When the sun's rays sent long shadows into the room, Marguerite finally told her that her mother would be worried and looking for her if she didn't go home. Elhrin gave Marguerite a hug, scooped up her book and shawl, and headed home.

Chapter Three

Gryzzl surveyed the desolate scene before him, knowing that he was stalling the inevitable. After the human had killed him in the cave, he had returned to Do'athra, the Realm of Darkness, where the dark souls of the living go when they die. This was the domain of the Dark God, Obsudius, who took pleasure in the suffering of his realm's inhabitants. A lost soul residing here could look forward to never-ending anguish, despair, hunger, and thirst for all eternity. Even now, Gryzzl yearned for just a sip of water from the cave where the human had killed him. But the yearning was fleeting because the feeling that was foremost in a lost soul's thoughts in this horrible place was fear, and right now, Gryzzl was consumed with fear. His master would be furious when he learned Gryzzl had failed to bring him the book. He knew that to anger his master was instant banishment to the Void. He wanted to find a place to hide, but knew it was useless. His master would find him. He had to go forward—he had no choice—here, a soul was forced to obey the will of his god.

He scanned the mountains surrounding the valley until his eyes were reluctantly drawn to his destination. A keep, black and ominous, rose up out of the ground like a walled monolith as it melded with one of the craggy, barren mountainsides that encompassed the valley. His master would be waiting for him there, and with the gait of the damned, he walked into the valley to face his destiny.

His master had been busy since he had last been here, before he was chosen to leave the realm in search of the book. Multitudes of souls were gathered on the flat plain of the valley floor awaiting the summons that would take them through the Rift and back into the realm of the living. His master was building an army for Obsudius, who wanted the human population destroyed and replaced with his own creation, the Do'athrim—human souls recreated into whatever form amused the God of Darkness. Glancing at the Do'athrim around him, Gryzzl thought it fitting Obsudius was deemed in the living world as the Wolf God or M'gelidia. He favored the wolf, and it was apparent in the throngs of Do'athrim choking the valley floor. But there were other types of

Do'athrim and some had not yet been converted and still retained their human form. Weaving in and out of the malevolent crowd of souls, he veered away from two lion-bodied creatures that had begun to fight, and shoved his way through a group of reptilian creatures with sharp fangs and long talons. Other than a few hostile hisses from the lizard men, no one noticed him as he passed. No one cared.

He continued through the army of dark souls until he reached the black structure on the far side of the valley, and stared with dread at the box tower that rose above the high walls surrounding it, knowing that most likely he only had a short time before he would cease to exist. With a brief glance at the square turrets flanking the gate far above, Gryzzl reluctantly ascended the wide stone ramp that rose high above the valley floor and entered into a courtyard that held hundreds of Do'athrim and human souls formed into ranks, all awaiting orders. Passing through the ranks, he approached the doors of the keep and saw a large human, devoid of any hair on his head or face, wearing full armor made of black leather. The man shouted obscenities at one of the Do'athrim wolven and Gryzzl stopped, hate filling his soul completely. Worelin, notorious for his cruel nature, was a favorite of his master, and took every opportunity to humiliate Gryzzl when they were in the master's presence. Gryzzl desperately wished he had the power to send Worelin's soul to the Void, but he was not N'gethwyn like his master. The Do'athrim had no magical powers.

Eyeing Worelin, Gryzzl tried to slip into the keep unnoticed, but had no luck. Worelin rested his hate-filled gaze on Gryzzl, making the Do'athrim wolven flinch. Despising himself for allowing Worelin to have an effect on him, Gryzzl acted like he did not notice the ugly human, and stepped through the open doors of the keep into a long corridor.

"Gryzzl," Worelin yelled. "Where have you been? You should have been back long before now. Master Cynder has been waiting for your return."

"I am here now," growled Gryzzl, pushing past a Do'athrim blocking his way, "and I am on my way to see him."

"You had best hurry, you puny dog. You know how he hates to be kept waiting," Worelin yelled at his back. "And why are you coming in through the gates? Shouldn't you be in the Rift Hall?"

Gryzzl growled under his breath and refused to answer. He did not want to give Worelin the satisfaction of knowing a weak human had killed him in the caves. Do'athra was a lifeless terrestrial replica of the living physical world, and when he had died, he had arrived in the realm of the dead exactly where he died—in the barren and now waterless caves underneath Casteal Island. Worelin had expected him to come back into the keep through the Rift Obsudius held open, but the truth was he had climbed out of the caves and traveled the extensive journey back to the valley of the keep. He had no clue how long the journey had taken him. Time was not measured in the realm of the dead, nor did it matter. This place was eternal.

He followed the long hallway until it opened into a large cavernous room filled with another troop of Do'athrim and dark souls all facing a large swirling mass of red energy embedded in the wall to his left—the Rift. He watched as they eagerly approached the mass and disappeared one by one into its maelstrom with a deafening roar. This was the portal Obsudius had created to allow his minions back into the living world. Once the souls of the dead reached the other side, they possessed living bodies that were subject to the laws of nature. For the tortured souls of Do'athra, any kind of living was bliss despite the relentless miserable existence they would lead on the outside. And even though they knew being back in the natural world was temporary and they had a specific purpose there, they reveled in the chance to enjoy all the pleasures of life that were denied them here while it lasted.

Across the room opposite him, Gryzzl warily eyed an arched doorway in the far wall and the fear inside his soul grew to a feverish pitch. Through that opening he would find his master.

He was trying to get himself to move forward when an enormous black reptilian head snaked its way through the opening and pierced him with fiery red eyes. If Gryzzl had been living he thought he would have succumbed to the enormous amount of fear overloading his soul and fainted. He stood rooted to the dusty flagstones, fixing his stare solidly on the long black fangs protruding from the beast's mouth, not daring to meet the blazing eyes. This was Cynder, but to all souls in the Realm of Darkness he was called Master, the favored one, the one who carried out the demands and wishes of the God of Do'athra.

"Gryzzl!" the Master roared, his rumbling growl reverberated off the stone walls of the room, causing the soldiers waiting to enter the Rift to immediately prostrate themselves on the floor. "Get over here now!"

As if that one command released his soul's frozen state like an arrow from a bow, Gryzzl shot across the room through the immobile troops and dropped to his knees before his master. He bowed his head to the floor.

"Master, I apologize for being late," he said into the flagstones.

"Get up, you fool," his master roared.

Gryzzl jumped to his feet, relieved to find he had a brief respite from his master's gaze because his master had noticed the soldiers had stopped going through the Rift and were prostrate on the floor.

"You, Sergeant, get everyone up and moving through the portal," he ordered the officer in charge of the troop.

A large Do'athrim in the form of a brown bear kicked the soldiers into motion. Once again the maelstrom of red roared to life as soul after soul rushed through the Rift to the other side.

Cynder shifted his attention back to Gryzzl. "I expected you back long ago. Let me see the book."

Gryzzl felt like his soul had turned inside out. "Master, I have failed. I do not have the book," he stammered.

Immediately, he was slammed to his back on the floor. His Master thrust his muzzle into Gryzzl's face, giving him an uncomfortable view of the sharp fangs.

"What do you mean, you have failed?" his Master growled low, sounding like an avalanche of granite rock tumbling down the side of a mountain.

"Master, I had the book. It was in the cave where you said it should be. There was a trap, and I was trying to get out when a pathetic human appeared and . . . uh . . . took the book from me," he whined.

"Took the book from you? And you let it go?" his master snarled. "Am I to assume you were killed in this encounter?"

Gryzzl was sure he was about to be zapped into non-existence. "Yes, My Lord, the human killed me. I failed," he whimpered.

His master reared his head and released a deafening roar of frustration, once again sending the soldiers who had not gone through the Rift to their knees and prostrate their bodies on the floor. Gryzzl squeezed his eyes shut. He did not want to watch his master send him to the Void. Stillness descended on the hall. Only the pulsating dull roar of the Rift and the distant voices of the army down the hall broke the absolute silence—until his master spoke, his voice barely above a whisper and filled with malicious purpose. "Gryzzl, twice you have failed me. First, you failed to retrieve the pendant from the So'ladiun you killed, and because of that failure, I had to send someone else to retrieve it. Now you fail to bring me the book. I should send you to the Void for your incompetence," his master paused and Gryzzl steeled himself for the inevitable. "But I am not. Not yet, anyway."

Gryzzl dared to open one eye. His master's shape began to shift and change until it morphed into a man-sized form dressed in a deep crimson, almost black robe with a cowl that concealed his face in dark shadows. He knelt down beside Gryzzl and reached out a green-tinged hand to grip Gryzzl's throat. His master's sharp talon-like nails pierced through his thick fur to prick his hide as he jerked Gryzzl's head off the stone floor. Having no choice, Gryzzl stared at his master's face. The dark recesses of the cowl prevented him from seeing any features but fiery red eyes.

"Gryzzl, did you recognize this human?" his master asked softly. His voice sounded almost human.

Gryzzl tried to shake his head no, but the grip of his master was too strong. His master did not require his answer, anyway.

"Could you recognize this human's scent if you came across it again?"

"Yes, Master," he managed to choke out.

"Then I am going to let you try again. You will go back, and you will find the human. You will kill it, and you will get the book and bring it back to me. If you fail this time, I will torment your soul for however long it amuses me, and then I will send you to the Void. Do you understand me?" his master said, squeezing Gryzzl's neck painfully.

"Yes, Master," Gryzzl wheezed.

"Good, you will go now," his master said, thrusting Gryzzl's head away. It connected with the flagstones with a sharp crack. Gryzzl nearly howled. Even though you could never die again in the Realm of Darkness, you could hurt, and it was horrific because pain was vastly amplified.

His master noticed that the rest of the troops were still lying on the floor. "I told you to get those troops out of here, Sergeant," he roared.

The soldiers scrambled to their feet and those closest to the portal ran through. Gryzzl got to his feet unsteadily and bowed.

"Thank you, Master," he said hoarsely.

His master did not acknowledge him, and turned to walk back through the arched doorway. "It would be in your best interest if you hurried," Cynder growled.

Gryzzl turned and sprinted across the room to the portal, knocking Do'athrim out of his way as he launched himself through the Rift.

Chapter Four

Elhrin stared into the swirling, lazy waters of the Green River and resolved once again not to cry. Taking in a calming breath, she decided it was time, and worked her way down the riverbank to a sandy beach and crossed over to a large rock not far from the water's edge. She focused on the sand and scattering of tiny various colored pebbles below her feet. She had not been here since last fall—since the day it happened. It had been too hard. Today, though, she felt like this was where she was supposed to be.

Lifting her satchel off her shoulder, she crossed her legs and sat down, using the smooth surface of the rock to rest her back. She couldn't help but glance at the far riverbank where the beasts had erupted out of the woods. The unusually warm weather that had caused all traces of snow to disappear in the last two weeks was having an effect on the land. There was a spattering of new growth popping up through the destruction of splintered trees and flattened dead undergrowth. She even spied a few blossoms and the traces of green on a cherry tree that had survived the explosion. She scanned the woods beyond. It wouldn't be long before all the trees fully regained their cloak of leaves. It was as if what happened here had not mattered. Life continued on.

She blinked her eyes against the tears that threatened to form despite her efforts not to cry. Getting a hold on her emotions, she thrust thoughts of that day out of her mind and opened her satchel, pulling out the *Book of Tolman* and propping it on her lap. It had been two weeks since Marguerite had given her the book, and although she read every chance she could, she still had not reached the middle. It seemed that for every page she read, ten more would appear. It felt endless. She wasn't complaining, though, because she had learned so much from its pages and didn't feel as lost as she had a few weeks ago.

She opened the book and found where she had left off. It was the writings from a mage that had lived several hundred years ago. She hesitated, and started to flip the pages to the end and read what Master Gryph had written.

"No, not yet," she whispered, and delved into the story on the page before her. For hours she was lost in the book's pages, dimly aware of the soft sounds of the flowing water beside her and the birds and insects singing in the countryside. Her eyes grew heavy, and the pages began to blur. She allowed her mind to drift, thinking how life must have been all those years ago for the man in the story.

"Elhrin," she heard a man softly call her name, and sleepily turned her head to look in the direction of the voice.

She yelled, immediately coming to her senses. She launched herself sideways away from him, and scrambled backwards on her hands and heels towards the river. Forgotten, the *Book of Tolman* thumped to the sand. She couldn't believe what she was seeing. She felt as if she had lost her mind and her heart hammered in her chest so hard she thought it would actually break through. She began to sob, and through the water that blurred her vision, she stared at a man who was supposed to be dead. He had a sad, but slightly amused expression on his bearded face as he sat next to the space she had just occupied with one forearm resting comfortably on a raised knee. He was wearing the clothes of his burial, a rich deep-blue doublet, fitted at the waist and trimmed in gold. Black trousers encased his overly long legs and disappeared into the tops of polished black boots.

"Master Gryph," she whispered.

He beckoned her to come closer. "Don't be afraid, sweetheart. I won't hurt you."

She did not know how long she hesitated, but finally, she crawled across the sand to him. She sat back on her knees and searched his deep blue eyes, unable to speak. How was he here? Why was he here? What is going on? Is he real?

A corner of his mouth lifted knowingly, but he did not speak. This was a technique he had used often. He was waiting patiently for her to come to terms with his appearance on her own—to speak her mind first.

Trembling, she reached out a hand to touch him. Her hand touched nothing, and she looked to see why. Her hand and the sand and the rocks underneath him were clearly visible through his body.

"What is happening?" she asked. At first glance he had appeared solid.

"It's a little unnerving, isn't it?" he said with that familiar suppressed chuckle that said he found something funny that shouldn't be funny at all.

"How can you be here?" she whispered through her tears. "I watched you die on this very spot."

"Yes, you did," he agreed with a sad smile. He looked across the river at the remnants of that day. "An unfortunate event, I must say, and a real low point for me, but you have to admit, I did go out with a bang, didn't I?"

"Don't do that!" she cried. He used any opportunity to make a joke. "Do you think this is funny?"

"No, Elhrin," his smile faded. "I don't think this is funny, and I promise I have no wish to upset you. I merely wish to see you laugh again." He reached out as if to wipe away her tears, but stopped when he realized he couldn't touch her. "I have watched you for a while, sweetheart, and it breaks my heart to see that my sunny, laughing young apprentice seems to have lost her smile."

"You have watched me?" Elhrin asked.

"You, Bayle, and Marguerite," he said wistfully. "I've got to make sure you all are doing well, don't I? Especially Bayle, that boy is going to hurt somebody or himself someday with all that clumsiness."

Elhrin couldn't help herself and smiled at the thought.

"There's that smile I longed to see," his face lit up. "I knew you had one in you still."

Her heart swelled with the love she had for this man. He always brought the best out in her, even when she felt her worst.

"Why are you here?" Elhrin asked.

"So you are not glad to see me then?" he asked, raising one eyebrow.

"No, that's not what I mean," Elhrin protested, she found that her emotions had turned into excitement because she was able to talk to him again, and she didn't want to make him think she didn't want him here.

"I know, Elhrin, I am only teasing. Solisius has been keeping me busy since I arrived in his realm," he said, "but now I have been given the opportunity to talk with you."

"What is it like? Ts'aura—The Realm of Light," she asked.

"It is a place that would exceed anything you could ever imagine. Its beauty is breathtaking, and the peace that fills your soul, Elhrin, is truly amazing," he patted his left leg, yet, there was no sound. "No more pain."

"Really?" she asked, knowing how much he had suffered with the old injury to his leg.

"Really," he responded, then pointed to the book lying face down in the sand. "I am glad to see Marguerite retrieved the book for you. How do you like it?"

Elhrin picked up the book and dusted the sand off its cover.

"It is a wondrous book, Master Gryph," Elhrin said, resting the book on her lap. "Marguerite said you wanted me to have it, but I don't understand why. It seems . . . I don't know . . . feels important. Why not give it to someone with more experience?"

"Because the book was not meant for anyone else, my dear, it was meant for you."

"Why me?"

"It might help you better understand if I tell you a little more about it. I'm sure from reading it you already know many ages ago it was started by Tolman Arahod, hence its title, *The Book of Tolman*. What you don't know, because for whatever reasons he did not include it in his writings, is that the God of Ts'aura requested that Tolman create this book for him."

"Why would Solisius need a book?" she asked, surprised a god would require a man to start a book for him, though there was the series of books the Church of Light used which follows the teachings of Solisius. Someone had to write those for him.

"Because of Obsudius, who is jealous of his twin brother—hates him for being the favored son of their father, The Creator of the Infinite Universe. The Creator chose his two sons to be caretakers of this world, and he deemed Solisius worthy of the eternal paradise of Ts'aura instead of Obsudius. He knew Solisius would be the best choice to preside over all souls of this world who are inherently good in nature. They are the ones who desire peace, are compassionate and understanding, but most of all have the ability to love. They are the ones who follow Solisius' teachings and end up in his realm when it comes time for them to pass. Obsudius would desire nothing more than for all that to come to a crashing halt, and does everything in his power to subvert human courage and resolve by using whatever means are at his disposal to create chaos and despair—ultimately trying to eliminate huge chunks of population if he can, and if he is successful, he hurts Solisius. But the reality is, Solisius can't fight his brother directly, he needs someone here in the physical world to fight against Obsudius' forces and keep the balance. Do you remember me talking to you about the So'ladiun?"

"You mean Solisius' Defenders of Light? I thought you made that up."

"No, the So'ladiun are very real, Elhrin, and Tolman was one of the first for the country of Anderan," he glanced at the book in her lap. "He had Tolman create the book because the So'ladiun are separate from the church. They are unique, and he wanted to give his special warriors something that could help them—guide them in their lifelong tasks. It was to be passed down through the years, to each chosen successor, and it was up to them to write their experiences and histories in its pages so that others could learn from them."

"You mean all the magicians who signed the book were chosen by the Lord of Light?" Elhrin asked as she opened the book to look at the signatures.

"Yes, they were," Master Gryph said.

"You were one of the So'ladiun, too?" Elhrin couldn't believe what she was hearing.

He lifted one corner of his mouth. "Technically, I still am, sweetheart."

Elhrin dropped her gaze to find his name last on the list. He was right, if this meeting with him was not her losing her mind or a dream, then Solisius' teachings were true. There was life eternal after passing from this world.

"Then you were the last living . . . ."

"No, Elhrin, I was not the last."

Elhrin looked up from the book, dreading what he was about to tell her. "What do you mean, not the last?" She was sure she knew the answer already, but asked the next question anyway. "Then who is the next So'ladiun?"

"You now possess the book."

"You mean me? That's ridiculous . . . impossible. Look at me. Do I look like a fighter to you? I am not a walking tree like you. I am shorter than most of the women in the village besides my mother and Triva, and I am not going to get any bigger. I have had very little training in hand-to-hand combat which, according to your own stories, you yourself had to use all your life to survive. There is no way that I have been chosen by the God of Light." Her tirade ground to a halt, and she stared at him, waiting for him to tell her he was only joking.

He merely stared back then said in a tone that screamed what he said was final, end of story. "Elhrin, you are So'ladiun."

He was not joking.

"I don't believe you. How am I supposed to fight against whatever evil Obsudius sends into the world," she said, jumping to her feet and starting to pace. "Physical fighting aside, you know my magic is not that strong. How could I ever manage to stand against anything like those creatures that came at us here?" She turned and swept her hand holding the book at the devastation across the river. "They killed you! You were powerful!" Breathing hard, she slapped her thigh with the book in frustration. "I don't even think I am capable of killing. You know me. I can't even slaughter a chicken."

"Believe me when I say I know killing is never easy, but you and I have been working towards this, Elhrin. Do you honestly think I would spend years teaching a young girl how to defend herself and fight with explosive and deadly forms of energy if there was not a reason? I regret being so busy that I did not get more time to teach you how to fight without using your magic." He sighed. "Time slipped from me. It would do you well to practice more in that area. There can be instances that you will have to forego magic in a situation, especially if your energy supply is depleted."

She turned back around. There was no humor in his features now. He meant what he said, and she had never thought about or questioned why he had taught her magical techniques beyond the basics of control for everyday use and safety. Still . . .

"I can't do this. You and the others in this book were Master Magicians. I'm not," she whispered.

"None of us started out as a master of our craft. As in all things, experience comes from diligent practice, and you must be patient. Do not expect instant results without hard work. And do not expect that there is ever an end to learning. It does not end. But do know that in time you will master each skill— you are that talented, and one day, my apprentice, others will call you master." He paused, allowing her mind to process what he was saying. He must have seen the doubt still clouding her eyes because he let out a small grunt of displeasure. "Elhrin, the one thing I seem to fail in getting across to you is that you are stronger than you give yourself credit. You have always held yourself back and doing so defeats your purpose. You are a smart young lady and your potential knows no limits—yet you can't seem to see it. If there is ever any one thing that I would have you remember I said it would be what I am about to say to you right now . . . Elhrin, believe in who you are—reach deep within and tap into a power that far exceeds the limits you have placed on yourself."

"I don't know how," she replied helplessly.

"You only think you don't know," he was not going to let her fall back into self-deprecation. "Keep studying the book. There are things in there that will help you, and never stop practicing and seeking new avenues." His face took on a strange look. "Reach for it. I promise you, it will come."

He was holding something back, but was not going to tell her what it was. She crunched across the sand and slid down beside him.

"Can you help me?" she asked, balancing the book on crisscrossed legs. "I need you. I'm scared."

"I know you are. I wish I could take the fear from you, but I can't. I want you to know, though, that I am never very far away and I am watching." She shook her head, something had happened to her hearing. His voice now seemed faint, as if he was talking from a distance. "Before I forget, Elhrin, a condition of being So'ladiun is to keep who you are to yourself. Solisius does not want the population or even the ones you love to know about who you are for fear you or they will become a target. You will find that there will be those who will know anyway, but it is just wiser to keep as low a profile as long as you can. Oh, and one other thing. Sign the book."

"What?" she asked, seeming to jerk awake as if she had been sleeping. He was gone. She couldn't believe it. It had been a dream? The whole thing was just a dream? Tears filled her eyes. It seemed so real.

She glanced where he had sat. No signs that anyone had ever been there. She stuffed the book into her satchel, and after dusting the sand off her trousers, she started for home.

When she reached her cottage she found it cold, dark, and empty. With an absentminded flick of her wrist, she lit the candles in the room with her magic and poured energy into the fireplace to set the smoldering logs left there ablaze. Elhrin remembered that her mother had said she had to go into the village for a church meeting, and Bayle still had to be at Master Toome's. She plopped her satchel onto the kitchen table, and went to pour a glass of water from the pitcher on the sideboard. Taking her glass back to the table, she sat down. Something from her dream kept nagging at her, and she couldn't quite figure out what. Going over the details, she reflected on what Master Gryph had said. He had told her she was chosen to have the book. That the owner of the book was one of Solisius' defenders and their destiny was to fight against Obsudius. Was this true? Is that what her having this book meant? That was impossible. Like she told Master Gryph in the dream, she was too inexperienced and had never used her magic to fight against anyone. The thought of killing a living creature of any kind revolted her. Surely she wasn't expected to fight whatever trouble the God of the Realm of Darkness created. But what was it he said that was nagging at her? Then she had it. He said for her to sign the book. She opened her satchel and slid the book from among her things inside and flipped open the cover. The signatures were scrawled neatly in two rows on the inside. Even if it had not been a dream, she could not sign despite what he had said. All these men were masters of magic. She was not. She was not even a good amateur. Besides, it wasn't real. It was just a dream. With a sigh, she closed the book and stuffed it back into her satchel. After taking the satchel to her room, she returned to the kitchen and began the mundane task of peeling potatoes for their dinner.

Chapter Five

The next day, Elhrin spent the morning doing her chores and delivering the finished work that did not require her mother's presence to customers. She then headed to Marguerite's cottage for an afternoon of practice. She had just made it to the lane leading to Marguerite's cottage when she heard a horse-drawn wagon approaching behind her. She stepped to the side of the road to let it pass, seeing that the lone driver was Bayle's boss, Master Toome. The wagon rattled up beside her and instead of passing her by, Master Toome pulled back on the reigns, bringing the wagon to a creaking halt.

"Good morning, Elhrin. How are you?" he asked, tugging on the wide brim of a soot-stained hat and giving her a grin that produced two deep crevices on either side of his unshaven face and a spray of lines around his eyes.

"I'm fine, Master Toome," she shielded her eyes from the glare of the sun, "I'm on my way to see Marguerite."

"Well, climb up here and let me give you a ride. I am on my way to Doogan's. I can drop you off." He slid to the side to give her room on the driver's bench.

"Thank you, sir," she said, chucking her satchel into the footboard of the wagon and hustling up to the bench.

Master Toome clucked his tongue and snapped the reigns. The wagon jolted into motion. "I haven't seen you in a while. What have you been up to lately?"

"I've been helping mother catch up on her sewing. With Myrim Junstall getting married next week, mother is loaded down with work," she replied, glancing sideways at his time-worn features that spoke of a lifetime spent out of doors.

"How is your mother?" He watched the progress of the horses and did not turn to look at her.

"She is fine. The work is wearing her out, but she loves it and it keeps her mind off of worrying about us. Which reminds me, we were talking the other day, and she was wondering about those creatures that attacked us last fall, have there been any more sightings of them anywhere?"

"Not that I have heard. We have kept an eye out for them, but haven't been able to find a trace of the beasts since last fall," he replied with a gruff sigh. "I don't like the fact that we didn't get the ones that survived Gryph's explosion. They ran like the wind for the Northreach Mountains, and our men lost them. It is a puzzle. No one in the country has ever heard of the beasts, and none looking for them have found evidence of their whereabouts. The tracks from the ones who attacked you stopped not far from where Gryph's explosion did not reach. It's as if they disappeared—as if they never existed at all."

"It still feels like a horrible nightmare I have yet to waken from," Elhrin darted a glance across Doogan's fields. It was unnerving, the entire mystery of what the creatures were, where they came from, and where they went, not to mention why they came here to attack them in the first place. She brought her gaze back to the road. The dense wood on the right side abruptly stopped as if the rock fence of Master Gryph's—no, Marguerite's small paddock had the power to hold back the advancing growth of nature, yet there were signs that the wood was defeating the fence's purpose. Winter had felled a few trees onto the wall, tumbling the rock down. Vine grew unhindered along the rest of the wall, and grass and briar grew wild inside the paddock itself since Marguerite did not often use this side for her cow.

Elhrin blew out a heavy breath. "Every time I come down here, I still have to remind myself Master Gryph is not here."

Master Toome glanced at her sideways. "Truth be told, I go through the same thing. I miss that old goat."

Elhrin smiled at the fond reference. "Me, too."

They fell into silence the rest of the way until the wagon rolled up to the front of Marguerite's cottage and came to a jerking halt.

"Thank you for the ride, Master Toome," Elhrin reached for her satchel just as she heard sounds of a fight coming from the back of the cottage. Marguerite yelled.

Master Toome jerked a sword from under the bench and jumped from the wagon at a dead run. Elhrin was right on his heels, tearing up the gravel of the path leading to the back yard. When they rounded the back of the cottage, Master Toome stopped abruptly in his tracks. Elhrin skidded to a halt, almost colliding into his back. Then she saw what he saw—something she never, ever thought she would see. Marguerite, wielding a heavy blade several hand spans longer than the length of her arm, was furiously attacking a hanging grain sack filled with hay. Dressed in a tunic the color of red clay and brown trousers, she moved with the grace of a dancer, thrusting and slicing at the swaying sack.

Elhrin was stunned by Marguerite's level of skill—she handled her blade as deftly as any seasoned fighting man.

With a low, throaty growl that increased in volume as she moved, Marguerite grabbed her weapon in both hands and spun her body completely around, neatly severing a huge gash all the way through the sack. Hay burst outward in a violent spray, scattering the strands in a wide arc as far as the other side of the tree. Breathing heavily from the exertion, she stared for a moment at what was left of the decimated grain sack, its limp and tattered form swaying erratically on the end of the rope, and then slowly turned her head to acknowledge the presence of Master Toome and Elhrin. "Well, did you two enjoy the show?" she asked, leaning on the hilt of her sword.

"Impressive. You still have a nice form, Marguerite, overreaching a little too much, as usual, but nice all the same," Master Toome commented. "Not bad for someone who has been out of practice for awhile. What brought all this on? Do you have a desire to return to a life on the road?"

"No, I'm just out of shape and needed some exercise," she slipped the sword into her scabbard and snatched a towel off a nearby limb. She used it to wipe sweat from her face.

"Is that so?" he asked suspiciously. "You sure it has nothing to do with what happened to Gryph?"

"No," she snapped a muffled reply. She lowered the towel from her eyes, flashing a warning at him to not argue with her. "Have you gone deaf? I told you I needed the exercise."

"Humph," he grunted, not believing her.

She glared at him a moment then turned her attention to Elhrin.

"Good morning, dear," Marguerite said, losing the heat in her voice.

"Good morning," Elhrin said. "Marguerite, I had no idea you could do that."

Marguerite barked a small laugh. "I am a little rusty. It has been a long, long time." She crossed the lawn and met them at a nearby wooden bench, sitting heavily and wiping her face with the towel once more. "Whew, and I'm definitely out of shape."

Master Toome picked up a three-legged stool he himself had made and given to them a few years back, and perched his large frame upon it. Elhrin joined Marguerite on the bench.

"I am reminded of the night at your inn in Kyndlewich, Marguerite. Has she ever told you that story?" Master Toome asked Elhrin.

"No, she hasn't," Elhrin said.

"Toome, she doesn't want to hear that old tale," Marguerite protested, shaking out her towel and folding it neatly into a square.

"Yes, I do," Elhrin said. She loved hearing about their past. Master Gryph had been full of tales and adventures. Most of which Elhrin suspected were made up.

"I will tell you then," he said, stretching out his long legs and crossing them at the ankle. "Years ago, Gryph and I were on our way to Yradin. We had met Marguerite in Kyndlewich where she worked in her family's inn on the way down, and Gryph fell head over heels for her, but he would not have admitted it at the time. On our way back, Gryph wanted to go back through Kyndlewich, even though it was out of the way from where we were. We made it into town late at night, exhausted and ready for a bed," he said, raising his hat to wipe sweat off his brow—his gray-shot dark hair was plastered in a damp ring around his head, "and had just settled our horses in the stables when a bunch of shady characters stumbled out of the inn and decided that the two of us looked like easy prey. They divided themselves between me and Gryph. We barely had time to draw our swords, but Gryph's magic always managed to make fighting a little easier. He sent a few of the villains sailing through the air into the side of the stables. The rest were temporarily stunned by his move, which gave me the opportunity to knock out my nearest adversary, and defend myself from the others. That was when I realized someone else had joined the fight, and was helping us. When it was over, Gryph turned to thank our new friend and the shock on his face was hilarious. I must confess, though, I was just as surprised as he to see Marguerite standing there with a sword in her hand."

"Just trying to help," Marguerite said, turning to Elhrin. "I was only nineteen at the time and could move a lot faster than I can now. They didn't know I had grown up in a family of men. My mother died when I was seven, and I was raised by my father and four brothers. They taught me how to use a sword because I always cried that they were leaving me out of their fun. I never knew just how useful it was going to be."

Elhrin was about to ask Marguerite if her family still lived in Kyndlewich when Bayle ran around the side of the cottage.

"Master Toome, I have been looking for you," he said, out of breath.

"What is it?"

"There are a group of soldiers at the inn," Bayle said. "They speak of trouble brewing north of the mountains, and are on the way to see King Goruth. Mister Dillingham thought you might want to talk to them before they leave town."

Voted mayor in last year's election, Master Toome handled the affairs of the village, and would need to know about any news that affected the country. He rose to his feet with a grunt. "I better see what this is about, ladies. It must be serious if Dillingham went to the trouble to send Bayle for me."

"Toome, I think I will go, too," Marguerite sat her cloth on the bench and stood.

"Marguerite, no, now don't go getting . . ."

"Toome, before you start in on me, let me tell you one thing. If what they have to say is related in any way to Gryph's death, I have a right to know."

"Now what would make you think the news is related?"

"Because Gryph was killed by strange creatures no one in Anderan has ever heard about, and there has not been one trace of them since. I don't know if what they have to say is related, but this is the first news since last fall of something unusual happening, and I intend to know what it is."

"I can tell you later what was said."

Marguerite's face was a mask of stone. She would not be denied having her way. Master Toome shook his head. "I bet you will show up at the inn right on my heels if I leave you here, won't you?"

"That's right," she said.

"Fine, let's go," he stalked off towards the gravel path, mumbling something under his breath that sounded like he was complaining about women being busy-bodies and needing to know everything.

"What did you say, Toome?" Marguerite called out to his backside.

"Nothing, I didn't say a thing." He held up both hands in mock surrender.

Marguerite slid her eyes to Elhrin, suppressing a smile. "Come along, dear."

The large common room of the Glimmerdale Inn was slightly smoky from pipe tobacco and the occasional puff of gray that would billow out of the two fireplaces located on either side of the room when the wind pushed a current down the chimney. Tables were placed in three rows spanning the length of the room, and since it was a popular place for locals and travelers alike, nearly all of them were occupied as was the long bar along the back wall.

Master Toome scanned the crowd until his eyes rested on a table of four uniformed soldiers from the King's Army. As he wound his way through the tables, one of the soldiers saw Master Toome coming and said something to a young officer next to him. They all stood and faced Master Toome saluting him formally, which surprised Elhrin. She wondered if they knew he was a former army colonel or if it was something they did to show respect to an older citizen.

"Put your hands down, boys, and have a seat," Master Toome said. "Which one of you is in charge?"

"I am, sir," answered the young officer. He remained standing while his comrades took their seats.

Something strange happened to Elhrin at the sight of him. She couldn't seem to breathe properly nor could she take her eyes off of the man. In a ragged state, she could tell he had been on the road for some time. His brown hair had the look of never seeing the right side of a comb, and his face and neck sported a thick growth of stubble. His uniform, while worn on his person properly as military required, it was wrinkled and stained with splashes of mud. He had the hard look of a fighting man—and he was beautiful.

"Son, I am Lee Toome, mayor of Glimmerdale. I would like to talk to you for a moment. Would you join me?" Master Toome indicated an empty table by a window in front of the room. He then turned on his heel and walked away without waiting for the soldier's reply. The soldier was expected to comply.

"Yes, sir," the young man said. Darting a questioning glance at his friends, he moved his chair to the side and followed the older gentleman.

Before they had time to settle comfortably in their seats, Gwendolyn Unger, the inn's barmaid, stopped by the table to take their order in her clipped hurry-up-and-tell-me-what-you-want style, then left them just as quickly to forge her way back through the crowd to the bar like a plow tearing up unbroken ground.

"What is your name, son?" Master Toome asked after introducing the two ladies and Bayle. Elhrin wasn't sure why Marguerite had insisted that she come with them to the inn. It wasn't necessary for her to be here like Bayle. Master Toome had ordered him to tag along so that he could drive Marguerite back home and finish Master Toome's delivery for him, and she and Bayle were going to wait outside until they were done, but Marguerite had told them to follow her, daring Master Toome to contradict her. Master Toome had not argued, growling that he guessed it didn't matter who was with him, anyway. They would hear the news eventually, and might as well hear it firsthand.

"Lieutenant Tomas Colkitte, sir," the young soldier replied. "You may know my father, Rolyn Colkitte. I believe he trained under you." That confirmed that the soldiers did know who Master Toome was.

"Yes, I know him well. As a matter of fact, he helped me with a problem in Greystone Village years ago, a good man and an excellent fighter. Sorry to hear of his accident. How is he doing?"

"He is well, sir, but the accident has affected his mobility. He has been reassigned to an administrative position and is not taking it well."

"I can understand that," Master Toome said, and then leaned in, indicating cordiality time was over, it was time to talk business. "I hear you are carrying important news from the north."

"Sir, I was told that this was confidential information and to give the news to the king only," he eyed them all warily. "We stopped here to replace missing shoes on two of our horses. We must be off as soon as they are done."

"If your orders were to keep your information confidential, Lieutenant, then how is it my young apprentice," he nodded his head at Bayle, "found out there is trouble brewing in the north?"

Tomas slid his eyes to Bayle. A quiet anger seemed to simmer just below the surface. "Sir, I would like to know the answer to that question myself. Aren't you the boy supposed to be helping shoe our horses?"

Bayle's eyes widened in innocence, and he held up a hand. "Hold on a minute. Mister Dillingham had to go back to the forge to get something and will finish as soon as he gets back. We heard two of your friends talking out back in the stable yard before he left. If it was a secret then maybe you should tell them to keep their thoughts to themselves. They knew we were there."

Tomas shot a glare at the backs of his companions across the room. "I will definitely have a word with them."

"Lieutenant, I respect your orders of confidentiality, but as mayor of this town and as a military consultant for the king, I am going to have to request that you share your news with me. Last fall, not far from where we sit, we lost our Minister of Specialized State Defense under unusual circumstances. I would like to know if your news is similar to that event."

Elhrin could tell that Tomas warred with obeying his direct orders or telling Master Toome his news. Master Toome saw it, too. "Son, who is your ranking officer?"

"Commander Barthe Nivle of the Lakeshore Glen Regiment, sir."

"I thought so. Lieutenant, I don't think your commander will have a problem with you divulging your information to me. It was on my recommendation that gave him his current rank and position as commander of Lakeshore Glenn."

That seemed to seal Tomas' decision to reveal his news to Master Toome—he nodded his head, but then hesitated again, looking skeptically at the others seated at the table.

Master Toome followed his gaze. "I will vouch for them as well, Lieutenant. Your news is safe with all here."

Tomas cleared his throat, "Yes, sir." Tomas' dark brow furrowed in concern. He leaned in and lowered his voice to keep it from carrying to nearby tables. "There is a strange, foreign army staging in the valley outside of Blackridge Keep."

"Is that so?" Master Toome huffed in displeasure and leaned back in his chair. "I would know the details. Start from the beginning."

"A few weeks ago, me and a friend of mine were given a short leave from our duties. We decided to go to the town of Blackridge. A friend of ours told us about some interesting places there to get, uh, well, to have fun," he flushed slightly, looking uncomfortably from Marguerite to Elhrin.

Marguerite caught Elhrin's gaze and rolled her eyes to the ceiling. The young man's obvious omission of what he referred to was not lost on the ladies.

"It was right at nightfall when we neared the town, and could see the valley toward Blackridge Keep. There had to be at least a hundred campfires. We knew of no friendly force in the area, and decided to go back to Lakeshore Glen to inform our commander. We had gone maybe a league when some kind of creature ambushed us and dragged my friend off his horse to the ground. I tried to turn my horse back to help him, but he was already dead, and the creature was coming after me."

"How did you get away?" Bayle asked, mesmerized by the soldier's tale.

"My horse was panicking, and I lost control of him. He ran us halfway back to Lakeshore Glen before I could control him. I did manage to get a quick look to see if the creature was following me, but it had given up on me and gone back to my friend. I don't even want to think about what it was going to do to him."

"What did the creature look like?" Marguerite asked.

"It reminded me of a big dog, only with a man's body."

"Do'athrim," Elhrin whispered.

Tomas turned his ocean blue gaze on Elhrin, and her stomach did a strange little flip immediately followed by a twinge of disappointment when Gwendolyn showed up at her elbow with their drinks, causing him to shift his eyes directly on the woman's buxom chest. Elhrin grunted silently. It was a wonder men ever accomplished anything, it seemed they only thought about one thing.

She looked away from Tomas to find Master Toome waiting for her to continue. "Master Gryph called them Do'athrim," she said, not understanding why she was just now remembering that detail.

"That's right," Bayle said. "When they came running out of the forest at us. I had completely forgotten he had said that."

Elhrin shot Bayle a puzzled look. What was wrong with the two of them? It was an unforgettable day that haunted her dreams. They should have remembered every tiny detail of that day.

"Do'athrim? The name sounds like the old language term for the Realm of Darkness—Do'athra." Master Toome turned to Marguerite, thinking she could add to the subject. "Did Gryph ever talk about them to you?"

"No," Marguerite took a sip of the spiced cider she had ordered, "I only learned of their existence when the rest of you did."

Master Toome drummed his fingers on the tabletop for a moment, thinking. He turned back to Tomas. "You said this happened weeks ago. Why are you just now heading to Muryne?"

"Sir, my commander wanted more information before word was sent out," Tomas said. "A patrol was sent to see if they could identify the force and determine its numbers. Only one soldier from that patrol made it back on foot. He reported that they had not been able to get close enough to determine numbers, but he confirmed my own story of strange beasts in the area and they were camping in the valley. Unfortunately, with the valley being mostly grassland, his patrol was seen and cut down. He was only able to survive because his horse ran off into a ravine, taking him down with it, and either they did not bother to look for him or he was lucky they overlooked him. The commander ordered an emergency fortification of Lakeshore Glen, and sent me to take word to the king."

"Forgive me, son, but I am having a hard time understanding something. How is it that your regiment did not know about this army before you and the other patrol was attacked? The town of Blackridge is sitting right there, and correct me if I'm wrong, there should be regular patrols running between the two towns." Scowling, he pressed two fingers onto the table top in front of Tomas. The military commander was coming out of Master Toome. "And even if the patrols did not notice, someone living in the area should have taken note of a crowd of beasts congregating in the countryside. There are farms all up and down that road."

"Yes, sir, I know. That is what makes all of this so unbelievable. As a matter of fact, my friend and I had passed a patrol returning from Blackridge when we were on our way. They were in no hurry and did not indicate there was something wrong, and Commander Nivle questioned each member of all patrols who returned before me. None saw anything out of the ordinary. The town was quiet and the valley was empty," Tomas fingered the handle of his mug. "It's as if the army suddenly appeared."

"Isn't Blackridge Keep just a ruin?" Elhrin asked, remembering the many tales she had heard growing up concerning the keep.

"It is. It was abandoned centuries ago," Master Toome said, staring thoughtfully out the window behind her. "And the valley where it sits is surrounded by mountainous cliffs on every side save the one facing the town of Blackridge, which means the mystery deepens. An army sailing in from Shimmerfin Lake or even coming down the lakeshore west of the Northreach

Mountains would have had to run over the town to set up camp in the valley. Lieutenant," his gaze flicked back to Tomas, "if what you say is true, we are in trouble for a fact. I think I will go with you to Muryne. I have business there, anyway. But first, I am going make sure our watch is increased. We have encountered these beasts before. I'll not have us unprepared again."

Master Toome drained his mug and slid his chair back with an audible scrape. "Bayle, take Marguerite back home and deliver that order to Doogan. Lieutenant, I will be back here within the hour. Your horses should be ready by then," he started to leave, then hesitated. "Marguerite, do you think Gryph would have anything at home that would tell us more about these Do'athrim?"

"I can look and see," she replied, "but I can make no promises. His study is just as he left it—an organized mess."

Master Toome smiled knowingly. "If you have any luck let me know when I get back." He disappeared through the front door.

"If Master Gryph knew about the beasts, why didn't he tell anyone?" Bayle asked.

"I don't know," Marguerite said with a sigh. "He was good at keeping things to himself. I suppose there are many things he has never shared with anyone."

Tomas picked up his mug and stood. "I should inform the others that Colonel Toome is expecting us to leave in an hour. It has been a pleasure to meet all of you."

"It has been a pleasure to meet you too, Tomas," Marguerite said, glancing over at Elhrin. "Hasn't it, Elhrin?"

"What? Oh yes, yes, it has," Elhrin stammered, feeling her face flush. Marguerite had caught her staring open-mouthed at him.

"Good evening, ladies, Bayle. I hope we meet again," Tomas said, and flashed a lopsided grin at Elhrin before he left to join his friends.

"Elhrin, what is wrong with you?" asked Bayle.

"What do you mean?" growled Elhrin. Somehow she knew he would jump on her behavior like a fly on honey.

"You kept staring at him as if you wanted to climb over the table and tackle him," said Bayle.

"I was not," she protested, wishing he would just keep his mouth shut.

"You were," he grinned and tapped a finger to the corner of his mouth. "You have a little drool right here. I think you are sweet on soldier boy."

"Shut up, Bayle," she snapped under her breath, darting a glance across the room to see if Tomas could hear them. He was deep in conversation, and didn't appear to hear Bayle's comments.

Bayle puckered his lips and made obnoxious kissing noises.

Elhrin's temper flared. He could be so annoying. "Bayle, I'm warning you. Don't push me or you will find yourself hanging from the nearest tree by the seat of your pants."

"Elhrin, you know Master Gryph said you weren't allowed to use magic on me . . . ."

"Children, not here," Marguerite sighed. She had more experience than she cared for with the two's heated exchanges over the years. She slid out of her chair and stood up. "Bayle, I need to get home."

Following Marguerite, Elhrin cast one last glance at Tomas. He had been tracking her through the room and raised his hand to wave. Embarrassed, she ducked her head in acknowledgment and rushed after Marguerite down the inn's rear hall.

After Bayle dropped both ladies at Marguerite's cottage, Elhrin wandered to the back lawn, wanting to practice something that she had never attempted before, and the cottage was far enough away from others in the village to give her privacy. She and Master Gryph had practiced here regularly and thinking of him reminded her of her dream. She wondered if she should tell Marguerite about the dream, but decided against it for the moment. Marguerite did not need to be reminded of her loss, especially now with the disturbing news they had just learned because whenever Anderan's peace was threatened in any way, Master Gryph was the first person the king turned to for help.

She sat her satchel down on the bench beside the cloth Marguerite had left earlier. Unexpectedly, the thought of Tomas flashed through her mind like a bolt of lightning. She was mortified at the way she had sat there and gaped at him like the silly young girls still in school who sat outside the Church of Light during noon break, giggling behind their hands whenever a boy strutted by like a rooster in a hen house. She stared down at the buckle on her satchel reflecting the sun's rays, but she didn't see it. Instead, she allowed Tomas' face to form in her mind, reliving the details from the wisps of brown hair that touched the collar of his coat to his bloodshot eyes that made the blue stand out like two beacons glowing in the night.

She physically shook herself to break free from the image. It was no use dreaming about someone you would never see again.

She turned to face the wooded area near the stream that was nestled in the back corner of the lawn. Two large blackened and dented steel targets sat in the tall grass just this side of the trees outstretched limbs. The white circles Master Gryph had painted on them for her to use as a focal point were long gone. It was a wonder that Marguerite had ever let him teach her back here, noting the many broken limbs, chunks notched out of some of the trunks, and burnt spots on the trees behind the targets. All were her fault from the many times she had missed while learning the various projectile forms of magic. There had been many times he had to put out fires, not only the physical ones that had erupted among the trees when she missed, but also the emotional ones when Marguerite became furious with him every time Elhrin scared the life out of her when things went awry. He had been so patient with Elhrin—had never condemned her when she had done something wrong, but had made her think about what she had done and many times asked her to come up with a solution to remedy the situation without showing her. He said she needed to think for herself, saying there would be times when she needed to rely on her own instincts and skills.

She sighed. Like now.

Calling on her magic, she formed a small ball of energy in her hand and fired it at the target, setting it ablaze just as it left her hand. It sizzled across the lawn and exploded against the center of the panel with a resounding crash, sending flames spiraling outward in all directions. Satisfied that she wasn't going to set anything on fire with the shower of sparks, she threw several more fireballs at the target to warm herself up. After practicing various techniques that Master Gryph had taught her, she then pulled the *Book of Tolman* from her satchel and opened it to a page she had marked earlier. The night before she had found instructions for a protective barrier between the magic user and any danger, thinking it had to be the shield Master Gryph had wanted to teach her last fall.

Skimming over the instructions, she memorized the way the flows of energy were supposed to go and decided to give it a try. She moved to an open space in the yard and took a deep breath, then willed her magic outward, focusing in her mind a wall as big as herself and placing it a few feet in front of her. She felt the energy course from her body and stop a few feet away as she wove the energy flows the way the book instructed. She could not see anything happening and let the magic go.

"I must not be doing it right."

She tried again and thought she could see some sort of shimmering a few feet from her, but couldn't be sure that it was really there. After a few more tries, she was about to give up when she heard a wagon rattling down the road in front of the cottage. Bayle was returning from making his delivery to Doogan, and instead of passing the cottage by, he hauled back on the reigns to bring the wagon to a halt. Marguerite rose from where she had been working in her herb bed, dusted her hands off, and leaned over the rock wall to take a package from him. Doogan, notorious for his generosity, always sent Marguerite meats or products from his gardens.

"Bayle," Elhrin called out, stepping to where he could see her through an opening in Marguerite's shrubbery.

"What?" he replied.

"Could you come back here for a minute and help me?" He nodded and jumped down from the wagon.

She walked down to the edge of the trees and used her boots to skim the ground, looking for last season's hickory nuts. She was in luck and found several hidden under the damp leaf cover.

"What do you need?" he asked, as he crossed the yard.

She placed the nuts into his hands. "I want you to throw these at me," she said.

His face spread into a wide grin.

"Don't get any ideas," she warned, "throw them when I tell you to."

"Gladly," he laughed. "This ought to be fun."

Elhrin moved away from him, making sure to put a safe distance between them. Bayle occupied himself while he waited for her, tossing the nuts in the air like a carnival juggler.

She smiled at him. "Not bad. Get ready." Elhrin called on her magic and focused on placing the barrier between them. "Okay, throw one."

Bayle did not go easy on her. He slung one hard. It made it half the distance between them when it hit something solid and ricocheted directly back at him. "Hey!" He jumped back and batted the nut down. "What was that?"

"It worked," Elhrin grinned, and let go of her magic. "I found out how to create something like a shield in the book Marguerite gave me. I didn't think I was doing it right because I couldn't see what I was creating."

"Well, it's good to know that you will be protected against anyone throwing hickory nuts at you. People can be so cruel sometimes," he smiled.

Elhrin narrowed her eyes at him. "I'm sure it will work against other things, too, you bone head," she said. "Do you have a sword in the wagon?"

He instantly became serious. "Elhrin, I am not swinging a blade at you."

"Why not? I need to know if it will work against a weapon."

"What if it doesn't?"

"I will place the shield far enough away, so that if it doesn't hold, then you will miss me."

"I don't know if this is a good idea," he protested, "but I'll do it." He retraced his steps to the wagon for Master Toome's sword. When he came back, Marguerite was with him.

"Elhrin, what are you doing?" she asked in a tone that revealed her disapproval.

Elhrin explained what she wanted to do and assured Marguerite that she wasn't in danger of Bayle slicing her in two. Reluctantly, Marguerite decided to let her try, and remained to supervise.

Once again, Elhrin created a barrier and let Bayle know she was ready. He exchanged a look with Marguerite then stepped toward Elhrin and pointed his sword at her. He slowly reached out with the sword until the tip met with a resistance. He then pressed the sword hard against the barrier, but it would not move. He tapped it a few times then stepped back and swung at the invisible barrier. The sword bounced off the barrier with a loud clang. Elhrin experienced a small uncomfortable jolt travel into her through her magic and let it go.

"Oh!" She shook her hands as if they had been burned.

"What is it?" Bayle asked.

"I felt the sword hit it," she said.

"What do you mean?" Marguerite asked.

"When Bayle struck the barrier, it sent an uncomfortable vibration into me. I don't think that is supposed to happen." She started for her book. "I'll look at the instructions again and see what I'm doing wrong. Maybe I need to adjust the flows of energy a different way."

"Not today, Elhrin." Marguerite held up a hand. "It's getting late. I'm not trying to run you off, but you know as well as I do, your mother will need you soon."

Elhrin had not noticed that the afternoon sun was on its way down.

Bayle hitched a thumb over one shoulder. "I need to go, anyway, to return Master Toome's wagon and finish up at the blacksmith shop. I can give you a ride if you want, Elhrin."

Reluctantly, she agreed to go—not wanting to stop before she figured out what went wrong, but Marguerite was right, her mother would be looking for her. If she had time later she would practice at home for a little while, but knew even then she wouldn't be able to for long. The day's events already had her tired, and magic was a major drain on her energy. She could only do it for so long before she was forced to quit. Master Gryph had always told her to never push using her magic too far because using it to the point of exhaustion was extremely dangerous. She could burn herself out or worse, she could make a mistake and kill herself with her own magic.

Elhrin stuffed her book into the satchel and slung it over one shoulder. "Marguerite, do you want me to help you look through Master Gryph's study tomorrow?"

"That would be lovely, dear." Marguerite placed an arm around Elhrin's shoulders and escorted her and Bayle to the wagon to see them off.

Chapter Six

Gryzzl slunk down behind a large, weathered rock. The stream beside him spilled over and through piled up debris and a wedged tree that had fallen amongst the stones in its waters, creating enough sound with its succession of tiny waterfalls to cover the inadvertent scrape of his boots on gravel as he had made his way along the stream's bank. He waited a moment, listening to the soft murmurs of human conversation coming from the road. They were relaxed, unaware of his presence. Taking his time, he peered around the edge of the rock. Two armed men were posted on this side of the stone bridge spanning the water. One stood with his back to a roaring fire, watching the road. The second man was on the bridge facing the other side, relieving himself.

Gryzzl studied the scene. The fire would be to his advantage. It was a moonless night, so he would be invisible to them in the deep shadows outside the fire's glow.

Silently, he pulled his bow off his shoulder and notched an arrow from the quiver on his back. He aimed at the man by the fire and let loose the arrow. It hit with deadly accuracy. The man grabbed his throat where the arrow protruded and fell with a thud onto the roadbed. He did not move again.

The man on the bridge turned his head at the sound. "Owen?"

Gryzzl notched another arrow and let it fly. The arrow thumped into the man's back before he had time to move. He stumbled forwards from the impact of the arrow and fell over the bridge. There was a brief crunching splash, then the silence of night returned.

Gryzzl listened to see if the noise had alerted anyone and sniffed the air to make sure he was alone. When he was satisfied that no one was coming, he went to the road and dragged the man to the stream below the fallen tree. Pushing away the hunger the smell of blood invoked, he rolled him into the water, briefly lamenting the loss of a good meal as the body slowly drifted away in the current.

He went back to the bridge and peered over the side. The other man was lying at an odd angle between two partially submerged boulders. Gryzzl thought he was concealed enough if anyone came along looking for them. He was hoping this mission would not take long, and he would be long gone before anyone noticed that these men were missing.

It had taken him days to find the scent of the bitch who had killed him in the cave, and he was surprised that the trail led from the lakeshore back here to the village where he had killed the So'ladiun. He would not fail his master this time. He would have the book—and the death of the female.

With one last glance at the road behind him, he slipped to the other side of the bridge, alert for any sound or smell that might suggest danger. Making his way into the night, he rounded a bend in the road. The woods thinned. He was able to see the cold pinpoints of lights from the distant village through the dark shadows of the trees bordering the roadway. Knowing that he could run into someone at anytime, he decided to slip off the road and walk along the tree line until he came across a lane leading away from the main road. Sniffing for the scent he was tracking, he realized the trail separated in two directions. One trail, the scent of the horse she had been riding, continued following the road. The other trail—her personal scent, led down the lane. That one was fresher. Gryzzl followed her trail. The narrow lane brought him to a rock cottage with a low, stone wall in front. His eyes flicked to a window, catching movement. A shadow broke the light filtering through the sheer curtain covering the glass. He growled in satisfaction. His search was over.

Silent as the night shadows surrounding him, he slipped through the open gate and carefully approached the window. The sheer curtain covering the window allowed him a gauzy view of inside. The bitch with the long hair braided down her back took a pot from the oven in the fireplace and placed it on a table. She pulled a chair out and sat down. She was alone. He growled softly, pleased with his good fortune. He backed away from the window and moved to the door. Gently, he tried the latch, but found it did not budge. She had it locked. Not about to be turned away by a mere locked door, he slammed a massive shoulder against the door. The door jamb shattered and he burst into the room. The woman screamed, knocking her chair over onto the floor as she vaulted out of it.

He jerked his sword from its scabbard and pointed it at her. To his liking, his intrusion seemed to have put the fear into her that she should have in his presence. She stood frozen in shock.

"Where is the book?" he asked. His guttural voice, unused to human words seemed foreign to his own ears.

Her eyes widened in surprise as she recognized who he was.

"You! How is this possible? I killed you in the cave!" She snapped out of her shock, sidling to the side, putting the length of the table between them.

He stepped towards her, assessing the options he had if she moved to one side of the table or the other.

"Killing me is not that simple. Where is the book?" he repeated. He stepped closer, hoping she would reveal which way she was inclined to go.

"The book is not here, and if it were, do you think I would give it to you?"

"Where is it?" he roared. Not being known for his patience, he chose the left side of the table and lunged for her.

She picked up the steaming ceramic bowl on the table and threw it at his head. He failed to duck far enough. It shattered against his rock-hard skull—boiling liquid drenched his face, soaking his fur and splashing into his eyes. A searing pain blinded him. Instinctively, he swiped at the pain, opening his eyes in time to see her blurred form grab a metal log poker leaning against the fireplace and swing at him with all her strength before he had the chance to defend himself. Pain exploded inside his head and Gryzzl went to his knees, roaring with anger that she had felled him so easily.

"I am going to kill you," he howled. He tried to stand, but found his legs did not want to cooperate.

The bitch tried to hit him again. He was ready for her this time, and wrenched the metal rod out of her hands. She jumped backwards and threw a nearby chair at him. He flung his arms up protectively, but the chair hung on the corner of the table and clattered harmlessly to the floor beside him. She seized the opportunity to take flight around the other side of the table and disappeared through the shattered doorway.

In anger, he grabbed the chair and smashed it repeatedly into the floor until it splintered to pieces. He could not believe she had defeated him once again.

He clawed at the table and used it to lever his bulk to his feet. The entire right side of his head was a throbbing mass, and he could no longer see out of his right eye. He touched his face gingerly—his fingers came away wet with his own blood.

She will pay for this, he fumed, stumbling out into the night after her.

Elhrin had just finished mending one of Bayle's shirts for her mother when she heard the faint sound of a scream coming from outside her cottage.

Wondering what was going on, she peered through a window, but it was too dark to see anything. She crossed the room to open the front door—and screamed. The hulking form of a scaly-faced reptilian man-creature filled the doorway. She tried to slam the door, but he caught it with a three-fingered claw and banged it open against the wall. The windows shuddered from the force. Elhrin backed away from the beast, trying to will her magic to respond, but her fear was blocking her ability to concentrate.

Behind her, Bayle's bedroom door flew open. When he saw the creature barging through the front door, he quickly grabbed his sword leaning against his bedroom wall and attacked.

"Bayle, no!" she yelled.

He swung wide. The Do'athrim side-stepped Bayle's blade and grasped him by the throat. He was jerked off the floor as if he weighed no more than a small child and flung against the wall. He landed in a heap on the floor, still breathing, but his eyes were glazed and unfocused as he stared at the floor.

In a panic, Elhrin tried to get her magic to respond. The creature pulled a long dirk from its belt, intent on finishing the kill. The door to her mother's bedroom flew open beside him. Startled, the beast whipped around and plunged his knife deep into the woman standing in the doorway.

"NO!" Elhrin screamed, watching in shock as her mother crumpled to the ground. She seized her magic, thankful it responded this time, and wrapped a magical flow of energy around the beast's body like a vise. She then lifted him into the air, flung him across the room and through a window, shattering the glass panes into a million pieces. She could only hope she had killed him. Letting go of her magic, she found Bayle had come to his senses and was crawling on his hands and knees to where their mother lay in a growing pool of crimson.

"No, mother, no," he sobbed over and over.

Elhrin ran to her mother's side and fell to her knees. "Mother, please, nooo!" she cried. She desperately tried to rouse her mother, but her mother did not respond.

Scraping footsteps came from the open door. The beast limped back inside, oozing a green fluid out of multiple cuts along his body.

"Which ones of you's has the pendants?" he asked in a lisping, gravelly voice. He now held a long, brutal-looking sword with an unusual hook on its tip.

Bayle scrambled for his sword. "What pendant?" he asked, as he placed himself between Elhrin and the beast. He shook with an uncontrollable rage. Tears flowed freely down his face.

"Bayle, no," Elhrin sobbed.

Bayle ignored her.

"The magician's pendants," the creature hissed. "Don'ts lies to me'sss. I knows you's has itss."

"I'm wearing it," Bayle yelled, and attacked the Do'athrim.

The lizard creature, weakened from his wounds, was hard pressed by Bayle's furious, out of control assault.

Elhrin watched the fight numbly, feeling like they were very far away and moving incredibly slow. She knew this wasn't right, that she should do something to help Bayle, but she could not get herself to focus and call on her magic. It was as if something inside her had shattered and sucked all coherent thought out of her mind.

Bayle managed to back the beast to the open doorway. The Do'athrim, sensing he was about to be pushed out the door, kicked Bayle's feet out from under him and sent him to the floor.

The lizard man pointed his sword at Bayle's throat. "Lets me haves itss."

"If you insist," said a voice from the doorway.

Elhrin heard a sickening crunch, and the lizard man started to fall towards Bayle. Bayle quickly rolled to his side out of the way as the beast crashed to the floor.

Marguerite stepped inside, holding a large piece of firewood in her hand. "Good thing you stack firewood by the door," she said, tossing the log back outside. "Oh, no," she breathed, seeing Xarah. She rushed over and knelt down, feeling for a heartbeat in Xarah's neck. Not finding one, she then reached for Elhrin and held her. "We have to leave. The village is being overrun by Do'athrim. One of them attacked me in my home looking for your book."

"This one was after Elhrin's pendant," Bayle choked out, running a shaky hand through his hair.

Marguerite made Elhrin look her in the eyes.

"Gryph gave both the book and the pendant to you for a reason. I don't know why, but I am certain it is important that these monsters don't get their filthy hands on them. We must leave right now."

"Mother," Elhrin sobbed.

"I'm sorry, dear, we don't have the time to take care of her properly," Marguerite said, sadly. "She would want you to be safe, Elhrin. We have to go."

"Where?" Bayle asked as he struggled to his feet.

"Let's try to make it to Toome's for horses. We'll go to Muryne. The king will give us protection."

Through the open door they could hear screams and the sounds of fighting coming closer from the direction of the village.

Bayle stepped by Marguerite and bent down to pick up his mother's small frame. "I'm going to put her on her bed," he said, his voice cracking with emotion.

"Elhrin, where is the book?" Marguerite asked.

"I'll get it," she sobbed. Climbing unsteadily to her feet, she staggered to her room and grabbed her satchel.

"All right, let's go," Marguerite said, waiting for them by the door.

Elhrin started for the door, but she couldn't bring herself to pass by her mother's room. It was wrong. If she left her mother . . . they would find her body . . . then what would they do? She could not walk out that door.

"Marguerite, I can't leave her like this!" Her mother lay on the bed, her face pale, yet peaceful despite the blood staining her gown. "I can't leave her for those beasts to . . . ," she choked off with a sob, unable to speak the unimaginable out loud. She willed her magic to respond. She was relieved when she felt the energy flow. Extending both hands in the direction of her mother, she sent an invisible flow of energy around the bottom of the bed. A wall of flames erupted from the floor, circling the bed. Fire engulfed the wooden frame and straw mattress, roaring high into the exposed beams of the roof. With a cry of anguish Elhrin let go of her magic. "Okay, now we can go," she said hoarsely, and rushed past them out the door.

They hadn't gone far when they heard the windows explode out of the burning cottage. Elhrin looked over her shoulder to see flames and smoke billowing out of the roof, windows, and the doorway. She couldn't breathe.

The grief she felt threatened to suffocate her as she ran with Marguerite and Bayle. When they reached the South Road, Elhrin glanced up at the village. Men and women were desperately fighting against a mass of Do'athrim. She started for them, but Marguerite grasped her arm and held her fast.

"As hard as this is to do, we can't help them, Elhrin. Those beasts know you or Bayle has the pendant, and if they see you, we are done. There are too many. We need to get you out of the village," Marguerite said, and pushed both Elhrin and Bayle in the direction of the blacksmith's home to get them moving again.

"Follow me. This way will be shorter. Elhrin, light," Bayle said, and veered off into the trees beside the road.

Elhrin waved a hand. A small globe of light popped into midair above Bayle's head and hovered close as they slapped their way through low hanging branches and tightly packed bushes. Bayle led them across a small brook, jumping the short expanse of water and clambering up a low rocky slope. Finally, they burst into the yard of the blacksmith shop. Marguerite yelled at Bayle and Elhrin to get four horses ready as she ran to Master Toome's house. She banged on the cottage's door.

"Maye! Open the door," she yelled. "Hurry!"

The door opened a moment later to reveal a short lady with gray hair pinned in a bun to the top of her head.

"What in the name of the heavens is wrong, Marguerite?" she asked.

"I'll explain on the way, come on," she said, and grabbed Maye's hand, dragging her along as she ran back to Toome's barn.

"Marguerite, wait, you're hurting me. What is going on?"

When they reached the barn, Elhrin and Bayle had two horses ready and were working on the other two.

"Bayle, we need weapons. Does Toome have any around here?" Marguerite asked.

"In the forge," he said, cinching the saddle on his horse.

"Maye, mount up. Elhrin, come with me," she said, and ran across the yard to Toome's forge. She thrust the forge's storage room door wide. It slammed against a barrel of raw steel rods with a bang. The barrel tilted to one side but remained upright.

"Light," Marguerite said, rushing inside.

Elhrin sent her light sphere zooming inside. A warm glow spread throughout the tiny room revealing a cluttered workbench and shelves filled with various tools and implements of the forge. In one corner was a barrel filled with basic, plain swords that Master Toome had not sold.

Marguerite grabbed three blades. "Let's go," she said, thrusting one in Elhrin's hand. She rushed back out into the yard. Bayle and Maye were already mounted and held the reigns for the other two horses.

Marguerite gave Maye one of the swords then mounted up.

Elhrin climbed into her saddle, unsteadily. It had been a long, long time since she had been on the back of a horse.

"You ready?" Marguerite asked

Elhrin nodded, wordlessly.

Marguerite kicked her horse and galloped out of the yard. Elhrin, Bayle, and Maye fell in right behind her, thundering down the road to Muryne at a dead run. Behind, the sound of screams, yells, and the clash of fighting receded with each fall of their horses' hooves. Over the din, a lone howl of a wolf sent freezing chills racing up Elhrin's spine.

Gryzzl reached the main road in time to see four riders burst out onto the road ahead and gallop away from him. One of them was the woman he sought. He lifted his muzzle to the sky and howled in frustration. He was too late.

After his fight with the woman, he had tracked her back to the village and had just reached its outskirts when he was surprised to see a band of his brethren fighting the villagers. At first, he wondered if the Do'athrim army had finally reached this side of the mountains, but then remembered this must be who his master had sent for the pendant. Dismissing his brethren from his mind, he had started to follow the scent of the woman again when one of his brothers had stepped out of a nearby copse of trees and stopped him. The burly beast had tried to order him to join the fight. Impatient to continue his hunt, Gryzzl killed his brother by severing the Do'athrim's head from his body. He had then continued the hunt for the woman, following her trail to a burning cottage and back to the road where he now stood. Watching the riders disappear into the night, he seethed with a blinding rage.

"I think I will kill this one slowly," he growled.

Chapter Seven

The journey to Muryne was like riding inside a living nightmare, running away from the monsters who were chasing you—not knowing if at any moment they would catch up and rip you apart. Elhrin remained on the edge of a hysterical breakdown, but she did not—could not give in to her emotions. Not yet. She had to remain strong this time. She had failed her mother, she could not fail them, too. They had to make it to Muryne safely and because the pitch black of the moonless night made it hard to see the road, it was up to her to provide light for their journey, even though she was almost too mentally exhausted to use her magic. But she did, regardless of the danger to her. Her small orb of soft white light hovered in the air above and in front of Marguerite. Giving off just enough light to illuminate the road and push away the darkness to the trees on either side, but it did not push away the horror of the night—the murder of her mother, or the fear of danger. Beyond the small circle of light, the forest was an impenetrable wall of varying shades of black. She was constantly looking behind them for signs of being followed or scanning the deep forests on either side of the road, listening for the sounds of movement among the dead leaves and limbs, wondering if the Do'athrim were among the tightly packed trees waiting to jump out and kill them. She kept envisioning a wolf head peering out at her from behind the gnarled, moss-covered trunks, but knew her exhausted mind was just playing tricks on her.

She scanned the forest beside her again. To her surprise, she realized she could make out the details of the nearest trees beyond her light. The long night had slipped away and the first traces of dawn were brightening the sky above the dense canopy of limbs and leaves. As soon as the natural light brightened enough, she released her magical light with a profound sense of relief. It popped out of existence as if it had never been, and it felt as if it took every last bit of her magical and physical energy with it. She felt hollow—lifeless inside.

"We are almost there," Marguerite's tired voice drifted back to her.

Elhrin peered past the two older women riding in front of her to see an end to the seemingly never-ending wall of trees lying ahead, and almost wept openly when they finally broke free of the shadows of the forest and rode out into the morning's first rays of sunlight and the rolling, dew-covered grassy hills overlooking the walled city of Muryne and the vast waters of Wyndermir Lake. They were here—they were safe.

She scanned the massive city whose rooftops of buildings and spires of the city's two cathedrals and the palace rose above the outer walls, thinking in another time, another place she would have been excited to be here. Eager to see the wonders she had heard of from those who had been here many times. The theatres, the outdoor arena, the marketplace, none of those things held any interest to her at the moment. All she wanted was to lie down and fall into a dreamless sleep, to forget just for a little while.

She shielded her eyes from the rising sun, trying to see as much of the lake as she could before the road took them to lower ground. Its immense size surprised her. She knew from the stories it was a large sea-like lake, but only having seen it one other time when she was just a child, she did not remember it being this big. Covered with a light blanket of delicate fog, it disappeared over the horizon to the east. And if she remembered correctly from the maps she had been forced to study of Anderan, it would eventually empty into the mighty Wyndermir River that connected the lake to the Yrahl Sea which made the city an important central hub for the shipping industry. Elhrin looked for the waterfront district, seeing a few ships anchored offshore, but it was hidden by the lay of the land and the walls hugging the lakeshore. The city was built on a large peninsula jutting out into the lake, and the docks would be located outside the city's walls along the entire tip of the peninsula.

After winding down and over low rolling hills, they approached the main gate trailing behind a lone wagon that had come from the opposite direction along the Eastern Road. This was the only way through the thick walls into the city from the main road. There were two more entrances into the city proper, but they were located on either side of the peninsula's tip along the waterfront to allow access from the docks.

One of the city's guards peered over the parapet high on top of the wall and took note of their arrival, but no one stopped them as they entered the long tunnel through the wall. The dirt of the road was immediately replaced with paving stones, making the clop of the horse's steel-shod hooves and the rolling wheels of the wagon in front of them echo loudly off the tunnel's walls.

When they made it through to the other side and back into daylight, the city spread out before them, and if her mind hadn't been clouded with grief and fatigue, she was sure its grandeur would have taken her breath away.

The last time she had been here was when she had been nine or so, and time had faded her memories of the city. She felt like she was seeing it for the very first time. The buildings near the walls were mostly private residences built two, sometimes three stories high, and were tightly packed against each other. Their exteriors were either a raw pale stone or plastered with a tan stucco and they had dark-tiled roofs unlike most homesteads in Glimmerdale which had thick thatched roofs. The occasional alley or roadway would break the rows of buildings as would the deep-water canals that gave the people of Muryne an alternate mode of transportation in and around the city.

As they moved deeper into the city, the buildings spaced out a little more, giving it a more open feel. Major roadways leading off to the far reaches of the city crisscrossed the main street they were on and common spaces for mini-marketplaces dotted several corners.

They rode by the Cathedral of Light, identifiable from almost anywhere in the city by a golden metallic replica of the sun perched high atop the church's single spire that brightly mimicked the fiery ball in the clear blue sky. The cathedral was a stunning architectural wonder with its pointed arch windows, carved adornments, statues of ancient leaders of the church, and a giant stained-glass mosaic depicting a burning sun on the front of the building.

On the far side of the church was one of the city's many parks. This one being of simple design with a lone sundial in the center of a carpet of green grass surrounded by rows of blooming pink and white dogwood trees. Above the top branches of the dogwoods, towards the center of the city, rose the spires and conical turrets of the Palace of Muryne, the home of the King of Anderan, and their destination.

She jogged her rattled mind for what she knew about King Goruth and his wife, Queen Egeria. She knew they had four children. Their eldest son and heir to the throne, Prince Cahail was in charge of the military garrison in the city of Tuhnichi. The two middle children, Princesses Destiel and Lexisa were married. Destiel was married to the Governor of the Southern Province, and Lexisa lived in the Western Province with her husband, an official of some kind. Their youngest son, Prince Movlin, was the same age as she, and she couldn't remember if Master Gryph told her he was in the army or studying at the University in Gildas.

Without warning, the unwelcome image of the beast plunging his knife into her mother and having to burn her mother's body flashed through her mind. She breathed in the chilly morning air and shivered. It was hard for her to grasp the reality of what she had been forced to do and it made her sick at her stomach.

Raking her fingers through her dew dampened hair, she darted a glance at Bayle. All color had washed from his normally suntanned face with the exception of a reddened nose and red-rimmed eyes. He had tried to hide the fact that he had been silently crying off and on throughout the entire journey, but they all knew. He had not spoken since leaving Glimmerdale, and had not responded to any of Marguerite or Maye's concerns for his welfare during the night.

She reached out a hand to him. At first, she thought he was not going to take her small offer of comfort, but finally he gave her a look of heart-breaking helplessness and took her hand. She squeezed his hand gently, he responded in kind then let go. They would have to talk soon. She did not want him to keep his hurt inside like he was prone to do . . . it would tear him to pieces.

She turned her attention back to the two ladies riding side by side in front of her. During their flight from the village, Marguerite had explained to Maye why they had needed to leave Glimmerdale. The older lady had been shocked to say the least, but she had not faltered, and Elhrin admired the strength and courage the two ladies possessed in the face of such horrible circumstances. She, on the other hand, was a shattered mess. It was her fault for not having the courage when she needed it most, and it cost her, her mother's life. She would never forgive herself for it as long as she lived.

They rode into the outskirts of the business district, and the area was alive with people starting their day. The shops were already open and their owners were busy setting up displays outside their doorways. The streets were increasingly becoming crowded, and they had to form a single line in order to go around a man and a woman pushing carts loaded with fresh baked goods.

As they neared an intersection, Elhrin started to feel strange. Her body seemed to go numb and her stomach roiled as if she were going to be sick. She covered her mouth and nose, thinking that a wagon of rotting fish parts was the culprit. She turned her head away from the stench and looked directly into the blue eyes of a deeply suntanned man riding in the opposite direction. Strangely, he tugged his cowl low over his face and turned his head away before she could get a good look at him. She frowned, thinking her mind was playing tricks on her because he had reminded her of Master Gryph. She turned in her saddle to look behind her. The man halted his horse and purchased a news sheet from a boy. He pulled a scarf up over his face as if he was cold then glanced her way once more before he turned to ride in the direction of the city gates. She lost sight of him when they veered off onto a street that paralleled one of the city's canals. Puzzled, she wondered why the look he shot her felt wrong, as if he hated her. She shook it off, thinking her battered mind was making up things and that she was just wishing that Master Gryph was here with her now. She needed him.

She looked across the dark and dirty waters of the canal to where the Palace of Muryne sat—its smooth, white stone exterior shone like a polished gem in the light of the early morning sun. Four stories high, it was adorned with spires and turrets placed on almost every corner of the many faceted building. There were no walls to protect it, and they were not needed. Its park-like grounds were completely surrounded by wide canals and were only accessible from two drawbridges spanning the water on either side.

Marguerite rode straight to the nearest bridge. Soldiers of the Royal Guard stood watch on both sides of the canal, and one stepped away from his post to stop them and ask for them to state their business. Marguerite told them who she was, and that they were here to see King Goruth. To Elhrin's surprise the man stepped aside and waved them through. Elhrin supposed being the wife of the late Minister Idwyr still carried some weight here.

Marguerite led them across the bridge and onto an avenue thrown into shadow from the row of age-old evergreen trees growing along both sides, creating a tunnel of dark green foliage. Meticulously kept lawns spread from the palace walls to the canals, broken only by crushed rock pathways, flower beds, and groomed hedges. At the end of the avenue was a gated archway leading into the main courtyard, and when they rode through, a forgotten memory of the last time she had been here surfaced.

In the center of the courtyard was a life-size fountain of four sculpted horses, rearing as if in anger on their hindquarters. Water spewed out of their mouths into a large catch basin below. It made her remember the reason for her first and only other visit to the city. News had reached Glimmerdale that Master Gryph had been ambushed and was dying from his wounds. Her mother had gathered Elhrin and Bayle into a borrowed wagon and traveled from Glimmerdale to see him, and she remembered being so worried about losing Master Gryph that she had cried nearly the entire way until she had fallen asleep. When they arrived at the palace, the fountain was the first thing she saw upon awakening, and its wild and ferocious feel had scared her. Even when he had recovered, she still associated the wild horses with her fear and did not like the fountain. She knew it was silly, knew it was just a fountain, but even now she did not want to look in its direction. Keeping her eyes glued to Marguerite's back, she followed the lady around it to the steps that led up to the palace's columned portico entrance.

Several palace groomsmen ran out to gather their horses as soon as Elhrin and the others dismounted. They brushed off as much dust and dirt as they could, but there was nothing they could do about the dried blood stains, so Marguerite guided them up the stairs and into the palace. A wide hallway led through open double doors to the left and right of the entrance, and was filled with people that either worked in the palace or were there for official business. No one gave them a second glance or stopped their progress, apparently too busy to reach their own destinations, and even if they had wanted to stop them it would have been difficult because Marguerite didn't slow down. Instead, she wound her way through the crowd with purpose and mounted a short stairway, obviously knowing exactly where she needed to go.

They entered the grand hall of the palace. The entire room, from floor to ceiling, was encased in marble tile with monstrous woven tapestries representing the five Provinces of Anderan on the walls. On either side of the room were matching marble stairways sweeping upward to a columned balcony. Directly over her head, in the wall of the entrance of the grand hall, was a stained-glass window depicting several kings and queens of Anderan. Sunlight streaming through the window cast a multitude of colors onto the marble tiles of the floor which became elongated and distorted onto Marguerite as she walked through them towards a set of doors with the carved crest of the state of Anderan. Two guards posted at the doors studiously watched them approach, but before they were halfway across the hall, one of the doors opened, and a man dressed in the royal colors of purple and gold came through. He immediately saw Marguerite striding towards him and narrowed his eyes. He met her before she made it to the doors, his displeasure obvious in the way he carried himself.

"Allow me to introduce myself. I am Osgar, the king's steward. Is there something I can help you with?" He flicked a look of distaste at each of them as if they had just crawled up out of the city's sewers and were fouling the air with an unpleasant stench.

Elhrin could see that the man's attitude was not going to go over well with Marguerite, and she almost felt sorry for the man. Marguerite straightened her spine and frowned down at the man who barely reached her chin.

"Could you be so kind as to inform King Goruth that Marguerite Idwyr and friends would like a private audience?"

"I am sorry, madam, but His Majesty has a full schedule today, actually, all of this week, and would not be able to accommodate you. If you could come back next week I may be able to work you in during the public audiences," he replied, and it was obvious he had no intention of helping them at all.

He started to turn his back on them, but Marguerite grasped a handful of the man's coat and jerked him around to face her. Furious, she leaned in close to his face. "Look here, you little runt of a man. This is important."

Osgar's eyes went round at the unexpected fury directed at him. "Madam, please unhand me," he stammered.

"Maye? Marguerite? What are you doing here?" a voice called from above. Master Toome leaned over the railing of the balcony.

"Lee," Maye cried, and had to push through a group of ladies who had stopped to listen to Marguerite and Osgar's heated exchange to reach the closest stairway.

Marguerite let the man go, but anger resonated from her like a burning furnace.

With an unpleasant scowl, Osgar brushed the wrinkles from his sleeve. "I told you, madam, His Majesty is busy."

"And I told you, it is imperative that we speak to him," Marguerite hissed low and deadly.

Master Toome met Maye at the top of the stairway and embraced her. "What are you doing here?"

"Glimmerdale has been attacked by those beasts, Lee. We rode through the night to get here," Maye said loud enough for all in the hall to hear.

Her announcement ignited an astonished flurry of whispers from the ladies.

"What?" he asked in disbelief, glancing down at Marguerite, who nodded her head in affirmation. He waved them up. "Come with me. I was on my way to drop off a requisition King Goruth had me write for the council last night. He will need to hear this, too."

"I told you this was important," Marguerite spat at Osgar. "Come along, children." She plowed through the group of ladies and mounted the stairs.

"Colonel Toome," Osgar protested, hurrying behind them, "his Majesty is expected in the council chambers momentarily."

"His Majesty was also expecting me five minutes ago. The council can wait," Master Toome said with authority and immediately turned to lead them down a long corridor lighted with oil sconces along the walls. He stopped at a set of double doors flanked on either side by two men from the king's personal guard. The steward, still sputtering about protocol, indicated for one of the guards to open the door. Elhrin and Bayle followed the men and ladies into a large, brightly lit sitting room. Several couches and chairs, upholstered in pale greens and trimmed in gold were placed in two seating groups near the dual marble fireplaces flanking each end of the room. In the center sat two massive tables with tall candlesticks, decorative glass globes, books, and vases filled with fresh-cut flowers on their tops. Dozens of paintings of people and places decorated the walls, and three multi-tiered glass chandeliers hung from the ceiling. A row of arched windows draped with heavy pine colored fabrics faced the centrally located royal gardens. From where she stood just inside the doorway, Elhrin could see a hint of the trees and shrubs through the windows.

The steward walked through the sitting area to a closed door on the right side of the room and knocked lightly. Elhrin heard a muffled male voice drift through the door. Osgar turned the brass knob and eased it open. He stuck his head inside. "Your Majesty, Master Toome is here."

"It's about damn time," a deep voice boomed.

Osgar stepped away from the door as the King of Anderan walked through concentrating on buttoning his coat. He was a stocky man of average height who exuded power with his mere presence, and Elhrin thought, a man you would not like to have for an enemy.

"Toome, do you think I have all day to wait on you? I need that requisition before I meet with council. Did you and Hascomb get it done for me?" he growled as he finished buttoning his coat and looked up to find Master Toome was not alone. "Good morning, ladies. I didn't know you were here." His ruddy face spread into a wide grin as he strode across the thick hand-woven carpets to greet them.

He offered a hand to Marguerite. "Marguerite, how are you faring?" he asked, bringing her hand to his lips and lightly giving it a kiss.

"I am well, Your Majesty," she replied.

"There has not been a day that I have not missed Gryph, especially now with our troubles to the north. I need him," he said with a sigh. "But we should not lament what we cannot change, can we? We use what we have." He let Marguerite go and turned to Maye, raising her hand to his lips, as well. "Like your husband, my dear Maye. He may think he is an old, worn out soldier destined to spend the rest of his days relaxing in Glimmerdale, but he is one of the best military minds we have. I will need that mind at my disposal and will do anything to convince him to return to my service full-time instead of the few instances he has spared me over the last decade."

Master Toome grunted under his breath in displeasure.

Smiling at Master Toome's obvious reluctance, he patted Maye's hand and let her go. "Egeria is not in the city at the moment and will be distressed that she missed you, Marguerite. She is in the Southern Province visiting Destiel. Tell me, what brings you to Muryne?"

"There has been another attack on Glimmerdale," Master Toome answered for her.

"What kind of attack?" he frowned, turning his steel gray gaze to Master

Toome.

"Maye said creatures like the ones before came back and overran the village last night."

"Damn it! What's next?" he exploded, then immediately held up a hand in apology. "Forgive me. Yesterday was a steady stream of upsetting news and it seems this day will start no better. Please sit down and tell me what has happened. Osgar, order refreshments for our guests."

Osgar bowed and left the room. King Goruth sat down and waited for the others to settle in their chairs. Elhrin was unsure of whether she and Bayle should sit or leave the room.

Marguerite noticed her hesitation. "Your Majesty, allow me to introduce Gryph's apprentice, Elhrin Caddoch, and her brother, Bayle," Marguerite said, as she sat in a chair next to the king.

Unused to royal protocol, Elhrin hoped she was doing the right thing and bowed. "Your Majesty." Bayle hesitated, then bowed, too.

The king nodded his head in acknowledgement and looked her over as if assessing her worth. "Gryph's apprentice—yes, I seem to recall him speaking of you, Elhrin. Please, have a seat, both of you." He turned to Marguerite, seeming to dismiss her and Bayle from his mind. "Marguerite, tell me about the attack?"

As Marguerite related the events of the previous night, Elhrin had a hard time keeping up with the conversation. Her fatigue threatened to overcome her, and she fought to keep her eyes open. She noticed Bayle doing the same thing, and it wasn't long before he lost his battle. His head slumped forward onto his chest. She couldn't believe that he had fallen asleep in the presence of the king, and was about to poke him when she realized that Marguerite had stopped speaking and Master Toome was now standing. She turned her attention back to the adults, and was startled to find the king staring intently at her as he listened to Master Toome. He had definitely not dismissed her from his mind. Frantically, she wondered if she had done something wrong—maybe she had fallen asleep and did not know it, but she didn't think so. She swallowed hard and looked anywhere in the room, trying not to meet his eyes. He wouldn't look away.

" . . . back to Glimmerdale," Master Toome said to the king, who nodded his head in agreement to whatever Master Toome had said. The king finally moved his gaze away from Elhrin, and it felt as if the weight of a full load of bricks had been removed from her chest. She breathed a silent, but deep sigh of relief.

"I will have a regiment ready to ride within the hour. You go with them and send me news of what you find," King Goruth said, his eyes flicking to the door as Osgar came back through with a servant carrying a tray of tea and an assortment of cakes, cheeses, and meat pies.

"Osgar, I need you to have Captain Loagyn meet me in the council chambers in ten minutes. Please make sure Madam Idwyr's apartments are habitable and find suitable accommodations near her for our young guests. Get them whatever they require. It appears they have had a rough night."

"Madam Idwyr's apartments, My Lord?" Osgar asked, not understanding.

"I keep forgetting you are new to this post." He leaned forward and lightly placed a hand on Marguerite's arm. "This is Minister Gryphon Idwyr's widow, and as you know, his apartment is right down the hall."

Osgar's eyes widened when he finally realized who Marguerite was, and that he had insulted the wife of the man who had been the second most powerful figure in Anderan as well as the king's closest friend.

"Yes, Your Majesty," he replied, and quickly left the room.

"Marguerite, I have a meeting with council members from the other provinces. We are going to plan a course of action to address the possible threat from the north. Would you accompany me and tell them your story and answer any questions they may have?"

"I would be happy to, Your Majesty," she replied.

King Goruth rose from his chair and the others rose too, with the exception of Bayle, who was still asleep.

"Wait here for Osgar to return and help yourselves to the food and drink," King Goruth said to Elhrin and Maye. "Toome, let me know what you find as soon as you can. Marguerite, if you will follow me."

After Marguerite and the king left, Maye grasped Master Toome's arm. "Lee, I am going with you."

"No, it is too dangerous. I don't know what we will find when we reach Glimmerdale. It will be best if I go with the troops alone. I will send word if I feel you can return." He took her hand. "Walk out with me."

Elhrin shook Bayle's shoulder. "Bayle, wake up."

"Wha . . . ?" his head snapped up in surprise. He blearily glanced around the room. "Where is everyone?"

"Marguerite went with King Goruth to a council meeting, and Maye went with Master Toome into the hall. He is leaving for Glimmerdale within the hour."

"He is? I would like to go back with him." He started to rise, but she put a hand on his shoulder.

"I don't think he will let you. Maye wanted to go, too, but he told her to stay until he sent word it was safe," she said, and glanced at the tray of food. "Do you want anything to eat?"

He eyed the assortment of snacks. "I'm not really hungry, but I think I will try one of these cakes," he picked up a small plate from the tray.

She watched as someone not really hungry consume two cakes, three pies, numerous pieces of cheese, and half of a pot of tea. At least, his appetite was okay. This made her feel somewhat better.

The maid that Osgar sent to guide Elhrin to her accommodations held open the door to her room for her. "If you need anything, just ask any of the maids who work on this hall. Oh, and if you wish for your clothes to be cleaned, place them on the floor outside the door," she said, perusing Elhrin's dirty tunic and blood-stained trousers.

"Thank you," Elhrin replied, as the maid closed the door behind her. She turned to look at her room.

It was a small interior space, no windows, but brightly lit by the numerous oil sconces hung on the walls and candles placed on the bedside tables. Far more luxurious than she was accustomed to, it was decorated with a feminine design. The walls were covered with a bright damask fabric of flowers on a cream base and the floor was a continuation of the marble tiles of the hallway, but covered with a large rectangular rug to match the rose and mint green color scheme of the room. The small fireplace across from the bed was topped by an ornately carved mantelpiece that held porcelain figurines and two tall brass candlesticks with thick pillar candles. A portrait of a young girl holding a small black dog in her lap and a tiny brown dog sitting obediently at her feet hung between the lit candles on the mantelpiece. In front of the fireplace were two mint-colored upholstered chairs and next to them sat a portable tub that had been brought in for her to bathe. She walked over to the tub and dipped her fingers into the warm water. Yes, more beautiful than back home, but it was not her home. She bit back her grief. She would not break down.

She glanced longingly at the canopy bed made of a dark, rich-looking wood, and draped with ruby velvet curtains tied to its four posts. A pale dressing gown and robe lay on the bed's matching coverlet. She sighed. She was so tired and her head hurt. All she wanted to do was sleep, but she decided that she needed to scrub the dust and . . . she swallowed hard . . . her mother's blood off her skin. She disrobed and slipped into the soothing waters of the tub, using her magic to douse all light save for the candles on the mantle and the bedside tables, wanting the comfort of the softer light to help calm her battered state of mind.

After her bath, she put on the dressing gown that had been provided for her, and remembered to put her clothes outside the door to be cleaned. Exhaustion was finally going to defeat her, so she climbed between the covers of the bed and curled up on her side to stare at the glowing embers of the small fire someone had lit for her.

Unable to stop them this time, the devastating memories of the night before flooded her weary mind. She gave in to her feelings and began to sob uncontrollably. Wailing at the unfairness of her mother being taken from her in such a horrible fashion, she couldn't believe that twice now she had to watch someone close to her heart die.

Why? she wanted to scream. She pounded a fist into the mattress, and then curled up into a tight ball as the racking sobs consumed her. She longed for the ability to go back and change what had happened. She should have never opened the front door and let the beast in. She should have helped Bayle. She should have done anything to keep the beast from her mother's door. She should have been stronger. She should have . . . was her last thought as sleep plunged her into a temporary reprieve from her grief.

Elhrin felt a presence in the quiet room and opened her eyes. Master Gryph sat in one of the chairs by the fireplace, facing her. Leaning forward with his elbows resting on his knees and his hands clasped together, he stared at the carpet beneath his feet, looking as if he had been waiting for her to awaken for some time. He seemed to sense her staring at him and raised his head to look at her. The sad compassion in his eyes told her he knew what had happened.

"Elhrin, I am so sorry."

Fresh tears formed in her eyes at the comforting sound of his familiar voice. "Master Gryph, I had to burn her body," she choked.

"I know, sweetheart, you were right to do so," he said.

"It's the hardest thing I have ever done, and Bayle—I don't know what Bayle thinks about it—if he thinks I'm a monster for burning her—if he blames me for her death."

"I'm sure Bayle does not blame you for what happened and understands it was a necessary act to burn her body. The Do'athrim are a nasty lot. You would not have wanted them to find her. Elhrin, do not blame yourself for any of this. It is not your fault."

She blinked several times to clear her vision. He didn't understand. It was her fault for not being strong enough to save her mother. "What will we do now? We have no home—no family," she whispered, dropping her eyes to look at the tiny flames of the dying fire that could be seen through his body. They were positioned exactly where his heart would have been and seemed to dance to the rhythm of an unheard heartbeat.

"You do have family. She may not be blood related and could never replace your mother, but Marguerite loves you just as if you were her own daughter."

"I know, but we can't impose on her."

"Never would Marguerite think you would be imposing on her. This will all work out, you'll see. But right now more important things are at hand, your destiny has found you, and the time has come for you to do what you were chosen for."

She jerked her eyes back to his. "What are you talking about?"

"Elhrin, I know you are hurting now, and this may not be the best time to talk to you, but I do not have a choice. I told you that you are So'ladiun. I was not kidding. You have been chosen to fight against any threat to the well-being of this country that Obsudius and his minions bring. As we speak, the army he is building at Blackridge Keep is expanding rapidly and already on the move. The army is very real, Elhrin, and so is the danger to the people of Anderan."

Stunned, she sat up.

"You mean I'm supposed to fight an entire army by myself?"

"No, Goruth will take care of the army. You have another task," he exhaled grimly, and stood to walk over beside her. "You have to go to Blackridge Keep and close the Rift."

"What is the Rift?" she asked, just as a knock rapped on the door.

"Elhrin?" The voice was muffled, but she was sure it was Bayle.

Elhrin glanced at the door then back to Master Gryph. He was gone.

"Elhrin?" she heard her name called again.

Her body twitched as if waking unexpectedly. She frowned, blinking several times to clear her eyes. She was sitting up in the bed, but the chair where he had been sitting had not been moved. It was in its normal position facing the fireplace.

Someone rapped on her door again.

"Coming," she called out. She slipped out of the covers and put on her robe. Cold tiles froze her feet as she padded across the floor. She opened the door to find Bayle on the other side, looking rested and clean, his color had returned and he appeared to feel better than he did earlier.

"Why are you wearing that?" she asked, uneasily eyeing the uniform he wore.

He looked down at the dove gray coat, buttoned to the collar, and charcoal trousers with a purple and gold stripe down the outside of the legs. "The steward had it sent to me since my clothes were ruined. It was the only thing available until I can get something new." He ran both hands down the front of his coat. "It's an infantry uniform. How do I look?"

"You look fine, but don't get any ideas," she said.

"I'm not," he said far too quickly for her comfort. He scrutinized her state of dress. "When are you going to get ready?"

"For what?"

"Marguerite said we are expected to dine with the king this evening."

"I didn't know that. I have been asleep, and no one has been to my room. What time is it?"

"Late afternoon," he said, "and we are supposed to meet in the main dining hall in a couple of hours."

"What am I supposed to wear?" she asked, glancing down to where she had left her clothes earlier and saw a package sitting in their place. "What is this?"

She picked up the package and carried it to her bed. Inside, was a pale-blue dress made of a soft silky material. A small note on top written in Marguerite's hand explained it had come from her.

Bayle admired the dress with a low whistle. "Are you going to wear it?" he grinned. "I don't think I have ever seen you wear a dress my entire life. Do you even know how to put one on?"

She stuck her tongue out at him. "Yes, I know how to put one on. Get out of here so I can change." She breathed a sigh of sad relief as she shut the door behind him. Bayle seemed like he was going to be okay, and he didn't seem to hold her at fault for what had happened. She wished she could do the same.

Not long after she finished dressing Marguerite came to her room and asked her if she felt up to a short walk around the grounds outside the palace before they were to dine with the king. Just the two of them, Elhrin suspected Marguerite wanted to give her a chance to talk about the night before. She blinked back moisture that threatened to build in her eyes. She didn't know if she wanted to just yet.

She glanced sideways at Marguerite, checking to see if the lady noticed her short bout of distress, but Marguerite was concentrating on keeping her dress from tangling with her feet as they descended the stairs to ground level. Unused to seeing Marguerite wear anything but simple durable work clothes, Elhrin thought she looked absolutely stunning in her midnight-blue velvet gown trimmed with gold scrollwork stitching. It set off the hint of blue in her gray eyes. Marguerite explained as they walked through the corridors and made their way outside, that both of their dresses were old ones she had left in her wardrobe in her and Master Gryph's former apartments.

"I must remember to ask Goruth why our apartment was not given to someone else," Marguerite said as she held open the door for Elhrin. She stepped out into the late afternoon air, smelling fresh with a hint of the chill night would bring. "He will have to find a replacement for Gryph soon. The country cannot go without someone to fill the role of Minister of Specialized State Defense. You would not believe the amount of correspondence from the far reaches of the country that I have had to forward here since Gryph's death."

"I can only imagine." Elhrin picked up the hem of her gown to keep it from dragging the ground as they walked down one of the many gravel paths. "I love the dress, Marguerite, but it is a bit long."

Marguerite grinned. "I apologize. It was the only one I had I thought you could wear. I have never worn it. The seamstress made a mistake and cut it too short for me. Honestly, I have no idea why I kept the thing." She reached over and rubbed Elhrin's back. "We will get you something tomorrow if you feel like shopping."

The two ladies crunched down one of the gravel paths to the canal in front of the palace and sat on a bench facing the water to watch the activity on the busy street across the way. Carriages and heavy wagons rattled noisily across the paving stones of the road as a group of men entered a nearby tavern nestled against an inn. Directly across from where they sat, a group of children ran down a set of canal access stairs across a boat landing and back up another set of stairs, playing chase.

A thought crossed Elhrin's mind as she watched the children play. "Marguerite, why did you and Master Gryph never have children?"

She heard Marguerite sigh.

"I'm sorry. I shouldn't have asked."

"No, it's fine," Marguerite replied, watching the children. "I wanted children—dreamed that one day I would have a houseful, but it was not to be. Gryph . . . he . . . well, he did not want any."

"That doesn't make sense. I thought he liked kids. He always had a mob following him around like a litter of puppies whenever he ventured into the village. He never seemed bothered by them."

Marguerite smiled at the memory. "Oh no, he was never bothered, quite the opposite. He loved to entertain, and you children could not get enough of his magical tricks. Those times were the highlights of his day."

"Then why would he not want any of his own?"

"Good question. To this day, I still don't know the bare truth of why. He avoided the subject at any cost, and for a long time I thought maybe it had to do with the difference in our ages because he always said that being ten years older he was too old for me and I figured he thought he was too old to start a family. But I guess that wasn't it. One day we had a difference of opinions on parenting after a mother publicly humiliated her child as a punishment here in the city. One thing led to another, and at one point I finally asked him why he did not want to have children with me. He looked at me as if I had slapped him. He told me that he wanted nothing more than for us to have children, but there was a reason why he couldn't. I know for a fact the reason was not that he was physically incapable, so I asked him what could possibly be stopping him if he wanted children. He said children were not in his future, and told me that he would understand if I wanted to leave him for someone who could give me the family I deserved."

"What did you say?" Elhrin asked.

"Nothing, I walked away," she said, sighing, "I couldn't grasp the fact he would say such a thing to me knowing how much I loved him. It took me some time to get over it."

"That must have hurt. Was that before or after you found out he had a son?" Master Gryph had an illegitimate son with a lady from his hometown of Pago Duhn, a small city on the east coast of Anderan.

"After, but I didn't use that against him. His son was born long before I knew Gryph, and he didn't know his son existed until about ten years ago when the young man showed up here. That was right before Gryph's injury. Do you remember meeting him?"

"No, I don't. I only remember bits and pieces of the time we spent here, and I only know about his son because Master Gryph mentioned that he was a sea captain one day when we were talking about how Anderan traded goods with other countries. I can't recall him saying anything else about him, and I don't remember ever seeing him visit you in Glimmerdale."

"Griffyn never came to Glimmerdale. His business kept him too busy."

"His name is Gryphon, too?"

"They are pronounced the same, but have a different spelling. His mother named him after his father. Griffyn Masstersun is his full name, and I'll never forget the look on Gryph's face when the young man told him that he was his son," she said with a small snort. "He certainly couldn't deny it. The boy looked just like how he must have in his early twenties with that thick black hair and blue eyes."

"Who is his mother?" Elhrin asked.

"She was a girl Gryph grew up with in Pago Duhn. I think her name was Lynh. I can't remember. Anyway, I think she thought they would marry one day until he left for Muryne when he was eighteen or nineteen. He didn't return to Pago Duhn until a few years later, after he had been employed by the king, and was sent there for some reason. That was when he met her again living alone in her parent's old cottage. He told me that she had led a rough life in the years after he left the first time. First her fiancée drowned in a boating accident, and then a year later, both her parents died from an illness within weeks of each other. He felt bad for leaving her again. He loved her in his own way and didn't want to hurt her any further, but he said he couldn't stay because his destiny was not in Pago Duhn, or with her. It's sad, really. The poor woman never married and lived a lonely life with her son until she passed away from the wasting disease the same year Griffyn found us."

Marguerite fell silent. Elhrin could almost read her thoughts, death was a guaranteed fate at some point in life, but there had been too much of it lately. Laughter from across the way drew her attention. The children were now throwing rocks in the canal. So full of life, nothing to worry about, Elhrin almost wished she could return back to those days, but then that would mean she would have to relive the horror of losing her mother, and Master Gryph last fall, and possibly others she loved who may not have survived last night's attack. No, that is not something she was willing to do over again.

"You know, destiny was a favorite word of Gryph's," Marguerite said, breaking the silence. "He used it the last time we talked about having children. He told me that he was who he was, and because of it children of his own were not destined to be a part of his life. I asked him what made him think that way, and guess what he did."

"He changed the subject," Elhrin replied.

"Exactly, he was so frustrating at times, never telling me everything, and I was furious for days that he would shut me out."

"Did he ever explain it to you?"

"No, but now, with everything that has happened and him giving you that pendant and book, I think it had something to do with you," Marguerite said.

"Me," Elhrin felt the blood drain out of her face. She averted her head, pretending to be interested in something far down the canal. This was too bizarre. Marguerite was talking about things similar to what he had told her in the dreams.

"Elhrin, did your mother ever tell you that Gryph and I were the ones who found your father?" Marguerite asked, surprising Elhrin with the abrupt change of subject.

"No, she just told me he had been killed by bandits on his way back from Muryne," she replied, wishing Marguerite hadn't brought up her mother, it hurt too much.

"That is true. Robbery was suspected because his wagon was gone. Gryph and I found him lying dead on the side of the road not too far from the village. We were coming from Muryne and were on our way to the Western Province, and we knew he wasn't just some vagabond left on the side of the road. Gryph put him on the back of his horse and we continued on to Glimmerdale to ask if anyone knew who he was. Turned out, we met Ralfe Yonge on the road before we reached the village and he directed us to your cottage. When we rode into your yard, we saw you outside playing. It was Gryph's reaction to seeing you that made me think about this now. He acted as if he was surprised by you, which looking back on it, knowing what I know now," Marguerite said, reflectively. "Strange."

Yes, strange would describe exactly the thoughts Elhrin had on the matter. She watched a man with a torch far down the street on the other side light a street lamp, noticing for the first time that the sun had dipped below the buildings across the way and dark was approaching. Elhrin glanced back at Marguerite, wondering why she had stopped her tale. This was the first time she had heard this story and she wanted to know everything. "What happened next?"

Marguerite shook herself out of her private thoughts. "When you saw us, you ran off inside the cottage and brought your mother out holding a crying baby. She saw your father on the back of the horse, and I thought she was going to faint and drop Bayle. Luckily, Gryph was close enough to catch her and the baby. I helped her back into the cottage while Gryph brought your father's body inside to be prepared for burial. I bet you don't remember him sitting on your front stoop talking with you that day, do you?"

Elhrin shook her head, wishing she could remember.

"I didn't think you would. You were so little and didn't understand what was happening. He stayed with you while I asked your neighbors for their help, and when we were sure you and the baby and your mother were in good hands, we went to stay at the inn. That night, Gryph informed me he liked Glimmerdale and asked what I thought about living there permanently. I was elated. I had been secretly longing for a place of our own because we traveled constantly, and the closest thing we had for a home was our apartment here. I hated living here, so I never questioned what prompted him to settle down in Glimmerdale. Looking back on it now, I feel like maybe he had been looking for you all along in our travels and had finally found you that day."

"Why would he have been looking for me, Marguerite? It doesn't make sense." Unless her dreams were true, but even so . . . .

"Elhrin, Gryph did a lot of things that never made sense to me. Sometimes he would do something, and I would think he had lost his mind, but it always worked out for the best in the end," she smiled. "His intuition simply amazed me, and I can tell you it got him out of many predicaments. I just wished it had worked for him last year."

"Me too," Elhrin sighed. "Still, if he was looking for me, why?"

Marguerite shrugged her shoulders. "The only thing I can think of is that you have the gift of magic, and it being rare in this world—maybe he needed to be around someone like him."

"But I didn't know I could do magic then. How would he?"

"I don't know, but I don't have any other explanation."

They sat in silence for a few minutes, each lost in their own thoughts, and Elhrin watched as the torch carrier lit the last lamp along the canal and then disappear down a side street. She was dumbfounded by Marguerite's words. Had he really been looking for her? Could the dreams be real? Could she really be one of Solisius' So'ladiun? And what made her so special that he could not have children of his own because of her? A horrible thought crossed her mind. "Do you resent me, Marguerite?" Elhrin asked quietly, almost afraid of the answer.

"What?" She gave Elhrin an incredulous look. "Why would I resent you?"

"Because, after my powers showed up, he spent most of his time with me when he was home. Maybe he would have changed his mind about you two having children of your own if I hadn't been around so much."

"You stop that line of thinking right now, Elhrin Caddoch," she scolded. "I love you as if you were my own. I would never, ever resent you." She squeezed Elhrin's hand.

An unexpected feeling of solace enveloped her. Master Gryph's words once again came true—Marguerite was family. "I love you, too," Elhrin said, tightly holding onto her hand. "Marguerite, there is something I've wanted to talk to you about, but just wasn't sure if I should. But now, after what you have just told me, I think I need to tell you."

"What is it dear? You can always talk to me."

Elhrin swallowed hard, hoping what she was about to tell Marguerite would not upset her.

"I have had dreams of Master Gryph."

Marguerite sighed. "Me, too, I dream of him all the time."

"These dreams are so different from all my other dreams. In them he is speaking to me of things that are happening here and now, and he is in the same room with me, or beside me wherever I have fallen asleep. It feels so real, like he is truly there."

Marguerite turned her body to face Elhrin on the bench. "Tell me about them."

Elhrin told her briefly about the dream by the river and in her room earlier, leaving out the part where he told her she was So'ladiun because, for some reason, she just couldn't bring herself to reveal it.

Marguerite turned her head to stare out at the street across the canal. Elhrin thought the lady was going to scoff at the idea of dreams being anything other than the manifestations of the mind.

Marguerite shook her head as if she couldn't believe what she had just heard then turned to look at her. "Elhrin, you are so much like Gryph it is uncanny. Don't be so quick to dismiss these dreams. I believe that some dreams come to you for a reason, and I feel that it is possible that he is truly talking to you."

"But if the dreams are real, and he is truly communicating with me, then he told me that I am supposed to close a rift and I have no idea what he is talking about. I just can't believe this is more than a dream."

"Let me tell you something, young lady. Living twenty years with a man who had magical capabilities taught me never to dismiss what most people would consider the impossible. I have seen the impossible most certainly become possible many times, and Gryph used to have dreams all the time he believed in. Some he would share with me and others he would refuse to tell me about no matter how many times I would ask him to tell me. I can now tell you for a fact that I have witnessed one of his dreams turn into reality." She shifted on the bench. "Years ago, when you were little, Gryph had a nightmare. He startled me from my sleep one night when he sat up in bed yelling the word, no. I can tell you having someone scream in your ear is not a pleasant way to be awakened," she said with a little laugh. "He was extremely upset over this dream. When I finally convinced him to tell me about it, he said he watched as monsters overran the village and threatened to kill me and you, and that he could not do anything to stop them. I told him it was just a nightmare that you were home safely tucked in bed, but he would not settle down. He said in the dream you were older, not a little girl, and the dream ended before he found out what actually happened to us. I had never seen him so upset over a simple dream like that before. I could not get him to go back to bed. He paced the floor the entire night."

"You think what he saw was what happened to us last night?" Elhrin asked.

"I do now."

"Then if that is so, do you think the reason he could not stop them in the dream was because he was not here, he was already dead?" she said.

"I do now," Marguerite repeated with a sigh.

"So, you truly think he thought his dream would come to pass?"

"I can't think of any other explanation why he would be so upset. You knew him, Elhrin. He rarely got upset over anything unless it had to do with us."

That was true. Forever the optimist, a problem had to be something major for him to worry. "I wonder if he knew that was the reason he couldn't help us. That he would be dead before the village was attacked."

"I think he did," she replied.

Elhrin could not believe what she was hearing. "Marguerite, did he tell you he thought he was going to die?"

"No, that is not something he would ever do, but when I brought the subject up he did not deny it or offer another solution. I can only assume he knew."

The children on the other side raced down the street, yelling at the top of their lungs like maniacs. Marguerite laughed at their silly, care-free antics.

"Marguerite, have you thought about remarrying? You are still young. There is still time for you to have a family."

"No, I will never remarry," she said, losing her smile. "I didn't just lose a husband. I lost my best friend, my soul mate, my lover, and in the process, I lost a good part of me. Elhrin, I loved him so much, and when he died, he took my heart with him. It will never be replaced."

"I understand," Elhrin said.

"Look at me. Sitting here talking like this when you have just lost your mother."

Elhrin bit back a lump in her throat. She did not want to do this right now—did not want to talk about what had happened. She needed to not think about it for awhile. "I'm fine. Should we be going?"

"Elhrin, I know you are avoiding the subject. I won't press you, but know that I am here when you are ready." Marguerite stood and smoothed the wrinkles out of her dress.

"I know," she entwined an arm around one of Marguerite's.

Arm-in-arm, they took a different route back, walking along the tree-lined avenue, stepping aside as a group of armed soldiers rode past and clattered over the bridge behind them. All Elhrin could think about was, if the dreams were real—did that mean she was truly a So'ladiun? A breeze shifted the ancient pines overhead, sounding as if they were answering her with the whispers of their boughs.

Yes, she heard a voice whisper.

Elhrin looked back. No one was on the avenue or the lawns on either side. They were alone.

"What is it?" Marguerite asked.

"Did you hear someone say something?" Elhrin asked with a frown.

"No, did you?"

Elhrin shook her head slowly. "I thought I did . . . must've been the wind."

Chapter Eight

Two days later, when Elhrin and Bayle felt ready to venture out into the city, Marguerite gave them money and directions where to purchase new clothes. They had just left the last shop with their arms loaded down with packages when they saw two soldiers gallop past, nearly running over an elderly lady in the middle of the street, making her drop a crate of produce to the paving stones.

The lady shook her fist at the men, but they did not look back. "You sons of bitches!" she yelled at the top of her lungs. "If I ever get a hold of you bastards, I'll cut your balls off and feed them to you for breakfast!" She put her hands on her hips and surveyed the damage to her food. "Run over an old lady like that," she huffed as a stooped old man shuffled into the street.

"I told you not to go," he said.

"Shut up, Laurence, and pick this mess up," she growled.

Bayle grinned at Elhrin. "I don't believe I have ever heard anyone threaten that before."

"Me either," Elhrin watched the soldiers disappear down the crowded street. "One of them looked like Tomas. Was he with those who went to Glimmerdale?"

"I have no idea," Bayle shrugged his shoulders.

"Let's find out," Elhrin said, trotting off down the street.

"Have a crush, do you?" he called.

"No," she said over her shoulder. She was not about to reveal to Bayle that, while she was trying not to have any feelings for a man she would never get to know, maybe she did.

They ran the entire way to the palace, and when they arrived, Maye and Marguerite were waiting on the balcony above the grand hall.

"There you are," Marguerite said when they topped the stairway. "Looks like you were successful. Did you find everything you need?"

"We did, thank you, Marguerite," Elhrin said, grateful for the woman's generosity which was something that was not new to her or Bayle. Master

Gryph and Marguerite had always given them money or gifts as long as she could remember. "We saw two soldiers head this way in a hurry and thought they might have been from Glimmerdale."

"I think you are right. We saw Osgar escort them to the king's apartments," Maye said, "and are waiting to find out."

They heard a door close down the hallway and turned to see Osgar standing in the middle of the hall, summoning them.

"Madam Idwyr, His Majesty requires your presence," he said, when they reached him. He opened the door for her to enter, but held out a hand to stop the others. "He requested you only, Madam Idwyr."

"They go where I go, and if this concerns the fate of Glimmerdale, then this concerns them, too," Marguerite replied in a tone that Elhrin knew meant the lady did not have any patience with the man, and dared him to argue with her. "If the king objects to them being with me, I will deal with it personally. Move aside."

Osgar's mouth thinned into a sharp line. Elhrin doubted he was used to being spoken to in such a fashion by someone who was not in a position of power. He motioned for them to enter.

King Goruth was sitting at a table near the windows, talking with the soldiers who stood a respectful distance away. Elhrin felt her face flush for no reason. As she had thought, one of the soldiers was Tomas. The other soldier, a fair-skinned, fair-haired man standing with his hand on the hilt of his sword, looked like he was no older than Bayle.

King Goruth turned his head at the sound of their entrance, tossed a napkin onto a half-eaten plate of food and stood. "Good, you are here, Marguerite. Osgar said you were waiting in the hall. These men bring news from Glimmerdale and Lakeshore Glen. I thought to save time and let you hear what they have to say first hand." He eyed each of them individually. "What is said here is confidential. I do not need rumors spread. Do I make myself clear?" His eyes fell on Elhrin last and remained there. She thought he was going to ask her to leave, but he did not, he merely waited until they all agreed before asking them to have a seat near one of the fireplaces. The two soldiers remained standing.

Elhrin reluctantly perched on the edge of her chair almost wishing she could leave. Being in King Goruth's presence made her feel uneasy. He always stared at her as if she had done something wrong, and she was beginning to think she had been right about him blaming her for Master Gryph's death, for not helping her mentor fight the beasts by the river.

When everyone was settled, his eyes left hers and he introduced the two soldiers. "This is Private Gerald from Lakeshore Glen and Lieutenant Colkitte who is also from Lakeshore Glen. It is my understanding you met him in Glimmerdale the other day and know the news he brought from the north. I had him return to Glimmerdale with Toome to verify the beasts attacking the village are the same as those he saw assembling at Blackridge. Lieutenant, tell us your news, beginning with what you have already told me."

Tomas flicked a quick glance her way, but then directed his news to Marguerite and Maye. "The news is not good. The beasts are the same as the ones being seen in the north. They destroyed much of the village and many of the villagers have been lost. Last count of casualties before we left was estimated at one hundred seventeen, not including the injured."

"Oh, dear heavens," Maye whispered.

"The only good news is that the village is now secure. All Do'athrim have been killed. The last of the beasts were found ransacking homesteads on the outskirts of the village yesterday afternoon. Colonel Toome has ordered double watch on the central village area as a precaution against further attacks and Major Riffkin has patrols combing the outlying areas."

"I must go back," Maye said.

"Maye, you can leave with the next troop to go out if you wish. Lieutenant, I would like to know which way the beasts entered the village?" King Goruth asked.

"It has not been determined, Your Majesty." Tomas lowered his eyes to the floor as if the lack of information was his fault. "The survivors report that they just appeared out of the night without warning, and as of yesterday evening, no one has found signs of a major passing anywhere outside of the village. They may know now."

King Goruth sat back in his chair and folded his arms over his chest. "Unbelievable. How many beasts were found?"

"Fifty-six, Your Majesty," Tomas responded.

King Goruth growled low in his throat. "If these are the same beasts as those at Blackridge we need to find out where they are crossing the mountains to get here. It does not appear they are using the pass. Did Riffkin send anyone to Greystone?"

"Yes, Your Majesty," Tomas said.

"Good." King Goruth turned his attention to the other soldier. "Private, you had to come through Greystone. How does it fare?"

The young man snapped to attention. "Your Majesty, there is nothing to report. The village is safe as of four days ago and no one indicated a problem when I stopped briefly at the Road Patrol house on the outskirts of Comahr Forest on my way here."

"I would be interested to hear what the news is now . . . what have you to report from Lakeshore Glen?"

"By now, the town will be under siege. Commander Nivle sent me here before they sealed the city. He had sent a troop to the town of Blackridge, and half of them returned to the city at a dead run. Captain Tull of the regiment reported that the town of Blackridge was gone and in the hands of the enemy. He reported seeing a beast I have only heard about in fairy tales." He shook his head as if he had a hard time believing the story.

"A beast different from these Do'athrim creatures?" King Goruth asked, frowning. Elhrin saw out of the corner of her eye that he looked her way. Why did he keep looking at her? She didn't know any more about the creatures than he did. She pretended not to notice and kept her eyes fastened on the young soldier.

"Much different, Your Majesty. He said this beast was bigger than any animal he had ever seen and reminded him of the old tales of the dragon of Styringill. It flies and attacks from above with magic. It destroyed buildings in Blackridge with ease."

King Goruth let out an explosive sigh and raked both hands through his thinning muddy gray hair. "This is all I need. A myth, come to life," he frowned at the floor and murmured something under his breath. It sounded like, "I need Gryph."

"What about the army? Do you have an estimate as to its size?" he asked.

"Your Majesty, the last report before I left suggested well over two thousand marching toward Lakeshore Glen. If there are more . . . ." The soldier shrugged his shoulders.

"I sent a regiment of three hundred men to Nivle. Did they stop in Glimmerdale?" King Goruth asked Tomas.

"Only long enough to speak with Major Riffkin, Your Majesty," Tomas said. "He told them to continue on their way."

"Good, they are still on the move, but if that army is as big as you say, they won't be nearly enough to compensate Nivle's troops. Osgar, gather the council, immediately, and my military advisors," he barked the order to his steward who responded so fast, he was almost out the door before the king finished his orders. "I had the council send a request two days ago to their provinces for men as a precaution. By law, they are to grant me a thousand men at my request outside of war. But it seems we are at war after all." Grunting as if the weight of impending war made it hard to move, he rose heavily from his chair. They all stood with him. "And we will need more men than I have requested."

"Marguerite, Maye, you all are welcome to stay here for as long as you like, but if you feel the need to return to Glimmerdale you may ride with my men. I will have them ready to leave at dawn tomorrow."

"Your Majesty," Bayle boldly spoke up. "I would like to join the army, sir."

"What?" Elhrin's mouth dropped open. He had never mentioned he was going to ask to join the King's Army.

Bayle frowned, but did not dare look her way.

"Son, I appreciate your enthusiasm, but it is my understanding that you and your sister lost your last surviving parent," the king said. "Wait on making any hasty decisions for now. Your sister will need you." He immediately turned on his heel, motioning for the soldiers to follow him out. "You men—with me. I have an edict of war to declare." He shot a quick glance at Elhrin as he passed, but said nothing.

Tomas flashed Elhrin a small smile as he followed the King out. Elhrin felt her face go red hot and hoped it didn't show. She stepped out into the hallway with the others and watched him until he was out of sight. She then rounded on Bayle. "What were you thinking? You know mother didn't want you to enlist in the army," she hissed.

"Back off, Elhrin," he retorted. "I know that, but I want to. This is war. You heard him. He needs soldiers, and I can fight just as well as anyone."

"Well, did you hear what else he said? I need you, too," she nearly shouted.

"That's enough," Marguerite said, as she put her hands on each of their shoulders. "Let's go back to my apartment. We can talk about this where it's private."

"I think I will go into the city," Maye said. "I need a few things before I leave for Glimmerdale in the morning. I will see you tonight."

"Okay," Marguerite propelled the two sullen youths to a door just a short distance down the hall.

Marguerite's apartment was one of the more spacious living accommodations in the palace given to the upper government officials or visiting dignitaries. It consisted of an open living and dining area, separate bedroom, and a luxury only the wealthy could afford—a private bath with running water.

Elhrin and Bayle flopped down in cushioned arm chairs situated in a seating arrangement around a low marble-topped table, and refused to look at each other.

Marguerite quietly closed the door behind her and contemplated the two for a moment. "Elhrin, maybe you should tell Bayle about your dreams."

Elhrin gave Marguerite a look of astonishment. She hadn't planned to reveal her dreams to anyone else.

"What dreams?" Bayle grumbled.

Marguerite returned Elhrin's look with a blank face. She nodded once. This was something she believed Elhrin should do. "Elhrin has been having dreams I am inclined to believe are more than mere dreams. There are too many events happening that confirm what Gryph has said to her."

Bayle turned in his chair to look at Marguerite. "Master Gryph?"

"Yes, Master Gryph," Elhrin spat out. She did not want to tell him.

"Elhrin," Marguerite warned. She touched Elhrin's shoulder lightly as she passed by on her way to a sideboard where wine bottles, a glass pitcher of water, and fine crystal goblets sat. She poured each of them a glass of water.

"What? He won't believe me," Elhrin grumbled. "Why should I tell him?"

"Because he is your brother and I think he should know what you are experiencing." She handed Elhrin then Bayle a glass. "And sometimes other points of views can help."

Elhrin hesitated, then reluctantly told Bayle a scaled down version of her two dreams, and as she expected, Bayle looked from her to Marguerite and back as if the two of them had suddenly turned insane and needed to be locked up in the Gildas Home for Mental Patients.

He blurted out his thoughts. "He told you all this in your dreams and you are considering going to Blackridge Keep to close whatever a rift thing is? That is just crazy. You can't do something based on a stupid dream, Elhrin. It's all in your mind."

"Exactly what I want to think too, Bayle," Elhrin sighed, slumping down in her chair, staring at the painted portrait of Master Gryph and Marguerite over the nearby fireplace. It was so hard to discuss her dreams without revealing the part of him telling her she was So'ladiun. "But what if this is what I am supposed to do? It feels so real. I wish he had told me more," she said, flinging a hand at the painting of a happy younger couple. Master Gryph looked about thirtyish with thick black hair, deep blue eyes, and a clean-shaven face. Marguerite looked like a young maiden barely in her twenties, dressed in a white evening gown, her long blonde hair coiffed elegantly on top of her head with strategic wisps draping down to frame either side of her face, one hand intertwined with his hand on her shoulder.

"Marguerite, you can't seriously be agreeing with her about this, can you?" Bayle asked.

"Bayle, as unrealistic and crazy as it all seems, yes, I do. I lived with the man for twenty years, knew him for a few years longer than that, and I have seen many, many strange things happen around him that were incredulous and some I would just as soon forget. Elhrin has the same gift as he did. Her dreams could very well be real."

He huffed loudly and shot out of his chair. "I can't believe this. Just because she can do magic you believe her." He stormed across the room and jerked open the door leading out to a private balcony overlooking the palace grounds and city beyond. He slammed the door behind him.

Elhrin eyed Marguerite. "That went well."

Marguerite shook her head. "He doesn't have to believe, but I think it best that you communicate with him more, Elhrin."

Elhrin nodded. "Okay, what now?"

"Now we try to prove your dreams are not real. As much as I believe you, I don't want to believe my husband wants you to do something as dangerous as to go to Blackridge Keep."

Esarai stumbled out of The Dancing Dog tap room and fell down the steps into the street. Grumbling, he picked himself up and gulped in a mouthful of the cool night air, then proceeded to cough violently. It was too crisp, too clean, and far different from the black fog of tobacco smoke he had just left behind. He turned around, unsteadily, and glared at the door.

"How dare she kick me out? S'not late," he grumbled under his breath, trying to button his coat. For some reason he couldn't find any holes for the buttons and was certain there had been some when he donned the coat that afternoon. He gave up, and belched loudly, then smiled, pleased with the two tones he had been able to achieve. He then lurched down the street dimly lit by the flickering street lamps lining the canal, wondering why the lights danced and weaved, and so did a night watchman walking toward him.

When the man drew near Esarai tried to salute him, but missed and hit himself in the eye. "Ow!" He clapped a hand over the eye, stumbled off balance, and careened into the wall of a nearby building, knocking over a rain barrel underneath one of the downspouts. Water splashed across the road.

"Get home, drunk," the night watchman growled as he dodged the river of water.

I'm not drunk, Esarai thought, and whirled around to yell at the night watchman, just barely keeping himself from falling over the overturned barrel. "I'll haf you know. I'm nah drunk!"

The night watchman did not acknowledge that he heard him, and disappeared down a side street.

"Don't know why peoples keep shayin m'drunk," he mumbled, and immediately tripped over the barrel, ran crazily across the road like a carnival acrobat trying to keep from falling off a tightrope, arms spinning. Miraculously, he managed to remain on his feet. He laughed at himself. "Tha' was close." He grabbed his crotch. The jarring of his bladder made him realize he had better empty it soon. "Canna' go home wet again. She'll kill me."

He spied a stack of barrels sitting by the wall, and thought it would be as good a spot as any. He looked up and down the street to check that he was alone and fumbled with his trousers to free himself, letting out a long groan of satisfaction when his stream blasted out onto the paving stones like a newly tapped keg. He grinned at the thought, swaying with his eyes closed, listening to the splattering of his stream hitting the ground—then the side of the wall—and back to the ground, wishing the bitch at the Dancing Dog would have let him have just one more pint. But he guessed it was just as well she didn't. It was long past time to get home to his wife. She didn't like it when he stayed out like this, but he deserved it, didn't he? He worked damn hard at that god-forsaken shit hole of a slaughterhouse, up to his eyeballs in blood all hours of the day. The last thing he wanted to do was hurry home to listen to her bitch about what a useless piece of horse-shit he was. No, he was in no hurry to go home. He forced the last bit of urine out and shook himself off.

He heard something move behind him. He peered over his shoulder—nothing there but the street lights and tendrils of fog drifting up out of the canal. He put himself away and adjusted his clothing. Another faint scrape came from the stairway leading down to a boat landing in the canal. It was too faint to be someone docking, so he dismissed the noise as being a tethered boat rubbing against the landing.

He made a decision. His wife be damned, he was a grown man. He was going to The Waterside. They stayed open all night and didn't care how much you drank. Then he heard the scraping sound again, like a faint scuffling of boot on stone. He blinked several times and shook his head to try and clear his vision.

"Who's there?" he asked.

Two red pinpricks of light, like floating eyeballs of fire peered over the canal wall.

"What the . . . ?" he slurred, and then an unbearable pain exploded in his abdomen. Staggering backwards, he crashed through the stack of barrels and slammed against the wall.

"Son of a bitch!" he gasped, looking down in shock to find an arrow sticking out of his stomach. He gingerly touched the area with a shaking hand and felt warm fluid ooze onto his fingertips. He brought his hand up to his face to inspect them just as footsteps echoed in the silence of the night. The red points of light came up the stairway and into the circle of light cast by a street lamp.

Esarai couldn't believe what he was seeing. A giant beast with the head of a wolf, covered in a thick, black fur that disappeared beneath the leather armor on its man-like body was coming at him. His heart slammed against his ribs and he couldn't breathe. His legs gave way, forcing him to slide down the wall and land in the puddle of urine he had created moments ago. He wanted to get up and run away, but none of his limbs would obey. He watched in absolute terror as the beast slung a bow over its shoulder and draw a sword from its side, never breaking stride as it approached. He heard a ghastly low moan like one of the slaughterhouse cows in intense pain from a poor kill, then realized it was coming from his own throat and was gaining in strength. The beast stopped at his feet and towered over him with sharp teeth bared wide into a menacing snarl. Trying to scream, Esarai briefly saw a flicker of light flash off the blade of the sword, then a searing pain in his chest, and before he drew his last breath, he insanely thought his wife was going to be extremely angry that he never came home.

Elhrin stuffed a new shirt into her satchel, packing for the journey back to Glimmerdale, and thought about the conversation she and Bayle had with Marguerite and Maye the night before. After dinner, the four of them had adjourned to Marguerite's room to discuss what they needed to do, but before they were able to, Marguerite had brought up the painful subject of Elhrin's mother's death. At first, Elhrin was uncomfortable and didn't want to talk, but Marguerite persisted with careful and compassionate prompting until she and Bayle finally gave in. Elhrin had to admit it had been a much needed conversation, especially for Bayle who had held everything in since that horrible night, and she could tell the talk had helped him. After they moved on from her mother's death, Marguerite steered the conversation back to what they needed to do, telling them that she had checked Master Gryph's old office in the council's office wing downstairs and it had been cleaned out of everything but the furniture. She said he hardly ever used it and felt if he had anything of importance it would be back home in Glimmerdale. When no one came up with a better idea, they agreed to return to the village despite Marguerite's hesitation about the dangers. The concerns for those that had been left behind overrode her fears and they all wanted to help the survivors in any way they could. Elhrin especially wanted to search Marguerite's cottage, hoping Master Gryph had left something that could give them some kind of answers or direction to what was going on now . . . and maybe more information on the So'ladiun because so far, none of the writers in the *Book of Tolman* had mentioned being So'ladiun.

A knock on the door startled Elhrin out of her thoughts, and she opened it to find Bayle dressed in a new slate gray tunic and brown trousers, and had a pack typically given to the soldiers in the army slung over one shoulder.

"You ready?" he asked.

"Yes," she replied, "just let me get my satchel."

"I passed Marguerite and Maye in the hall. She said to meet them in the courtyard," Bayle said, as they left her room. "Have you heard the news this morning?"

Elhrin shook her head.

"They found a man floating in the canal across from the palace. He was murdered," he said, as they walked down the hall and descended the stairs of the grand hallway, explaining in detail the state the body was in and how the fish in the canal was already picking at the flesh.

"That's horrible," Elhrin said when he finished, "do they have any idea who did it?"

"I don't think so," Bayle replied.

They descended into the entrance hall and could see Marguerite and Maye standing just outside the door deep in discussion.

Marguerite saw them coming. "Elhrin, I need to talk to you," she said, and pulled her aside. "I couldn't sleep last night. I can't get past the fact that those beasts came to the village looking for the items you possess, and if we go home, others looking for it will have no trouble finding you again. Are you sure going home is what you want to do?"

"I don't know what else to do?" Elhrin said.

"We can always stay here for a little while. Give it a little more time and try to figure out from here why those items are so important to these creatures."

"I know, but both of the items came from Master Gryph and he gave them to me for a reason. You said yourself that if there are answers to be found from him it would most likely be back home. I want to know why?" She put a hand to the solid lump under her shirt. "The book has given me direction somewhat with my magic, but the pendant . . . why did he want me to have it? Marguerite, I want to go through his study and see if he left anything behind that could give us answers. I want proof my dreams are not real. My intuition tells me to go home."

Marguerite smiled slightly then nodded. "I won't argue with your intuition, dear. I couldn't tell you how many times I have relied on Gryph's. We will go, but I want us to be alert. The lieutenant said all Do'athrim were killed, but they have no way of knowing for sure if any may have escaped. It makes me extremely uneasy that the beast that attacked me in my cottage was the same one . . . ." Marguerite cut off her words, as if she said more than she meant to.

Elhrin frowned. "Same one . . . what?"

Marguerite clamped her lips together, hesitating. "I wasn't going to tell you this, but I suppose there is no point in it now. My trip to Muryne before your birthday was not for personal reasons. It was to retrieve your book from Gryph's hiding place."

"Hiding place? I thought you got it out of Master Gryph's study."

"No, Gryph hid it earlier last year. He said it was extremely important that the book was kept safe until it was time for you to have it," she stopped, staring off in the distance. Elhrin watched her face go from astonishment to anger.

"Gryph knew," Marguerite burst out. "The overgrown walking tree . . . he did know!"

"Knew what?" Elhrin was puzzled. Bayle and Maye stared at them curiously.

Marguerite faced her and lowered her voice to a hoarse whisper. "That he was to die last fall."

Elhrin's eyes widened. "I thought you were just guessing about that."

"I was guessing, but apparently he did know. Why else would he go to all the expense and trouble to hide it like he did if he didn't think he would be around to keep it safe himself? Why didn't I realize that at the time?" she fumed, looking past Elhrin at the crowd of people in the courtyard. "Why did he have to keep so many secrets from me?"

"I guess to keep you from being sad," Elhrin said, shrugging her shoulders. "You said you worried about him after his dream. Maybe he wanted to protect you from counting the days when he would go."

"Yes, I know." Marguerite lost her anger. "He was a protector." She sighed. "But sometimes he protected me too much. I'm a tough old bird." Marguerite winked at her and nodded her head at their horses across the courtyard. "We had better mount up if we are going to go. I don't want to hold up the soldiers outside."

In a copse of trees outside the city walls, Gryzzl watched a long line of soldiers and the ones he followed ride out of the city gates. A low growl rumbled deep in his throat. The night before had frustrated him immeasurably. It had taken him too long to find a way into the city without being seen by the humans along the walls, and then, of all things, a drunk saw him and left him no choice but to kill it and dump it into the canal. Afterward, he had tried to find a way into the palace where the female was staying, but there had been too many guards on the palace grounds. By the time he realized he was going to have to find another way to reach the female, the sky started getting lighter, and he had to go back outside the walls to wait for the next night and try again.

Now, watching as his quarry disappeared out of sight, he wanted to howl in frustration. This was taking far longer than he expected. His master was not going to be pleased. Rising to his feet, he sprinted through the trees, once again in pursuit.

Chapter Nine

Elhrin and Bayle stared helplessly at the remains of their cottage. It had burned completely. Only parts of the outer wall and foundations were left. Everything else was ash and charred stumps of wood. The past few days had not been a nightmare from which they could awaken. It was real. Their mother was dead. Their home was gone—and now, so were many of their beloved friends and neighbors.

"Goodbye, mother," Elhrin said softly, and glanced up the lane where the other cottages nearby had also been destroyed, the dim light of dusk making their blackened exteriors look like oversized tombstones, which they were. No one on this row had survived, including her friends, Nolina and Sib.

She felt like she could hardly move. The weight of how her life had been turned upside down was almost too much to bear. She patted Bayle on the back, and turned to go back to the inn. Bayle followed silently a moment later.

It was going to take a long time for the village to recover from all the damage. Master Toome had given them a brief update on everything that was happening, and had told them a strange story about how the bodies of the Do'athrim had somehow disappeared, and no one could figure out what had become of them. Elhrin wondered how fifty-six bodies could simply disappear without anyone noticing what happened.

Another question with no answer, she thought, as she and Bayle cut through the rows of burned and damaged homes to the main street of the village where a major cleanup was underway. Master Toome was in the street with several men, directing a wagon near a pile of debris outside his and Maye's weapons and hardware shop. It had burned completely to the ground. The acrid stench of burned and charred wood permeated the air. Fires had ravaged many of the shops, and those that still stood were burned out shells with some of the outer walls caved inward.

Luckily, the Glimmerdale Inn was still intact, only singed on the outside where the bakery nestled up against its left side had burned to the ground. Triva's place was still standing, as well, but the interior was a mess, and

Marguerite's apothecary shop had the front window busted out and the front door hung precariously on one hinge. It had been ransacked, but not burned, and Marguerite had been able to salvage some of her wares to help the injured being cared for in the inn.

"I'll meet up with you later, Elhrin," Bayle said, and ran to lend a hand with the clean up.

Elhrin crossed the street and entered the Glimmerdale Inn. It was absolute chaos inside. Most of the tables had been cleared out of the common room to make a place for the injured. She recognized many familiar faces in pain or sleeping on blankets placed on the floor, and Triva, Father Jerome, and several other ladies of the village were busy helping them.

Elhrin searched the room until she finally located Marguerite in all the confusion. She was in the back near the bar, kneeling next to a man, bandaging his arm.

Elhrin made her way through the maze of injured on the floor. "Marguerite, is there anything I can do to help?"

"Maye, Kara, and Eleanor are in the stable yard washing bed clothes and making bandages. They could use your help," she replied, briefly glancing up from her work.

Elhrin made her way down the dark back hall and out the door. She found Kara, the baker's wife, ripping a bed linen into strips for bandages right outside the door. "Kara, do you need help?"

The woman shook her head without looking at Elhrin or stopping her work. Normally, an enthusiastic, almost overly friendly woman, Elhrin couldn't blame her for her stoic demeanor. Her baby girl had been among those killed, and she was keeping busy so she would not have to confront her loss. Elhrin could sympathize. She was doing the same thing.

"Let me know if you do." Elhrin patted the woman on the shoulder and walked across the stable yard to where Maye had two boiling cauldrons of water over hot fires. She looked exhausted. Sweating from the heat and exertion of washing linens, her skin was bright red and her hair had fallen in wet tendrils around her face.

"Maye, I'll help you do that," Elhrin said, taking the washing paddle out of Maye's hand.

"Thank you, dear," she replied, wiping her forehead with the back of her sleeve. "A shame isn't it?" She nodded her head at Kara. "So many loved ones lost."

Elhrin turned the cloth in the cauldron. "Yes, too many," she whispered.

Maye leaned in and wrapped an arm around Elhrin's shoulders. "We will get through this, love. We will get through this together." She placed a kiss on Elhrin's cheek and walked away to help Eleanor hang linens on a nearby line.

Elhrin rolled the bed sheets in the water, grateful to have something to occupy her mind other than her personal worries and losses. Both her best friends had perished in the fight. She punched air bubbles out of the linens. She should have stayed. She should have helped to fight the beasts, not run like a scared puppy with her tail between her legs to the safety of the city. Why? Why did she run? Was she right in what she said to Master Gryph? That she was incapable of killing even something as horrible as the Do'athrim? Tears of loss, frustration, guilt, and who knows what else flowed down her cheeks. She glanced up at Kara. The woman ripped cloth as if each piece was a limb torn from the beasts that killed her baby. What if she had stayed and fought, would the baby still be alive?

She punched the linens again. She knew she couldn't turn back time— couldn't take back what she had done, or more accurately, not done, but she could shape her future—she could make sure that whatever happened from now on, it wouldn't be because she did not try. One thing about her dreams of Master Gryph she knew was true. He had taught her how to fight with her magic, and she would never—ever—back down or run again. She hoped.

"It's ready," Bayle said, placing the last log in the dark fireplace. Elhrin sent a tendril of magic to the fireplace, and tiny flames appeared among the logs. When she was satisfied that the wood had caught and would burn on its own, she let go of her magic. For the first time since returning to the village, they observed the disaster inside Marguerite's cottage. The place had been ransacked, and the floor was covered with broken furniture, crockery, and rotting food.

"Let's light some candles, and I'll see if I can find a usable lamp," Marguerite said with a sigh.

As tired as they all were, none of them wanted to leave the cottage in a mess. It took them an hour or so to clean up the living area and bedroom, and when they were through, they sat down in front of the fire exhausted.

"It has been a long day," Marguerite said, closing her eyes. "Elhrin, you and I will sleep in my room. Bayle, I'm sorry we don't have another bed. Will you be all right in here tonight?"

"Yes, I'm so tired I could sleep anywhere," he said, stretching and yawning.

"Before we retire, we need to barricade the doors and windows somehow," Marguerite said, and opened her eyes to look at the two teens.

"Master Toome said there had been no signs of any more Do'athrim," Bayle said.

"I'm not taking any chances. There weren't any signs last time, either," she replied and stood up. "Let's get this done and go to bed. I want to get into Gryph's study as soon as I can tomorrow. It will take awhile with the state it is in."

The next morning, they ate a small meal of salvaged fruit and tea, then Bayle left for the village to help Master Toome, and Marguerite and Elhrin began the cleanup of Master Gryph's study. They had been working silently for almost an hour when Marguerite finally spoke.

"What's this?" she asked, frowning down at a piece of folded and creased parchment.

Elhrin, who had been returning books to a bookcase, glanced at the woman sitting cross-legged on the floor behind Master Gryph's desk.

"Did you find something?" Elhrin asked, stepping over a pile of books she had sorted and stacked on the floor. The Do'athrim had ripped every last book in Master Gryph's collection from the shelves and dumped them on the floor.

"It's an old letter from Gryph's son. Let's see, it's dated five years ago. He says he will have a ship ready by the time Gryph arrives in Pago Duhn," she said, glancing up at Elhrin. "He asked Gryph if there was anything special he needed for such a long journey. Gryph never mentioned to me about leaving the country when he went on that trip." Marguerite sat there for several minutes staring at the page. "Humph," she said finally.

"What is it?" Elhrin asked.

"I knew he had to go to Pago Duhn, but I wonder why he had to leave Anderan. No wonder he was gone so long. It was the longest we had ever been separated since being married."

"That must be the time I waited day after day on that big rock at the end of the lane looking for him to come down the road from Muryne," Elhrin said. "I hated it when he left Glimmerdale."

"You know, Elhrin, as I recall, he came back wearing the pendant he gave you. That was when he gave me this ring," Marguerite said, and lifted her hand to show Elhrin a deep blue oval sapphire set in a gold ring. "He said he got these from a merchant in the east. I guess he went a little further east than I assumed."

"I wonder where it came from?" Elhrin asked, pulling the pendant from under her shirt. Dangling from the gold chain, the gem was oblong in shape and green in color, and had an almost imperceptible inner glow to it. "Have you seen the strange glow it has? It's not very bright at all, but you can see it in the dark."

"Yes, I have. Gryph would never remove it. I told him it looked like he slept with a firefly sitting on his neck," Marguerite replied with a tiny smile, and started to get up off the floor when she noticed something underneath a nearby bookcase. She reached under it, and pulled out a long sword with worn black leather wrapped around its hilt. A dark blue almost black sapphire was embedded in its pommel and its polished steel guard was carved in the shape of two eagle heads, the sharp tips of their beaks pointing towards the point of the blade. "Here's Gryph's sword. I hadn't noticed it wasn't hanging on the wall where he kept it." Grunting, she used the desk to pull up off the floor. "My back is killing me. Let's take a break."

Elhrin watched as Marguerite hooked the sword's hilt onto brackets behind his desk. "Marguerite, when he gave me this pendant he said to never take it off. I wonder what is so special about it?"

"Good question. How about asking him the next time he visits you in your dreams, and while you are at it, tell him I have a bone to pick with him about all these secrets he has kept from me. Oh, and if you don't mind, mention to him I think it would be nice if he visited me in my dreams," she said as she disappeared through the doorway.

Smiling, Elhrin followed her into the kitchen.

Marguerite surveyed the meager rations left in the cupboard. "You know, we need supplies. Triva told me yesterday she was expecting a wagon from the south this morning, and Doogan said to stop by his place if we need anything. I think I will take him up on that offer. He was lucky they missed his place. We could use some eggs." They had discovered her own chickens had been eaten on the spot by the Do'athrim, and the coop was sickening to see. Blood, feathers, and uneaten body parts were strewn everywhere. They still did not know what had happened to her cow, and hoped it had escaped and was roaming unharmed in the countryside somewhere.

"I can go for you," Elhrin offered.

"That would be lovely, and I can continue to work on straightening Gryph's study while you are gone," Marguerite said. "Tell Triva to let Father Jerome know I will be in town to help in a little while as I promised."

An hour or so later, Marguerite was grimacing at the mountain of papers on Gryph's desk when she heard someone come into the cottage.

"Elhrin, you should see the pile of papers I have gone through. I think that man saved everything he ever wrote or received," she called out, then stopped to listen when Elhrin didn't respond. "Elhrin?"

Footsteps trod across the living area floor. The loose floorboard in the hall creaked.

"Elhrin?" Marguerite called again—a trickle of unease crept up her spine.

A large figure then filled the doorway. Marguerite's eyes widened, and she quickly whipped around and jerked Gryph's sword from its brackets, but he was too quick for her. She was slammed face first against the wall. His arm pinned the back of her neck, making it difficult for her to breathe.

He lowered his muzzle to her face and snarled, "I am going to ask you one last time. Where is the book?"

She glared into his blood-red eyes, noticing one was glazed over. "Do you know your breath stinks?" she asked.

He roared in fury, gripped her shoulder painfully, and threw her across the room into a bookcase. It cracked and splintered, sending its contents flying. Gryph's sword jarred out of her hand and clattered to the floor just out of reach. Pain ignited in her back as she landed in a heap amongst shards of wood, books, and papers.

The Do'athrim sidled past Gryph's desk and pointed his sword at her. "I should kill you like I did your mate. Tell me or not, I will still find the book."

Marguerite's head snapped up, hate filling every fiber of her body. The son of a bitch killed Gryph. "Then kill me, you monster, because I am not going to make it easy for you," she spat out and lunged for Gryph's sword.

The Do'athrim tried to stab her. The blade nicked the side of her neck and embedded into the wood of the ruined bookcase. Marguerite's hand wrapped around the leather of the hilt and she started to swing, but was surprised when the beast suddenly soared through the air and crashed hard onto the desktop, scattering a mountain of papers across the room.

"Thank the light," Marguerite breathed.

Elhrin stood in the doorway with her hands outstretched before her. She jerked the beast off the desk with her magic and slammed him hard against the wooden beams of the ceiling. The wolf barked in pain. She lowered him halfway to the floor then slammed him back into the wooden beams with an audible crack. He howled.

"Elhrin, stop," Marguerite commanded. "I need to ask him questions before we kill him."

Elhrin pinned him forcefully, high against the wall. He snarled and howled, trying to break the invisible bonds that held him, but found he was unable to move.

Marguerite glanced at Elhrin. The young girl was terrified. Sweat ran down her face and her arms trembled as she concentrated on holding the massive beast against the wall. Marguerite had a sinking, dreadful feeling that the girl would need to overcome whatever barriers she was placing on herself before long. Gryph did nothing without reason, and giving that book and pendant to Elhrin was not a whim. Marguerite had known all along, especially after the day he died, those two items he possessed were special, but what she did not know was why.

The beast barked in frustration.

Marguerite struggled to her feet, and the pain that shot through her back almost sent her to the floor again. She limped over to the snarling beast and pointed her sword at him.

"Now it is my turn, dog," she said. He emitted a low growl deep in his throat. She pushed her sword tip tight against his throat. He shut up. "I want to know why you want the book."

Hate-filled eyes glared at her, and when he did not answer, she pushed her sword point into his neck until it drew blood. He barked a startled yelp of pain.

"Answer me," she shouted.

"My master sent me for the book. You pathetic humans should be very afraid. My master is going to destroy you," he rasped.

"Who is your master?" she asked.

He laughed. At least, she assumed it was a laugh. It sounded more like a maniacal series of yips and barks. "He is the one that will eliminate your race for the God of Do'athra."

"Marguerite, he's heavy. Hurry, I'm getting tired," Elhrin said, gritting her teeth.

"Why does your master want the book?" Marguerite asked.

He said nothing, but continued to try and wriggle free of Elhrin's hold.

"Marguerite," Elhrin said, desperately.

Marguerite glanced at Elhrin. She would have to hurry. Elhrin was not used to holding someone against their will. The strain of his strength fighting against her must be tremendous. "Elhrin, try to hold him one more moment," she said, and turned back to the beast. "I know I killed you in the cave. How is it that you are not dead?"

He bared his ugly stained fangs, and she thought he wasn't going to answer her. She pressed the sword tip a little harder against his neck. "I came through the Rift," he choked.

His body abruptly slid down the wall causing her sword to drive through his throat. Choking, he grabbed her blade with both hands trying to remove it, but she gave it a twist. He gasped, and his body went limp. She let him drop to the floor.

"I'm sorry. I couldn't hold him any longer," Elhrin said out of breath as if she had run at top speed a long distance.

"You did fine," she said, looking with distaste at the dead beast. "He confirmed what Gryph told you in that dream, Elhrin. He said there was a rift. Do you still believe you are only having dreams?"

Wordlessly, Elhrin shook her head no.

"Help me get him outside. Then I want to find Toome. He needs to know what we have just learned," she said, ignoring the pain in her back to reach down and grab one of the beast's arms.

In the end, Marguerite stayed at the cottage to tend to her own wounds and sent Elhrin to find Master Toome. Elhrin reluctantly agreed. The thought of leaving Marguerite alone with the beast made her uneasy, even though she knew he was dead.

She found Master Toome and Bayle on their way out of town in a wagon loaded with burnt bits of lumber and destroyed pieces of furniture. She quickly told them what had happened and climbed in the wagon to ride back to Marguerite's with them. When they arrived at the cottage, Marguerite was waiting outside her front door beside the dead beast.

"Marguerite, are you all right?" Master Toome asked, jumping from the wagon.

"Yes, thanks to Elhrin," she replied, and repeated the events of the fight that Elhrin had already told them, adding what they had been able to learn from the Do'athrim about the rift.

Master Toome blew out a huge breath and rubbed his eyes. Elhrin hadn't noticed before just how tired and how much older he looked. "So, he was sent here after Elhrin's book by someone answerable to Obsudius, the God of Do'athra? I find that hard to believe. Where is his master? And what is a rift?" he asked, folding his arms across his chest.

"I couldn't tell you for sure, Toome. He said his master was carrying out the will of Obsudius, which I took to mean the army that has been discovered outside of Blackridge Keep. So, my guess would be, his master is there. As for the rift, I honestly don't know exactly what it is, but maybe it is some way for a dead being to enter back into the world living again," she said, reaching up to touch the bandage on her neck.

"Have you lost your mind, Marguerite?" he asked. "Tell me, how is it possible for the dead to walk out of the spiritual realms, living and breathing again?"

"I don't know the logistics of it all, Toome, but this is the second time I have killed this particular Do'athrim and he said he came through the rift," she said, pointing at the beast.

He stared at her opened mouth for a moment, and then narrowed his eyes. "Second time? Suppose you tell me about the first time."

Marguerite sighed and related her story of retrieving the book from a cave on Casteal Island.

"What were you thinking by not telling anyone where you were going? That was a dangerous thing to do. What if you had been killed? No one would have ever known what happened to you," Master Toome admonished her.

"It wasn't supposed to be dangerous. I knew how to disable Gryph's mechanism, and besides, how was I supposed to know he was going to be there ahead of me?"

Master Toome crouched down for a closer look. "How can you be sure he is the same one? There have been a good many that look like this."

"Toome, I know for a fact this beast is the very same one who attacked me in the cave," she replied defensively. "How else would he know I had the book? Gryph never told anyone but you and Goruth he even had that book. I'm fairly certain neither of you told anyone about it, have you?"

He stared up at her for a moment as if she would ever doubt his trust. "No," he drawled out the word, "that is something you know I would not do." He grimaced at the beast. "Fine, I will not argue with you on the matter, but I still do not believe someone can come back from the dead." He pushed himself up with a grunt. "What do you want to do with him?"

"You can leave him for the carrion fowl for all I care," she replied, bluntly. "Do what you think best."

"Bayle and I have a load of debris we are dumping in a ditch outside of the village. We'll just bury him under it," Master Toome said. "There is no need to raise anymore fears with our neighbors by letting them see that one more creature has been in the area. Bayle, help me load him."

For the next few days, the three of them spent time helping with the cleanup of the village, taking care of the wounded, and rebuilding homes destroyed in the attack. Marguerite could hardly move from her bruises and cuts, but still went into the village to help. She and Elhrin spent the evenings sorting through Master Gryph's things in his study, and Elhrin studied the *Book of Tolman* in her spare time, searching for anything that would tell her about the Rift.

Each day, they saw several army regiments passing through the village heading west. Master Toome told them the king was gathering his forces south of Kilmyn Pass in the North Reach Mountains, and the king himself was to pass through Glimmerdale on his way to join them in the coming week.

Late one night, Elhrin sat alone at the kitchen table with her book. Marguerite and Bayle had already retired, exhausted from the day's work, so she had decided to take advantage of the quiet to skim through Master Gryph's writings again. She had finally been able to get herself to read them, and found that he had actually already told her a lot of what he had written. She almost knew his chapter by heart, but had decided to once again look through to make sure she had not missed anything.

She propped her elbows on the table, placed her chin in her hands, and stared blankly at the far wall, listening to Bayle breathe noisily through his mouth as he slept by the fireplace. She couldn't quit thinking about the pendant. Why would the Do'athrim want it?

Elhrin slipped it from under her collar. Its faint inner light was slightly brighter in the dim light of the oil lamps and candles in the room. She turned the natural gemstone in her fingers. What was so special about it?

Knowing she would not find the answers to her question, she decided to go to bed, and called on her magic to extinguish the candles near the fireplace.

A bright glow erupted from the pendant just as the flames atop the candles winked out leaving a tiny trail of smoke from their wicks. Letting go of her magic, she stared at the pendant in surprise, wondering why it had responded to her use of magic. The stone's inner light receded to its original state of a miniscule glow.

She called on her magical energy, holding it in check. Again the pendant responded by intensifying its inner light, casting a soft green glow across the top of the table.

What does this mean? she wondered, and noticed a new light coming from the table. The page where the book was open began to glow green, and the words started to swirl and distort. She let go of her magic and rubbed her eyes, thinking she must be overly tired and was seeing things. The pendant lost its glow, and when she looked back to the book, she saw only the handwriting of Master Gryph.

She decided to try again, and called on her magic. As the pendant began to brighten, the words on the page once again started to swirl and distort until the entire page was covered in a soft glow that began to reveal a distorted moving image. Astonished at what was happening, she watched as the image started to sharpen and focus until, finally, it revealed Master Gryph moving through the darkened corridor of a cave, but it was a younger Master Gryph. His hair was almost completely black with just a touch of gray, and he did not have the beard she was used to seeing him wear.

"This is incredible," she murmured, watching as he moved through the cave, lighting his way with a small sphere of light floating in front of him. He wound his way through the tunnel until he came upon a narrow crevice in the cave wall and stopped. He sent the light sphere inside the crevice, and then dropped the pack he was carrying and turned himself sideways to squeeze through the narrow opening and work his way through until he reached a small grotto where the cave ended. On the far side of the grotto, a vein with a faint green glow trailed down the rock wall and ended on the floor where a mass of sparkling green crystals had formed. He squatted before the crystals, and used his knife to gently dislodge one from the mass. He held up the crystal in front of the light sphere and inspected the gem. Nodding to himself, he seemed satisfied with its quality.

The image she watched, flickered, winked out briefly, but then reappeared to show Master Gryph standing on a rock, high over a jungle of trees and a turquoise blue sea beyond. The image flickered again, and she saw an older Master Gryph, the one she clearly knew, standing on a riverbank. His arms were spread before him, and he faced Do'athrim across a river. Elhrin immediately let go of her magic and sat back in her chair.

"I do not want to relive that day," she whispered, as the pendant's light diminished.

Excited, she picked up her book and hurried into the bedroom. Marguerite was sleeping on her side facing the door, one hand tucked under the pillow at her chin. Elhrin skirted the bed and sat on the opposite side.

She gently shook Marguerite's shoulder. "Marguerite?"

Marguerite stirred, and sleepily turned over just enough to look at her. "Is something wrong, Elhrin?"

"No, I have found out what the pendant can do. Look," she said, and opened the book on the mattress of the bed. Marguerite turned completely over to watch.

Elhrin held the pendant and called on her magic. The pendant brightened and the page of the book once again swirled before Elhrin.

"Do you see, Marguerite?" she asked. The book was showing the same scene of Master Gryph walking through the cave.

Marguerite scrutinized the page. "What am I supposed to be seeing?"

"You don't see Master Gryph walking through a cave?"

"I don't see anything different except your pendant is now brightly glowing."

Disappointed, Elhrin let her magic go. "I could see it. I don't understand why you couldn't see it, too."

"Maybe it's something only you can see. I don't possess the pendant nor do I have any magical abilities."

"Maybe you're right," Elhrin said, glancing down at the book. "I wish you could see it, though. It's like seeing him alive again."

"Describe it for me." Marguerite leaned back on her pillow.

Elhrin related what she saw to Marguerite in as much detail as she could, but decided to not mention the part where it began to show the day of his death. That image was already ingrained in their heads.

Marguerite stared at the ceiling, saying nothing. Finally, when Elhrin had almost given up on her making any comment, she turned her head and looked at her. "Well, we now know he didn't get the pendant from a merchant in a faraway city," she said. "I wonder what else he has lied to me about."

"I suppose he had his reasons for not telling you, Marguerite."

"Maybe so, but I can't think of one good reason for not telling me the truth," she said, and turned her head back to stare at the ceiling. "You better come to bed. We have a lot to do tomorrow."

Elhrin donned a night gown then lay down beside Marguerite, realizing as she pulled the covers over her that she had forgotten to extinguish the lamps in the other room. With a slight wave of her hand, the lights winked out and the bedroom was thrown into a sea of dancing shadows from the flickering fire in the bedroom's small fireplace.

"Gryph used to do that." Marguerite's voice drifted softly out of the dark. "Never could remember to extinguish the lights before getting in bed."

Chapter Ten

Elhrin opened her eyes to the darkened room. The only light came from the dying coals in the fireplace. Behind her, she could hear the quiet, even breathing of Marguerite sleeping, and Bayle's snores in the other room. Elhrin's thoughts quickly turned to her discovery of the pendant showing her the moving images in the book. She couldn't believe how amazing it was to see an actual event from the past happen as if you were there. She wondered if she were to use the pendant with writings of the other magicians, would the book show images of them.

"Not necessarily, it will only show you images of people or events that you need to know to fulfill your destiny if they reside within the book's pages," a quiet voice said behind her. "Solisius designed the pendant to only answer to its owner's individual circumstances."

Elhrin flinched from the unexpected voice—glad she didn't give in to the scream that wanted to burst forth and awaken Marguerite. She rolled over to see Master Gryph standing on the other side of the bed.

"You can hear my thoughts?" she asked, not in the least surprised to see him. "I don't know if I like that."

He grinned, put a finger to his mouth for her to be quiet, and shrugged his shoulders.

"So, does that mean Solisius controls the pendant?" she whispered.

"Not directly. The crystal is his creation and he has imbued it with a magic that will help with tasks relating specifically to its holder. That is why he sent me to get it."

"He sent you to get it? How did you know he wanted you to go get it?" Elhrin asked, trying to grasp the idea of a god speaking directly to a mere human.

"That particular request came to me in my dreams," he said, and sat on the bed beside Marguerite, smiling fondly down at her sleeping form. Elhrin noticed the bed did not sink or move under him.

"Elhrin, have I spoken to you about dreams before?"

She shook her head.

He grunted, displeased. "Well, I should have. Dreams are important for the So'ladiun. While you will have ordinary dreams like anyone else, there will be those that stand out in your mind. Those dreams you need to pay attention to because they very well could mean something important is going to happen in your life, and you will need to do something about it."

"Is that the reason you are in my dreams?"

"Who says I am a dream?" he smiled, and cocked his head to one side.

"You aren't a dream?"

"Yes and no. I suppose I am more of an awareness on your part, sort of a waking dream."

"So you aren't something my mind is conjuring up just because I miss you?"

His smile widened. "I miss you, too, and no, I am not your imagination. Elhrin, I am here because Solisius wants you to understand, once and for all, that you are who he has chosen to fight for his cause. Normally, I would not be allowed to speak to you because the dead are not allowed to speak to the living. He made an exception for me because I was not finished with what I needed to do."

"What did you leave unfinished?"

He sighed. "The list is endless. I wanted you to be more prepared for your destiny and I have failed you, and I have failed Marguerite, too."

"How can you say that? I do feel lost, but I don't feel that you have failed me, and Marguerite, well, she is angry with you right now, but I don't think she feels you have failed her." Elhrin propped up on her elbows.

"I bet she is angry with me," he gazed at his wife with a sad smile. "The woman does have a magnificent temper."

Marguerite shifted in her sleep, and turned her head in the direction of Elhrin letting out a soft sigh. Master Gryph frowned at the bandage on Marguerite's neck. "What happened there?" he asked, sounding slightly angry.

"She was attacked by a Do'athrim. He was after the book."

Master Gryph sat in silence for a moment, staring at Marguerite, and then nodded to himself as if he was answering to something only he could hear. "Elhrin, the book is irreplaceable. You must keep it safe. Obsudius has had his N'gethwyn try throughout the years to steal the book away from Anderan's So'ladiun. He believes that there are secrets hidden within its pages that he should know, and he is probably right."

"What kind of secrets?" she asked.

"I don't know. They have never been revealed to me and won't be revealed to you unless you are the one that is supposed to know them. Obsudius thinks he can overcome the magic that keeps the secrets hidden, but I am sure Solisius is far too smart to allow his information to be revealed should the book fall into enemy hands. That being said, I don't think we should risk it."

She agreed. "Who are N'gethwyn?"

"The N'gethwyn are Obsudius' answer to the So'ladiun."

Elhrin groaned, "Are you kidding me? He has fighters capable of magic, too?"

"Yes, he does, and they are scattered all over the world, as are the So'ladiun."

"You mean there are others?"

Master Gryph chuckled, "Did you expect for you to cover the entire world as one of Solisius' So'ladiun? Anderan alone is a monstrous undertaking. Don't you think one against the entire world would be overwhelming?"

"I don't know what I think."

"Well, rest assured that you only have to worry about Anderan's safety for the moment."

"Only have to worry about Anderan's safety, he says," Elhrin raised her eyes to study the ceiling. "Master Gryph, you talk about the book giving guidance, yet I have had a hard time finding anything in it to help me."

"Is that so? Have you not learned anything from it at all?"

"Well, yes, I have learned a good bit of history about the men, and some new magic, but I have not found anything to do with the Rift, or Do'athrim, or what I am supposed to do."

He gave her one of his famous stares that told her he knew she could do better, and suddenly she felt like she was twelve years old again.

"So, you think what you have learned so far has not been helpful at all."

"No, I didn't mean that. What I have read so far has helped me to not feel as lost with my magic, but still, I thought it would help me more with what I am supposed to do with this destiny you say I'm supposed to fulfill," she said, and reached up to brush a stray hair away that had fallen in her eye.

"Elhrin, ultimately the book's purpose is to finally go to the one who will unlock its secrets. For the rest of us it is a guide only, a tool to help the So'ladiun with the tasks they are given. It is not a step-by-step map of how to fulfill your destiny, nor are you to think that it will hold the answer to every question that may arise. Life is not like that. There is no one place, thing, or individual that will ever have all the answers, and sometimes what you seek will only be revealed when the time is right. It is the path of fate. Let's set this aside for the moment, I don't have much time left, and I need to talk to you about Cynder."

"Cynder?" Elhrin asked.

"Cynder is one of Obsudius' N'gethwyn, and is the beast in charge of the army ravaging the north."

Marguerite shifted again and moved her arm to her side. Her hand fell right through Master Gryph's leg and rested on the bed. Master Gryph closed his eyes for a moment and sighed, and when he opened them to resume his tale, he did not bother to hide the naked longing in the look he gave his wife. "Centuries ago, Cynder was a favorite pet of Obsudius when the beast lived in our world during the lifetime of Tolman Arahod. Where he came from originally, no one knows, but one day he made his home in the Styringill Islands off the coast of the Southern Province. For years, he terrorized the local citizens of the islands. They tried to kill him, but were unsuccessful, and most were forced to leave. The stubborn ones, who braved his wrath trying to save their homes, died miserable deaths leaving the islands deserted. With the people gone, Solisius knew Obsudius would have Cynder turn his attention elsewhere so he sent Tolman Arahod to kill him. It was a difficult battle for Tolman, not only because Cynder is powerful, but because he is also a shape-changer and can become any being he has a mind to. The battle was long, and in the end, they killed each other."

Elhrin felt the blood drain out of her face, and her mouth went dry. It took her several tries before she was able to get words to come out, and even then, it was less than a whisper. "Master Gryph, I . . . how . . . there is no way."

"No way for what?"

"No way I could possibly defeat Cynder. Wait a minute. Didn't you just say he was dead?"

"Yes, I did, but he is dead no longer. Obsudius has done the forbidden, and has opened a portal from the realm of his spirit world to the realm of the physical world. It is the Rift I spoke of at the palace, and it is allowing the souls that reside there back into the world, living and breathing as if they had never died. Cynder is here now, wreaking havoc on the north with thousands of Obsudius' followers, and the time has come for you to meet your destiny. Elhrin, you cannot wait any longer, you must leave Glimmerdale."

"Leave Glimmerdale?"

"Yes. The longer you wait means more of Anderan's citizens die. The army will have an endless supply of fighters until the Rift is closed," he said. "You must close it before the army crosses the mountains and gains access to the heart of Anderan."

"Do I have to fight Cynder? Can't the King's Army kill him?"

"Cynder is a magical creature, and it will take someone strong in magic to destroy him."

"I knew you were going to say that," she said, resigned.

"You must travel as quickly as you can to Blackridge Keep. The Rift is inside," he said, and glanced over his shoulder to the window beyond. "I have to go now. Dawn is arriving and Marguerite will awaken soon, but before I go, know that you can and you must do this. I have told you all along that you are far stronger than you know. You just have to start believing it yourself. And don't worry, you won't be alone. There will be others who will be with you. You'll see."

He stood up, gazing at Marguerite's face as if he was ingraining every single detail into his soul.

"Elhrin," he said, a touch of sadness crept into his voice, "it will be a while before I will have the chance to see you again. Do me a favor, and tell her I miss her, and not to be too angry with me. I hated keeping secrets from her, but there are some things the So'ladiun cannot reveal, even to the ones we love most. I hope one day she will find it in her heart to forgive me for hurting her."

He lifted a hand to wave goodbye, and was gone. It was then she realized that he had not told her how she was to close the Rift.

The next morning, Elhrin sat at the table with Bayle while Marguerite placed plates of eggs and a slice of smoked ham in front of them, and then sat down with her own plate. Bayle immediately began shoveling his food into his mouth as fast as he could.

"Bayle, your food isn't going to get up and run away. Don't you think you should slow down before you choke?" Marguerite asked.

"Sorry, Marguerite," he said around a mouthful of ham. "Master Toome wanted me to help the men pull down the walls of Mister Younges shop this morning, and I didn't want to be late."

"I think you will have plenty of time. At least, slow down to chew."

Bayle grinned at her, looking like a chipmunk with his cheeks full.

"Elhrin, you are quiet this morning. Is everything all right?" Marguerite asked, as she raised her cup of tea and took a sip.

"I had another dream last night," Elhrin said quietly.

Marguerite's hand froze as she was setting her cup back down. "Is that so? Are you going to tell us about it?" She sat her cup on the table with a tiny clink.

Elhrin looked from Marguerite to Bayle then back again. She knew Bayle was not going to like what she had to say.

"Master Gryph said it was time for me to leave Glimmerdale and go to Blackridge Keep."

"What?" Bayle leaned forward in his chair. "Elhrin, you are not going anywhere because you had a dream, especially not Blackridge Keep. I don't know if you have heard, but there is an army of beasts up there ready to kill any human on sight," he said, sarcastically.

"Bayle, calm down and let her finish," Marguerite reached out to pat him on his arm. "Elhrin, what else did he say?"

"Marguerite, you were right about the Rift. It is a portal that allows the dead back in the living world, only it is the dead from the Realm of Darkness, and until it is closed, they can keep coming back into the living world. He said I have to close it. He also said that the dragon-like beast in the north is named Cynder, and he is the one guiding the army. Only someone with magical abilities can defeat him," she blew out a huge breath.

Marguerite stared at her cup, tracing her finger around its rim. Bayle sat back in his chair and crossed his arms over his chest.

"Well, he doesn't want too much from you, does he?" he retorted.

"Bayle, I know this is hard for you to comprehend. Believe me, I find it hard, too, but I can't explain it any better than the fact that I now know without a doubt, that my dreams are more than just my imaginings."

"Did he tell you how to close the portal?" Marguerite asked.

"No, he left before I could ask him."

Bayle threw up his arms in exasperation. "Well, there you go. You can't just run up to it and tell it to close. How does he expect you to accomplish this feat?" he asked, leaning his chair back on its back two legs.

"I don't know," she said, "but I have to trust him. I can't just sit here and not do anything."

"It's a dream, Elhrin," he said. "I can't believe you think it's real."

"Bayle, I also think it is real," Marguerite said, "and I think we need to make a plan."

"A plan for what?" he asked.

"A plan for reaching Blackridge Keep without getting killed," she replied, and gave him a look that told him there would be no more arguing.

"I can't believe this," he said, starting to set his chair down. The back two legs of the chair slipped. Off balance, his weight carried him backwards to the floor with a crash.

Elhrin clapped both of her hands over her mouth.

"Bayle, are you okay?" Marguerite asked, as she rose to help him.

"Fine, lovely, couldn't be better," he griped, as he rolled over onto his knees and rubbed the back of his head where it had smacked the floor. Marguerite grasped his hand and helped him to his feet.

"Elhrin, please don't do this. It is too dangerous," he pleaded as he reached down to pick up the chair.

Elhrin lowered her hands. "I think I have to, Bayle. I can no longer believe my dreams are coincidence. Master Gryph told me about the Rift in Muryne before the Do'athrim wolf said he came through it . . . the Rift is real, and as far as I know, there is no one else who has the gift of magic that can close it besides me."

He nodded and went to the door, opened it, then stopped and looked back at her. "Just so you know, if you go, I go too," he said, slipping out the door before she could reply.

"Marguerite, I can't let him go with me. Like he said, it would be too dangerous. I am going to have to go alone."

"No, you are not," Marguerite said in a tone that she had never used on Elhrin before. "You better get used to the idea that I am not going to allow you to go somewhere this dangerous by yourself. I for one am going with you. As for Bayle, I don't think you are going to be able to stop him."

Elhrin was flabbergasted. "Marguerite, I . . . you . . . what?"

"Elhrin, stop stammering. I am going, and that is the end of the matter," she tapped a finger to her lips. "Let's see, we need a map, and we need to make a list of supplies we will need. Elhrin, was there anything else Gryph said that could help us?"

Elhrin found her voice, "Um, the only other thing he said was to pay attention to my dreams, that they could be important, and to keep the book safe. Um, what else, oh yeah, he told me more about Cynder. He said, that Cynder and a magician by the name of Tolman Arahod killed each other long ago, and that Cynder was a shape-changer and could assume any form he wanted. I wasn't too happy to hear that part. I knew this journey was going to be difficult, but I didn't know it was going to be impossible."

"Gryph wouldn't send you if he didn't think you were capable," Marguerite left the table and went into his study. A moment later she came back with some paper, pen and ink, and sat back down at the table.

"He also had a message for you," Elhrin said.

Marguerite dropped the ink she had just opened, causing it to spill onto the paper. She ignored the spill and stared glassy-eyed at Elhrin, waiting for her to continue.

"He said to tell you he missed you, and he was sorry for having to keep things from you, but he did not have a choice. He hoped you would not be too angry with him, and that one day you will be able to forgive him. It was never his intention to hurt you."

Marguerite lowered her head and stared at the spill on the table.

"I'm not angry at him for keeping things from me," Marguerite whispered, and Elhrin could see tears drop onto the paper and mix with the ink. After a moment Marguerite wiped her eyes with her hands. "Elhrin, you are going to have to excuse me, I need to be alone for a bit. We will do this later," she retreated to her bedroom and closed the door behind her.

After Elhrin cleaned up the ink spill, she retrieved her satchel and started to go outside, but noticed dark clouds building up in the sky. Afraid it might rain, she decided to take her book into Master Gryph's study. Sitting down at his desk, she moved a pile of papers out of her way and opened the book. Since Master Gryph had mentioned Tolman Arahod, she wondered if the pendant would reveal anything in his pages.

She pulled the pendant from under her shirt and called on her magic. The pendant immediately brightened, the page below her hand began to swirl and images started to emerge. When the images came into focus, she was unprepared for what was happening in the scene.

Trees exploded across the page, making her jump in her seat and she had to remind herself that this was not happening now, nor was anything going to come out of the book at her. At least, she hoped it wouldn't. Smoke filled the scene, making it difficult to see, and she thought it was in a dense forest somewhere, but couldn't be sure. Then an old man limped through the smoke. Blood flowed like a river from a gash across his forehead, down his face, and into a long white beard, immediately turning the hair a deep crimson. The long blue and gray robes he wore were blood-stained and ripped to shreds as if someone had thrown a thousand knives at him. He stopped in the middle of the page as the smoke swirled around him.

"This must be Tolman," she whispered. "What is going on?"

He was having a difficult time standing up straight, but he drew back his arm and fired a ball of fire through the smoke and out of Elhrin's view. The scene flashed, then cleared, just as the ball of fire exploded into a large hooded figure, sending him flying backwards through dense underbrush and out of sight. A moment later a creature as tall as the trees came crashing through the underbrush.

Elhrin was stunned. "Is that Cynder?"

The creature looked like an enormous lizard running on two legs. His mouth, open wide, revealed sharp black fangs, and when he neared Tolman, he spewed a green liquid out of his jaws. Tolman outstretched his arms before him and took a step back, but lost his balance and fell to the ground. Elhrin was amazed he had managed to keep his arms in front of him and knew he had created a shield when the liquid hit an invisible barrier dangerously close to his body, but flowed away from him onto the ground, burning anything it touched. Tolman then shoved his arms outward, sending his barrier slamming into the beast. Cynder flew backwards into the trees behind him, snapping branches as he crashed through.

Tolman staggered to his feet, carefully avoiding where the liquid had fallen, and stumbled through the clearing Cynder's huge body had made in the trees. When he reached Cynder, the beast had changed back into the hooded figure and was waiting for him. Simultaneously, the two figures sent magic colliding into each other. Elhrin didn't know what Tolman was doing, but Cynder was choking and gasping as if his throat was being crushed and he could not get any air. Cynder was sending waves of white, spidery light reminiscent of lightning into Tolman's body, causing him to crash to his knees.

Elhrin could tell they struggled to increase their magic on the other. With one final effort, they both forced out all of the magical energy they had left. A tremendous flash obliterated the scene, causing Elhrin to see spots before her eyes. When the page cleared, and she could see beyond the spots, she noticed something strange.

The scene now showed a place that was desolate and gray. A valley sat between high craggy mountains, and off in the distance she saw an ebony keep built on the side of one mountain. On the flat ground of the valley floor stood the hooded figure of Cynder, and the resigned figure of Tolman was on his knees. Beside them both was a remarkably handsome man. His raven black hair hung in waves to his shoulders and he was dressed in rich, black robes trimmed in crimson. When she looked closer at his pale face, she shuddered. The malevolence in his coal black eyes was pure evil.

She wondered who he was and where they now were. The place was devoid of any plants, grasses, or trees.

"My Lord, I don't know how he came with me," Cynder laughed. His raspy voice was uncomfortable to hear, sounding almost as if forming words was difficult and unnatural for him.

She leaned closer to the book. *My Lord? That is Obsudius?* She couldn't believe what she was seeing. Surely he couldn't be the God of Do'athra?

"I opened a portal, Cynder, and pulled you both through to me. So'ladiun, it seems you have found yourself in quite a predicament. Let's see how my brother likes it when I send his precious Defender of Light to the Void," the dark god said, and flicked his hand in the direction of the doomed magician. Tolman didn't have time to react. Suddenly, he was no longer there.

"Oh no!" Elhrin gasped, letting her magic go. The page reverted back to its normal state. Elhrin felt like she was going to throw up. Shaking, she pushed herself away from the desk, and went to the kitchen for a drink of water.

Obsudius sent him to the Void. That meant that Tolman's soul no longer existed. Elhrin shook her head. The concept was too big, too horrific to grasp.

The bedroom door creaked open and Marguerite came out into the kitchen. Elhrin could see she had been crying. "Marguerite, are you all right? I'm sorry if I hurt you," Elhrin said, as rumbles of thunder from an approaching storm shook the cottage.

"Elhrin, you didn't do anything wrong. I'm fine. I just needed a little time to myself to process Gryph's message." She produced a weak smile. "I'm happy that he had one for me this time. Are you ready to work on our list? You know, we probably need to talk to Toome and see if he has any ideas we could use. He won't like any of this, but he will just have to accept it."

"He may not let us go," Elhrin said.

"He won't have any say in the matter," Marguerite stated, and went to get more paper.

Elhrin knew that when it came to an argument with Marguerite—Marguerite invariably won. Master Toome did not stand a chance.

Marguerite returned with the paper and they both settled down at the table. Without warning, the door burst open and Bayle rushed in soaked from head to toe, dripping large amounts of water on the floor. The storm had arrived, and lightning flashed outside the door behind him. A crack of thunder shook the cottage.

"Bayle, shut the door. My floor is getting soaked," Marguerite scolded, but then saw the worried look on his face. "What's wrong?"

"Marguerite, something has happened and I'm not sure how to tell you," he shut the door against the storm and situated himself behind the end chair at the table.

"I don't understand why everyone is so scared to tell me things. What is it?"

"Marguerite, you know I went to help Master Toome in the village, right?"

"Yes, and . . . ?"

"Well, the storm came and Master Toome suggested we go to the inn and wait on it to pass so we could finish clearing out the walls we had demolished. Most of the injured have been moved out of the common room, and the inn is back open for business."

"Bayle, I know that, I helped move them, remember?" she said, becoming impatient with him not getting to the point.

"Right, so anyway, we were eating when Nute, who was sitting in the corner behind us, started talking to himself. At first I thought it was funny because he had too much to drink and I couldn't really understand him, but then Master Toome jumped up, dragged him from his chair and pinned him to the wall, asking him to repeat what he had just said," he paused, uncomfortable with what he was about to say.

"Go on," Marguerite prompted.

"Uh . . . well . . ."

Marguerite slapped the table with the palm of her hand. Both Elhrin and Bayle flinched.

"Bayle, what did he say?" she ordered.

"He said that he wasn't supposed to tell anyone, but when they went to fill in Master Gryph's grave, he wasn't there," Bayle spoke in a rush. "The grave is empty."

Elhrin watched Marguerite's face go deathly pale, feeling the blood drain out of her own face at the same time. Marguerite jumped up without a word and ran out the front door into the storm. Shocked, Elhrin shot out of her own chair, grabbed cloaks off the pegs beside the door, and ran after Marguerite. "Come on, Bayle," she shouted, covering herself with a cloak as she ran through the downpour.

They caught up with Marguerite just before she reached the shops and followed her into the inn. Standing just inside the door dripping wet, Marguerite scanned the room. Master Toome was not there, but Doogan Phisk sat at a nearby table watching them curiously through the smoke wafting up from the pipe clasped in his mouth.

"Doogan, have you seen Toome?" Marguerite asked the elderly man.

"Yeah, he hauled Nute Fleunk upstairs by the scruff of his neck," he said, pipe firmly clamped in yellow-stained teeth.

"Thank you," she said, and rushed for the stairs. Elhrin and Bayle followed close on her heels.

Marguerite put her ear to each door, listening for Master Toome's voice until she found the one she wanted and burst through without knocking. Master Toome whirled around at the intrusion. In the far corner of the room behind Master Toome, sat Nute Fleunk, a scrawny cane pole of a man with hair the color of wheat, looking as if his life was about to come to an end. Two soldiers from the King's Army stood off to the side, next to the only bed in the room. They reached for their swords, but Master Toome gestured for them to stand down when he saw who the intruders were. He crossed the room and grabbed both of Marguerite's arms before she had taken two steps into the room.

"Calm down, Marguerite. I am still trying to get the story straight. He is so drunk and scared that half the time I can't understand him."

"What did he say?" she hissed.

"So far, I have been able to determine that he and Graem Soot were supposed to fill in the grave and couldn't. He mumbles something about lightning and keeps repeating that he was gone. I am assuming he means Gryph. These two men are going to go get Graem and bring him back here," he jerked his head toward the door. The soldiers saluted and left, closing the door behind them.

He led Marguerite over to a vacant chair beside the small fireplace in the room. There was no fire burning so he draped a blanket around her shoulders. "You are soaking wet. Sit here and I'll see what else I can find out."

Marguerite sat on the edge of the chair. Elhrin and Bayle moved out of the way to the other side of the room. Briefly glancing at the two young people,

Master Toome turned to contemplate the man hunched in his chair. Nute blearily eyed Master Toome as he nervously chewed on a fingernail.

"Nute, tell me again why you couldn't fill in Minister Idwyr's grave after the funeral?" Master Toome asked.

"I tole yew," Nute slurred and waved a hand in the air. "Lightnin'—boom! We run. He say, shhhh, don' tell nobody, they'll hang ush."

"Two grown men were so scared of a storm that you had to run for cover and leave a grave open?"

"Tha' tree blew up right beshide ush," he said with a suppressed burp. "How wush we s'posed to know if tha lightnin' washn't going to get ush next?"

Marguerite grunted in displeasure.

"I don't give a damn if lightning struck you in the ass a dozen times!" Master Toome yelled so loud that everyone in the room jumped. "You don't leave a grave open, especially not one that holds one of Anderan's top officials. Are you two that stupid?"

Nute shrank as far away from Master Toome as his chair would allow. Elhrin had never seen Master Toome so angry. He stood rigid as a post, and opened and closed both fists by his side as if contemplating hitting the man. "Nute, when did you and Graem finally go back to fill in the grave?" Master Toome growled, low and deadly.

"Nex' morning," he said quietly.

"The next morning?" Marguerite sputtered in disbelief.

Master Toome shot a furious glance at her. "Do you know who this lady is?" he asked, pointing a finger at Marguerite.

Nute jerked his head once in abrupt affirmation, but refused to look at Marguerite.

"Do you understand the amount of tremendous pain she has had to live through? And now she has to sit here and endure the unbelievable story of two men who were stupidly careless with her husband's body. Do you care?"

Nute lowered his eyes to the floor in shame."Shorry ma'am," he mumbled.

Marguerite sat stiffly in her chair, her hands were clasped together so tightly in her lap that her knuckles were white from the pressure.

"Sorry is not good enough," Master Toome growled. "Tell me what you saw when you went to the grave the next morning."

Nute shifted uncomfortably in his chair. "The casket wush open and wushn't no body inside. Jus' a bunch of water in it."

"Why did you two decide to fill in the grave without telling anyone that his body was missing?" Master Toome asked, bending over to get eye-level with Nute.

"Like I shaid, Graem shaid we'd be hanged, an wouldn' let me tell."

"Well, he may have very well been right," Master Toome muttered. Nute's eyes widened with fear.

There was a knock on the door. A soldier stuck his head inside. "Colonel Toome, can I speak with you a moment?"

"Don't you dare move, Nute, or I will nail your hide to the wall with my sword." He glanced at Bayle. "Watch him for me."

Master Toome slipped out into the hallway and closed the door behind him. No one said a word after he left. The shock was too overwhelming. Marguerite never took her eyes off Nute. The man, fully away of her intense displeasure, started to gnaw on another fingernail.

A moment later, Master Toome came back in the room.

"Graem is gone. His wife told them he left the day before the village was attacked, and has not returned. She has no idea where he has gone, and apparently doesn't care. Can't say as I blame her, he beat her enough. I'm surprised she didn't leave the bastard long ago."

Master Toome scrubbed both hands over his face making a rasping noise from the beard stubble on his jaw. He let out an explosive sigh, "Marguerite, would it upset you to dig up Gryph's grave just to make sure this idiot's story is true?"

Marguerite shook her head. "I have to know, Toome."

"Right then, come morning, if the weather clears, we'll dig it up. Why don't you and the kids go home and get some rest. I am keeping Nute here, temporarily under arrest until we straighten this mess out."

Chapter Eleven

The next morning dawned with a fog so dense that, when she looked out the window, Elhrin couldn't see the low rock wall separating the yard from the road. The atmosphere of the room behind her was one of dreaded anticipation. All wanting the truth to hurry up and be revealed, but at the same time, there was the anxiety of having their fears confirmed. What if he is not there? How could his body possibly be missing? What would that mean and what happened to him? How could this be happening in the first place? The same questions kept rotating in her mind over and over, and she couldn't get them to stop.

She turned from the window. Marguerite sat at the kitchen table staring at the untouched food on her plate. Bayle, across the table from her, was cleaning his own plate as if he would never get the opportunity to eat again. Elhrin was like Marguerite. Her nerves were too raw to even think about food. She wondered if there would ever be anything that would affect Bayle enough to stop him from eating.

Probably not, she thought.

The rest of the morning passed at a snail's pace as they all worked on one mundane task after another, trying to kill time, waiting for Master Toome to come for them. Finally, near midday, he arrived in his wagon and drove them to the graveyard on the hill.

Two men were already there, uncovering the grave. Elhrin and the others climbed down from the wagon and stood off to one side to wait. She glanced at the village below. The sky had cleared, but fog still hung in the low recesses of the countryside and over the river, reminding her of the fairy tale story her mother used to tell her when she was a little girl about a city in the clouds. Far off in the distance, the uppermost peaks of the Northreach Mountains rose above the tree-lined horizon. Elhrin sighed. She was going to have to leave the village soon and travel over those mountains to face a fate that terrified her to the core of her being.

She noticed movement along the road leading up the hill to the graveyard. A dozen or so riders emerged from a bank of fog, one bearing a flag with a gold lion emblazoned on a purple background.

"The king," she announced, and everyone turned to watch the riders until they reached the top of the hill.

The King of Anderan dismounted from his horse and strode through the damp, high grass of the graveyard. The others in his party remained with the horses.

"Your Majesty, I wasn't expecting you until later this afternoon," Master Toome said as he bowed.

"I left sooner than I had anticipated, and decided to ride ahead of my army. I wanted to have a little more time to see the damage from the attack. I didn't realize that when I got here, I would be greeted with distressing news. What is going on?"

Master Toome related the unbelievable story Nute had revealed the day before. The king's scowl deepened as the story progressed, until Master Toome ended by telling him that they were digging up the grave just to make sure the story was true.

"Mayor, we have reached the casket," said one of the men in the grave.

Master Toome, King Goruth, and Bayle stepped to the edge and peered down. Marguerite and Elhrin stayed behind, both too frightened of what they might see in the hole.

The men in the grave tossed a few more shovelfuls of dirt out of the grave before they stopped. Master Toome cursed under his breath and smacked his fist against his leg in frustration. He and King Goruth turned to face them.

"Marguerite, he is not here," Master Toome said grimly.

Marguerite sank to her knees before Elhrin could catch her, and doubled over to sob uncontrollably in the grass.

After they had managed to get Marguerite on her feet again, King Goruth had insisted that they follow him to the Glimmerdale Inn, since it was the closest place suitable for them to discuss what had happened to Master Gryph's body. On the ride back into the village, Marguerite worked through her shock and despair so that by the time they had reached the inn, she was fighting mad and had strode into the inn without responding to Triva's call from across the street, jerked a chair out from under an empty table, and sat stiff as a board without looking at anyone in the common room. The room was then quickly cleared by one of the king's men to give them privacy.

Master Toome, who had not followed them straight into the inn, slipped through the front door a short time later, cutting off a broad ray of sunshine when he closed the door, returning the common room back to its normal gloomy daytime state—the only light coming from a single iron chandelier filled with candles over the bar and the inn's two front windows. "I sent men to search the area to see if they can come up with evidence of any kind, but I doubt after all this time that they'll find anything. If only those two had told us immediately, we may have had a better chance," he said, pulling an empty chair from a nearby table to join them.

"Marguerite, I am sorry you have to go through all this. Gryph was a good friend, and I loved him like a brother. I promise you that if I were not facing such a serious situation in the north, I would launch a full-scale investigation into this matter. But right now, I have to secure the safety of Anderan," King Goruth said.

"I know, Your Majesty, I fully understand your situation. I have a feeling that this is related to what is happening in the north. I just don't know how," she said, wrapping both hands around a warm mug of spiced cider.

"Do you think the Do'athrim took him?" Bayle blurted out.

Elhrin wished that just once he would keep his thoughts to himself. "Bayle, hush," she frowned at him.

Marguerite placed a hand lightly on her arm. "He doesn't have to hush. As horrific as it is to think about, that is a legitimate possibility," she said, then frowned at her mug. "And if so, one more act they will be held accountable for."

"Don't get your bonnet set on revenge, Marguerite," Master Toome warned. "We will find out what happened, and I will take care of whoever is responsible."

Marguerite leveled her gaze on Master Toome. "Toome, I know you will. In the meantime, Elhrin and I have business of our own to attend to. We are going to Blackridge Keep."

"You are going to do what?" Master Toome sputtered. Both he and King Goruth stared at her as if she had just sprouted a second head and declared herself queen of the entire world.

"You heard me, Toome, I didn't stutter," she replied, calmly taking a sip of her cider.

"You will do no such thing," King Goruth said. "What has gotten into you, woman?"

Master Toome narrowed his eyes at her, suspicious of her intentions. "Marguerite, I know Gryph's death has been hard on you, but . . . ."

Marguerite raised an eyebrow. "I do not have a death wish, Toome, if that is what you are thinking, and I certainly have no desire for getting Elhrin killed, either."

"Then why would you suggest such a crazy idea?" he asked.

"You both are aware that Elhrin was Gryph's apprentice, right?" she asked, looking from one man to the other.

"Yes. So?" King Goruth asked.

"I am not going to tell you how we came by this knowledge, Your Majesty, you wouldn't believe me anyway, but there are some things you need to know. Elhrin has learned the name of the beast to the north is Cynder, and no matter how many men you throw at it, the effort would be futile because it is our understanding that only magic can destroy it. Elhrin has to be the one to fight him, and she has to do it at Blackridge Keep. I am going to go with her."

Master Toome snorted in contempt. King Goruth held up a hand to stop him from saying anything further. "I know you said that I wouldn't believe you, but humor me, anyway, and tell me how you came by this information."

"Just suffice it to say that the information came from Gryph and leave it at that," she said defiantly, daring him to call her a fool.

"From Gryph." King Goruth leaned back in his chair and studied Marguerite's face. Then his gaze drifted to Elhrin. "I am going to remind you both that I am your king and any information you have that is vital to the security of this nation is not to be kept from me. Elhrin, what say you?"

Marguerite placed a hand on Elhrin's arm. "She agrees with me."

He continued to stare at Elhrin, waiting.

Elhrin cleared her throat, nervously. "I . . . ."

Marguerite squeezed her arm warning her to remain silent.

King Goruth noticed the gesture. "Marguerite, you do realize I could arrest you for withholding information."

Marguerite shocked Elhrin by producing both her arms for him to chain together as if the king had shackles on his person, and would haul her off on the spot.

King Goruth huffed in frustration. "Very well, Marguerite, you are more stubborn than a thousand mules. Put your hands down." He frowned. "I will let this go for now, but do not begin to think this subject is closed." He nodded at Elhrin. "So, this beast has to be killed with magic and you think that Elhrin here is the one for the job?"

"Your Majesty, I don't think so, I know so," Marguerite pronounced, she crossed her arms on top of the table and leaned in.

Elhrin couldn't believe how bold the woman was in front of their monarch, and thought it was a good thing the room had been cleared because she didn't think the king would have allowed such insubordination from anyone in public.

The king raised his eyebrows and barked a short laugh. "Woman, I must say you are as tough as any man I've ever met. I can see why Gryph could not let you get away from him all those years ago. Nevertheless, I cannot in good consciousness allow you and a teenage girl go to certain death."

Master Toome spoke up. "I agree. Marguerite, this is ridiculous. I know Elhrin is probably very capable of handling herself magically, but it is just too dangerous."

"No offense, you two, but this is how it is. You do not have a choice. If she doesn't do this and succeed, then Anderan is lost. Also, you have not let me finish what I needed to tell you. There is more." She spread a hand palm down on the table. "I know you think I have lost my mind, and this next part is not going to help matters one bit, but I tell you I know what I have to say is truth, and if you ignore me, then you might as well lay down here and wait for the Do'athrim because no matter what you do, they will keep coming until you are dead."

"What are you talking about now?" Master Toome asked, exasperated.

"The Rift, Toome. I was right about it being a portal to the Realm of the Dead, or more specifically, the Realm of Darkness. Obsudius opened this portal and the army is coming through it from him, and will keep coming unless the portal is closed."

"And Gryph gave you this information, too?" Master Toome asked.

"Yes, he did."

"How? Gryph is dead," Master Toome said.

"I am well aware of that, Toome," Marguerite snapped.

"Yes, I know. I apologize. But you have to understand that from where I am sitting, all this sounds mad," he said, sweeping an arm through the air. "A god opening a portal, beasts coming from the realm of the dead, vital information to an impending war coming from a dead man, how can you expect us to believe you? If I didn't know you, didn't know Gryph, I would immediately recommend you be sent to the mental institute."

"Your Majesty, Master Toome, what Marguerite is telling you is true. I have to go. I know of no other choice," Elhrin said, quietly. "Magic is what is needed to stop the war, and that means me."

The king stared at Elhrin for so long she began to grow a little uneasy at his steady gaze. Finally he spoke. "Young lady, against rational reasoning, I am going to choose to believe you for the moment. I think to totally ignore you would be a mistake. You are Gryph's apprentice and I knew him like no other," he eyed Marguerite, "including his wife. However, since I don't have a complete confirmation of your story as of yet, I am not going to let you go anywhere on your own."

"Your Majesty . . . ," Marguerite began.

"Wait, I am not finished. I want you to accompany me to Kilmyn Pass where I have ordered all battalions from across the country to meet. We can discuss this further along the way, and possibly have more answers by the time we reach the pass. I had not planned to stay the night here, but since it is this late in the day, I will not leave until daybreak. Will this give you enough time to get ready?"

"Yes, Your Majesty," Marguerite replied.

"Toome, I know you have many responsibilities here, but is there any way I can talk you into joining me on this campaign?" King Goruth asked.

Master Toome was surprised by the request. "Your Majesty, I would be honored. I don't think my wife will be pleased, but I think she will understand."

"Good. What do you plan to do with the young man you have locked away upstairs?"

"I would like to hang him for his negligence."

"No!" Marguerite exclaimed. "As angry as I am at what he has done, I do not want him executed."

"Then what do you suggest?" Master Toome asked.

"I don't know, just don't kill him," she replied.

King Goruth spoke up, "How about I recruit him into the infantry and give him the honor of being in the front lines?"

"Excellent idea," Master Toome smiled. "Marguerite?"

"I suppose," she sighed, resigned. "What if he runs?"

"Oh, I can guarantee he won't run," the king said, and picked up his mug of ale to take a long drink.

Chapter Twelve

Elhrin couldn't suppress an audible groan of relief when King Goruth called for the army to halt and set up camp late the following afternoon.

Marguerite turned around to give her a grin. "My thoughts exactly, dear."

Living in a small community where one could walk everywhere, Elhrin was not used to riding horses for long periods of time. The ride to Muryne and back had made her aware of muscles she didn't know she had, and it seemed this time was going to be no different.

"I am glad we are finally out of Comahr," Bayle said as he dismounted. "It's too dark in there, makes me uneasy."

"Since when are you afraid of the woods?" Elhrin asked, stretching her tired back and aching legs.

"I'm not afraid. It's just that with all that is going on and, you know, since what happened . . ." he trailed off, glancing at Marguerite, who was nearby, removing her pack from the back of her horse.

"Bayle, you don't have to tiptoe around me about Master Gryph," Marguerite said, slinging her pack over her shoulder. "I don't want either of you to feel uncomfortable talking to me about him or anything else. Agreed?"

"Agreed," they replied.

"Good," she smiled.

"Madam Idwyr?" a young boy, dressed in the king's livery, trotted up.

"Yes, sir?"

He blushed happily at the formal title of respect she had given him. "I am to show you where you and your party are to sleep tonight," he said, and escorted them to a tent being set up for their use.

After they had settled in, the page returned to tell Marguerite that the king wished to speak with her alone.

Elhrin watched Marguerite and the page disappear behind a row of tents. "Do you want to have a look around before the sun sets?" she asked Bayle.

Bayle's huge grin answered her before he did. "I sure do."

"I figured you would," she grinned. "Let's go."

They walked back to the road. Grassy meadows on either side of the rutted dirt road were alive with the activities of a large force setting up camp for the night. Rows of tents had sprouted up within an hour and hundreds of campfires had been lit, creating a low cloud of smoke that drifted east with the light breeze. They passed a line of supply wagons with a row of cooking fires topped with black cauldrons. Army cooks were busy preparing a meal for the men.

The smell of food set Bayle's stomach off. It rumbled audibly. "I am about to starve," he said.

"You? Hungry?" she poked him in the side. "We better remedy that soon. You are a bit scrawny."

"Stop," he grinned, slapping away her offending finger.

"Elhrin," she heard someone call her name. She searched the crowd of soldiers around her. Her heart skipped a beat when she saw Tomas and an extremely tall, ebony-skinned soldier slip through the crowd.

"Bayle, wait," she yelled for her brother who had kept on walking and hadn't noticed she had stopped.

"Elhrin, I didn't expect to see you here," Tomas grinned.

An unnatural warmth spread over her cheeks as she considered his smile, thinking it had to be the most beautiful smile she had ever seen. "I didn't expect to be here," she replied, hoping her face wasn't as red as it felt. She was grateful when Bayle joined them and Tomas turned his attention to her brother.

"Bayle, right?" Tomas asked, offering to shake Bayle's hand.

"Yes," he replied.

"Elhrin, Bayle, this is my friend Sergeant Jag Soryn. He is in the Second Bow Regiment," Tomas said.

"Good to meet you," Jag said in a deep voice and with a wide grin that nearly made his dark brown eyes disappear. He leaned on an unstrung bow that was almost as tall as he was.

"What are you two doing here?" Tomas asked.

"She . . . ," Bayle pointed at Elhrin.

"It's a complicated story. We are here at the request of the king," Elhrin interrupted quickly. She didn't want him to reveal their plans and have people start asking questions she didn't want to answer.

"Okay," Tomas drawled the word out, and Elhrin could tell he knew that she had intentionally interrupted Bayle. "We were on our way for a little bow practice. Would you like to join us?"

Her first instinct was to decline the offer because she wasn't sure when Marguerite would return and did not want her to worry about where they were, but she could see the excitement in Bayle's eyes and decided to accept. They followed Tomas and Jag to a practice area of portable targets where other bowmen seemed to be competing with each other and good-naturedly making bets on who would have the better shot.

Tomas found two open targets on the far end of the line. The two readied their bows and fired several arrows apiece. Jag's arrows landed around the center of the target while Tomas had one arrow hit near the center, with others all over the target, and the last he fired, embedded in the leg of the target stand.

"You keep firing low like that, Tomas, and we might recruit you to shoot the legs out from under our enemy," Jag teased, as he ambled to the target to retrieve his arrows.

Tomas smiled at Elhrin. "I guess you can see why I am not in the bow ranks." He went to retrieve his own arrows. "Make fun of me all you want, Soryn, but the laugh will be on you the next time I watch you fall off a horse during mounted drills."

Jag pointed an arrow at Tomas. "You won't let that go, will you?" Jag laughed, his white teeth flashing against his dark skin. "I fell once." He held up a finger. "One time."

"Well, it is unforgettable. I still don't know how you could have come out of the saddle. The horse was only trotting when you hit the ground."

"I told you my foot slipped out of the stirrup when I went to stand up and fire."

"Sure it did," Tomas smiled.

Elhrin and Bayle continued to watch Tomas and Jag practice, enjoying the easy teasing banter they tossed at each other, and it dawned on her how relaxed she felt. How she had forgotten her worries for the moment. She was musing on this, and the fact that she loved the way Tomas' mouth tilted a little every time he smiled, when she realized he had been speaking to her and she hadn't been paying attention to his words.

"I'm sorry, were you talking to me?" she blushed.

He flashed a pearly smile, revealing the tilt she had just been contemplating. "I asked if you would like to give this a try." He held up his bow.

"No, I'm afraid I don't know how," she declined. "Besides, I'm too short."

"Nonsense, come on, I'll teach you," he said, waving her over.

"Ha, if you let him teach you, you'll be shooting at worms," Jag teased.

"Really, no, but I'm sure Bayle would like to try," she said, not really sure why she felt so embarrassed. "He has never had the chance to shoot a longbow."

"If you change your mind, the offer stands. Okay, Bayle, want to give it a go?" Tomas asked, and Bayle was more than eager to try a true bow, having only hunted squirrels with homemade bows back home with his friends.

Tomas demonstrated how to hold the weapon and draw the arrow. He explained how to sight the target, and then gave the bow to Bayle. Bayle readied himself and pulled back on the bowstring, not realizing that it was much harder than he was used to until he felt the taught resistance of the string pull against him. Shakily, he managed to pull the string back, take aim with one eye closed, and let loose the arrow with an audible snap.

"Ow!" he yelled, and hopped around holding his left forearm where the string had snapped him. "That hurt."

Elhrin put her hand to her mouth, trying not to laugh. Tomas and Jag bit back smiles, and Jag took off a leather arm guard and handed it to Bayle.

"Now you give this to me," Bayle complained.

Jag grinned and shrugged his shoulders.

Bayle tried again and successfully launched the arrow toward the target, but it fell well short of reaching it. He tried several more times, but never got the arrow anywhere near hitting the target.

Elhrin could see that he was getting frustrated. Back home he had been the best shot among his friends. After several more attempts and failures of hitting the target, Elhrin took pity on him. When Bayle let loose his next arrow, Elhrin sent a small stream of her magic, and navigated the arrow to strike the exact center of the target. Bayle was stunned. He then let out a whoop of laughter and Tomas and Jag slapped his back, congratulating him.

Bayle whirled around. "Elhrin, did you see that?"

"I did. Nice shot," she replied.

He grinned like a little boy, but then he narrowed his eyes and the smile slowly left his face. "Wait a minute. Did you do that?"

"Do what?" she replied innocently.

"Did you help me hit the target?"

Tomas and Jag traded confused glances.

Apparently, Elhrin was no good at hiding the truth because Bayle became angry. "Elhrin, don't do that again," he yelled, then jerked off the arm guard and handed it and the bow back to Tomas, and stormed off into the camp.

"Bayle, wait. Don't go. I'm sorry," she called after him. She darted a helpless glance at Tomas and Jag. "I'm sorry. I had better go after him."

She left the two men staring after her in confusion.

Jag leaned on his bow. "What was that about?"

"I have no idea," Tomas replied. He flashed a grin at his friend. "Nice form, though, don't you think?"

Jag eyed Elhrin's retreating backside. "Indeed, my friend, indeed."

Elhrin caught up with Bayle before he reached their tent. "Bayle, stop. I'm sorry. I shouldn't have done it. Please stop," she begged and nearly collided into him when he suddenly halted and rounded on her.

"Elhrin, why did you do it?" he asked, exasperated. "Why are you always helping me when you think that what I am doing is not good enough?"

"I didn't think that you weren't good enough. I saw how frustrated you were and just wanted to help."

"I don't need your help," he yelled. "Just because I am not perfect like you, doesn't mean I can't do anything on my own."

"What? I am not perfect. Why would you say such a thing?"

"Because everyone is always carrying on about how you can do this or that and making fun of me because all I can seem to manage is to trip over my own feet."

"I would never make fun of you. I am proud of you. If it hadn't been for you when the Do'athrim came I would probably be dead, too. You never hesitated when he came into the cottage. I froze," she jabbed a finger to her chest. "I was terrified, and because I didn't fight like I should have, our mother is dead."

He dropped his head to study the ground. *Damn, he does blame me.* "Bayle, I am sorry—so, so sorry for everything. I would never intentionally hurt you."

"Elhrin, it is not your fault what happened to mother." He raised his eyes to look at her. "And I know you would not hurt me on purpose, but don't you see what you do? You are always helping me, making my life easier, trying to protect me. Don't get me wrong. I am grateful. But you are making it difficult for me to find my own way. That is why I wanted to join the army. I knew that I would finally be able to stand on my own and not have my sister to take care of things for me." He looked away again, finding it difficult to meet her gaze.

Elhrin was stunned. "I had no idea you felt this way. I guess I think of you as my baby brother who needs me, especially now with mother gone." She placed a hand on his arm—relieved that he did not try to draw away from her touch. "But now, I do see the man you are becoming, and I guess I am just going to have to get used to the idea that you can handle things on your own."

"Thank you," he said quietly, then slowly his mouth spread into a small grin. "You know, I appreciate you giving me the chance to find my own way, but let's not go overboard. You will still help me with Father Jerome's home studies when we get back, won't you?"

Elhrin smiled, knowing how much Bayle detested the school studies Father Jerome sent home so Bayle could work, but impressed, nonetheless, that he still intended to continue his last year of education despite all that had happened. She hoped joining the army had left his plans, too. "Well, we'll see," she punched him playfully on the arm, "but I'm not making any promises. You did want to be independent, after all."

By the time they returned to their tent, the sun had almost disappeared below the horizon, casting a golden red hue across the camp. They found Marguerite back from her meeting with the king, stirring a stew of root vegetables and smoked ham in a small black pot over their campfire.

"Good timing, you two. This is just about ready," she said.

"Great. I'm starving," Bayle said, and flopped down by the fire.

Marguerite filled each of them a bowl from the pot, and then lowered herself to the ground to eat.

"What did the king say?" Elhrin asked.

"Many things, not all of which I agree with," she replied. "He is still skeptical of our story, but has not dismissed it yet, at least. He is still refusing to let us travel to Blackridge Keep. I'm afraid if he does not change his mind by the time we reach Kilmyn Pass, we are going to have to take matters in our own hands whether he likes it or not. Elhrin," she blew on a steaming spoonful of stew, "he is going to ask you to demonstrate your abilities."

Elhrin lowered her bowl to her lap. "When?"

"He said he would wait until we reach his staging ground."

"What should I do?" How could she make the king believe she had the skills to complete this mission when she didn't even think she did?

"Impress the boots off of him." Marguerite winked at her. "You are more than capable. Believe me, I know. I think my hearing is damaged from you and

Gryph blowing up my back yard. The wildlife still won't come around—too scared. Why even the birds make a wide circle around my place."

Elhrin had to laugh. Marguerite had made that up. There was nothing wrong with the wildlife around her cottage, and the birds terrorized her grapevines. She loved it when they scared them off for her.

Marguerite yawned. "While I am thinking about it, there is something I've been meaning to talk to you two about," she said. "I know being in the middle of all these soldiers feels safe, but we have to be on our guard constantly. Elhrin, your," she hesitated, looking around to see if anyone was listening to them and lowered her voice, "special items are still wanted. If what we think is true about the Rift, then the Do'athrim we killed in Glimmerdale or any of his companions could come looking for us again. We need to try to stay together and no one is to go off by themselves at any time. Do I make myself clear?"

Elhrin and Bayle nodded.

"Good. It will take us about three or four more days to reach the staging ground where King Goruth has designated for his army to assemble. Prince Cahail will be leading troops from the Tuhnichi garrison and a General Dulok from Fort Denmar is supposed to already be there waiting with his men. Even with this many troops, Goruth is not sure his force will be big enough to handle the size of the Do'athrim army. He is hoping the other Provinces will send men before he has to engage the enemy in a battle."

"What happens if they don't arrive in time?" asked Bayle.

"I don't think the army will stand a chance, and that was the point I was trying to get across to him. If what Gryph told Elhrin is true, we need to hurry. People are dying as we speak. I don't know what it is going to take to convince him of the urgency."

Bayle studied his empty bowl.

"It would be nice if Master Gryph talked to King Goruth in his dreams," Elhrin said, knowing her brother still thought they were crazy—wondering, once again, if maybe she was.

"Wouldn't it, though," Marguerite replied.

Chapter Thirteen

By mid-afternoon the next day, Elhrin's backside was screaming for relief. The short break in the village of Greystone had done nothing to ease her sore muscles. She made a promise to herself that if she lived through this whole ordeal, she would never, ever ride a horse again. She shifted in her saddle, but no matter how she sat, she was uncomfortable.

"Having problems?"

Elhrin glanced over her shoulder as Tomas rode up to join her.

"No, not really," she replied. She was not willing to admit that her rear felt like someone had beaten it with a big stick.

"Haven't ridden much, have you?" he asked.

"Is it that obvious?"

He held up a thumb and forefinger. "Just a little." He grinned. "Don't worry. It gets easier with time."

"My butt sure hopes so," she replied with groan as she shifted in her saddle again.

Tomas burst out laughing. "Can I ask you something?"

"You can ask me anything, but that doesn't guarantee I'll give you an answer."

"Fair enough," he said. "What happened yesterday with you and your brother?"

"I apologize for that. We just had a little misunderstanding."

"But why did he get angry with you, and what did he mean about you helping him hit the target?"

Elhrin debated whether or not to tell him she had magical abilities, knowing not everyone was open to the idea of someone having the kind of power she possessed. In the end she decided to tell him because he would find out, anyway, when she had to perform for the king. She grimaced at the thought.

"Do you know who Minister Gryphon Idwyr was?" she asked.

"Doesn't everybody? The man was a hero, wasn't he?"

He was to me, she thought. "That's what some people would say," she said with a small smile. "Those on the receiving end of his wrath wouldn't agree. Like the rebels holding out in the town of Rheine during the western civil war sixteen years ago. Rebel sympathizers started rumors that he blew up the entire town, killing hundreds of women, elderly, and children before they were forced to surrender."

"I've heard the stories," he said.

"But it wasn't true. What really happened was, the rebels had engaged his troops in combat in the mountains and when they saw they were outnumbered, retreated back to Rheine and holed up in the town's stockade. He blew the gates off their hinges so the men with him could get in. The town was left intact and no innocents were harmed, but those that believed the rumors still hate him."

"People do tend to think the worst of a person. Can I ask what that has to do with what we were talking about?" Tomas asked, amused.

"I was his apprentice," she replied, watching his face for his reaction.

He looked amazed. "No kidding, you have magical powers?"

"Yes, and I made Bayle's arrow hit the target. That was a mistake I won't make again."

"Huh," he grunted, and fell silent.

She guided her horse around a washed out hole in the road, fearful of what his silence meant. She realized how sheltered she had been in Glimmerdale. There had been very few who did not like her or the fact she was different. She couldn't take it any longer. She had to know. "Does it bother you?"

"Does what bother me?"

"My magic."

"Why should it bother me?" he asked. "Are you going to set my hair on fire or something?"

She laughed, "No, I wouldn't do that."

"Good," he swept a hand through the brown waves on the side of his head. "I happen to like my hair."

Me, too, she thought, wishing she could touch it.

His grin widened as if he had heard her thoughts. "You have a lovely smile," he said.

Heat rushed into her face. Suddenly, she felt shy. "Thank you."

He leaned over and touched her cheek. "It brings out your dimples."

"Stop it," she said, leaning away from his hand, embarrassed. "Or I might change my mind about setting your hair on fire."

He jerked his hand back. "Yikes, the woman is dangerous," he laughed.

King Goruth, riding at the head of the army, chose that moment to turn in his saddle and check on those following him. Frowning, he caught Elhrin's eye and then glanced at Tomas. He turned back around in his saddle. She had the feeling he did not like Tomas being near her.

"Do you need to leave?" she asked.

"I don't think so," he said. "Do you wish for me to go?"

"No, absolutely not," she said, quickly. "But aren't you supposed to be in the line with your regiment or something?"

"My regiment may all be dead by now," he said with a sigh. "They are defending Lakeshore Glen."

She winced inwardly for her callous mistake. "I'm sorry. I forgot that was where you were stationed. What are you supposed to do now?"

"For now, I have been assigned to His Majesty as a messenger. I will stay with him until I can rejoin my regiment." He paused. "Elhrin, I know you didn't want to tell me before, but is your magic the reason why you are here?"

You could say that, she almost blurted out loud. "It's hard to explain," she said. "I really don't think I can talk about it."

"Hmm, you are mysterious," he gave her a lopsided grin. "I like it."

"I'm not as mysterious as you think."

"No?"

"No, truth be told, I'm far more mysterious than you think," she said. "And, far more dangerous," she added with a mischievous grin.

"I'm going to have to keep a close eye on you, then," Tomas laughed—a hearty sound that drew the king's attention.

He turned in his saddle. "Lieutenant," King Goruth beckoned.

"Duty calls," Tomas said with a grin. He spurred his horse forward to join the king. They discussed something for a brief moment, and then Tomas turned his horse and rode back down the line. "I'll talk with you later," he said as he rode past.

Elhrin couldn't help but feel disappointed that he had to go. She realized that Bayle may have been right. She had known all along she found Tomas attractive, but there was something more to her feelings and whatever it was grew stronger each time she saw him.

That evening, after Marguerite and Bayle retired for the night, Elhrin sat on her bedroll going through the *Book of Tolman* by the light of a single candle. She had tried the pendant again on Master Gryph and Tolman Arahod's writings, but the scenes they showed were no different than the ones she had already viewed. She wondered why the pendant kept showing her the day of Master Gryph's death. She already knew what happened that day, and she didn't want to watch it happen again.

She decided to go through each chapter after Tolman's, one by one, and see if anything turned up. After a dozen or more with no luck, she decided to call it a night. She put the pendant back inside her tunic, and was closing her book when the page turned and the word *Blackridge* caught her attention. She scanned the page again, and there it was in the writings of a magician by the name of Lleiff Halite.

She thought that she had read his writings before, but for some reason she did not remember this particular passage. She went back to the beginning of the passage and began to read.

It has been some time since my last entry, but there has been a most distressing turn of events in the Northern Province that has kept me busy for several months. Let me start from the beginning so that you will better understand what has transpired.

Last fall, Worelin, the High Lord of Clan Terinov of Blackridge, called a truce to the constant feuding and bloodshed with their neighbors the Clan of Oynh of Lakeshore Glen. This was met with great relief by the High Lord of Oynh, Horat, who had written to the King of Anderan of the news, but had added a note of skepticism as to the trustworthiness of Worelin Terinov's intentions. It seems his reservations were well founded.

Earlier this year, after the snows melted and the days began to warm, Worelin proposed a celebration of peace and asked the Oynh clan to join him in a valley on the border of the two clans' territories. Oynh readily accepted the offer and most of the clan attended the celebration. It was said the celebration was a spectacular affair, with games, music, food, and plenty of ale. However, late in the evening, when the majority of Clan Oynh had become impaired from hours of drinking, the men of Clan Terinov, who had not consumed the ale as the Oynh clan had thought, became hostile and attacked the men of Oynh. They did not stop until every man, woman, and child of Oynh had been murdered in cold blood. Only two managed to survive. Horat Oynh's daughter, Cameall, who Worelin took prisoner back to Blackridge Keep, and a young boy who managed to escape into a nearby wood and carried the horrible news to Lakeshore Glen.

When the King of Anderan received word of the event, he organized an army to lay siege on Blackridge Keep. Worelin was a cunning adversary. He was able to thwart my magical efforts to gain passage for the king's men into the keep, causing the siege to last far longer than hoped. Changing tactics, I looked for another way in and was successful. The result allowed me and my companions the element of surprise and we were able to take Worelin into custody, thus ending the siege and sealing Worelin's fate. He was sentenced to death for his treachery, and the king wasted no time in sending his message to those who betrayed trust. Worelin was drawn and quartered in full view of the remaining members of the Clan of Terinov below Blackridge Keep, the clan was disbanded, some were taken to the prison at Fort Denmar, and Blackridge Keep was ordered to be abandoned.

Horat's daughter, Cameall, was found locked in the master chambers of the keep and taken into the protective care of the king back to the City of Muryne. Unfortunately, due to the trauma of her ordeal, she was despondent, refusing to speak, and upon closer examination, it was discovered she was with child.

Recently, I found out from a prisoner who had been privy to Worelin's intentions, that the High Lord of Terinov had planned the truce and the massacre expressly to take the daughter of Horat. He knew the High Lord of Oynh would never agree to a marriage otherwise.

Elhrin was surprised at how Blackridge became abandoned. The tale she knew was very different from Lleiff's version. She thought it had been abandoned because of the actions of an evil lord who once lived in the keep. The story was, he went out into the night and abducted young girls from the surrounding countryside. The girls were never seen again, and supposedly he had tortured and killed them. Then after his death, the local citizens believed the keep was haunted by the evil lord and the missing girls' ghosts, and no one was willing to go near the place anymore. She scanned down through more of

Lleiff's writings, but he had moved on to other subjects. She was nearing the end of his chapter, when she noticed a brief paragraph mentioning the young girl, Cameall.

I am sad to say Horat's daughter, Cameall, died today giving birth to a son. I suppose it is for the best. I don't think she would have ever recovered from the trauma she suffered at the hands of Worelin Terinov. As to the fate of her young son, the king feared for his safety, so had him whisked away to be given into the care of an unnamed family.

Elhrin closed the book, blew her candle out, and burrowed down into her blankets. She was tired, but sleep was elusive as her mind played and replayed her short conversation with Tomas. Her lips spread into a small smile. She hoped he would keep a close eye on her.

She was running down a dark stone corridor, the only light coming from smoking torches placed at great distances from each other along the walls. Her heart beat furiously and she could not breathe. Something was chasing her, something horrible, something she was too afraid to turn around and see. On she ran down the never-ending corridor, she was too slow, it was going to catch her. She could hear its footsteps pounding the flagstones behind her and knew it was closing in.

Something sharp grabbed her shoulders and she started to scream. Then something slammed into her back and sent her sprawling to the ground. A massive weight landed on top of her and crushed her into the flagstones. She thought her bones were going to break, but suddenly it was lifted off and she heard a horrendous crash, followed by a downpour of rubble and dirt. She had to cover her head to protect it from falling debris.

Coughing from the cloud of dust filling the corridor, she raised her head and saw a figure slowly rise from the floor. Reptilian in form, the creature was a menacing figure. This was the thing that had been chasing her, and it now stood just a few paces away.

The creature laughed, "Well met, So'ladiun."

She started to rise and run again.

"Elhrin, stay down," a deep voice ordered.

She jerked her head around. Master Gryph stood in the middle of the corridor behind her.

"Cynder, it is time for you to go," he said.

"Oh, I think not, So'ladiun," Cynder raised a sharp scale-covered claw and shot a sizzling sphere of green at Master Gryph.

Master Gryph threw both hands forward defensively. The green orb hit something solid in front of him in a deafening explosion of multi-colored sparks that scattered along the corridor. Master Gryph raised both hands above his head and clapped them together, then pushed outward, creating an orb of dazzling white that grew in size as it passed Elhrin. Cynder dodged to the side, trying to move out of the way, but the sphere slammed into him and sent him tumbling down the corridor with crackling bolts of white traveling along his entire body. Master Gryph walked past Elhrin without looking at her, a grim determined look upon his face.

Movement on the corridor floor made Elhrin glance back at Cynder. His body began to shimmer and change, until he transformed himself into a beast resembling a huge insect. He had a triangular-shaped head with large multi-faceted eyes, mandibles that dripped a slimy liquid, and he stood on bent grasshopper-like hind legs with four legs along his torso waving in the air.

"That one was new to me, So'ladiun. I'll have to remember it for the future," Cynder rasped, his mandibles snapping.

"There is no future for you," Master Gryph raised his left hand in the direction of Cynder. Elhrin could not see anything happening, but Cynder started to scream. Master Gryph closed his fist tightly. One of Cynder's flailing legs snapped off and crashed into the wall. A dark liquid spurted out of the remaining stump in a long stream, splattering across the floor. Cynder retaliated with bolts of lightning out of the remaining three appendages and caught Master Gryph off guard. He dropped in agony to his hands and knees.

"No," Elhrin tried to yell, but her voice created no sound. She wanted to get up to help him, but found she could not move no matter how hard she tried.

Master Gryph slowly raised his hand, fighting against the agony of the currents coursing through his body. Cynder began to gasp for air, his mandibles snapping back and forth furiously, and he too fell to the floor. Neither let up on the other. Helplessly, Elhrin watched the battle of wills until Master Gryph shouted out in pain immediately followed by a blinding flash of light that disrupted her vision. When she could see again, she found she was no longer in the corridor, but was in a bleak valley, barren and gray, surrounded on all sides by high, craggy mountains. Off in the distance was a dark citadel, and on the valley floor stood the most handsome man she had ever seen. Beside him stood a hooded figure that she recognized to be Cynder, and facing them both, on his knees, was Master Gryph.

"Well, Gryphon, it seems you have found yourself in quite a predicament. Let's see how my brother likes it when I send his precious So'ladiun to the Void," Obsudius said, and flicked his hand in the direction of Master Gryph. Master Gryph didn't have time to react. Suddenly, he was no longer there.

"NO!" she screamed, and sat up in her bedroll.

"Good heavens, Elhrin, what's wrong?" Marguerite asked.

Elhrin's heart was racing, and she realized she had just been dreaming. She could barely make out the dark figures of Marguerite and Bayle who were both sitting up in their bedrolls.

"Are you okay?" Bayle asked.

"I'm sorry, it was just a bad dream," she said, shaking uncontrollably.

"Do you want to tell us about it?" Marguerite asked.

"No, I'm okay," she said. The last thing she wanted to do was tell Marguerite Master Gryph had been sent to the Void, even if it was just a dream. The mere thought of spending an eternity without your loved one would be horrific. "I'm sorry I woke you."

"If you change your mind, let me know," Marguerite said, her blankets rustled as she lay back down.

"You sure you're okay, sis?" Bayle asked.

"Yes, I'm sure," she said, "you better go back to sleep."

Elhrin lay back on her blankets, staring blankly into the inky darkness. Why would she dream about Master Gryph fighting Cynder like that? He was dead.

Was it possible for him to fight in the realm of the dead? She remembered with a start that he had said he wouldn't be visiting her for awhile.

Please, please, please, don't let that dream be true.

She lay wide awake for the rest of the night until she heard the sounds of soldiers moving outside her tent, breaking camp. She could not lie there any longer. She had to get her mind off of the dream. Numbed with fatigue and fear, she rolled out of her blankets to get ready for what promised to be a long day.

Chapter Fourteen

Over the next few days, King Goruth's army wound its way slowly through the foothills of the Northreach Mountains, following the winding, rutted and rocky road north over grassy hills and knolls and through the deep shadows of musky smelling forests filled with tall ferns and prickly holly. As she unhooked the clasp on her cloak, Elhrin noticed that it would not be much longer before they reached the edge of the tall mountains, and that meant soon she would have to demonstrate her abilities for the king. She frowned as she rolled her cloak into a ball, not knowing why she dreaded the event. She was capable of handling herself, but would she measure up to his standards? He knew what Master Gryph had been capable of, and she certainly wasn't that talented. What could she do that would be comparable? She had no idea. She turned to fasten the cloak to her pack resting on the rear of her saddle and saw Tomas and a rider in a blue and white surcoat galloping for the front of the line. Tomas smiled at her when they passed. She smiled back, wishing that they could talk again. The last few days had only been brief hellos and passing smiles as the king had kept Tomas busy with one task or another. The two men skidded to a halt next to the king.

Bayle, who was riding right next to her, leaned in close. "He must be from Tuhnichi. He's wearing the colors of Prince Cahail's regiment."

"Shh, I can't hear what he is saying," she said.

"Your Majesty, Prince Cahail is a day's ride behind you near Greystone," Elhrin heard the soldier say, "and General Wyrinfell from Gildas sent word to the prince that he was outside the village of Glimmerdale, which puts him about a day behind the prince."

"Do you know how many men General Wyrinfell has with him?" King Goruth asked.

"According to Prince Cahail, he has seventeen hundred fifty men, Your Majesty."

"How many are with Cahail?"

"Twelve hundred, Your Majesty. He emptied the garrison in Tuhnichi of everyone he could spare."

The king did not respond to the news and was silent for so long, Elhrin thought he had forgotten about the soldier riding beside him.

"Has Cahail received word from the Southern Province as to whether they have men on the way?" King Goruth finally asked.

"The Prince did not indicate that he had, Your Majesty."

King Goruth grunted in displeasure at the news. "Ride back to Cahail and tell him to send word to Councilor Idora in the Southern Province. If she does not already have her men on the road, then she needs to do so, quickly. As it stands now, if they have not already made it into the Midlands, they may not reach us before we have to engage the enemy."

"Yes, Your Majesty," the soldier bowed in his saddle and wheeled his horse around to gallop past her in the direction of Greystone.

"I'm afraid we may not have enough men," King Goruth said to no one in particular.

"We need to close the Rift, Goruth," Marguerite said, surprising Elhrin with her familiar use of his given name without his title, but guessed it was only because of their friendship and the fact that they were out of earshot of the rest of the army. The king had asked the three of them and Master Toome to ride with him and had ordered his entourage to fall back so they could speak privately.

"Marguerite," he sighed, "please, we have just been over this. I cannot agree to let you and Elhrin go off to Blackridge Keep without knowing any more than I do now. I have not had substantial evidence that this Rift you keep raving about exists and, even if it did, and everything you have told me is true, I still don't think I would let you go."

Tomas shot a puzzled look at Elhrin, but she kept her face impassive.

"Goruth, sometimes you can be like a boil on the backside of a mule," Marguerite spat out. "How does Egeria live with your stubbornness?"

King Goruth looked at her sideways and raised an eyebrow. "She takes notes on a day to day basis, and then lets me know in excruciating detail how far I fall short of her expectations each night," he said, without smiling.

Marguerite burst out laughing and the king grinned, then frowned, "What have we here?"

They had reached the summit of a steep rise and were greeted with the sight of a large group of people on the road, moving in their direction. The group moved slowly, silently, as if each step took more life out of them and it would be only a matter of time before they collapsed into the dust of the road. The crying of a child broke their silence, and as they drew near, Elhrin saw that there were very few men, most were women and children.

"Refugees," Master Toome observed.

"Tomas, let the men know we will be taking a break. Then I want you to see that these people get any supplies or medical attention they need," King Goruth said pulling back on his reigns.

Elhrin edged her horse beside Marguerite's.

"It breaks your heart, doesn't it?" Marguerite said.

"Yes, it does," Elhrin replied.

Each man, woman, and child had the haunted look of one who had lost everything, including hope. When they neared the army they stopped, unsure of what to do. King Goruth beckoned them forward. Two men separated from the party and bowed before the king.

"Your Majesty," said one of the men. He was covered in dirt and dried blood that had seeped from a bandage around his head. "I am Dolph Oberson and this is my neighbor, Alyn Tolb."

He indicated the older man beside him, who was covered in cuts and bruises, and had a bloody bandage covering his entire right hand.

"Where are you from, Dolph?" the king asked.

"I have a farm just south of Lakeshore Glen, but it is gone now," he said. "We were attacked last week, and my entire family was killed. If it hadn't been for Alyn here dragging me out of my burning home, I would be dead, too. The countryside north of the mountains is crawling with monsters straight out of a nightmare. We decided to come south, hoping to find safety."

Tomas returned. "We are ready, Your Majesty," he said, dismounting from his horse.

"Have your party follow the lieutenant here, he will give you anything you need," King Goruth said. "There is a farmstead not much further down the road. I'm sure they will let your party rest there for the night."

"Thank you, Your Majesty, the generosity of your military has been appreciated. This morning we left an encampment near Kilmyn Pass, and a General Dulok provided us with a few supplies," Dolph bowed once again and gestured for the party of refugees to follow him.

In silence, they watched the refugees shuffle away. King Goruth turned to Master Toome. "Good. Dulok has beaten us to the staging area," King Goruth said. "We'll rest briefly here, then we must be moving on. I want to be there before nightfall."

Sitting cross-legged in the high grass on the side of the road with Marguerite and Bayle, Elhrin experienced a sudden feeling of nausea. She frowned at the half-eaten apple in her hand wondering why it was not sitting well on her stomach. She tossed it away.

"Something wrong?" Marguerite asked.

The woman was very acute when it came to anyone starting to feel sick. Master Gryph once joked that Marguerite could sense someone coming down with a cold in Agadar, a city on the west coast of Anderan, from Glimmerdale.

"I don't know. I feel weird," she said. She uncorked her waterskin and took a sip of water.

"Weird, how?" Marguerite leaned forward to place a hand on her forehead.

"You aren't warm."

Elhrin shook her head. "No, I don't have a fever. I don't know what it is."

Marguerite gave her a small smile. "Maybe your nerves are catching up to you."

Elhrin grimaced at the reminder. "Maybe," she said. King Goruth had told her to be prepared to demonstrate her abilities first thing the next morning.

"Elhrin, do you see that?" Bayle blurted out louder than he needed as she was sitting right next to him. He pointed towards the mountains.

Master Toome, who was nearby with the king and other members of the king's war council, glanced his way. He turned to look at the mountains.

From their vantage point on the high knoll, they could see something large soar like a hawk over the peaks of the mountain range in the distance. When it banked to skim the face of a mountain and circle around, Elhrin saw it was the creature the soldier had described to the king back in Muryne. Black as night with a long muscular body, it resembled the lizards she was used to seeing crawl along the rock fences back home in search of insects—only this monster had a gigantic wingspan propelling its huge body over the earth at a fast rate. The beast swooped down low on the horizon and sent a series of bright orbs of fire raining down on something out of their line of sight.

"Your Majesty, you need to see this," Master Toome said uneasily.

The king, engrossed in conversation with one of his officers, turned to look.

"Cynder," Elhrin whispered, as a thin veil of fear settled over her. She felt like vomiting in the grass. He looked nothing like any of the versions she had seen thus far, and he was far larger than she expected.

The creature made several more passes at the unseen target on the ground before lifting up and flying away over the mountains from which it came. Tendrils of smoke rose above the treetops in the area where he had attacked.

King Goruth turned to face her, his face grim and angry. "That was the creature you have been calling Cynder?"

Swallowing a huge lump in her throat, she nodded.

"The damn thing just hit my army. Mount up," he yelled, jogging to his horse.

They scrambled up out of the grass and ran to their mounts. King Goruth turned his prancing steed around to face her. His face was red with fury. "Elhrin, you ride with me and tell me everything you know about this creature and how you know it. No more playing games. I want to know exactly how you came by your information. Do you understand me?"

"Yes, Your Majesty," she said, trembling. She looked helplessly at Marguerite, who gave her a reassuring glance before climbing on her own horse.

They pushed the horses as hard as they could without killing their mounts, and along the way Elhrin told the king about her dreams and the viewings she had seen from the *Book of Tolman*, only leaving out the fact that Master Gryph said she was one of Solisius' So'ladiun. Every once in a while, Marguerite would interject to remind him of times past, instances with Master Gryph that he was aware of, hoping to give credence to Elhrin's story. King Goruth never took his eyes off the road, never spoke or asked questions, just listened to what she and Marguerite had to say. His silence scared her.

When she was through, he finally spoke, his anger evident in the low, even tone of his voice. "In the future, you are to share all information with me, even if you think I won't believe you, or it is strange or unimportant. You let me decide what to do or think about the information you give me."

"Yes, Your Majesty," she said, blinking hard against the tears that were threatening to form.

"Marguerite, why you felt it necessary to leave this out, I have no idea. I have been friends with Gryph for over thirty years—have spent half my life with the man," he seethed, almost shouting. "I know what he is capable of as well as you do. As a matter of fact, I know things you or anyone else will never know. Your lack of faith in me is disappointing."

Marguerite spread her lips in a thin line, but said nothing.

He pinned Elhrin with eyes of gray steel. "When I say you are to share all information, I mean everything. Do you understand me, young lady?"

"Yes, Your Majesty," she whispered, realizing he knew she had left something out, but still she could not bring herself to voice something she felt could not possibly be true.

It was deep in the afternoon when they rode through a thick haze of smoke to reach the devastated camp. Tents and wagons had been destroyed and burned, some still smoldering, and debris was scattered everywhere. Craters, looking like tiny burned out waterless ponds, dotted the ground throughout the camp from where Cynder's magic had exploded. Hundreds of men and horses were lying dead across the wide meadow. The stench of blood and feces mingling with the smoke was nauseating.

The surviving soldiers were busy putting order back into the camp and gathering their fallen comrades for burial in a pit being dug near a patch of woods across the field.

King Goruth ordered his men to fall out and help. She, Marguerite, and Bayle were commanded to stay with him, and followed his entourage to a tent where General Dulok, who had been wounded in the attack, was being cared for.

The three of them stood just outside the open flap of the tent, listening to the general relate the events of the attack.

"I heard the first explosion, and was on the way out of my tent to see what had happened when it blew up behind me. The next thing I knew, I was flat on my face with a piece of tent pole sticking out of my leg. Then the creature flew over me so close I thought I was dead, but he passed me by. I have never seen anything like it. He looked like one of the alligators you find in Blackwater Swamp down south, only with wings. At any rate, the thing flew by several times throwing down exploding balls of green fire. You can see what that did to us," he paused to cough. "The men tried to fight it, but arrows and spears bounced off its hide like it was made of stone. Only the ones hitting its wings seem to do any damage, but I don't think it would have been enough to kill it. Thank the Light of Solisius, the thing decided to leave when it did. I really don't know if we could have brought it down."

Marguerite stepped to the tent's doorway. "King Goruth, Elhrin . . . ."

"Not now, Marguerite, we will talk later," King Goruth snapped. He turned his attention to the officers with him. "Captains, I want a double watch around the perimeter of the entire camp at all times. Everyone is to remain battle ready. Move the horses into the trees. If this thing comes back, I want them out of the way. At daybreak, we will decide what we need to do while we wait on the others to arrive."

"Yes, Your Majesty," two of the officers said, and left the tent to carry out the king's orders.

"Dulok, I'll be back later," the king rose to leave.

"Your Majesty, there is other news. I had a messenger arrive from Captain Jilken's regiment before the attack," General Dulok said.

"What did he say?" he asked, halting at the tent's entrance.

"They never made it through to the city, but were able to clear out bands of the monsters south of the city before they were forced to retreat back into Kilmyn Pass with about fifty men. They have set up a fortified outpost, and are going to stay there to observe the enemy movements and fend off any who enter the pass if they can. They will send messengers to you as they learn new information and are awaiting your orders. From their vantage point, they can see Lakeshore Glen. The siege continues on the city, but won't last much longer as most of the city is on fire and more of the enemy is marching from the direction of Blackridge."

King Goruth ducked out of the tent. "Tomas, find me this man and have him await me in my tent. Marguerite, you and Elhrin come see me in about an hour. I have a few things I want to discuss with you before you retire for the night." He strode off through the tents, issuing orders to the group of officers following in his wake.

Right after dusk, Tomas arrived to tell Elhrin the king was ready for her and Marguerite to join him. She handed the end of a rope to Bayle. "Marguerite isn't here," she said, wiping her hands on her trousers. "She went to the surgery to see if she could help."

"I'll find her after I escort you to King Goruth's tent," Tomas said, watching Bayle attach the rope securely to a stake in the ground.

"Can you finish this by yourself?" she asked Bayle. The outer lines were all that was left to finish stabilizing their tent.

"Yes, go ahead," he said, snatching up another stake to pound in the ground.

She followed Tomas through the new rows of tents being erected. He glanced at her sideways. "How have you been?"

"Good, considering all this," she sighed with a small smile.

He nodded grimly. "War is difficult to get used to in any form, but this," he shook his head in disbelief at the destruction left behind by Cynder, "is utter madness."

"It is a nightmare," she said, looking across the camp lit by hundreds of smoking fires. There was no doubt the cleanup would continue late into the night. "I never thought I would be a part of something like this."

He reached out to grasp her arm, pulling her to a halt. "Please tell me the king is not using you against your will," he said, frowning.

"No, he's not," she said, surprised by his concern. "I'm here of my own accord."

"Why would you want to come here?" he asked.

"Have I told you I'm crazy?" she asked. Frowning, she touched her stomach. She was starting to feel sick again. What was wrong with her?

Tomas smiled. "No, I think you mentioned being dangerous and mysterious. Crazy is a new one." He tugged on her arm. "Come, crazy lady, your king is waiting." He led her down another row of tents then turned to skirt between two supply wagons.

"Did he pitch his tent in Bald Mountain Quarry?" she asked, thinking they were taking a long time to get to it.

"I'm taking you the scenic route. I'm enjoying your company," he grinned at her just as horns trumpeted from the direction of the mountains. His face fell. "We are under attack! Come." He turned and ran, disappearing in the sea of tents.

Elhrin started after him, but then skidded to a halt when she heard the flapping of giant wings. She had a vow to keep. She looked for Cynder, but cloud cover and the smoke from numerous campfires made it impossible to see anything in the sky. Then a green orb appeared over the northernmost edge of the camp, briefly lighting the sky and illuminating the giant black creature soaring above. The fiery orb sped down across the camp and exploded somewhere in the center with a ground shaking boom. Fire shot high above the tents. Screams and cries from the injured rose above the pandemonium of hundreds of men bracing for battle.

Arrows were launched into the night sky. The beast roared. Cynder was now behind her. She whirled around in time to see another orb slam into the far side of the camp, followed by a second volley of arrows, some of which had been set on fire. Briefly, they illuminated the sky, showing her where the beast was flying. Without stopping to think if she could do it or not, Elhrin remembered the white orb Master Gryph had used in her dream. She quickly built the energy of her magic and raised her hands over her head to clap them together and force them outward. A crackling white orb shot like a comet into the sky, leaving a trail of sparks. Cynder saw it coming and veered out of the way. It zoomed into the clouds and disappeared. A moment later, a faint distant report echoed from the mountains when her orb finally connected with something and exploded.

Cynder pulled up to hover in one place. She could tell he was looking for the one who had sent the sphere of magic at him. She sent another blazing ball of energy flying toward the beast. He rapidly beat his wings to back out of the way, but the orb clipped a wing in an explosion of white sparks that showered down onto the camp and sent him spinning out of control through the air into the dark. She listened for the sound of him hitting the ground, but it never came. Over the uproar of the camp, she heard the beating of wings again steadily thumping louder, closer. She turned in circles, trying to determine the direction from which he was coming.

The next thing she knew, she was hit from the side and tumbled with someone across the ground as explosions hit the ground where she had just been standing. Bayle pushed himself off of her. "You almost got yourself killed," he hissed, angrily. "He knew precisely where you were, and you just stood there. Come on, we have to move before he comes back."

He jerked her to her feet and pulled her through the maze of tents. As they ran, she could hear Cynder flying nearby through the noise of the continuous volley of arrows and the chaos of the camp. The wing beats thumped closer. The popping of arrows striking something solid became louder. Green orbs blossomed in the darkness above, shooting from the sky to explode into the camp, sending men and wreckage flying all around her and Bayle. Elhrin jerked her hand out of Bayle's grasp and faced the silhouette of Cynder, visible in the sky from the blazing light of the fires ravaging the camp. This time, she poured as much energy into the orb as she could, and fired it at Cynder. It flew upward at a tremendous speed and caught him in his hindquarters with a blinding flash of light and a broad spray of sparks. Cynder trumpeted a deafening roar of pain as he tumbled out of the sky and landed heavily in a copse of trees near the road.

Elhrin bent over and propped her hands on her knees, breathing hard. That last one had taken a lot out of her. She was not used to expending this kind of energy at one time and could tell her supply for her magic had diminished considerably. She wiped a sleeve across her sweaty brow, listening to the cheers that roared across the camp. Everyone thought that the monster had been defeated, but then a tremendous bellow trumpeted from the stand of trees, silencing the cheers. Cynder was alive and furious. Once again, the thumping of wings sounded in the dark as he rose out of the trees.

"Stand ready," a nearby officer shouted. His order was echoed by others throughout the camp.

"Bayle, I don't know how much more I can do," Elhrin huffed desperately, trying to catch her breath. She was terrified.

Cynder's wing beats were erratic as if he could not fly normally. The men let loose their arrows, pelting him as he zoomed low over the camp, barely clearing the tops of the tallest tents and speeding in the direction of Elhrin and Bayle. Elhrin sent a series of fiery orbs at the beast. Cynder zigzagged back and forth, dodging her attack, but one caught him on his foreleg. He roared with pain, but did not slow down. He was coming after her.

Bayle grabbed Elhrin's arm and forced her to run. Behind them Cynder opened his mouth, and like the dragon fairy tales of old, spewed out a plume of searing flames, igniting everything in its path. Bayle changed course and pulled Elhrin to the left through a row of tents and supply wagons. Cynder banked to follow right behind them. Elhrin gathered what little energy she had, knowing it wasn't much, hoping it would be enough. She then tackled Bayle and landed on top of him as they hit the ground. Remembering how Tolman had protected himself from Cynder, she formed a magical barrier over both of them, praying it would be enough. Cynder spewed fire, engulfing them in flames as he sped by. The heat was intense, almost unbearable, and she could barely breathe, but her barrier kept the flames away from their bodies. She closed her eyes, concentrating hard to keep it in place because the strength of her magical energy was almost gone.

"Elhrin, get up," Bayle grunted. "Get up."

Elhrin let go of her magic and nearly passed out, the world around her going gray. She felt Bayle wriggle out from under her and then grab her arms and drag her away from the flames. The tents around them were on fire. When her eyesight cleared, she saw two worried faces—Tomas and Bayle.

"You okay?" Tomas asked.

She nodded. "Cynder?"

"He's gone," Tomas said. His lips spread into a grin. "You were magnificent."

"I don't feel magnificent," she coughed, propping up on her elbows.

Marguerite ran through the burning debris, skidding to a halt when she saw Elhrin lying on the ground. "Elhrin," she yelled, rushing over. She dropped to her knees and jerked Elhrin into a tight embrace. "Thank heavens you are safe." Elhrin had never seen Marguerite this frightened and could feel her body tremble. "Are you hurt?"

"No," Elhrin croaked. Her throat was dry. "I'm just tired."

"Come, let's get you back," Marguerite said, releasing her and allowing Bayle and Tomas to pull her to her feet.

The camp spun crazily around her. If Tomas and Bayle hadn't been holding onto her, she would have dropped back to the ground, which was not good. If she was going to battle Cynder, she needed her magical stamina to be stronger.

"Lean on me," Tomas said, looping his arm underneath hers. "Can you walk?"

"Yes," she nodded. She was sure she could walk on her own, but it felt nice to have his strong arms around her. "Aren't you supposed to be with the king?"

"He sent me after you," he said. "I thought you had followed me to his tent, but when you started firing back at the beast I saw you hadn't. I tell you, Elhrin, I think you have impressed him this night. I know I'm impressed."

For some reason, hearing that her near escape from death impressed the king made her angry. She knew it was irrational, but it was what it was.

They reached their tent to find it undamaged, and Elhrin crawled in alone and fell on her blankets, exhausted. Tomas left to inform the king that Elhrin was safe, and Marguerite stayed outside to rummage through their pile of belongings for food and water. Bayle plopped to the ground just outside of the tent. She could feel him staring at her. She rolled her head to look at him. Still sweating, there were clear trails of moisture from forehead to chin in the black soot covering his face. He was grinning from ear-to-ear.

"Why are you smiling?" she asked.

"I don't know. I can't seem to help it. That was the most scared I have ever been in my life, but I have to admit, it was a little bit exciting."

"If you say so. Tell that to all the dead men."

"I didn't mean it like that," he lost his smile. "I didn't say I wanted to do it all over again. Why are you so angry?"

"I don't know," she huffed in exasperation. "Maybe, I'm scared. Cynder is still out there and I am going to have to face him again. He is so strong. I don't have the magical energy to match his. I don't know if I can kill him."

"Yes, you can. What you did tonight looked like something Master Gryph would do. Didn't I hear Master Gryph tell you one time that your magical energy grows and builds with use and practice? I have never seen you do anything like this before. I think you are gaining in strength. You gave him something to think about, that's for certain. He turned tail and ran."

"I highly doubt he was scared of me, but you are right, I haven't done anything like that before." She had to admit there was something there—inside her. What she used against Cynder, she had only seen in a dream. How did she manage to do it without guidance? And Cynder did leave. Why would he leave when he could have finished her off quickly? She knew she had hurt him, but she didn't think it had been enough to drive him away. A thought crossed her mind—was he limited in energy supply, too? She realized Bayle was still staring at her. "Your belief in me means a lot. Thanks for saving me back there."

"Right back at you."

She heard a deep voice call to Marguerite.

"Yes, she is," Marguerite answered, turning to look at Elhrin. She gave Elhrin a small smile.

A large shadow flitted across the outside of the tent's canvas then King Goruth stooped to look inside the front opening. "Well, young lady, that was a remarkable display of courage you provided for us tonight," he said.

Elhrin sat up on her bedroll and rested her arms on her knees. The frustrated anger she was feeling seemed to escalate by his appearance. "Thank you, Your Majesty. You did want me to prove to you that I was capable of handling myself. I hope that was sufficient," she snapped. She was not quite sure why she felt angry at the king. It wasn't his fault they were attacked, or that Cynder had come within a breath of killing her and Bayle, or that she was here in the first place.

Frowning, he narrowed his eyes at her tone. "More than sufficient," he said, evenly. "I can certainly tell Gryph had a hand in your education."

"He was the best," she hissed. Maybe she was angry at his lack of faith in her. Or the fact he had demanded that she prove herself.

"That he was," he agreed, contemplating her for a moment as if he wanted to say something, but decided against it in the end. "Are you well? Tomas said you suffered no injuries."

"I am fine, just tired," she said, tersely. Or, maybe that was truly the core of her anger—she was tired, and terrified, and desperately missed her mother.

"Good. You hurt the beast enough for him to break his attack. I do believe he fairly limped back across the mountains. Get some rest now. I don't think we have to worry about him returning tonight. Tomorrow, you and I have a few things to discuss." He stood up straight and left without another word, leaving Marguerite to frown at her through the tent opening, arms crossed over her chest.

Marguerite raised an eyebrow at Elhrin. "Did that make you feel better?" she asked, letting Elhrin know that her less-than-pleasant attitude was uncalled for.

"No," she sighed with regret and fell back on her blankets.

"I didn't think it did," Marguerite said and walked away.

Chapter Fifteen

The next day dawned with a cool mist drifting down over the land, creating a thick blanket of fog that gave the unusually quiet camp an eerie feel, as if the souls of those that had died the day before still walked among them within its fine ethereal wisps.

Elhrin shivered and pulled her cloak close as she, Marguerite, and Bayle made their way to King Goruth's tent. Even the men they passed seemed to sense the feeling of death that lay over the camp like a living entity. The boisterous mood of the last few days had been stamped out completely. There was no laughter, no joking, and if anyone spoke it was in a hushed manner. Cynder's attack had shown them a reality of war that none had ever faced. An enemy with a cold steel weapon they could understand—knew how to fight against, but a beast that was resistant to their efforts, and could kill on a massive scale with ease, was new to them.

Elhrin stopped abruptly to look at a broad path of blackened earth. Bayle nearly collided into her back. "Elhrin, warn me when you decide to stop."

"If you would quit walking on my heels, Bayle, there wouldn't be a problem," she said, absently, as she stared at the trail Cynder's fire had left. The path, as wide as two supply wagons, end to end, disappeared into the fog to her left and right. She could understand what the men around her were feeling. *How can you defeat something that can do this kind of damage?* She and Bayle were lucky to be alive.

"Elhrin, we will be late," Marguerite said, waiting.

Reluctantly, she stepped onto the sodden black path and followed the lady to a large, purple and gold-striped tent. Master Toome, Tomas, and several officers waited outside the entrance. Master Toome saw them coming and hurried to meet them. He pulled both Elhrin and Marguerite into a bone-cracking hug.

"Toome, you are hurting us," Marguerite grunted.

"I'm just glad you are both safe," he said, releasing them. "I didn't have the chance to check on you last night. Elhrin, I had no idea you could do what you did, but I am glad you can."

"Thank you, Master Toome," she said, a little embarrassed.

"Colonel Toome." Tomas called. He held the flap of the tent to one side, waiting for them to enter.

"These boys still insist on calling me Colonel," he said, with a twinkle in his eyes. He put a hand on Marguerite's back. "Shall we go?"

The large tent was crowded with the army's top officers, and Elhrin, Bayle, and Marguerite had to squeeze in behind Master Toome just inside the tent opening. The king was addressing those assembled, but because of her short stature she could not see him. Master Toome saw her predicament and beckoned for her to stand in front of him where there was a space. From her new position she could see that King Goruth stood behind a portable table. General Dulok was seated on one end with his wounded leg propped up on a stool. Both men and those officers closest to them, hovered over a large map of Anderan spread out on the table.

"Like I said earlier, we are going to have to move the army. He knows where we are and I don't want to sit here and wait for him to come back. What do you think, Dulok?" the king asked, lifting his head to scan the crowd. His bloodshot eyes stopped briefly on Elhrin, taking note of her arrival, before he looked back down at the map. She could tell he was exhausted and guessed he probably had not slept the night before.

Master Toome patted her shoulder, then squeezed through the crowd so that he could study the map.

"What if we moved into the pass? The forest along the road would provide some cover from overhead," General Dulok suggested.

"I don't know if that is a good idea. There are areas that would bottleneck the army and we would be at a disadvantage if we were attacked," Master Toome said, and leaned over to point at the map. "Especially, here in Rusty Rock Gap. There is nothing but cliffs rising on both sides of the road for at least three leagues. If he catches us there, we won't stand a chance."

King Goruth studied the map, weighing their options. "We are going to have to alter our normal tactics to counter this beast's might," he said, finally. "The pass does offer more protection than out here in the open for the most part, and we are going to have to get through the mountains at some point, anyway. It might be best if we break up the army in smaller groups and spread out. The old pass road is rough but still usable. Dulok, have your cavalry and infantry take that route. We can reassemble near the other side in Blythe Mountain Cove." Tiredly, he rubbed his eyes with his fingertips. "After that, we will decide our next step. Does anyone have any objections to this plan or have any suggestions otherwise?" He waited for a moment, but no one had anything to add. "All right, what I want to do is to get the camp disassembled as quickly as possible and move out. I am hoping the cloud cover and fog will help hide our movements. If the beast decides to come back today, I want him to have to hunt for us." King Goruth picked up a correspondence packet from the table and handed it to an officer in the crowd. "I want two runners to carry these for me to Cahail and Wyrinfell. Those letters tell them what has happened thus far, but they will need to understand our new plans and to follow us into the pass. Unless anyone has any questions, let's get moving."

"Your Majesty, who was the one that drove off the dragon?" someone on the other side of the tent asked.

"That would be the apprentice of the late Minister Idwyr. Elhrin, come here." He beckoned her with two fingers.

Elhrin was caught off guard by his summons and felt her mouth go dry as everyone's attention shifted to her. She squeezed through the men in front of her to stand by his side. There was a low murmur of surprise when they saw her. She knew a short, slim-statured teenage girl was far from the warrior they expected to see. King Goruth placed a hand on her shoulder and gave it a reassuring squeeze.

"We were lucky to have her with us last night," King Goruth said, and Elhrin was surprised when a few murmured an agreement. "She and Minister Idwyr's wife have been traveling with us since Glimmerdale, and have been providing me with some useful information concerning our enemy. On that note, I have a few things to discuss privately with the ladies, so if you gentlemen don't mind, I would like for you all to get our men ready to leave. Toome, Dulok, I would like for you to stay."

The men filed out of the tent, and Tomas closed the tent flap behind them, but remained inside.

"Lieutenant, find the ladies a seat," King Goruth sat down wearily and propped his arms on the surface of the table. "Last night was a bit of an eye opener for me, and I have been thinking about your argument. I want to know what your plan is, Marguerite? How is it that you propose to get to Blackridge Keep safely, allow Elhrin enough time to kill a powerful beast and close this rift you say exists, all without getting yourselves killed by the hundreds if not thousands of Do'athrim swarming in the area?" he asked, as Tomas placed two folding stools beside the table.

"We don't have an actual plan yet, Goruth. You have sidetracked us, and we haven't had the chance to formulate a plan," she replied, taking the seat nearest to him.

"I didn't think you did. Maybe I can help you with one."

Elhrin glanced at Marguerite in surprise. It sounded as if he was letting them go.

He rubbed a hand over the short beard stubble on his chin. "As strong as my instinct is to keep you within the protection of my army, I think Elhrin will have a better chance of defeating this animal when he is least expecting her. So, I am going to agree to let you go ahead with your plan to travel to Blackridge Keep."

Master Toome sputtered in protest.

King Goruth glared at him, daring him to speak. "If she remains with me, he will know where to find her. That won't do us any good," he continued.

"Don't we need her to stay to fight him?" asked General Dulok. "She was the only one who seemed to hurt it."

"Yes, I know, but we will have to do the best we can without her. I am hoping that once he sees there is no one using magic against him, he will assume he killed her last night."

"We are talking about a magical creature." Master Toome spread his arms wide in supplication. "What if he finds out she still lives? He will hunt her down like a hound after a fox. How can you let two women and a young boy go off on their own unprotected?"

"Did you hear me say anything about them going off unprotected? Shut up, Toome, and let me finish," King Goruth snapped. "Lieutenant Colkitte has informed me of a Sergeant Jag Soryn who grew up in a small village not far from Laurel Grove and is familiar with the terrain. I spoke with the sergeant's commander, and he highly recommends him for the job. I believe he will be more than capable of getting them to Blackridge Keep. Ladies, would you two agree to let a few select men of my choosing accompany you?"

"No, we wouldn't mind . . . oh!" Marguerite flinched when Master Toome pounded the table with a fist.

"This is unbelievable, men or not, you are going to get them killed, Goruth," Master Toome shouted.

The tent fell silent as a tomb. King Goruth stared coldly at him without blinking an eye. "My friend, I know you are concerned for their welfare, but I think it would be in your best interest if you calmed down before you push me too far," King Goruth said low and even, matching the glare that Master Toome was giving him. "If what Marguerite says is true, we have no choice. I am more than happy for Elhrin to stay with us, if she so desires, but I am certain she will have a better chance for success away from us."

"Is that the real reason, Goruth?" Master Toome asked. Seething he leaned over the table, seeming unafraid of his monarch. "Are you sure you are not trying to save your army, hoping he finds out she lives and is elsewhere and that his desire for her death will draw him away?"

"Toome," King Goruth growled, "you are treading dangerous water here. There is more to this than you know."

Elhrin wondered what he meant by that last statement as she stepped closer to Master Toome and placed a hand on his arm. "Master Toome, please understand." The hard look in his eyes made her falter, but he had to see the truth. "If I stay and kill Cynder here, it won't matter. As long as the Rift is open, he will just come back through and start all over again. I need to be at Blackridge Keep so I can close it and prevent him or any of the others from coming through again. I have to fight him there."

"We don't know for sure that the Rift exists," Master Toome said, throwing up his hands in frustration.

"Yes we do, Toome. I have told you time and again, but you refuse to let it sink into that thick skull of yours. Gryph told Elhrin in her dream that it did, and I told you the day she and I killed the Do'athrim in Glimmerdale that he had said he came through the Rift. What more do you need to start believing it?" Marguerite asked.

"Marguerite, you are basing this on the contents of a dream. Your love for Gryph has blinded you to reality. He was just a dream. It wasn't real."

"Not real?" she scoffed. "Then explain to me how it is not real when Gryph told her in a dream that she needed to close the Rift, *before* I killed the Do'athrim and he also told her exactly who Cynder was *before* she was able to see the exact story he told her unfold before her eyes in the book he gave her. Now, if these events had happened before her dream of Gryph, then we might be able to say it was not real and that she was dreaming about something that was on her mind. But it didn't happen that way. Just because you don't have substantial evidence that you can touch or see to verify the truth doesn't mean it is not real. Before yesterday, we only heard reports of Cynder. Have you ever seen anything like him in your lifetime? Do you have enough proof that he exists?"

"Don't patronize me, Marguerite, I also have proof of exactly how dangerous he is," he growled at her. "Goruth, again, this is just too dangerous for them, even with the best of men. If you insist on going through with this, then I am going with them."

King Goruth shook his head. "No, I need you here. We will just have to rely on her expertise and those of my men to see them through. If they fail, and what they say is true, then we are going to have a hard time winning against an endless enemy."

Master Toome leaned heavily against the table, and dropped his head to stare at the floor. "Madness, I say," he growled low under his breath.

King Goruth glanced at Tomas, who had positioned himself by the entrance. "Lieutenant, has your friend arrived?"

"Yes, Your Majesty," Tomas replied, and opened the tent flap to beckon Jag inside.

Jag ducked through the opening. His black, curly hair brushed the roof of the tent where it swooped down from the center pole. "Your Majesty," he bowed before the king, then saluted his superiors.

"Sergeant, Lieutenant Colkitte tells me you are familiar with the Northreach Mountains," King Goruth said.

"I am familiar with a large part of them, Your Majesty. I grew up west of Kilmyn Pass and spent much of my time hunting and fishing across the southern range."

"I need you to tell me what you think would be the best way for a small party to reach Blackridge Keep from here if you wanted to stay away from the pass and remain as hidden as possible?" King Goruth asked, once again perusing the map on the table.

Jag frowned, thoughtfully. "There are a few ways, but the easiest would probably be the old mine road by the Poitoo River. It leads to the abandoned gold mine on Hugeot's Mountain which is halfway through. The rest of the way to the forest on the northern edge is a tough hike, but not undoable. I would not advise horses, though. The terrain is too rough, and they would be more hindrance than help. Once you reach the other side, it is a matter of skirting the mountains and staying out of sight until you get to the valley that holds the keep. That is when it will become nearly impossible to reach without being seen. With the exception of the north side facing Shimmerfin Lake, the valley is surrounded by steep cliffs, and there is very little tree cover anywhere. If the enemy has anyone in the valley," he shrugged, leaving the obvious unspoken.

"Do you have another suggestion?" King Goruth asked.

Jag shook his head. "Nothing comes to mind, Your Majesty."

"What about over the mountains and down to the keep from the backside?" General Dulok asked.

"I just don't know. I haven't been in that part of the mountains since I was boy. We could try it, anyway, but if the backside is as steep as the rest of the valley it would be difficult to get down."

"Sounds like that is your only option at this point, however, you may get there and find another way," King Goruth rubbed the back of his neck and yawned. "Elhrin, what do you think of this plan?"

"Um, I think it is a good one," she shrugged. Having no experience in any of this, she was going to have to rely on their expertise. She leaned forward to look over the map. "Where is the mine road and Blackridge?"

"We are here," Jag tapped a finger on the map, "and the road is here. This is Blackridge." He pointed out each place.

The distance was further than she expected. "How long will it take us to get there?"

"Hmm, I would say two weeks, more or less, providing we don't run into any trouble," Jag replied.

Grunting in exasperation, Master Toome ran a hand through his hair. "This is insanity. The north is crawling with Do'athrim, who's to say the mountains aren't either. Those that killed Gryph and ravaged Glimmerdale had to get there somehow. There have been no reports of any being seen roaming the pass."

"Toome, you do have a good point, but we are going to try, anyway," Marguerite said, then glanced at Elhrin and Bayle. "We do have to be on our toes. If the Do'athrim I killed follows the same pattern as before and can come back through the Rift, then he will be tracking us down again."

"What is this you speak of?" King Goruth asked, frowning.

"There is a big black wolf who thinks I have the book Gryph gave Elhrin, and he is trying to retrieve it for his master, who I am inclined to believe is Cynder. Now that I think on it, Elhrin, since Cynder now knows about you, I bet it won't take long for him to figure out that you have the book," Marguerite said.

King Goruth closed his eyes and sighed heavily as if the news did not please him. He opened them and looked directly at Elhrin. "Is there anything else you need to tell me?" he asked her, pointedly.

"No, sir," she said.

"Very well," he grunted. He placed both palms on the table and pushed himself to his feet. "If what you say is true, he will most certainly be looking for you." He walked around the table. "Lieutenant, gather the men we discussed earlier. Make sure to take whatever you will need and have everyone meet at Marguerite's tent when you all are ready. I wish for you to be far away from me before nightfall."

"Yes, Your Majesty. Bayle, we could use your help," Tomas said, motioning for Jag and Bayle to follow him. He caught Elhrin's eye and gave her small smile.

Surprised, yet pleased that he would be going with them, she watched him push the tent flap open and hold it for Jag and Bayle. He flashed her one last smile and stepped out, letting the flap drop back in place.

King Goruth placed a hand on her shoulder. "Elhrin, it is with a heavy heart that I send you off on such a dangerous mission. I hope Toome is wrong in his accusation of me sending you to your death. If you want to change your mind and stay, I will gladly accept."

"No, Your Majesty, this is my destiny," Elhrin said.

"I couldn't tell you how many times I have heard Gryph say those very same words to me. Very well, I wish you a safe journey, and when this is all over, I want you to come see me." He wagged a finger at her. "You and I, we have much to discuss." He turned to Marguerite. "My dear lady, keep yourself safe. I couldn't imagine what Gryph would do to me if he knew that I was sending you off like this."

"I am almost certain he knows. He told Elhrin that she had to go, and he knows good and well I wouldn't allow her to go alone," Marguerite smiled. "We had better go get our things. Thank you, Goruth, and make sure to stay safe, as well."

"I will walk you out," Master Toome offered, and held open the tent flap for them. "Is there anything I can say or do to make you change your mind?" he asked, once they were outside.

"No, this is what must be," Marguerite said.

"I didn't think so," he sighed, and gave Elhrin then Marguerite a hug. "I expect to see you two safe and sound once you are finished."

"I expect the same thing from you, Lee Toome," Marguerite said, giving him a kiss on the cheek.

Chapter Sixteen

Exhausted, Elhrin trudged behind Marguerite, wondering when the woman would call for another break from their strenuous hike. She had only allowed them to stop twice since leaving King Goruth's army the day before. Once for an hour or so to catch their breath during the night, and then a short break sometime around midday for a quick bite of cheese and flatbread before she insisted they move again. Elhrin knew Marguerite wasn't trying to push them until they collapsed, but wanted to put as much distance between them and the army as quickly as possible, however, the hilly terrain of the foothills south of the mountain range was taking its toll on them all. Even the men King Goruth had sent with them seemed to be dragging a little, and they were used to long hours of rigorous exercise.

"Marguerite, I don't know about you . . . but I've about had it," Elhrin said, breathing hard. The hill they were climbing felt like it went straight up.

"I'm going to agree. We will . . . stop . . . when we reach the top," Marguerite said, winded.

Willing her legs to keep moving, Elhrin stared at the sword strapped to Marguerite's back and wondered why she had brought Master Gryph's sword in addition to her own. She had been meaning to ask Marguerite about it, but had forgotten to until now. "Marguerite . . . ?"

"We need to take a break when we reach the top, Jag," Kyne Pittwold called out.

Startled, Elhrin jumped with a little yelp. She had not known Kyne Pittwold, one of the new men in their party, was right on her heels, almost breathing down her neck.

Jag, leading the party, raised his hand without turning around to let Kyne know he had been heard.

Elhrin heard a low laugh and glared over her shoulder at the wiry man. As she suspected, he had that greasy smirk of self-satisfaction she wanted to slap off his pale face. It was going to take all of the patience she could muster to get used to this particular man who had made it painfully clear in the few short hours since he joined them that he was unhappy with his assignment.

She turned back around, grimacing in distaste. He made her uneasy. She knew he was probably boring a hole through her back with those soulless black eyes. Shivering inwardly, she made an extra effort to move up beside Marguerite.

Marguerite raised her eyebrows at Elhrin's sudden burst of energy.

"Just ready . . . to reach the top," Elhrin huffed. She heard him laugh quietly again. He knew she wanted away from him, and was enjoying the fact he could get under her skin.

Thankfully, the four others sent by the king were more to her liking and, admittedly, a huge relief to her mind—they did not ease the suffocating terror that threatened to bubble up whenever she allowed herself to think about what she was doing, but at least she did not have to do this alone. At first, she had wondered why King Goruth had not sent more men, but then she realized the small number of the group was on purpose to keep signs of their passage to a minimum. He had hand-picked each man for their individual skills, and she trusted his instincts, but why did he send Kyne? Why send someone that did not want to be here and did not seem to fit in with the others? Tomas and Jag were a given. They knew the area and were experienced fighters. Then there was Fuller Beame. A man she started out being a little skeptical about because of his short stature when Tomas had introduced him as an archer like Jag. She had thought in order to handle the length of a long bow an archer needed to be a certain height, and he was just barely taller than her, but then Jag had laughingly joked that Fuller had been born with a bow in his hand because it seemed like an extension of his arm, claiming that Fuller could shoot a fly off a horse's butt. She liked Fuller. He was quick to smile and funny. The stories he and Jag had shared helped keep their minds off the rigorous hike.

The last man that completed their party was Michell Strow. With the exception of Marguerite, he was the oldest of the group. He was probably in his late twenties or early thirties, and Elhrin had no doubts as to why he had been chosen to join their party. She couldn't recall ever seeing a man so large. He stood nearly as tall as Jag, with shoulders wider than she and Bayle standing side by side. His neck alone was as thick as a bull's. He carried a massive two-handed sword on his back. Its pommel rose above the back of his shaved head and its tip reached well below his waist. The thought of the damage that sword could do to a man made Elhrin glad he was on her side.

"Thank the Light," Marguerite groaned, when they finally reached the top of the hill. She sank to the ground with an audible sigh of relief.

Elhrin slipped off her pack and sat next to a pine tree, using its rough trunk as a backrest.

"I think I lost the feeling in my feet over an hour ago," Marguerite said, rubbing an ankle through her boot. "Of course, that is better than the pain they were in right before I lost feeling."

"What I am regretting is the fact that I ever complained about riding horses. I am so tired, I feel like we have been walking for a week," Elhrin said, watching

Bayle drop next to Fuller in a tired heap. Kyne, true to form, squatted a short distance away from everyone, making it clear he did not want to be a part of their group.

"We are all going to have to rest tonight. I think maybe we have put enough distance behind us for now, and I don't want everyone to be so exhausted no one could lift a sword if it came to a fight," Marguerite said, and turned to speak to Tomas, who had just emerged from a stand of nearby brush where he had gone to relieve himself. "Tomas, the sun is getting low in the sky. Tell Jag and Michell we need to find a good place to camp soon."

"Yes, madam," he said. He plodded through the thick grass covering the hillside and disappeared over the next knoll to find the two men who had gone ahead to assess their position.

Elhrin closed her eyes and allowed her body to relax.

"Shh, everyone be quiet and nobody move," Fuller whispered.

Elhrin opened her eyes. Fuller slowly removed his bow from his back and notched an arrow, aiming directly at Kyne.

"What do you think you are doing?" Kyne tensed, ready to spring if Fuller fired on him.

"Shh, be still," Fuller hissed, and let his arrow fly.

Kyne ducked as it whizzed by his head and sped downhill to impale a rabbit, flipping it head over tail into a nearby bush.

"That was great," Bayle whooped with laughter.

Fuller stood up grinning. He started to go retrieve the rabbit, but Kyne jumped up and blocked his passage.

"Don't you ever do that again," Kyne spat, jabbing a finger into Fuller's chest.

Fuller slapped Kyne's hand away. "Piss off, man, I wasn't going to hit you." He shoved a shoulder into Kyne as he brushed past, pushing him hard to the side.

Kyne pulled his knife and started after Fuller, ready to fight. Fuller heard him coming and whirled around. He immediately crouched in a defensive position.

"Kyne!" Marguerite barked. "We will not do this!"

Elhrin leaned forward and grabbed her magic.

Kyne jerked to a halt. He glared at the lady, clearly debating whether or not to listen to her orders.

Marguerite saw his struggle. "Will it be worth it?" she asked.

Kyne ran a hand through his thick black hair, thinking. He then slammed his blade back into the sheath at his side and turned on his heel. He stalked across the far side of the hill and headed for the edge of a wood.

Fuller watched him go, then shook his head in disgust, and left in the opposite direction to find his kill. Bayle scrambled to his feet and followed Fuller downhill.

"That was close," Elhrin said, releasing her hold on her magic. She had been prepared to knock Kyne on his tail if he had moved one step closer to Fuller. "I don't understand why Kyne is here?" she asked.

Marguerite sighed. "I don't know, either, but I'm sure Goruth had his reasons."

Elhrin grunted skeptically. Kyne had shown up unexpectedly on their trail about a half-hour after they had left the army, not offering any information other than the king had sent him. He handed Marguerite a note stamped with the royal seal that said he was to join their party. Elhrin had asked Tomas when Kyne had lagged behind if he knew him, but he had just met him when she did, and couldn't tell her anything more. The king may have had a good reason for sending him, but that didn't change the undefined ill feelings she had towards the man.

"I wish I had the energy he has," Marguerite commented, pointing at Bayle. He ran up the hill carrying the dead rabbit by its ears.

"Looks like rabbit for supper," Bayle said, grinning when he reached them.

"It's not enough for us all. I'll keep my eye out for another," Fuller called out as he made his way back up the hill.

"I don't know that we should cook. The last thing we need is smoke drifting up over the trees and alerting anyone of our location. I don't want to take any chances of Cynder flying over and seeing us."

"Don't fret about that, madam," Fuller said, slinging his bow over his shoulder. "There is a way to do it with minimal smoke, and we'll smother it after we're done cooking."

"Then I will leave that task to you," she smiled. "If you three will excuse me, I'm going to see where the men have gone." She rose off the ground with a grunt, and followed the path Tomas had taken.

"Bayle, help me up," Elhrin said, holding a hand out for him to pull her to her feet. "Nice shot, Fuller, but I don't think you are popular with Kyne right now."

"I'm not worried about him. He needs to lighten up—too serious for his own good," Fuller said.

"Do you know him?" she asked.

"No, I never met him until yesterday."

"I wonder why he was sent to go with us?"

"I haven't a clue. I've tried to talk to him, but you see how sullen and close-mouthed he is. I think I would have an easier time getting an answer from the dead rabbit," he said.

Elhrin eyed the rabbit with a grin. "I think you are right." She picked up her pack and slipped it over her shoulders. "Come on, let's join the others."

They found Marguerite standing with Michell and Tomas on a gigantic natural rock mound, looking out at the landscape on the other side of the hill. The view was magnificent from their high vantage point. The forest that spread across the foothills was broken in spots by large grassy meadows, and in the far distance to their south, she could faintly see the northern shore of Wyndermir Lake.

Jag pointed to a place midway between the lake and the south face of the mountains to their north.

"We will travel due east through the woods until we reach the Poitoo River," he said. "The road to the mine follows its banks into the mountains."

"Let's save that for tomorrow," Marguerite said, scanning the surrounding area. "Everyone is tired. I think we should find a place to camp for tonight and start fresh in the morning."

Elhrin nearly came out of her skin when a voice spoke just over her shoulder.

"There is an area of boulders with a good size overhang in the trees behind us. I think it would be a good place to make a camp," Kyne said.

Damn, the man is quiet when he walks, Elhrin grimaced, wondering why he was in the army when he could make a profitable career out of stealing or as an assassin.

"Let's go take a look," Michell said. "Lead the way, Kyne."

They headed into the trees and down an incline strewn with rocks and underbrush that hung on packs and clothing as they plowed through. On one occasion the small sword at Elhrin's side hung on a branch and slapped her leg painfully when it released. She rubbed her thigh. Wearing the weapon was hard to get used to, but Marguerite insisted she carry it for added protection.

When they rounded a stand of densely packed half-dead scrub, she could see why Kyne had chosen the spot for a camp. The boulders he spoke of were situated on a hillside and tumbled on top of each other like a god had thrown them into a pile and left them there. One of the huge rocks hung out over the ground and created a dry space underneath that could easily fit their group with room to spare.

"Excellent spot, Kyne. I'll check to make sure it's safe. Wouldn't want to crawl under there and end up sleeping with a family of skunks," Michell said. He slapped Kyne hard on the back in approval as he went to inspect the area under the overhang.

"Umph!" Kyne grunted. He glared hatefully at the large man's back as if he itched to pull his dagger again.

"It is a good spot," Tomas agreed, turning in a circle to scout the area. He pointed below where the land fell into a crevice. "There might be a creek down there. I'll go take a look and fill our waterskins if it is."

"Bayle, let's you and I hitch back to the meadow and see if our dead friend has family." Fuller nodded at the rabbit Bayle was holding. He glanced at Marguerite. "We'll be back before dark."

"Make sure you do," she replied.

"Here," Bayle handed Elhrin the dead rabbit he had been carrying. Grimacing, she held it far away from her as she watched them disappear into the woods.

Jag dropped his pack and untied a small hatchet he had attached to its back. "I'll get firewood. Kyne, give me a hand."

"It's clear." Michell called from underneath the overhang. Hunkered down on all fours, he turned to look at them, laughing when he saw Elhrin's lip curled in utter distaste at the rabbit. "I take it you don't have the stomach for gutting and skinning it."

Marguerite glanced at her, eyes sparkling in amusement.

"Well, I can try, but . . . ," she almost gagged at the thought. Try as she might, she had never been able to handle cleaning animals well.

"But Minister Idwyr ruined that sort of fun for her years ago," Marguerite finished with a short laugh.

"I still do not understand why he forced me to learn about all the inner parts of those animals," she shuddered from the memory.

"He said you needed to get over being squeamish," Marguerite held out a hand for the rabbit, "and it wouldn't hurt for you to know how a body worked."

Elhrin handed the rabbit over. "He said I needed to get over being squeamish?"

Marguerite slipped a dagger from the sheath at her side. "That he did." She found a fallen log nearby and placed it on top to gut the animal.

"I'm not that squeamish," Elhrin mumbled, watching Michell clear out the space underneath the overhanging rock. "It's just that he opened things, and stuff fell out and . . . ."

Marguerite laughed. "You don't have to justify yourself, dear. Not everyone can take the sight of blood and guts," she called over her shoulder.

"I know," she said, thinking she was going to have to get past being squeamish. She had no doubt this journey would be filled with instances of blood and guts, and she could not afford to falter. Then what Marguerite had said about him needing her to know how a body worked registered in her thoughts. It made sense. He had wanted her to know where to find vital organs not only in animals, but in humans, as well, and had pointed out where to find a heart, lung, stomach, and bowels on himself when he had slaughtered a pig one fall, using the pig's organs as a visual tool. He wanted her to know where the kill spots were—*ugh*—she did not want to think about having to kill a human. If it came down to it, she knew she would, but she wasn't going to dwell on it.

She dropped her pack and started to help Michell, pushing piles of leaves to the side that he tossed from under the overhang. Once he had it cleared, he then dug a deep, narrow pit for the fire.

"The ventilation should help eliminate much of the smoke and the overhang will help dissipate what rises. Hopefully, it won't be enough to alert anyone of our location, but we will keep it small, nonetheless," he said as he crab-walked from underneath the rock and walked over to Marguerite. "Madam, if you and Elhrin will gather kindling to start our fire. I will finish this for you."

She handed the bloody knife to him. "I will accept that offer with relish." She smiled.

Tomas crunched through the dry leaves, returning from his search for water. "I was right. There is a small creek down there," he dropped the waterskins by Elhrin who was snapping sticks in two and dropping them in the hole. "I also found something else."

Elhrin and Marguerite stopped what they were doing to listen.

"There was a set of boot prints heading east—fairly fresh. It is probably nothing to be concerned about. It could just be a hunter."

"Or it could be our Do'athrim friend. We need a double watch tonight at all times, and I don't think any of us should wander off alone," Marguerite said, scrutinizing the surrounding woods, watching as Jag and Kyne trudged out of the trees. "I really wish Bayle and Fuller had not left."

"What's going on?" Jag asked as he and Kyne dropped an armload of wood by the fire pit.

"Tomas found a set of boot prints down by the creek," Marguerite said.

"Really? Show me," he said, and the two hiked downhill towards the small ravine.

Michell skewered pieces of meat on a sharpened stick. "Kyne, you and I will take the first watch."

Kyne had dragged his pack well away from them and briefly flicked an eye at Michell without saying a word as if he wanted to tell the man no.

"I'll take that as a yes," Michell said with a shake of his head. "Man, you are one unique individual."

"Exactly," Kyne growled under his breath. He sat on a rock and pulled out his knife and a short leather strop. He started to sharpen his blade, ignoring them all.

Elhrin picked up a pile of sticks and dropped them in the fire pit. She thought about giving Kyne a quick slap in the back of his head with her magic for his lack of manners, but knew Marguerite would not like it. Instead, she lit the tinder with her magic, keeping the flames hot until the larger pieces caught and burned of their own accord.

Marguerite pulled out a small pot from her pack, and filled it with water and dried beans. She then seasoned them with herbs she had brought from Glimmerdale, and nestled the pot off to the side over some of the coals.

Michell fashioned a short spit and placed the meat over the flames. Soon the smell of the food entered the air and Elhrin felt her stomach rumble in anticipation. All of them carried enough rations to hopefully last the journey, but fresh, cooked food was always welcome over the dried and smoked staples they had in their packs.

While she waited on dinner, she decided to look through the *Book of Tolman*. She pulled it from her pack, and proceeded to sit on a nearby rock, but noticed Kyne followed her every move with his black eyes and changed her mind. With a small smirk directed his way, she slipped to the other side of a tree and out of his line of view. She heard him chuckle silently—pleased with himself. Yes, a quick smack on the back of his head wouldn't hurt anything, would it?

"Ow!" he yelped.

She smiled to herself.

"Elhrin," Marguerite called out, "don't do that again. You know Master Gryph would have not approved of such use of your powers."

She peered around the tree. "Sorry, Marguerite."

Marguerite jerked her head at Kyne. "Not me, child."

Elhrin glanced at Kyne. He glared at her while rubbing the back of his head. "My apologies, Kyne."

He narrowed his eyes, but said nothing.

She leaned back against the tree with a smile. That smack had definitely been worth it.

She opened her book, knowing that it was hopeless to think that she would find anything in its pages about the Rift and how to close it because she was almost positive that none of the magicians before her had any experience with one.

She skimmed through the writings of Odrun Jorme, Master Gryph's predecessor, and found nothing. She stared at the first page of Master Gryph's writings, lost in thought, turning the things she already knew over and over in her head, wishing that somehow she could come up with an answer to her problems.

Mindlessly, she started to flip the pages and her eyes rested on a passage describing an event that had almost taken his life. He had fought another person of magical abilities by the name of Grom Kyryloh and had killed him. Grom had been the leader at the time of a secret religious faction dedicated to the service of Obsudius called the Brothers of M'gelidia. Elhrin had never known of their existence until she read about them in the book.

After the death of Grom, the Brothers of M'gelidia focused on revenge, and had nearly killed Master Gryph in Muryne with a poisoned arrow. This was when her mother had taken her to Muryne as a girl. The news of his impending death upset Elhrin so much, that her mother felt it necessary for the three of them to go to the city to see him.

She sighed. After Master Gryph's unexpected and miraculous recovery, being in Muryne had been one of the happiest memories of her childhood. The three of them had been allowed to stay in the palace, and she and Bayle spent many afternoons playing with the other children in the Royal Gardens and on the palace grounds.

She turned the page. Her eyes widened at what she saw and she slammed the book shut, nearly dropping it.

Marguerite called out, "Elhrin, are you all right?" She rounded the tree. Her face lined with worry.

"What, Marguerite?" Elhrin asked. She realized her hands were shaking, and pressed them to her thighs to still them.

"You shouted as if something was wrong," Marguerite said.

"I did?" Elhrin hadn't realized that she had made a sound.

Marguerite nodded.

Elhrin decided to show Marguerite what she had seen in the book. "I hope you can see this," she said, knowing Marguerite had not been able to see the moving pictures when she used her pendant. Elhrin opened the book to find the page again. She pointed to a note that Master Gryph had scrawled across the top margin of the page.

"Can you see this?"

"Yes."

"It wasn't there before," Elhrin said and read the note out loud. "Elhrin, if you are reading this, then your destiny is at hand. Heed me, that when the time comes, you must remain focused on your task. Do not hesitate, no matter what happens around you."

"Interesting, it sounds like he is giving you a warning," Marguerite said.

"Do you know when he wrote this passage about his encounter with the Brothers of M'gelidia?" Elhrin asked, pointing below the note.

Marguerite read the passage Elhrin indicated. "As a matter of fact I do. It was during his recovery right after it happened. He couldn't leave his bed, so writing in this book was one of the few things he could do at the time," she smiled. "That and be the grouchiest patient in all of Anderan."

Elhrin snorted. "That sounds like him. I remember he always had a hard time lying around if he was sick or hurt."

"Wasn't that the truth?" Marguerite shook her head. "Sitting still and having nothing to do always drove him crazy which meant he would do things that drove me crazy. He thought it was funny, but I got so tired of him moving this or that around, making me hunt all over the apartment thinking I had misplaced whatever he had moved."

"Actually, it was funny," Elhrin grinned, remembering Marguerite desperately hunting for her brush one morning and the whole time Master Gryph kept it hovering right over her head where she couldn't see it. She only found it when she walked by a mirror and saw it in the reflection.

"Of course you would think so," Marguerite huffed good naturedly, "you two were always thick as thieves together."

Elhrin smiled fondly at her. "I miss those times."

"Me too." Marguerite's smile drooped a little.

Elhrin glanced back at the note he wrote.

"Marguerite, if he wrote this warning to me at the same time he wrote the passage about the Brothers of M'gelidia, then I would only have been nine years old. How could he know?" Elhrin stared off into the distance. "Even if he wrote it right before he hid the book, how could he know what I would be up against now?"

"Dear, my guess would be that he had one of those famous dreams we keep talking about." Marguerite patted Elhrin's shoulder. "Come on. While you were reading, Bayle and Fuller returned successfully from their hunt, and your brother is busting to show you his kill."

"I'll be there in a minute," she said, trying to sort through all the turmoil that was racing around in her head.

He knew all along that she was going to be one of Solisius' So'ladiun and never said anything about it in all the years that he had been instructing her. Why? Why not tell her? Why let her flounder around like this? Especially if he knew he was going to die last year.

And the dreams, he told her virtually nothing in her dreams. Here she was, heading for a battle that could very well end not only her life, but any of the lives of the ones that were with her, and she was not prepared. What about Marguerite? He had to know that Marguerite would not let her travel without her. Did he not care for her safety?

She felt herself grow truly angry with him for the first time in her life, and she did not like it. Why had he left her without the knowledge that she needed to complete this so called destiny, and where was Solisius? If she was chosen to fight for the God of Light, then where was his guidance?

Unwanted tears slid rebelliously down her cheeks feeling cool as a sudden breeze sifted through the air, drying the tiny rivers on her cheeks. She furrowed her brow. She could have sworn she heard a voice whisper, "I am here," among the rustling of the leaves around her.

Tomas squatted on his heels beside her. "You okay, Elhrin?" he asked.

She rushed to swipe away the tears, hoping he wouldn't notice. It must have been him she heard.

"Yes, I'm okay. Just having a little 'Why me?' time," she sniffled and plastered a smile on her face, feeling a little embarrassed.

"I can certainly understand that. Everyone needs a little 'Why me?' time. Honestly, if I had been told that I was the only one who could stop a flying magical monster, I hope that I would be as brave as you are, but I have a strong suspicion that I would just run like a banshee all the way to Nabafin as fast as I could," he said, flashing that crooked grin she loved.

"That would be something to see, since Nabafin is out in the middle of the Yrahl Sea," she snorted out loud without meaning to, and was instantly mortified.

"My point exactly, I wouldn't need a boat," he reached out to wipe a stray tear from under her eye. The humor left his eyes and the smile faded as his lips parted slightly. He stared at his fingers on her face then lifted his eyes to hers. She could not define the look he gave her. All she knew was that one look, whatever it was, whatever it meant, made her body feel weak and warm and— excited?

"Elhrin, I know nothing I can say will make what you have to do any easier, but if there is anything I can do to help, I will," he whispered.

"You are helping me," she said softly.

"I am? How?" he tilted his head to one side.

"You are here, aren't you?"

"Yes, I am here." Abruptly, he stood up and offered her his hand. She took it and he helped her to her feet, surprising her when he pulled her hand to his chest and closed the distance between them. He dropped his face close to hers. Elhrin's heart skipped a beat, then started to speed up as she stared into his eyes, noticing for the first time tiny gray flecks sprinkled within the blue.

"Just so you know, the king did not order me to come with you. I volunteered," his voice deepened and the warmth of his breath caressed her cheek.

"You did?" she croaked, swallowing hard and dropping her gaze to his lips. She wondered what it would feel like if he kissed her, and without thinking, she leaned closer to him.

His lips spread into a lazy grin. "You had better go see Bayle's rabbit. He has been waiting for you." He stepped back and released her hand. She hoped the wave of disappointment washing through her didn't show on her face, but if it did, he didn't say anything, only smiled handsomely at her and motioned for her to follow as he turned and walked away.

She mentally kicked herself for her stupidity in thinking he might be interested in her. She must have misinterpreted his look, his reason for admitting to volunteering for this journey. What must he think of her now? He knew what she wanted. She grunted in disgust at herself and headed into camp. Bayle saw her coming and grinned like a little boy who had been given a new toy.

"Elhrin, look, I killed one."

"You did?"

She glanced at the bloody carcass of the rabbit he was gutting and inwardly cringed. She really needed to work on getting over being squeamish.

"Fuller let me use his bow when we spotted this one and I actually hit it," he laughed.

Amused, Fuller confirmed Bayle's kill. "Luckiest damn shot I ever saw. The boy let the arrow go too soon, and the thing skimmed a branch before hitting the rabbit."

"Does it matter how it was killed?" Bayle asked.

"Nope, dead is dead. Doesn't matter how it got that way," Fuller said.

Late that night, Elhrin was startled out of a deep sleep when a hand clamped across her mouth. She opened her eyes to darkness, barely making the outline of a face inches from hers. She flung her blanket off and reached for her magic.

"Shh," Tomas hissed, holding her firmly in place. He leaned in close. "Cynder," he whispered, letting her go.

She eased to a sitting position, allowing her hold on her energy to dissipate, and took a deep breath to calm her jangled nerves, but couldn't seem to get a hold on the fear he had caused by jolting her awake. It made her feel sick.

She noticed the woods surrounding them were deathly quiet. The noisy symphony of insects and tree frogs had stilled completely. All she could hear was the whisper of a light breeze rustling the leaves in the treetops and the quiet movements of her companions. Her fear seemed to build deep inside as she strained to listen for Cynder, then she heard it—the distant beating of giant wings, and they were coming closer.

Is he looking for me already? she wondered, silently.

The pale sliver of the moon and a sky full of stars did not give off much light through the boughs of the trees. She could barely distinguish the forms of the others in the darkness. She heard, more than saw, Jag and Fuller quietly ready their bows. A large shadow that had to be Michell was crouched down near the edge of the overhang watching the sky. Marguerite and Bayle both sat ready on their bedrolls. She heard Bayle quietly slide his sword out with an almost imperceptible metallic hiss.

Cynder approached their camp from the east. The thumps from his wing beats drummed louder and louder, seeming to match the tempo of the blood pounding furiously in her head. Then the sound of rustling and shifting limbs reached her as if he were running along the tops of the trees towards them. She was not ready to face him again. It was too soon. But he was coming and there was nothing she could do about it but prepare herself and pray that she was strong enough to defeat him this time. She shifted to her knees, grabbed her magic, feeling the energy course through her limbs, and waited for him to arrive.

Even though it felt like an eternity, she did not have to wait long. He flew directly overhead and she had to stop herself from attacking him first. The draft from his wings shook the trees around them so violently that limbs snapped and popped creating a downpour of leaves and sticks.

She swallowed hard against the nausea created from the mixture of intense fear and the raw energy of her magic. *Please go away. Please go away,* she plead silently.

Cynder flew past, but then banked around and came back.

Fuller or Jag pulled a bow taught.

"Hold still," Michell hissed.

The beat of wings moved south of them back to the east then headed north once again as if he was circling them.

"He might be picking up the scent of our fire," Michell whispered.

Elhrin glanced where the fire had been. It was hours cold and covered in a thick layer of dirt that Jag had thrown over it before they had gone to bed. She didn't see how Cynder could catch a scent from it.

"Or us," she breathed in horror.

"Aye," he agreed. "Or us."

The wing beats were coming back. This time she heard both bows being drawn.

Elhrin held her breath, waiting, listening as he thumped closer. Again the trees started to shake in the distance, rattling louder as he drew near, but this time he zoomed past north of their location. Elhrin turned her head, straining to hear which direction he was headed as his wing beats thumped away.

Michell and Jag eased out from under the overhang. They cautiously backed away from the rocks to see the sky.

Elhrin wondered how well Cynder could see in the dark. If they had not been under the overhang, would he have seen them when he flew over?

The sound of his wings circled west of them a few times then headed off into the night. Patiently, they waited to see if he would return.

A lone cricket chirped somewhere close by as if to signal the all clear. Others soon joined him, returning the forest back to its normal nighttime state.

Elhrin pulled in a shaky, deep breath and released it slowly, letting her fears and her hold on her magical energy slide away with it.

Jag walked back to the overhang. "That was close. There are only a few hours before dawn, Madam Idwyr. I think it might be a good idea to leave while it is still dark. I would like to travel a little further south and east to get away from the edge of the mountains. It seems as if that is where he is searching."

"Sounds like a good idea," she replied, pushing to her feet. "Let's pack up."

Elhrin felt a hand slide down her arm and squeeze her hand on her thigh. Tomas had not left her side the entire time. She wrapped her fingers around his, taking comfort in the warmth of his hand.

Chapter Seventeen

A day and a half later they reached the old mine road, and Elhrin was grateful that they had not seen or heard Cynder flying around them again. She hoped they would never see him again. She was tired of the ill, nauseating feeling she got every time thoughts of the beast flitted through her mind since the night he flew over. She wished that some miracle would occur and he would drop dead before she reached Blackridge Keep, but she knew that was useless thinking and turned her attention to what Jag was saying as he cut a trail through the tall grasses and undergrowth that had sprouted up in the roadbed.

"The gold mine shut down about thirty years ago," Jag said. "Now, it's just a place to camp for the hunters and trappers that travel through. Hopefully, we will be able to reach it by nightfall tomorrow."

"I bet this area is prime for game," Fuller commented, scanning the countryside. "I've about had my fill of flatbread and dried beef that tastes like I'm eating my boots. Maybe we can get Bayle to bounce a few arrows off trees and nail us something fresh to eat tonight."

Bayle laughed. "Hey, I may not be an expert bowman like you and Jag, but tell me, have either of you ever ricocheted an arrow off anything to hit your target?"

"Can't say as I have, Bayle, but Tomas," Jag pointed a thumb over his shoulder at Tomas who was walking with Elhrin, "did one day when we were going through training together as new recruits."

"Hey, leave me out of this," Tomas called out.

Jag turned to walk backwards and grinned at Tomas. "Oh no, my friend, I am telling this story."

"Then let me warn you. I have a few stories I can tell about you," Tomas said, seeming annoyed at Jag, but his lips twitched as if he was trying not to smile.

"I consider myself warned," Jag said, unconcerned. He turned back around to pick his way through a stand of briars. "Anyway, it was the very first day we had target practice. I don't think Tomas even knew what a bow was before that day."

"Oh, come on! I did too," Tomas scoffed good-naturedly. He smiled at Elhrin as he stomped a stray briar down to let Elhrin pass. "My sister wears big pink ones in her hair all the time."

Elhrin laughed at his joke as she scooted past.

Jag used his bow to shift a clump of briars out of his way. "Hey, did you just interrupt my story?" He turned around and pointed his bow at Tomas.

"Tell it right, and I won't interrupt."

"Keep moving, fellows," Marguerite said from the back of the line.

"As I was saying, the bow was new to Tomas. So when it comes his turn, Tomas steps up with the cockiness of someone who thinks it looks easy, as if anyone with half a brain could hit a target as large as the ones we were using. He let that arrow fly." Jag demonstrated with his bow. "Ping! It ricocheted off the top of the stand, and landed squarely in the butt of Captain Barren's horse."

Bayle and Fuller whooped with laughter.

"That horse reared straight up and threw the captain to the ground. The bad part was, his trousers had caught on something on his saddle, and ripped half of them right off his body," Jag was laughing so hard he had a hard time finishing the story. "There he lay, half-naked on the ground, and his horse is running across the practice field with a part of his pants flapping in the wind like a flag. I don't think I have seen anyone so mad. He jumped up cursing us for all we were worth, and demanding for the one who shot the arrow to step forward."

"Yes, and you all sold me out," Tomas huffed with a short laugh.

"Hey, we weren't about to be taken down with you," Jag stopped to catch his breath. "Everyone pointed at Tomas, and the captain hauled him off the field into the barracks. What did he end up doing to you? I forgot."

"After a day full of regiment exercises, I had to move mountain size piles of horse manure out of the compound for three weeks straight, and then I had to clean all the latrines every night—alone." He grinned at Elhrin. "That was worse than hauling the horse manure. You wouldn't believe what men can do to a latrine. It is a nightmare. I thought I was going to smell like shi . . . , uh, dung for the rest of my life."

"I'm glad you don't," she said, wiping tears of laughter from her face. "Whew. I needed that laugh."

"Glad my misfortune could provide you with some humor," he smiled as he reached down to pick up a rock in the roadbed he had dislodged with his boot. He reared back and threw it down the steep embankment that separated the river from the road, and landed the rock neatly into the center of the river.

"Let's keep moving," Marguerite reminded them again.

"Yes, Madam," Tomas bowed elegantly to her.

Marguerite chuckled with a shake of her head. She motioned them forward with a wave of her hand. "Go."

Elhrin glanced back down at the river as they trudged after the others, seeing a swirling pool that Master Gryph would have claimed as a perfect spot for a spotted trout.

"You know, being here," she gestured at the river, "reminds me of home." It felt like a lifetime instead of a few days since she had left the village—lost her mother.

"What was it like growing up in Glimmerdale?" he asked.

"Quiet. Not much goes on in a small village, but we were happy even though my mother struggled every day to support us with my father gone. I think we were lucky that we had Marguerite and Master Gryph in our lives," she said, and looked over her shoulder to where Marguerite trailed behind Michell with Kyne. "Unless they were out of the village, Bayle and I were always with them whenever we had free time."

"If you don't mind my asking, where was your father?"

"My father was killed when I was only three."

"I'm sorry to hear that."

"Don't be. I don't remember him at all."

"Did you miss not having him around?"

"No, not really," she reflected. "I suppose Master Gryph became like a father to me and Bayle. He certainly acted like one at times." She smiled, remembering when he had made them hug without letting go for a whole day after he caught them rolling around in the yard fighting. Elhrin could still recall her mother's reaction when they walked through the door that afternoon holding each other. She had asked what they were doing, and when Elhrin told her that Master Gryph had said they had to stay that way until supper, she had clapped a hand over her mouth and went in her room and closed the door. They could hear their mother laughing, anyway. "How about you? Where did you grow up?" she asked.

"For the most part in Muryne, but I was born in Gildas. My father is career military, and we traveled wherever he was stationed. For awhile, we lived in Yradin, and then moved to Tuhnichi before he was given a permanent post in Muryne."

"I've only been to Muryne twice. Once when I was a little girl, and I only remember bits and pieces about that trip, and then just a few weeks ago," she said. "It's a beautiful city. One day, I hope I can go back to see it all."

"Maybe, after all this is done, we can go together, and I'll be your guide."

"Maybe," she smiled. "What about your family? You mentioned your father and a sister. Are your parents still living? Do you have any other brothers or sisters?"

"Both of my parents are living. My dad suffered an injury a few years ago that makes it difficult for him to move around. He was given an administrative job, and it almost killed him when he was prevented from joining this campaign. My mother stays home and takes care of my younger brother, Gideon, and my baby sister, Prynne. She wasn't too happy to learn that I was going off to war. I was able to visit them when I was in Muryne, and she begged me to quit the army. I tell you, the hardest thing I have ever had to do was leave my mother crying on our doorstep and keep on walking."

"I can only imagine," she said, softly.

"Elhrin, I don't think I have ever said how sorry I am about your mother. You have had one rough year, haven't you?" he asked, lightly brushing her arm with his fingers.

"I certainly have had better ones," she said, watching Bayle laugh at something Fuller had said. "At least, I haven't gone through it alone. Without the support of Bayle and Marguerite, I don't know what I would have done."

"Bayle seems to have weathered well," Tomas said. "He told me he wants to join the army. As tall as he is, I think he would make a good bowman, if he could ever get it under control."

"There is something by the river," Kyne called out and everyone stopped in their tracks.

"Where?" Jag asked.

"I saw something move on the other side, over in that stand of trees by the boulder that sticks out of the river," Kyne said.

Elhrin scanned the opposite riverbank, but saw only a blue jay flitting through the gnarled trunks.

"Kyne, I don't see anything," Michell said, moving to the edge of the road.

"I tell you, I saw something," he snapped.

"I'm not doubting you. Don't get so defensive," Michell said, frowning as he peered across the river, trying to see anything in the shadows of the forest on the other side.

"Let's keep moving," Jag said after a moment. "It could just be an animal trying to get to the river, but everyone keep a lookout, just in case."

Kyne mumbled something under his breath, and noticed that Elhrin was watching him.

"What?" he snapped.

"What did you just say?" she asked, sure he had just called them all stupid backwoods simpletons.

"I wasn't talking to you," he growled, and pushed by her to follow Jag up the road.

"I wasn't talking to you," she mocked under her breath.

Marguerite gave her a look only an annoyed mother could give. "Elhrin, you need to give him a chance. He hasn't done anything to you."

"No, but he makes it hard to like him."

"Not everyone has the disposition to be sunny and cheerful all the time."

"Well, he certainly isn't sunny or cheerful any of the time," Elhrin mumbled, and was glad that Marguerite let the subject drop.

By late afternoon, they had traveled through a grassy valley and reached the point where the road began the steep climb into the higher elevations of the Northreach Mountains. Still following the Poitoo River, the old roadbed skirted the cliff face of a mountain until it disappeared from view around a curve in the distance.

"I don't particularly like this spot for making a camp. It's too open," Jag said gauging the location of the sun in the sky, "and we only have a few more hours of daylight. Madam Idwyr, do you want to stop?"

"No, let's keep going," she said between breaths, and gestured wearily for him to lead the way.

After another hour or so, the sun sank below the peak of the mountain, sending dark shadows through the dense foliage of the musky, damp forest they had entered. Exhausted, they followed the road upward as it wound its way around large boulders and natural rock walls on the side of the mountain.

Bayle stopped to take a quick drink from one of the tiny rivulets of water that fell steadily down the face of the rock.

Elhrin pulled the strap of her waterskin over her head. "Fill this up for me, will you?" She pulled out the stopper.

"Sure," he said, taking the waterskin.

"Oh, for goodness sake," Marguerite growled when she heard Kyne and Fuller start to argue. "There they go again."

"Just because I don't feel the need for constant chatter like you, Fuller, doesn't mean anything," Kyne said.

"Well, all of us have revealed our backgrounds, but you. You avoid any personal questions. I would like to know why? What are you hiding?"

"I am hiding nothing. I am Kyne Pittwold and I have been ordered by King Goruth to accompany you on a senseless suicidal mission. That is all you need to know. The rest isn't any of your business."

Fuller halted and placed a hand on Kyne's chest to stop him.

"It is definitely my business," Fuller said, "and the business of us all. Why did King Goruth send you long after we left his army?"

Kyne glanced down at Fuller's hand on his chest with distaste. "You better remove that," he warned, balling up his fists.

Michell stepped between the two and shoved them apart. "You two stop arguing. We don't have time for this right now."

Marguerite blew out an impatient breath. "It's going to be a long journey if they can't find a way to get along," she said with an annoyed shake of her head, and started back up the road alone.

Bayle handed Elhrin her waterskin, raising his eyebrows. "I wonder how long it will take before she smacks their heads together," he whispered.

Elhrin stifled a laugh, looping the strap of her waterskin over her head.

"Michell, don't you think he needs to tell us what his purpose is here?"

"Fuller, the king knows his purpose, and sent him for a reason. Let it rest."

Marguerite screamed.

Elhrin whirled around in time to see her fall to the ground. They all raced to her side—the men pulling weapons as they ran.

Elhrin dropped to her knees. There were no wounds visible. "Marguerite?" She gently shook the lady's shoulders.

Marguerite did not respond.

"Marguerite?" She shook her again. "What's wrong?" she asked the men. They stood protectively in a circle around her, looking for enemies in the deep shadows of the forest. "She has no injuries."

Bayle knelt down and lifted Marguerite's head onto his lap.

"She looks like she fainted," Kyne said, sparing a quick glance at the fallen lady.

"Fainted?" Elhrin asked. "Why . . . ?"

"We have company," Jag said quietly, nodding his head in the direction of the road before them.

Jag and Fuller raised their bows, sighting in the newcomer.

"Steady men," Michell said in a low voice. "Whoever it is, is alone. We don't want to kill an innocent man."

In the dim light of the dusk-darkened forest Elhrin could see the silhouette of a tall figure on the old road bed.

"Oh, my god," she breathed in disbelief and pushed herself to her feet. She could not yet see the features of the figure, but his shape and the way he walked, with an almost imperceptible limp, was all too familiar. Elhrin felt numb and her body hummed as if she, too, would join Marguerite on the ground. She drew in a breath to steady herself. "Bayle, am I dreaming? Do you see what I see?"

"Elhrin, it couldn't be who you think," he said, staring in shock at the approaching figure.

Marguerite moaned.

"I think she's coming around," Bayle said.

"Elhrin, what do you need us to do?" Tomas asked, taking a step toward the figure.

"Do nothing. Stay here," she croaked, and only took one step before Tomas grabbed her arm.

"Elhrin, wait," Tomas said, not willing to let her face the stranger alone.

She covered his hand with hers. "I will be careful." She patted his hand and gently pried his fingers from her arm. With a deep steadying breath, she walked to meet the newcomer.

His features began to materialize out of the dim shadows the closer he came, the dark hue of his naturally tan skin, a product of his origins from the south coast of Anderan, the prominent straight nose, the gray peppering his black hair and beard, and those eyes that were always lit with good humor unless he was provoked, but he was no longer dressed in the entire outfit they had buried him in. He now had on a homespun shirt underneath a durable gray coat a little short at the wrist, and a long, black cloak that almost brushed the ground. A slouchy leather pack was slung over one shoulder.

"This can't be real," she whispered as tears filled her eyes and silently spilled down her face. A man she knew to be dead stopped mere paces away from her. This time he was not a dream or a ghost, or whatever he had been whenever she had seen him. His body was solid as a rock.

"Elhrin," he acknowledged her and slipped his pack from his shoulder, dropping it to the ground. He waited for her to make the next move.

She scrutinized him carefully—unsure if this was a trick. He had told her

Cynder was a shape changer. Just in case, she reached for her magic.

"Elhrin?" Tomas called, uneasily. He did not like her being that close to him alone.

She held up a hand to let him know it was okay. For some reason she was not afraid.

"Are you real?" she asked the man.

"Absolutely," he raised one corner of his mouth. A gesture so familiar she knew no one, especially a malicious beast, could duplicate it if he tried.

"How can you be here?" she asked, still hesitant.

"It is a long story that I will tell you later. Right now you can rest assured I am no enemy, but if you need proof that I am not Cynder I can tell you that there was a day, during a hot summer afternoon a few years back, that one of Marguerite's pies went missing from the cooling shelf and it was not Horace the goat who ate it." His eyes crinkled as he smiled, knowingly.

She covered her mouth, stemming the sobs that wanted to burst forth. Only the two of them knew the truth of that story, since they were the ones who took the pie and had cleaned up the mess before Marguerite had made it back inside from where she was hanging clothes on a line. They had claimed the goat had come through the front door that had been left open to allow a breeze in and ate the pie.

He held out his arms. "I could use a hug."

Knowing without a doubt he was who he said he was, she rushed into his arms. He was warm and solid. She could hear a strong heartbeat within his chest. He was real. He was alive!

He kissed the top of her head. "What's wrong with Marguerite?" he asked, squeezing her one last time before relaxing his hold.

Brushing tears from her face with a sleeve, she reluctantly left the comfort of his arms. "I think she fainted," she sniffled.

Concerned, he moved to Marguerite's side and knelt down without worrying about the armed men around him. Trusting Elhrin's judgment, they gave him room, but remained battle ready if he made one wrong move.

"Thank you, son," he squeezed Bayle's shoulder then lifted Marguerite from the boy's lap and gathered her to him.

The men backed away, apprehensive and confused by his appearance.

Without taking his eyes off Master Gryph, Tomas edged closer to Elhrin. "Is that who I think it is?" he whispered.

"Yes," she smiled tremulously. This was too surreal.

Bayle rose shakily to his feet. He shot Elhrin a look of utter disbelief.

"Marguerite," Master Gryph said gently, ignoring them all. He stroked her face and hair. "Marguerite?"

Marguerite's eyes fluttered open. A small whimper escaped from her lips. Tears began to stream freely down the sides of her face. She raised a visibly trembling hand to touch him lightly on his cheek. "Gryph," she whispered. "Am I dreaming?"

"No," he answered softly, and leaned down to kiss her tenderly.

Chapter Eighteen

Sobbing silently, Marguerite slid her arms around Gryph's neck and clung to him as if she were afraid he would disappear.

"I love you, Marguerite," he whispered into her ear, wishing he had the power to make all her painful memories disappear and replace them with nothing but joy.

"Oh, Gryph, I love you," she said between sobs, "so much. I can't believe this . . . ." She couldn't stop crying.

He kissed her, wiping her tears with his thumbs. "Don't cry," he said. "All is well."

"Please," she whispered, "please tell me again I am not dreaming. Tell me I will not wake to find you gone once more."

"You are not dreaming. I am here," he said, turning his head to look up the road. Elhrin and Bayle were standing alone a short distance away to give them privacy. "They are waiting. Are you ready to get up?"

She nodded, wiping the moisture from her face with her hand.

He helped her to her feet, holding tight to her trembling body. He then waved for Elhrin and Bayle to join them. "Come here, you two. Where are the others?"

"They went ahead to find a place for us to stop for the night," Bayle said, pointing behind him where the road disappeared into the dark shadows of the forest.

"Come here, boy," Gryph grinned wide and hauled Bayle into a hug, pounding him on the back. The boy's head now reached his shoulder and that was saying something, since he himself stood taller than most in the country of Anderan. Bayle might reach or surpass his height before he was through growing. "You have grown taller since I last saw you."

"Yes, sir, I suppose I have," Bayle smiled with a shake of his head. "This is hard to believe. We thought you died by the river. How did you make it look so real? I bet it was magic. Did the king ask you to fake your death?" he rambled in one long breath without pause.

Gryph barked a short laugh. He loved Bayle's adventurous imagination. "I didn't fake it, son, it really happened." He let the young boy go, regretting the fact they had been forced to witness his death.

"It did?" Bayle cocked his head to one side, puzzled. "I don't understand. Then how are you here?"

"Well, that is an interesting story. Let me begin by letting you all know that my death that day was not supposed to have happened."

"What do you mean, not supposed to have happened?" Marguerite asked, wiping her nose with a kerchief she had pulled from her coat pocket.

"How could you know that?" Elhrin asked.

"When I reached Ts'aura I knew something was wrong because Solisius was surprised by my presence, and asked me what I was doing there," he chuckled. "I didn't know what to think about that. I thought if anyone should know why I was in the Realm of the Dead, he would."

"Then if you weren't supposed to be there, what happened?" Elhrin asked.

"You don't know?" he asked, surprised by her question.

"No, how should I?"

"I was under the impression you figured out how to use the pendant with the book."

"I have, but . . ." her eyes widened as it dawned on her, "So, that's why the book kept showing me the day of your death. I always quit when it began because I didn't want to watch you die all over again."

"I can certainly understand that," he said. "However, had you watched, you would have seen that soon after the arrow hit me I lost control of my magic."

"I can see how getting hit would do that to you," Bayle commented.

"No, son, you don't understand. The arrow was not the problem, painful, yes, but it did not go in deep enough to do any major damage, and I could have easily pulled it out had I been given the chance. The problem came from the poison on its tip."

Marguerite gasped, "I didn't realize you had been poisoned. It never occurred to me when they brought you home. Was it the Uihrian poison?"

"Yes, it was."

"Uihrian poison? What is that?" Bayle asked.

"It is the poison that almost killed him years ago, when those M'gelidia bastards attacked him in Muryne and busted his knee," Marguerite said with heat behind the kerchief she was using to wipe her nose.

Gryph arched an eyebrow at her choice of words. She rarely used harsh language in front of the children. "It has the ability to cut a person with powers from their source of energy and at the same time paralyze their limbs," he said, sliding an arm around Marguerite's shoulders. He had caused this woman enough pain to last several lifetimes, and knew that was the reason behind her heated outburst.

"So the poison killed you and not the arrow like we thought," Elhrin said.

"In the end it was both. When the poison cut me from my source of energy, the sphere I was building exploded too soon, and I could not control the direction of the force of the explosion. Luckily, the bulk of it went in the direction I had intended. Had it not, I would not have been there for you to find. At any rate, the explosion threw me against the boulder and to the spot where you found me. The arrow was forced deeper into my chest and I believe punctured my lung because I could not breathe. That combined with the poison, well, you know what happened."

"I didn't realize how much you suffered," Marguerite said.

She had wrapped an arm around his waist underneath his cloak and was softly rubbing his side with her hand. Her touch was worth the agonizing decision he had made to find them. "I didn't, my love," he squeezed her shoulders, reassuringly. "The only thing that caused me any concern was knowing I wouldn't have the chance to say goodbye to you."

Marguerite swiped a stray tear from her eyes with her kerchief, smiling.

"You still haven't answered my question," Bayle said after a moment.

"You asked a question? No . . . when did that happen?" Gryph grinned at the sandy haired young man. Bayle was notorious for asking one question after another. He did not mind the questions, but he also loved any opportunity to good-naturedly aggravate Bayle. He had missed this young man tremendously.

"Gryph, you know what his question was," Marguerite squeezed him. "Don't tease him."

"It's been awhile since I have been able to, I couldn't resist," he chuckled, and she dug a finger in between his ribs. "Okay, okay, I will tell him. It was Solisius' idea that I come back. He was not pleased with Obsudius for causing my early demise, so he opened a small rift for me to pass through. This is something he would not normally do because it is forbidden for the dead to walk again on the earth once they have passed. He made an exception with me because it was not yet my time, and because there is something he wants me to do for him."

"That is amazing to think one minute you're dead, then poof, you're alive again," Bayle said, wide-eyed with wonder.

"Well, don't go getting any bright ideas, young man. If you die it will be permanent, and the same goes for me. Like I said, this is a one-time exception."

"I wasn't planning on testing it, Master Gryph. I like living too much."

"That's good to hear," Master Gryph smiled.

"So, is this why your body is missing from the grave in Glimmerdale?" Bayle asked.

"Ah, you found out about that, did you?" he glanced down at Marguerite. "I'm sorry, that must have been hard on you, but it was necessary for Solisius to . . . well, I won't go into what he had to do. Let me just say that there cannot be two of me in the world, dead or alive."

"Is that true for the ones who come through Obsudius' portal?" Elhrin asked.

"Yes, it is," he said.

"Is that so? We keep running up against this one particular Do'athrim that I have killed twice. How is it he is able to return if his body is still rotting somewhere?" Marguerite asked.

"Twice?" he raised his eyebrows. "I'm impressed. Elhrin said you had an encounter with a Do'athrim looking for her book. What happened with his body?"

"Well, the second time Toome buried him under a pile of debris from the village, but the first time I left him floating in the caves below Casteal Island," she replied.

He looked out at the shadow-filled forest, mulling over the answer he had to give them. He knew exactly what happened to the body, but he could not reveal the whole truth. "My guess is that Obsudius has fashioned a condition of life within his portal. If so, then the magic that gives them life when they pass through also has the ability to somehow destroy their body if they are to die on this side," he said, pausing to gather his thoughts. "Because if he doesn't, his minions would be stuck in the Realm of the Dead and would not be able to pass back through the Rift until time takes care of their bodies naturally. Like I said before, there can't be two physical forms of anyone in the world at the same time."

"Why not?" Bayle asked.

"That is just the way it is. Think about it. Each individual has only one soul, and that soul can only have one body." He raised both hands and two tiny orbs of light popped into existence, each hovering just above his palms, one a pale blue color, the other a soft white. "That means you can only be alive in the physical world if the two are joined." The orbs floated towards each other and combined into one light, changing color to a deep blue with a white center. "Otherwise, your soul has to be in one of the spiritual realms." The light disappeared with a tiny pop.

Bayle shook his head and held up his hands. "I am sorry I asked. This is too complicated."

Gryph chuckled, feeling Marguerite rub her hand up and down his side again as if she could not get enough of touching him. He checked a sigh before it left his lips. He longed to be alone with her.

"Gryph, you said that Solisius wants you to do something for him. What does he want you to do?" Marguerite asked.

Elhrin nodded her head. "I was about to ask the same question."

And that was one question he was not ready to answer. "It is nearly dark. I think we need to find the others," he said, and indicated for Bayle and Elhrin to lead the way.

"I hate it when you do that," Elhrin sighed and shot him a look that told him she knew he had not answered the question on purpose. "Come on," she motioned for Bayle to follow her down the road.

Marguerite held him back. "Gryph, I have always believed you and the teachings of the church that Solisius and Obsudius were real entities and not something someone from times past made up. You being here is so amazing it takes my breath away and proves that Ts'aura is real." She slid her hands to his chest, slipping fingers underneath the fabric of his shirt between the buttons, touching his bare skin, not knowing that single touch set him ablaze. "I have always trusted you, but this last month I have found one secret after another that you have kept from me and it hurts me to the core to think you do not trust me. Why is that? What have I done to make you think that I am incapable of handling your secrets?"

He placed both hands on either side of her face and kissed her long and deep.

"Gryph, please don't shut me out. Not now," she breathed against his lips when he gave her a chance to breathe.

He sighed and leaned his forehead on hers.

"Marguerite, I have always trusted you. I will explain everything soon, I promise. Just not tonight, tonight I only want to be with you."

"Okay," she whispered, "but I will hold you to that promise."

He smiled. "I know you will, my love." He gave her one last brief kiss before he reluctantly let her go. He noticed Elhrin still waited a short distance down the road, and smiled at her obvious attempt of trying not to look in their direction. He nodded for Marguerite to look at Elhrin.

"You know, Gryph, she is one frightened and confused young lady who needs your guidance," Marguerite said, waiting for him to retrieve his pack.

"I know. I can't change her destiny, but I hope I can help," he reached for her hand and held it tight.

Elhrin was so happy that, for once, she thought her heart would burst with utter joy instead of the heart pounding fear she had been experiencing the last few weeks. She couldn't stop herself from grinning at him as they walked.

He cut his eyes her way, seeing her grin, and reached out to drape a long arm around her shoulders to pull her close. "Looks like they found a place," he said, pointing out a flickering of light among the tree trunks and foliage.

The men were setting up camp on a flat, sandy place in the road which turned out to be the perfect spot because it was sheltered on one side by a rocky outcrop that was overgrown with trees. The foliage above created a dense canopy and blocked the sky. The other side of the road was filled with trees and bushes along a gentle slope, leading down to the rushing waters of the river below.

Michell knelt on one knee to add wood to the small fire that gave off just enough light to push the shadows to the edge of the roadbed. The others busied themselves with staking out a spot to sleep for the night. When the men heard them coming, everyone stopped what they were doing to stare at Master Gryph with obvious disbelief and maybe, distrust.

Master Gryph grunted with humor and dropped his arms from Elhrin and Marguerite's shoulders. "It's not every day you see a dead man walk up, is it, boys?" He stepped close to Jag and offered to shake the man's hand. "I'm

Gryphon Idwyr."

Jag hesitated for a second, and then shook Master Gryph's hand. "Yes, sir, I know who you are, Minister, and no, I don't think I have ever heard of a dead man appear alive again, but then I have not known of dragons or half-men, half-beast armies before, and they are out there."

"That they are," Master Gryph agreed.

Jag released Master Gryph's hand. "I'm Sergeant Jag Soryn, and this is Sergeant Michell Strow," he pointed to the large man by the fire. Michell saluted respectfully.

Tomas walked over to introduce himself. "Sir, I am Lieutenant Tomas Colkitte."

"Good to meet you, Lieutenant," he said then narrowed his eyes. "You wouldn't happen to be related to Rolyn Colkitte, by chance?"

"Yes, sir, he is my father."

"A good man, your father. I met him in Greystone years ago. He helped Colonel Toome and I with a little matter the king wanted us to take care of for him. The man certainly is talented with a sword. I was sorry to hear he had been injured. I know it must have been hard for him."

"Yes, sir, it was," Tomas said, stepping back.

Master Gryph turned to Fuller, who held out his hand to shake Master Gryph's but had forgotten he was holding a hatchet he had been using to chop firewood from a dead branch on the side of the road.

"Are you going to use that on me?" Master Gryph asked, pointing at the hatchet.

"No, sir," embarrassed, Fuller transferred the hatchet to his other hand. "I'm Corporal Fuller Beame, sir."

"Good to meet you, Corporal," he said, and peered into the darkness at the silent man standing just outside of the firelight behind Fuller.

"Kyne?" he asked.

Kyne dipped his head once in affirmation.

"You know Kyne?" Elhrin asked, incredulously.

"Sure I do," he stepped over to Kyne and clasped the man's hand. "Why does that surprise you?"

"I guess because he has been vague about who he is," Elhrin said.

"Marguerite, you don't remember Kyne?"

"I'm afraid I don't," she replied.

"What's wrong with you, boy?" he furrowed his eyebrows at Kyne. "Why haven't you told them who you are?"

"Didn't think it was important," Kyne said, shrugging his shoulders.

"Now why would you think that?" Master Gryph's frown deepened. "When traveling with a group whose survival depends on being able to trust one another, don't you think it becomes important for everyone to know their companions?"

Kyne ducked his head. "Yes, sir." He actually appeared contrite. This was a side of Kyne that Elhrin didn't think he possessed. There was no smirking, or sneering, or blatant contempt.

Master Gryph patted him on the back with a shake of his head. "Well, let me introduce you, since you didn't do it yourself. Kyne is Queen Egeria's nephew."

Elhrin felt her mouth drop open.

"The queen's nephew?" Fuller asked with a loud snort, finding the information hard to swallow. "What are you doing with us?"

"Incredible, Kyne, you really do need to work on your social skills," Master Gryph sighed. "I imagine Goruth thought his expertise would be needed."

"And what would that be?" Fuller asked with a laugh. "I think we all could do without his expertise as being a major pain in the ass."

"That does it," Kyne started for Fuller, who spread his stance and readied his fists for a fight. Master Gryph grabbed Kyne by the arm and held him fast.

"Settle down, both of you," he ordered, sternly. "Save your energy for the enemy. We do not fight amongst ourselves. Is that understood?"

"Yes, sir," Fuller said, relaxing his stance.

Kyne jerked his arm from Master Gryph's grasp and backed away. The Kyne Elhrin knew was back.

"Fuller," Master Gryph said, "Kyne has a keen eye and a sharp mind. He is a serious asset to this group. I know well why Goruth would choose him." He shot a look at Elhrin. "Believe me, he will be needed."

"What can he do?" Elhrin asked, wanting a more specific answer. If she was to trust him, she wanted to know more about him.

"For starters, the boy could climb up the sheer face of Chance's Mountain if he wanted to and . . . ."

"Ahem," Kyne interrupted quietly. "Actually, I already have."

"Well, there you go," Master Gryph turned to face Kyne. "I remember the first time I saw you climb when you were just a lad. I needed to go to Yradin and since Martaline was on my way, Goruth wanted me to escort Egeria and your family on a visit to her and your mother's eldest sister living there. We stopped for the night near the old castle ruin outside of Thistle Meadows and you decided to crawl up the only standing tower it has left." He glanced at Marguerite. "He didn't even use a rope. His mother, Elene, screamed the entire time for someone, meaning me, to get him down."

"Why didn't you?" Marguerite asked.

"I was so amazed at what he was doing, I wanted to see if he could make it, and he did," he grinned at Kyne. "If I remember correctly your father had a long talk with you after I brought you safely to the ground, and you walked a bit funny for a few days."

"Yes, sir," Kyne said, "my father was pretty mad at me. Sitting was quite uncomfortable after that."

"Your mother was pretty mad at me, as well," Master Gryph said. "Elene hasn't spoken to me since. Do you still climb?"

"Every chance I can get," Kyne said. "Minister, earlier today I thought I saw something move on the other side of the river before we started into the mountains but I couldn't be sure. Was that you?"

"No, it wasn't me," Master Gryph said. "Did you cross for a closer look?"

"No, sir, we moved on, but I kept an eye on the shore. Nothing appeared again," he said.

Master Gryph frowned. He looked in the direction of the rushing waters of the river, invisible in the darkness. "You should have taken the time to get a closer look. You cannot afford to let your guard down." He purposely caught each of the men's eyes one by one. "This mission is serious. You are keeping a watch schedule, aren't you?"

"Yes, sir," Jag answered.

"Good," he motioned for Marguerite to follow him, "my wife and I will take a look around and make sure no one is out there while you finish up here." A tiny sphere of light popped into the air just above his head as he and Marguerite stepped off the road and made their way down to the river.

"Elhrin," Tomas said after they had gone.

Elhrin found she was the object of everyone's attention. "What is it?"

Tomas skirted the fire and stood next to her. "We are a bit confused as to how Minister Idwyr is here—alive."

"Oh," she said, wondering how she could explain something she was having a hard time grasping herself. "I know this is hard to believe. I don't even know if I understand it, but do you all remember Marguerite and me telling you why we are traveling to Blackridge Keep?"

Kyne sneered, "Of course we do." He sauntered into the light. "As I recall, my dear, you said something about closing a portal into the Realm of Darkness because the god of Do'athra is sending armies of Do'athrim out of it as we speak. Please," he huffed, "like we are supposed to believe such a thing can exist."

She knew he had not believed the story when he heard it the first time, and she really didn't expect any of them to believe her, but the smirk on Kyne's face pushed her over the edge. She had, had enough of his sour attitude. "Kyne, no one is forcing you to believe anything. Just what is your problem?"

"My problem is that I was ordered on this farfetched mission and told to go along with whatever you say. You are just a girl who, until recently, sat in her sheltered home at her mother's knee. I don't care what powers you possess. I for one am not inclined to follow the lead of an inexperienced baby who can't even look at something bleeding much less be the one to cause it. I think we are on our way to meet with our own deaths without just cause."

"Kyne, remember I didn't ask you to come along, and you may be right. We all may die on this mission, and I am inexperienced, but aren't you forgetting something?"

"What?" he asked, curling his lip as if the word had a bad taste.

"I am no longer at my mother's knee," she fumed. "I am right here with you—ready to die if I must to save our country. You know what? Forget this. I'm tired of defending myself." She ripped her gaze away from his mocking black eyes. "Tomas, Master Gryph is here because, as unbelievable as it is, he came through a portal just like the Do'athrim are doing, and his presence is proof that a rift can exist."

Shaking with rage, she turned her back on Kyne, trying to stamp out the strong desire to rip off his nose.

Tomas gently squeezed her arm. "I believe you, Elhrin. I have seen the beasts. We all saw Cynder and his power. If they are real, then I have to think that it is possible the Rift is real, too. Don't you agree men?"

Everyone nodded with the exception of Kyne. "You all are crazy to believe a god is actively involved in all of this," he fumed and stalked out of the circle of light to where he had laid out his bedroll.

"Don't let Kyne get to you, Elhrin," Tomas said. "He's not worth it."

"I know," she blew out a huge breath and let her anger go with it. "Thank you for believing me, Tomas."

"I never doubted you," he said and squeezed her arm again. "I'm just sorry my question caused so much trouble. Listen, I am going to take the last watch tonight. Do you want to join me?"

"Sure, as long as I don't have to take a watch with Kyne."

"Well, thanks a lot," he grinned. "You sure it wouldn't be a burden?"

"I didn't mean it the way it sounded."

"I know, I'm only teasing. You had better eat and get some rest, our watch will be here all too soon," he said, and left her to set up his own spot for the night.

"Wake up, sleepyhead," Elhrin heard somebody say, intruding in on a rare, pleasant dream she was having of her mother, alive and well, back home in Glimmerdale. Someone shook her arm.

"Elhrin," he said, shaking her again.

"I'm awake, Tomas," she growled, and opened her eyes. He was kneeling beside her. "You don't have to shake me to death."

He grinned. "My, don't we wake up in a lovely mood?"

She sat up, yawned and stretched, then stuck her tongue out at him. He laughed as he got up to add wood to the fire that was barely burning. She crawled out of her blankets, careful to not wake Bayle who had placed his bedroll beside hers.

"Why is there still a fire?" she asked, extending her hands out to warm them.

"The minister said it was fine to keep a small one," Jag yawned, as he pulled a blanket over him. He and Michell had the previous watch, and were settling in their bedrolls.

"Where is he and Marguerite?" she asked, noticing the couple was not among the sleeping bodies around the fire.

"I don't know." Tomas shrugged.

Jag leaned up on one elbow. "Hey, you two, they are safe down by the river, and uh, you might want to steer clear of the area. I believe they want their privacy."

"Got it," Tomas grinned knowingly at Elhrin. "You ready?"

Elhrin grimaced at the unwanted image Jag's information conjured. "Yes."

"You okay this morning?" Tomas asked as they left the light of the fire to patrol the outlying perimeter of their camp. "I know last night was a lot to take in, and Kyne didn't help with his stupidity."

"Yes, I'm fine—I think," she chuckled. "The world I have known all my life seems to no longer exist. Monsters running over the countryside, portals opening and allowing the dead to come back to life—things I thought could never happen, has. I guess maybe I had a glimmer of hope that the rift really would not exist." She shrugged her shoulders. "I hate to say this, but I wish Kyne was right that it couldn't."

"It is a bit like living inside a dream, isn't it?"

"Exactly," she said, and then pointed a finger at him. "Don't you dare tell Kyne I wanted him to be right."

Tomas laughed, "I won't."

Something crashed to the ground in the woods above the road. Tomas drew his sword. Elhrin grabbed her magic. They listened for more movement, but heard nothing out of place.

"Sounded like a limb fell," Tomas whispered.

Elhrin conjured a light sphere and sent it zooming towards where they heard the sound. A branch on a tree trembled. Elhrin lifted the light higher and two pinpoints of light reflected back at them.

"It's just a raccoon," Tomas breathed, sliding his sword back in its scabbard. The furry gray animal climbed higher up the tree, scattering pieces of bark to the floor of the forest.

Relieved, Elhrin let the light wink out. "I think I almost wet my pants."

Tomas chuckled softly. "Me too."

They continued their patrol in silence for a while, making a complete circuit around the camp, listening to the sounds of the forest to make sure there was nothing unusual in their surroundings. Crickets and frogs sang noisily in the darkness around them, adding their melody to the sound of the swift waters of the river spilling over rocks below. Not hearing or seeing anything else that suggested danger, they turned to go back to the camp. Tomas led her outside the fire's circle of light to the exposed large roots of an oak where they could sit and watch the area.

"Elhrin, can I ask you something?" Tomas asked, keeping his voice low.

"You can, but I can't guarantee I'll give you an answer," she grinned, turning to face him. His face was dimly lit, mostly in shadows—the flickering light of the fire behind her reflected in his eyes.

"I seem to recall hearing you say that before," he said, and cleared his throat. "Do you have anyone—is there someone you care for back home?"

"If you mean someone that I like or am in love with, the answer is no," she said.

"That's surprising considering how pretty you are," he said.

She felt her face flush from the compliment. "To tell the truth, there was a boy I thought I had feelings for at one time, but he intends to marry another girl. I realize now he is not my type." *You are*, she thought. "Why do you ask?"

"I just wanted to know," he replied and moved his face where he could see her eyes. "Elhrin, there is something, I don't know, I just can't quit thinking about . . . ."

He was babbling and it made her laugh. "You are making no sense."

"I know. My brain is not functioning right. All I can think about is this," he leaned in, hesitated to see if she would back away and when she did not move he closed the distance to shyly place his lips on hers.

His kiss was soft and tender, non-intrusive and nothing like Micah Promint's unpleasant slobbery mauling she had endured last summer. This felt right and wonderful, something that had been missing in her life without her knowing it until now. A simmering heat blossomed in the core of her body and flowed like a river of lava to her extremities.

He deepened the kiss, pressing closer to her, but then without warning he jerked his head back. "I'm sorry."

She frowned, wondering what had just happened. "Why?"

"I didn't mean to be so forward," he looked away as if he couldn't meet her gaze. "I should have asked you first."

Her inexperience made her nervous, but she wasn't about to let him become the shy one all of a sudden. She placed a hand on his unshaven cheek and made him look at her. "Do you want to kiss me?"

"More than anything else," he smiled.

This time, she leaned forward, and he met her halfway. Their lips melded together, and something seemed to click into place as if they had known each other for a long time. An undefined feeling rose inside her—buzzing, tingling—familiar and unfamiliar at the same time. She placed a hand on his chest to steady herself, amazed that she could feel his heart race through his shirt and uniform jacket, matching the tempo of her own blood pounding in her veins. His lips pressed into her and he wrapped an arm around her, pulling her closer.

"You know," a deep voice said uncomfortably close to her ear, "it is a better idea to watch for danger with your eyes open and being aware of your surroundings at all times."

She yelped in surprise at the unexpected intrusion. Both she and Tomas broke apart to find Master Gryph standing over them. Tomas scrambled to his feet.

"I, uh, I'm just going to go," Tomas stammered, pointing in the direction of the road behind him, "walk down the, uh . . . ."

"You do that, Lieutenant," Master Gryph growled.

Tomas turned around and disappeared into the dark as fast as he could without breaking into a run.

Master Gryph frowned down at Elhrin. "Young lady, you need to watch yourself."

Elhrin felt heat flare in her face, and she wanted to sink into the earth.

Master Gryph turned away to walk back to the fire where Marguerite stood waiting. Marguerite shifted her eyes to look at him then quickly placed a hand over her mouth to hide a smile and turned her head away from Elhrin.

What was so funny? Elhrin wondered.

Master Gryph squatted down beside the sleeping form of Bayle and shook him. "Bayle, wake up."

"What? Is it time to go?" Bayle asked, sleepily.

"No, not yet. Do you want to go fishing with me? I saw a pool that looks promising, and we have a little time before we have to leave."

"Yes, I do," he said, instantly wide awake, and leapt out of his bedroll.

Amused at Bayle's enthusiasm, Master Gryph picked up his pack and rummaged through its contents to pull out fishing line and homemade fishing flies.

Bayle's eyes widened at the sight. "I thought Ts'aura was not a physical realm."

"It isn't," Master Gryph replied.

"Then where did you get your things?"

Master Gryph cocked an eyebrow. "I am a man of means and resourcefulness, my boy. Come, we are pressed for time. Talk while you walk."

Elhrin watched the two slip through the woods to the river. He had not looked her way again, and she wondered what to do next. Should she find Tomas and see if he was okay or follow Master Gryph down to the river and apologize? But for what? She didn't do anything wrong. Drawing in a nervous breath, she noticed Marguerite sitting by the fire, warming her hands and watching her.

"Would you care to join me?" Marguerite asked, patting the ground beside her.

"Yes," she said, glancing in the direction where Tomas had disappeared, but it was too dark to see where he had gone.

"Marguerite, I didn't mean to make him mad . . . I'm sorry."

Marguerite reached over to pat Elhrin's knee when she sat down next to her. "Relax, Gryph is not mad. Men are a bit protective when it comes to their girls kissing boys. I imagine seeing you and Tomas together was a bit of a shock for him."

Elhrin stared into the flames of the fire. "I wasn't thinking. It just happened."

"That seems to be what every girl says when faced with the same situation. I think I even said it when my father caught me kissing the ale delivery boy behind our stables one morning. I was so scared. He had never laid a hand on me in my life, but I thought he might make an exception that day. But he didn't, he just made sure I was too busy to have time for boys. Of course, I still found time, anyway."

Elhrin glanced sideways at Marguerite, and found her smiling.

Elhrin managed a grin. "Do you think Tomas will come back?" Being on the wrong side of Master Gryph's anger was a scary prospect for anyone who knew him, and more so for those not accustomed to him.

Marguerite chuckled, "Of course he will, but I have a feeling he will stay as far away from Gryph as possible."

"Yes, that's what I think, too," she said, wondering if he would stay far away from her as well. She hoped not.

A short time after dawn lifted the impenetrable blackness around them, Master Gryph and Bayle returned wearing matching grins on their faces. Elhrin had not seen Tomas yet, only heard him make wide circles in the forest as he patrolled the area.

"Hey, everyone, look what we have," Bayle said, and held up his catch. Four slick-bodied trout dangled from his make-shift stringer of vine.

"Looks like you two had good luck," Marguerite observed.

"Well, I did. He cheated," he laughed, nodding his head at Master Gryph.

"Bayle, you aren't supposed to reveal a fisherman's secrets," Master Gryph said, dropping his catch of three on a nearby rock.

"How can you cheat at fishing?" Fuller asked.

"You know," Bayle said, wiggling his fingers, "magic."

"Just for that, young man," Master Gryph pointed at the fish on the rock, "you are cleaning them all by yourself."

"So, you had to resort to magic, did you?" Marguerite teased.

"I didn't have a choice. He was hogging all the good spots, and it was getting late. If I had more time, I wouldn't have needed to."

"I think he's using that as an excuse. He's just mad I not only caught mine the regular way, but my fish are bigger than his," Bayle said, as he placed his fish beside the others on the rock for comparison. "See?"

"Boy, you are getting too smart mouth for your own good," Master Gryph growled with a straight face, then grinned and ruffled Bayle's hair. "Seriously, though, you are going to clean them."

Bayle groaned and rolled his eyes at the thought. He liked to catch them, but hated cleaning them.

As they gathered to eat a quick breakfast before breaking camp, Fuller entertained the group with a humorous story of his childhood involving a pig sty.

Elhrin took a bite out of a crispy piece of trout, glancing once again at Master Gryph wishing he would say something, anything to let her know he wasn't mad at her. But he didn't, he was laughing at Fuller's animated recount of being stuck in mud up to his knees all day long with pigs who wanted to smell his face with nasty, snot-dripping noses, and then of all people to rescue him was a girl he fancied and her flock of friends. The kids had tossed him a rope and hooked it to a horse. When Fuller was jerked from the mud, his boots had remained behind and his pants had slid below his buttocks exposing his bare bottom.

Chuckling, Master Gryph turned to his wife. "Marguerite, is there a hole right here?" He pointed at a spot on his cheek.

"No, why do you ask such a thing?"

"Because Elhrin has been staring at me for so long, I thought maybe a hole had started to form," he grinned and cut his eyes at Elhrin.

Elhrin flushed and looked away, embarrassed to be caught, but was he not ever going to talk to her? The waiting was agony.

"We need to leave if we want to make the mine before nightfall," Jag announced, tossing fish bones in the fire.

Reluctantly, everyone rose to break camp. Elhrin remained to help Fuller chunk sand and dirt on the fire. A hand, strong and callused, entered her line of view. She glanced up.

"Coming?" Master Gryph asked. She took his hand, and he hauled her up. Smiling, he hugged her. The relief she felt almost took her breath away. He kissed the top of her head. "Elhrin, I have made many mistakes over the years where you are concerned, allowing the busyness of my life to demand my attention. Because of this, I have failed to tell you far too many things that are important for you to know. Have I ever told you that I love you?"

She shrugged her shoulders. She knew he cared for her, his actions throughout the years had shown her that, but she did not know just how much he cared.

He breathed deeply as if he was dissatisfied with himself. "I never had the opportunity to have a daughter of my own, but you know what?"

"What?" she whispered.

He tilted her face so he could see her eyes. "That didn't stop me from having one, you understand?"

Her breath caught in her lungs. He had never told her that before. Like she had told Tomas, was it only yesterday? She considered Master Gryph a father figure, but she never knew he thought of her as anything beyond his apprentice. It was all she could do to keep from bursting into tears of joy. She squeezed him so hard he grunted.

"Will you walk with me?" he asked.

She nodded.

"Grab your things before the others leave us."

Elhrin looked to where Marguerite stood behind him, smiling. "I told you he wasn't mad," she mouthed the words silently.

Chapter Nineteen

"Marguerite, why did you bring my sword?" Master Gryph asked, slipping his sword belt around his waist, adjusting the scabbard so that it rode comfortably on his right hip.

"I used it to kill the Do'athrim in our cottage. He bragged about killing you, and I have to admit, it just felt good that it was your sword that ended his life. I liked the idea of having it with me. It was a reminder . . . for some reason, I couldn't leave it behind . . . you know."

He slowly shook his head in disbelief. "No, I don't know. Why burden yourself with two swords?" He pointed at hers strapped to her waist.

"It felt like the right thing to do," she shrugged her shoulders. "I can't explain it any better."

He stared at her for a brief moment as if he couldn't believe what she had done, then lifted one corner of his mouth and lowered his head, concentrating on buckling his belt like it needed all of his attention. "Manipulator, he knew what I would do all along," he mumbled under his breath.

"What did you say?" Marguerite asked.

"I said, did you think to bring the antidote?"

Elhrin frowned, puzzled, wondering why he just lied to her. She had heard what he had really said, but didn't know what it meant.

"Of course, I did. I carry it with me all the time," Marguerite patted a small pouch at her side. "I didn't stop after you died. Old habit, I guess."

"What are you talking about?" Elhrin asked.

"She has the antidote for the Uihrian poison," he said.

"You mean there is an antidote? We could have saved you that day."

"I don't think having the antidote would have mattered. The wound in my chest was too serious," he said.

"We should have tried, right, Marguerite?" she asked. "Bayle or I should have gone to get you."

"I would have done anything in my power to save him, but he is right, the blood filling his lungs would have been beyond my skills to stop."

Not satisfied with that answer, Elhrin looked away and found Tomas at the head of the line right behind Jag—as far away from her as he could get. She allowed her thoughts to drift back to the night before, wondering what would have happened had they not been interrupted. The two of them had not had the opportunity to speak all morning, but Tomas had mouthed the words "I'm sorry" when Master Gryph had not been looking. She hoped he meant he was sorry they were caught, and not sorry that he had ever kissed her.

She decided to not borrow trouble as her mother used to say whenever she fretted over something that hadn't happened yet, and looked up at patches of blue sky visible through the boughs of the trees. She wondered if they had seen the last of Cynder. She hoped so. She needed this brief interlude of peace and wasn't ready for the real world to intrude just yet.

She glanced sidelong at Master Gryph. He and Marguerite had fallen silent and he was scanning the forest around them. She had so much she needed to discuss with him, but didn't know where to start. It was funny. Just two days ago she had been so mad at him for leaving her without answers, and now here he was, and she found it difficult to talk to him.

"Elhrin, you are thinking so hard, I can almost hear your thoughts," Master Gryph said, unexpectedly, breaking the relative silence of their trek. "Are you ready to ask me your questions?"

Elhrin flinched. He had been scrutinizing the mountain above them with his head turned away from her. "How do you do that? How do you know what I am thinking?"

He turned his head to look at her. "Lucky guess."

"I don't believe you," she narrowed her eyes at him. He did this too often to her for it to be sheer luck. "I honestly don't know where to begin. There is so much."

"What were you just thinking about?" he asked. "Other than Tomas."

See? How did he know that? She felt her face go red, and wondered why she embarrassed so easily. "I wasn't thinking about Tomas," she denied.

He hiked up one eyebrow, not believing her.

"Okay, I was," she snapped, a little irritated that he had been able to get her to reveal the truth. "Do you have the ability to read my mind now, like when you visited my dreams?"

"Settle down, I'm teasing you, and no, I cannot read your mind. However, you might want to work on your facial expressions. Sometimes they reveal far more than you might wish. Let's stick to the subject. What else were you thinking about?"

Elhrin touched her face in shock. She never realized she moved her face in any way. "Uh, I was thinking about Cynder, and how I hoped he was not near us."

"You should know he is nowhere near here right now."

"How could I possibly know that?"

He stopped abruptly in his tracks. He stared at her as if he was angry. What did she do now?

"What is it?" Marguerite asked, concerned.

"I can't believe I forgot to teach her something as important as this," he growled, tilting his head back as if he was talking directly to the canopy of limbs above. "What did I do all those years to leave her this unprepared?"

Elhrin wasn't sure, but she could've sworn she heard soft laughter within the breeze that rustled the leaves around them.

"This is not funny," he said under his breath.

"What are you talking about?" Elhrin asked.

"Just a minute," he frowned. He called out to the boys who had not noticed they had stopped, "Hold up, men. I need to stop for just a moment." He turned back to Elhrin. "Elhrin, you and I have the ability to sense when others with magical abilities are near. As strong as Cynder is in his power, you should have no trouble recognizing when he is nearby. As a matter of fact, you should be feeling my presence. Do you not feel me?"

"I don't know. What is it I'm supposed to be feeling?" she asked.

"Now that is a good question. For me, it is like seeing someone, only I don't need my eyes. It may be different for you. All I can say is that it is an awareness that is very different from any of your other senses. For instance, with Cynder you may have associated the feeling with fear, but . . . ."

"I was afraid."

"I'm sure you were, but I bet it was amplified with your ability to feel Cynder's magical energy," he said, crossing his arms over his chest.

"I did feel almost sick whenever he was near. Is that it? I don't feel sick now. Wouldn't it be the same with you?" she asked.

"I would hope not. Your feeling sick with him is a result of who he is—his black, evil-tainted energy. It would feel repulsive, I'm sure."

"I guess it does feel like that," she recalled. "But why don't I feel you?"

"You probably do feel me, but don't recognize it because you have known me since you were knee-high to a grasshopper and are used to my energy. We need to work on you separating my energy from what you deem normal. Once you know what you are looking for it will become second nature for you and you will be able to recognize it immediately."

"Knee-high to a grasshopper? That's a new one," she grinned. He was always coming up with little sayings like that one.

He raised a corner of his mouth. "Something my father used to say."

"Okay, how do I do this?" she asked.

"Do you remember how I taught you to close your eyes and clear your mind of everything around you and concentrate on your energy?"

She nodded.

"Okay, I want you to do that, but don't touch your energy. You don't need it for this. Relax, and don't think about anything. I just want you to concentrate on what you are feeling inside."

"Okay," she said, closing her eyes.

"I am going to move away from you—distance makes a difference, so as I move away the feeling will diminish. This might help in recognizing me faster.

Listen inside. Pay attention to anything that feels different. If you do figure it out, I then want you to concentrate on exactly where my energy source is without looking for me with your eyes."

Elhrin heard them moving away and smiled. "You do realize you limp, don't you? I can recognize you from the others."

He grunted, "Believe me, I more than aware of my limp than I wish to be, young lady. Cover your ears. I don't want you using your other senses. Bayle, help me out."

Elhrin opened her eyes and watched Bayle walk back to them. "What do you want me to do?" he asked.

"Use that pretty voice of yours," he winked at Bayle. "Hum, sing, whatever comes to mind. Didn't I tell you to close your eyes?" he asked her.

"Yes," she shut her eyes and placed her hands over her ears. Bayle started to hum one of her favorite songs. She grinned, loving her brother's voice, realizing it had been far too long since he last sang. "Good one," she said.

"Thank you," he replied, and continued the song, effectively drowning out everything else.

She turned her thoughts inward and shut out everything around her. Bayle's humming barely registered on her awareness as she delved deep inside herself, trying to concentrate on what she was feeling. Hearing only her own breathing and heartbeat, she went deeper and searched for any feeling that was different. At first she felt nothing, then she realized there was a slight tingling feeling, sort of like a faint humming or buzzing inside her that didn't seem real, but yet it was—an awareness of something not of her but recognizable and familiar, and it seemed to be fading somewhat as if slipping away from her. He was right. It was like seeing without having to look—like turning a face to the warmth of the sun with eyes closed, she could tell the direction of the source. Testing herself, she blindly turned in a circle then stepped a few paces to either side. The direction of the source did not move no matter which way she faced. She turned to face the direction of the source, but did not open her eyes.

"I have it. You are back the way we came," she said, dropping her arms.

"He didn't hear you," Bayle said.

"You are back the way we came," she called out.

"Excellent," she heard him say faintly, and opened her eyes. He had moved nearly out of sight far down the road, and was walking back. She paid attention to the newfound feeling and realized the tingling was increasing the closer he got to her. It was then that she realized this particular feeling had crept in on her awareness before. Twice that she knew of in the last day. The first time was when he first arrived, and the second, to her dismay, was when she was kissing Tomas. She had thought at the time, it had to do with her feelings for Tomas, but no, it was because Master Gryph was approaching, and now that she recognized it for what it was, his energy felt powerful, like a storm approaching. She couldn't believe she had not noticed it before. In all the years she had known him, not once did this ever attract her attention as being unusual. The only explanation she could come up with is that her awe of him, who he is, overpowered her own senses. As far back as she could remember she was always extremely excited to be with him. She thought it was anticipation of learning new things with her power, but now she knew part of it was just feeling his energy.

"So, what do you think?" he asked when he neared. "Do you think you could recognize someone with magical abilities now?"

"I think so," she said.

"I hope you know so," he said as he passed them without slowing down, "your life may very well depend on it."

She and Bayle fell in behind him, and a horrifying thought crossed her mind. "Can Cynder do this?"

"I don't know," he said.

"Elhrin, if Cynder could, wouldn't he have sensed you when we were with King Goruth or the night we camped under the rock overhang?" Bayle asked. "He flew directly overhead but didn't stop."

"That's true," she said. "What do you think, Master Gryph?"

"Cynder is very different from you or me. He is not human, and it certainly would be helpful if he couldn't, but to be on the safe side, let's be prepared in case he can. By the way, Marguerite told me about your fight with Cynder. I am proud of both of you. I told you, Elhrin, that you were stronger than you thought. I'm sure you gave him something to think about. This war of theirs is not going to be as easy as they planned," he smiled, scratching the stubble on his neck under his beard. "I certainly could use a shave."

"Yes, you could," Marguerite said, hearing him. "And I certainly could use a nice hot bath to wash off this thick layer of dirt, but I don't see that happening anytime soon."

"Your swim in the river last night wasn't good enough? It was for me," Master Gryph gave her an unmistakable look that left no doubt as to what he was referring to.

For the first time in her life, Elhrin witnessed Marguerite's face go blood red. "Gryph, shut up," Marguerite snapped and stalked away.

"Will you look at that?" Master Gryph said, watching Marguerite's hips sway from side to side, her anger evident in every step she took. He flashed them a mischievous grin. "I love it when she is on fire—a fine sight, indeed," he said, whistling happily as he strode after his wife.

Elhrin and the others all traded smiles. She knew why Marguerite was mad. She was a very private person and she did not like it when personal things were made public, just as she did not like showing her private emotions around anyone. That was why she moved away from people if she was upset, and why Master Gryph had to hurry to catch up to her now.

"I guess it's time to go," Michell said, and Tomas fell in beside Elhrin.

"Hey," he said, almost shyly.

"Hey, yourself," she replied.

"Are you mad at me?"

"No, why would I be?"

"You know, because of what happened. I mean, I pushed myself on you, and then Minister Idwyr shows up. I just thought you might be mad."

"Are you regretting kissing me?" she asked, scared he was going to say yes.

"No, of course not," he protested, "I just thought maybe I was going too fast for you."

"Believe me, I will let you know if you go too fast," she said, clasping his hand.

He grinned wide. "I have no doubt you will."

They hiked steadily the next day and a half, climbing higher into the mountains as the road wound back and forth following the river's path. By mid-afternoon of the second day, a strong breeze shifted the trees around them, announcing the arrival of a blanket of dark gray clouds and the possibility of rain.

Jag glanced at the sky, then spoke over his shoulder, "I think we may reach the mine shaft before the rain hits us. It shouldn't be more than an hour from here."

"Sounds good, son," Master Gryph said, but then held up a hand for them to halt. "Jag, hold up."

"What is it?" Bayle asked.

"Silence," he commanded in a low voice. He tilted his head in concentration then scanned their surroundings.

It was then Elhrin realized the tingling sensation humming inside her was different, and wasn't coming from Master Gryph. Now that she knew what to look for, she could differentiate his energy from a new source, a source that felt sick and foul as if diseased. Shuddering in disgust, she concentrated on pinpointing where it was coming from, but it was so faint that all she knew was its general direction on the mountain above and ahead of them, coming closer at a steady pace.

"Elhrin," he motioned for her to join him, "do you feel it?"

"Yes, is it Cynder?" she asked, thinking the source felt similar, but she wasn't sure.

"No, I recognize this energy source, and my guess is that he is not alone," Master Gryph said, and glanced at Jag. "You men get yourselves ready. We have company and they will force us to fight."

"We can't avoid them?" Marguerite asked.

Master Gryph leveled his gaze on her. "It's Grom. There is no use in running. He has the ability to sense Elhrin and I, and knows we are here. He will hunt us down."

Marguerite's face lost its color. "I thought he was dead."

He raised an eyebrow at that statement. "You thought the same of me."

Realization dawned on Marguerite. "Ah, right, he came through the Rift."

"I believe he has," he said matter-of-factly. He turned to the men, pointing far up the road where it disappeared around a sharp bend. "Keep an eye on the bend. He will be above us on the mountainside, but he may have others using the road."

Elhrin wondered what they were going to do about cover. There was nowhere to go except up or down the road. Sharp embankments rose and fell on either side of the road with few trees on the river's side to hide behind for protection, and Grom's energy source was getting stronger at an abnormally rapid pace. The men spread out in a defensive position. Tomas, Michell, and Kyne moved to her right, Jag and Fuller to her left.

"Elhrin, do you know how to form a shield?" Master Gryph asked.

"I do, but I have only practiced with small ones," she said, swallowing a huge lump in her throat. She realized what he was asking her to do—she was the protection.

"Make it as big as you can to cover you, Jag, and Fuller without sacrificing its strength. If there are archers firing on us you will have to put it in place in a hurry then drop it so our boys can fire back. Get ready," Master Gryph ordered the others, scanning their surroundings. "We are not going to have time to find a better vantage point. Marguerite, you and Bayle go back down the road and get out of the way."

"I'm not going anywhere," Marguerite stood her ground, sword ready.

Master Gryph frowned at her. "You never listen to me. Very well, stand behind me." He glanced at Bayle, but Bayle planted himself beside Marguerite, refusing to run. He growled under his breath at their stubbornness, but then turned his attention to the mountain slope above them. The enemy had arrived.

Elhrin heard the distant snapping of limbs and footsteps rustling through the leaves as the enemy moved closer, not bothering to hide their advance, but the laurel and rhododendrons were too dense for her to see anyone.

"Halfway up and to the right near the rock," Master Gryph murmured as he shifted his cloak off his shoulders to free his movements. "Wait for my command."

Jag and Fuller aimed their bows at a large boulder jutting out of the side of the mountain exactly where she felt the diseased energy source move. The bushes shook then parted and a large man stepped out onto the rock alone, moving calmly as if greeting friends, only no friend would look down upon them with such a vile look of contempt on his hideous face. Elhrin thought the man could have stepped out of a nightmare. He had skin so pale he looked dead. His long black, greasy hair, with one wide streak of gray in the front, reminded her of a skunk. He was dressed entirely in black leather armor, and draped across his shoulders was a cloak made from the pelt of a black bear. A childhood memory shot through her mind, and Elhrin couldn't believe her eyes. She now understood what Marguerite meant when she thought he was dead. This was the man Master Gryph killed long ago in Glimmerdale.

"Look who we have here," the man said with a mock bow. "I am honored. I thought you died, Minister."

"I could say the same for you, Grom, yet here you are," Master Gryph replied.

Grom threw back his head and laughed. The coarse sound, like a dull saw drawn through hard oak, echoed down the mountainside. He turned his smile on them.

"Damn, look at that," Fuller hissed under his breath. "Bet he's not popular with the ladies."

Elhrin had to agree, revolted by the sight of Grom's teeth. Every one of them had been filed to sharp points and plated with silver.

"I give thanks to Obsudius, God of Do'athra, for my return," Grom brought both hands together in homage, "and he will be pleased with me when he finds out I have exterminated two of the So'ladiun today."

Marguerite drew in a sharp breath of surprise.

"Ah, arrogant as always, I see. Before you exterminate me, Grom, will you answer a question?" Master Gryph cocked his head to one side.

"Anything, for an old friend," Grom flashed his metallic smile.

"What are you doing so far away from your army?"

"Don't pretend ignorance, Minister, it doesn't work for you. You know we are after the *Book of Tolman,* and if my information is correct, your young apprentice wears a certain pendant My Lord covets as well."

"And might I inquire as to how you knew my young apprentice would be here?"

"Oh, it wasn't that hard. Gryzzl knows your wife well and we knew they were together."

"That still did not answer my question of how you knew they would be here," he pointed at the ground, "and you managed to be here waiting."

Grom smiled maliciously, shrugging his broad shoulders. "Sometimes the hand of fate is kind. I was on my way to your village to remedy the failures of others sent before me, but Cynder discovered your apprentice was with your king in an encampment near the mountain pass. He found out that she left his protection and thought they might be headed this way, so I sent Gryzzl to scout ahead. He returned this morning and said you were on the road. You made it easy by coming to us, and this time, we will have the book and the pendant." He waved someone forward. "Men, show yourselves."

A large Do'athrim with the black head of a wolf joined Grom on the boulder. He removed a bow from his back, and as if he had all the time in the world, loaded an arrow and took aim at Master Gryph. Along the mountainside, men stepped from behind trees, aiming drawn bows at all of them.

"And there he is," Marguerite said quietly.

"He is your Do'athrim?" Master Gryph asked her softly, not taking his eyes off Grom.

"Yes."

Master Gryph breathed deeply and raised his voice to Grom. "Grom, do you think it will be that easy? Did Cynder tell you how his meeting went with my apprentice? She ran him off, and if I recall the last time you and I met it ended badly for you."

"Not this time, Minister, not this time."

A small troop of Do'athrim appeared around the curve in the road, the lead wolven barked rapidly when he saw them on the road. They charged at a dead run.

In a voice just loud enough for the party surrounding him to hear, Master Gryph said, "Everyone wait on my command to move. Elhrin, the bows must go first. Do whatever it takes. Follow my lead."

The next thing she knew, the Do'athrim called Gryzzl dropped his bow and howled—an agonizing, lonely sound. Clutching his chest, he toppled off the boulder and landed with a crash of snapping limbs in the underbrush below.

As soon as he hit the ground, everyone moved at once.

"You will die this time, Idwyr," Grom yelled. He launched a bolt of red fire down the mountain. At the same time, his bowmen loosed their arrows.

Master Gryph and Elhrin conjured their magical barriers. Grom's red fire bounced upward off the invisible shield in front of Master Gryph, sizzling leaves and branches as it skimmed out of control through the canopy of trees. The arrows Grom's men fired fell like rain all around them. Fletched shafts pelted her shield with audible cracks against the solid surface and ricocheted harmlessly away. Her shield held.

"Elhrin, drop it," Master Gryph ordered her to let go of the shield. "Now!" he roared as soon as she lowered her arms.

Jag and Fuller launched arrows back up the mountain. With deadly accuracy, Jag's arrow lodged in the eye of an archer, causing him to drop like a stone to his knees. Fuller's arrow struck a man in the middle of his chest, sending him sprawling backwards to the ground.

Master Gryph sent two sizzling comets of blue in different directions, simultaneously. One at Grom, which was shot down immediately with a bolt of red fire from the man, the other comet sped down the road at the advancing Do'athrim. It detonated into a thunderous spray of sparks, killing the animals in the lead and causing the others to skid to a halt. Michell, Tomas, and Kyne ran to fight those left. Bayle decided to follow them.

"Bayle, wait," Marguerite yelled. She huffed in frustration and ran after him.

Elhrin had to let him go, praying he would remain safe. The men on the mountain had moved to a closer vantage point and were sighting them in. She sent her magical energy up the mountain, and created an invisible line of heat along the ground in front of the remaining archers. She poured a wave of energy into it. A wall of flame burst furiously up from the ground. Surprised, the archers jumped back from the intense heat of the fire wall and away from their cover, giving Fuller and Jag the perfect opportunity to hit their targets. The screams that erupted from the dying men made Elhrin's blood run cold. She watched them drop lifelessly into the flames and abruptly catch fire. The remaining archers recovered quickly and she barely erected her shield in time before they fired again. An arrow pinged off her barrier as the archers quickly reloaded and fired again. Someone down the road cried out in pain.

Master Gryph deflected another attack from Grom, and then fired back. Two more comets of blue raced up the mountainside. Grom raised his hands against the attack. The first orb hit an invisible barrier to explode in a thunderous flash of light, while the second ball exploded on the surface of the boulder, sending chunks of rock into Grom's shins. He screamed and fell to his knees.

"That was stupid to not extend the shield to the ground," Master Gryph muttered, firing more orbs up the mountain. Grom was trying to get to his feet when he saw the blue flames coming at him. He threw himself out of the way, rolling off his perch and disappearing into the undergrowth beside the rock. The balls of blue flame exploded into the trees behind where he had stood, snapping them in half and bringing their tops down in a deafening crash.

Master Gryph moved in front of Elhrin and to her left, not taking his eyes off the mountain, heedless of the arrows zooming up and down the mountainside. She felt Grom's magical energy move to the left. He was changing his position, but she couldn't see him among the mountain laurel and various shrubs that covered the mountainside.

"Elhrin, the archers," Master Gryph reminded her as he moved slowly down the road, following Grom's energy source.

She returned her attention back to the fight. Jag and Fuller had moved further away from her, trying to get a clear shot at the enemy. Grom's archers had placed themselves behind tree trunks, using them for cover. Suddenly, a red flame shot down the mountain to explode onto the roadbed. Jag and Fuller both cursed and protected their heads from the dirt and rock the explosion had kicked up and did not see the next round of arrows flying their way. Elhrin quickly formed a shield to protect them, but then there was a painful ringing of steel in her ear. She instinctively ducked down and whirled around. Kyne and a Do'athrim wolven had locked swords right next to where she had just been standing. Shaking with the knowledge that she had almost been killed, she sent out her magic to snake along the ground like an invisible rope come to life, and used it to jerk the feet out from under the beast he was fighting. The beast fell to the ground, and without hesitation, Kyne thrust his sword into the beast's chest and gave it a wrenching twist.

Jerking his sword out of the dead beast as if he was in a furious rage, he shot Elhrin a smoldering glare. "Still can't kill anything, little girl?" he seethed, then ran off without waiting for an answer to meet another Do'athrim who had slipped by Michell and was heading their way.

Angry at herself because she knew he was right, she faced the mountain, determined to overcome her hesitance—their lives depended on it. Luckily, Jag and Fuller were safe. The roadbed was full of arrows sticking out of the ground, so the two men used them to their advantage. Moving constantly, they jerked up the enemy's own arrows and fired the projectiles back at them on the run. Another archer fell to his death. There were only four men left.

Seeing that the enemy had their attention focused on dodging Jag and Fuller's barrage of arrows, she flung a ball of flame at the one closest to her. He never saw it coming. The ball of flame caught him in the face and exploded, igniting his entire head into a mass of fire. Unbelievably, he did not die instantly. Instead, he started to scream in agony, slapping at the flames in desperation. He started to run down the mountain in her direction as if he could douse the flames by running from them. The flames on his head grew stronger, and he tripped and fell, rolling down the steep slope and off a ridge directly in front of her, landing with a sickening thud in the roadbed. The flames never went out.

Elhrin stared in shock at the gruesome sight of the dead man's burning face. Flesh blackened, eyeballs melted like wax out of their sockets, gaping holes appeared as fire consumed layers of skin and muscle, revealing bone and teeth. Was this what her mother's body had gone through? Her stomach roiled at the knowledge that she was capable of this kind of power.

Someone slammed into her, knocking the both of them onto the ground.

FWAP! An arrow lodged into the ground by her head. Another thumped into the roadbed at her feet.

Kyne grabbed a fistful of her shirt and rolled with her to the side, placing his body protectively over hers.

"Never take your eyes off the living enemy, you fool," he hissed. His face was blood-red, his body shook with rage. He pushed himself to his feet, placing himself between her and the archers. "Get up!"

She scrambled to her feet, ashamed for her mistake. She scanned the mountainside and sent a blast of energy at the archer taking aim at her. It exploded into the tree he used for cover. Scared, he ran. Elhrin launched an orb of blue fire at him. It blasted into the mountainside behind him. He dove onto the ground and rolled.

Kyne shifted quickly behind her.

Elhrin heard his sword meet another, but she concentrated on the archer who was scrambling across the ground for the nearest tree. Even though the distance was almost too great for her, combined with his weight, she still managed to grasp him with her magic and jerk him down slope into a rock jutting out of the ground. He crashed into it headfirst with a sickening crunch. He did not move again.

A short distance down the road, Fuller grunted and jerked back when an arrow hit him. He stumbled and fell flat on his back.

Elhrin ran to protect him, flinging a barrage of fiery comets up the mountainside. The archers ducked for cover. One died as the explosions burst trees in two and sent a mass of arm-length splinters into him.

Jag fired as the last man ran for new cover. His arrow lodged into the back of the man's neck. "Got him," Jag yelled.

Elhrin turned to help Fuller, but the man was already standing and pulling his sword from his scabbard.

"Are you all right?" she asked.

He flashed a grin at her, pointing at a large ornate buckle on his quiver strap. "Everyone always made fun of this, but I knew it was good for something. It saved me."

"No time to talk," Jag ran by them to the fight still raging on the road. Fuller took off after him.

Torn as to which way to go, she decided Master Gryph could use her help more and ran to fight Grom.

Dangerously close to the edge of the road and the steep slope that did not end until the river, Marguerite and Bayle fought side by side against a Do'athrim who looked like a furry bull with four arms. The beast had two swords he swung with such strength that Marguerite had a difficult time holding onto her blade every time she blocked one of his swings. Bayle tried to strike at his legs, but the bull beast knocked his sword aside. He cried out in pain as his sword arm was forced wide, spinning him around and almost over the edge. He scrambled to remain on the road.

Seeing that the move had left an opening for her, Marguerite thrust her sword between the buckles of his breastplate. Her blade carved a long gash into the beast's side. He trumpeted a roar of pain and sliced downward with the second blade. Marguerite dropped to the ground. The sword whistled by her head, coming close to slicing off her ear.

Bayle took advantage of the beast's attention on Marguerite and swung his blade with both hands. He severed its muscular arm at the wrist, causing its sword and hand to fly out over the edge of the road. The beast roared in furious pain. Blood spewed out of the wounded stump, spraying Marguerite and Bayle with warm red fluid. From her position on the ground, Marguerite gripped her hilt and thrust upward. Her blade caught the beast in the space below his breast plate. She pushed her sword into his torso with all her strength until her blade could go no further. The beast made a choking sound and blood poured out of his mouth. He collapsed on top of her, pinning her legs under him.

Bayle pushed the beast off her. "Are you hurt?" he asked. The fear in his voice made it crack.

She swiped her sleeve across her brow to wipe blood out of her eyes. "No, I'm fine," she said, blinking the dark haze away only to see that his face was also covered in blood. "I bet I look as good as you do. Is any of that blood yours?"

"I don't think so," he said.

Marguerite jerked her sword out of the dead beast and rose to her feet. Taking in a calming breath, she surveyed the fight around her. Tomas kicked his opponent to the ground and sliced the beast's throat. Jag was kneeling next to an immobile Michell, and Kyne and Fuller were fighting with the only remaining Do'athrim who looked as if they wanted to run instead of fight. The bodies of the dead littered the road around them. Sure that Tomas would help Kyne and Fuller finish their fight, she hurried to check on Michell.

Meanwhile, Gryph followed the path of Grom with his senses, but was caught off guard when the bolt of flame Grom hurled at them had come a little to his right and exploded onto the road between him, Jag, and Fuller, showering them all with dirt. He scanned the forest in the area where the bolt had come from.

"Why are you hiding?" Gryph called out just as he heard Jag say something about getting an archer and run to join the fight on the road.

Grom shifted to the left. He saw a bush shake, but Grom did not appear. The vegetation was making it difficult to find the man, and even though his magical senses told him the general area where Grom hid, it did not pinpoint him precisely. He was not going to waste precious energy firing aimlessly. "Are you scared this will end the same as last time? I thought you said you were going to exterminate me. Well, here I am. Exterminate away. Frankly, I don't think you are strong enough or smart enough to kill me," he taunted, knowing Grom had an ego the size of the sun.

Grom responded as expected. "Shut up, Idwyr, you think too highly of yourself. This fight is not over," he yelled, and from the cover of the trees, two bolts of pure white shot down the mountain.

Gryph launched himself sideways to the ground and rolled. The bolts passed harmlessly across the road where he had stood, hitting something down in the forest with a boom. He reared up on his knees, scanning the area where the bolts had appeared. There was an unnatural shadow among the bushes. He sent an invisible stream of magic speeding up the mountainside and wrapped it tightly around Grom. Grom let out a howl of anger just as Gryph tightened his hold and jerked him out from his hiding place and slammed him against the nearest tree. Grom ricocheted to the ground and rolled into a thicket of mountain laurel. Gryph lost sight of him again, and started to rise to his feet, but a force slammed him in the chest and landed him flat on his back completely knocking the wind out of him. He tried to breathe, but couldn't seem to get his lungs to work. Gryph felt Grom shift with his senses, and knew he had to move because he was too exposed on the roadbed. With a gargantuan effort, he managed to haul in a lung full of air and roll across the road just as an explosion hit the roadbed, deafening him and covering him with dirt.

That was too close. "Enough is enough," he growled softly to himself as he rose to his knees and searched the thicket where Grom was hidden. He smiled without humor when he caught a flash of silver among the shadows. "Ahh, there you are, snake."

Knowing Grom probably held a shield in place for protection, Gryph poured a large amount of energy into a flow he directed at the thicket. Instantly, the laurel burst into a flaming inferno. Grom shouted in furious surprise and jumped out into the open.

"Damn you, Idwyr," he roared, flinging a rapid succession of flaming balls of energy down the mountain. Gryph raised a shield in time to deflect the barrage of missiles, and they scattered in all directions with a series of concussions.

Gryph quickly glanced up the road, relieved that no one was in the path of the wayward missiles, but then noticed Elhrin running toward him. A fierce force of concern for her welfare hit him hard. He knew she was capable of handling herself, but the protector in him wanted Grom dead before she became involved in the fight.

The N'gethwyn stood out in the open. He raised his hand for another attack, but Gryph was quicker. "Goodbye, Grom," he yelled, as he sent a beam of crackling green light up the mountain.

Grom could not create a shield in time. The beam hit him in the torso and bored a hole straight through armor and flesh. Surprised, he opened his mouth to speak as he looked incredulously at the gaping wound in his body. No sound came out as he dropped to his knees and toppled lifelessly onto the forest floor.

"Humph, that worked better than Phagen described," Gryph murmured, as he wearily dragged himself to his feet. His last attack had been a technique he had never used before. A long dead predecessor, Phagen Ryarthe, had met with him in Ts'aura before he left the realm and had told him about the intense bolt of energy that burned holes through solid objects instead of exploding, but Ryarthe had failed to tell him that it would cause a massive drain on his magical energy.

Elhrin skidded to a halt by his side. "Is he dead?"

"Yes," he glanced up the road. The fight was over. They had persevered against the odds. He placed a hand on Elhrin's shoulder and squeezed. "I'm proud of you, young lady, you fought well. Let's go check on the others."

Marguerite broke away from the group huddled around a mass of dead bodies when they neared. "Gryph, Michell is dead."

"Oh, no," Elhrin gasped, looking past Marguerite.

Michell lay entangled with several Do'athrim, an arrow was lodged into his shoulder and his head had been nearly severed from his body. The man had certainly been a fighting force before he fell.

Angered, Gryph rumbled low in his throat, knowing without a doubt what had happened to fell the giant man.

"It was the poison, wasn't it?" Marguerite asked.

"Looks like it," he said.

"What do we do with him?" Kyne asked.

"I'll take care of him," Master Gryph said, rubbing a hand over his eyes. "Get your gear and move out. I will catch up."

"Hey, do you all see this?" Bayle called out.

One-by-one, the dead enemies littering the ground began to dissolve. Sounding like sand falling across a sheet of paper, they slowly disintegrated until nothing was left but a lump of dust on the ground.

Stunned into silence, nobody moved.

"Well, Gryph, I guess your theory was right," Marguerite said, breaking the silence.

He cut his eyes at her and grimaced. "It won't take long for them to return to the Rift. They will tell Cynder of our location. Jag, we need to change direction. What do you suggest?"

"If they came from Blackridge, I'm sure they used the trail that I had originally planned to get us down the north side . . . by the mine." He pointed north. "If they were to return, I bet they will come the same way because it is the quickest route back here. We could head east, sticking to the mountains, but the terrain will be more strenuous and it may take us longer."

"I don't think we are going to have a choice. Does the river follow the road all the way to the mine?"

"No, sir, it veers away east not too much further up the road."

"Right, let's follow the road until then and head east from there. Go ahead and go. I will be along shortly."

Everyone except Marguerite wearily retrieved their packs and trudged down the road. He waited for her to leave, but instead, she poured water onto a cloth and used it to wipe dried blood off her face.

"Marguerite, you need to go," he said, hoping he would never see blood on her face again.

"I'm waiting for you," she said, eyeing him sidelong, calmly rewetting her cloth and squeezing the dingy excess water out.

He held her eyes with his for a moment, still finding it hard to believe that he was lucky to have a woman like her stand by him. He nodded his head and looked down at Michell's lifeless form. It angered him that he had to do this, and understood how hard it must have been for Elhrin to have done it for her mother. With a grim sigh, he set Michell on fire with his magic, consuming the body with intense blue flame. He did not let the flames die out until there was nothing left but a scorched place on the ground. He bent over and picked up Michell's massive sword. Grimly, he impaled it into the ground above the scorch mark as Marguerite came to stand beside him, holding his pack. Without a word, he took the pack from her, placed his arm around her waist, and started after the others.

Chapter Twenty

The night surrounding Elhrin was black as pitch. She could barely make out the silhouette of Tomas in front of her as they wound their way through a forest of trees smelling strong of pine. The ground beneath her feet felt padded, and the sound of their footsteps were muffled as if the forest floor were a carpet made of moss and pine needles. Which it probably was, but she couldn't see to confirm it. Earlier, when night first fell, she and Master Gryph had taken turns conjuring small spheres of light to light the way, but now, after the fight and hours of the demanding trek through the mountains, both of their energy supplies were gone. She felt if she had to use one more ounce of energy for magic she would probably lapse into unconsciousness.

Someone tripped up ahead.

"Whoa there, Bayle," Fuller said.

"Thanks, Fuller," Bayle replied.

That figures, she thought. *He has a hard enough time keeping on his feet in daylight.*

No sooner had that thought flitted across her mind when she stumbled over a tree root. A small burst of pain flared up in her big toe. "Ow."

"You okay?" Tomas asked.

"Yes," she winced, trying to walk off the pain. *Serves me right for thinking Bayle is the only clumsy one here.*

"Low branch," Jag's voice warned.

A whisper of a moving limb broke through the darkness, then a dull thump.

"Damn, that hurt," Kyne fumed.

"I warned you, Kyne."

"Not soon enough, damn it! It would have been nice if somebody had thought to make or bring torches with us. How did you people expect to see at night?"

"Kyne, you are a spoiled ass. If you complain about that one more time, I'm going to smack you in the back of the head," Fuller growled. Tempers were flaring.

"I wouldn't recommend it, Fuller. I would hate to have to kill you," Kyne replied in a low deadly tone.

Fuller snorted in contempt, "As if you could."

"Boys, please don't start again. It's hard enough to walk without listening to you two argue," Marguerite said from behind Elhrin.

"Master Gryph," Bayle's disembodied voice drifted back, "what did you do to the Do'athrim that was beside Grom?"

"Bayle, leave it to you to expect me to speak when I can hardly breathe," he said, winded.

"Gryph, the limb," Marguerite said.

"Oomph, yes, I found it," he grumbled. "All right, I think we need to stop before someone breaks something."

Moans and groans pierced the night as everyone found a place to rest.

"Gryph, are you going to answer him? I want to know what happened, too," Marguerite asked, breathing heavily.

"Can you give me a minute?" he asked, trying to catch his breath. "I'm not as young as the rest of you."

Marguerite laughed low, under her breath. A heart-warming sound after the stressful day they had endured.

"What's so funny?" he asked.

"Nothing," she said, "I'll tell you later."

He grunted and drew in a deep breath, then let it out explosively as if that last breath could rectify his exhaustion. He cleared his throat. "Bayle, I blew up his internal organs."

"You did what?" Marguerite asked.

"You did? I didn't see you do anything," Bayle asked at the same time.

"I don't have to be obvious when I use my magic. And I certainly did not want them to know what I was doing beforehand," he said, rustling leaves as he moved closer to Marguerite. "Marguerite, do you have any water?"

"Yes," she said, "here."

"Okay, you are going to have to help me out. I don't know where 'here' is. I can't even see my own hands, much less wherever you have that waterskin, and I'm too tired to conjure a light."

"Oh, for heaven's sake, here," she said, and Elhrin heard something land with a thud.

"Oomph! Woman, do you realize where you threw that?" he complained. "I need those parts."

Everyone burst out laughing, now knowing what happened.

"I didn't mean to," Marguerite laughed.

"You want to kiss it and make it better?" he asked.

The men roared with laughter.

"Stop it right now, Gryph," Marguerite's voice shot back, not amused.

Laughter rose and fell all around Elhrin for a few minutes releasing the tension of the day. Finally, everyone drifted into silence.

Elhrin filtered through all that she knew, but could not figure out what he had done to kill the Do'athrim. "How did you do it?" she asked.

"Well, it is a tricky technique. I honestly did not know if I would be able to pull it off." She heard him take a swig from the waterskin and swallow. "I noticed Gryzzl was panting, so I sent a fine thread of energy through his open mouth and down his throat. When I thought I was far enough inside his body I expanded the end of the thread and caused it to explode from within."

Elhrin recoiled inside, "Ow!"

"I know, not a pleasant thing to do to anyone, even an enemy, but it was necessary," he said.

"What do you mean you expanded the end of the thread?"

"I pooled a concentration of energy on the end of the stream and forced it outward."

Elhrin frowned. This technique was new to her. "You never taught me how to do something like that."

"Yes, I know," he said. "I've never tried it before, myself. Like I said, I didn't know if I could do it. It took a tremendous amount of control and far longer than I wished. I was lucky it worked."

"Why didn't you do it to Grom instead?" Bayle asked.

"Two, no, three reasons why. One, Grom would be able to detect what I was doing to him and would cut it off before it worked, which means I would have had to focus on a fight with him first. I did not want to do that because Grom wasn't my primary concern, Gryzzl was."

"Why is that?" Fuller asked.

"Because I was fairly certain his arrows were poisoned, and I personally knew he was good with that bow, not to mention that it was a quick way to eliminate one adversary."

"Well, someone else had arrows laced with poison, too," Kyne observed.

"Yes, Kyne, they did. Elhrin, Jag, and Fuller did their best to eliminate the archers. What happened to Michell was unfortunate," Master Gryph said.

Elhrin sighed as her companions fell silent. Mulling over the fight, she wondered if Michell might still be alive if she had been just a little stronger and not been so hesitant to kill someone. She clamped her lips firmly together. It wasn't going to happen again.

"Master Gryph?" Bayle asked.

"Yes, Bayle," Master Gryph said with a slight yawn.

"You just mentioned two reasons why the Do'athrim had to die first," Bayle said. "What was the third?"

"He attacked Marguerite, twice, and that made me very unhappy."

"Okay, now you've made me sorry I hit you," Marguerite said with a small laugh.

"Good, you should be sorry," he chuckled. "You sure you don't want to kiss it?" he whispered.

"I mean it, hush!" she ordered.

He chuckled again.

Elhrin felt something wet hit her on the cheek.

"Great. Now it's starting to rain," Kyne complained.

Drops pattered through the forest canopy, and Elhrin pulled her cloak from her pack, donning it just in time as the rain started to steadily fall. Tomas scooted closer to her, and she felt him pat her leg to see where she was.

"Here, put this over you," Tomas said, draping a blanket across their legs. "Are you covered?"

"Yes, it feels good," she replied, tugging her hood low over her head and snuggling closer to him, laying her head on his shoulder.

"Tomas, keep your hands to yourself," Master Gryph said.

"Yes, sir," he replied.

"Gryph, leave him alone," Marguerite said, and then let out a little squeak. "Ouch! Leave me alone, too."

"Never have, my dear, and never will," Master Gryph said.

"I certainly hope not," Marguerite whispered.

Elhrin found Tomas' hand resting on his leg. She twined her fingers between his, feeling rather than seeing him smile as he squeezed her hand tight.

"If anyone can sleep in this, go ahead," Jag said. "Fuller and I can take the first watch."

Tomas put his free arm around Elhrin and pulled her closer. She rested her head against his chest and closed her eyes. He felt so good and warm that, despite the cold, clammy rain pelting her head and seeping through crevices to her skin, she fell asleep.

"Elhrin, wake up," she heard Master Gryph call her, and tried to open her eyes, but she was so tired her eyes refused.

"Elhrin," she heard him say again, and finally, was able to force her eyes open. He was crouched beside her with firelight dancing behind him, and for a moment, she thought she was back in the King's Palace in Muryne having another dream.

"Am I dreaming?" she asked, yawning wide.

She saw the white of his teeth as he smiled, understanding what she meant.

"Not this time," he reached out to tweak her nose like he used to do when she was little and rose to go back to the fire. "Get up. You and I are taking the last watch together."

Elhrin sat up, making Tomas' arm fall away onto the wet ground. She had forgotten that he was beside her and he shifted a little to compensate for her leaving him, producing a tiny snort through his nose, but he didn't wake up. She realized that sometime during the night, they had slid down to lie on the ground, and he had put his pack under his head and had cradled her in the crook of his shoulder. She took a moment to study his features visible in the soft flickering light cast by the fire behind her. His rain-soaked hair curled around his face in dark wisps, and the strong line of his chin was covered with thick stubble. Thick eyelashes rested on his cheeks, and she thought it unfair that a man could have better looking lashes than she did.

She smiled to herself, realizing that her feelings for him went far deeper than a schoolgirl crush, and wondered how that could have happened. Was it possible she fell in love with him the first time she saw him in the inn? That thought was ridiculous—love at first sight only happens in fairy tales and romantic stories, right? She glanced at those around the fire. Seeing that Master Gryph was preoccupied with Kyne and Bayle making their way back into the camp, she quickly leaned in to place a light kiss on Tomas' lips. He smiled slightly, but did not open his eyes.

"Did you boys see anything?" Master Gryph asked. He sat down by the fire, leaning comfortably against a tree and crossing his long legs out in front of him. Marguerite moved her blankets closer to lie next to him, laying her head on his lap, watching the fire sleepily.

"No sir," Bayle answered, settling into his bedroll by the fire. "It's too dark to see—like staring at a black wall, and we didn't hear anything unusual. We circled the area several times, keeping the fire to our left, everything seems okay."

Kyne spread out his bedroll near Bayle, all the while following Elhrin with his black eyes as she slipped from Tomas' side into the chilly, pre-dawn air and moved to warm herself by the fire. She knew by the look of utter distaste smeared across Kyne's face that he had seen her kiss Tomas, but she didn't care. Then she remembered that he had saved her life, and the least she could do was thank him for it no matter how much she wished she could make warts pop up all over that face.

This was not going to be easy. "Kyne, I, uh, I want to thank you for what you did yesterday . . . you saved my life."

He froze, then shrugged his shoulders as if it had been about as important as swatting a pesky fly. "Just doing what I was ordered to do."

"Whatever the reason, thanks," she said, frowning at his rude indifference. She sighed and looked to Master Gryph, wondering what he thought about Kyne's behavior. If she had been rude, she was sure either Master Gryph or Marguerite would have called her on it, but Master Gryph remained silent as he watched Kyne hunker into his bedroll. He had that familiar position she had seen so often when something was on his mind. Eyes squinted, the right eyebrow hiked upward a little, right arm crossed over his chest while his left hand smoothed the hairs of his beard.

"Kyne, didn't you tell me you wanted to own your own shipping company one day?" he asked.

"Yes, sir."

"What happened to that idea?"

"My parents decided that being a simple shipping merchant was not good enough for the nephew of the queen. They thought I needed to follow the protocol of royal tradition and be an officer in the army for awhile and, since I have no link to the throne, they expect me to go into what they consider the next best thing," he curled his lip in distaste, "politics—as if I want to be the next governor of the Western Province or sit on the High Council."

Master Gryph had a peculiar look on his face. "Well, Kyne, you have a brilliant mind and would be excellent in either of those positions, but it is up to you to do what you want—nothing is ever set in stone."

"Tell that to my mother," Kyne grunted.

Elhrin was surprised yet again. Kyne hid his background well. "You're an officer?" she asked, glancing at his attire. He did not wear the gray army uniform like the others. He wore russet colored trousers, and a long forest green tunic topped by a thick vest of dark leather. Elhrin never pictured him as a true member of the King's Army. Actually, she never pictured him as anything beyond the image of the thief she had conjured early in their journey.

"Unfortunately, yes. A captain in the Third Cavalry Regiment of the King's Personal Guard, and temporary personal bodyguard of yours truly," he said, with a mock bow of his head.

Stunned, Elhrin didn't know what to say, and it must have shown on her face because when she looked at Master Gryph he had a knowing smile on his face.

"You could do worse than Kyne for a bodyguard, Elhrin," he said. "As you saw yesterday, he is excellent with that sword of his, and I have had the pleasure of watching him train a few times. No one was able to defeat him. Goruth knew what he was doing when he picked these men to accompany you."

"I suppose so," she said, staring into the fire. She didn't like having to trust someone who made her feel so . . . so angry all the time. Even thinking about him making her angry made her feel angry.

"Elhrin," Master Gryph said.

"What?" she spat out the word with heat.

He raised his eyebrows at her explosive answer.

"I'm sorry," she apologized. Kyne was making her crazy. "Sir?" she answered politely.

"Where is the *Book of Tolman*?" he asked.

"It's in my pack," she replied.

"Would you get it for me?"

"Yes, sir," she got up and retrieved her pack, bringing it back to the fire where she dug out the book and handed it to him. "I guess I should have given it back to you sooner."

He glanced at her sharply. "Why would you do that?"

"I just thought that now you are back . . ." she said with a shrug of one shoulder.

"Elhrin, nothing has changed. This book is yours, and what it means to have it has not changed, either. You are who you are," he said.

"You can quit talking in general, Gryph. We all heard Grom call you two So'ladiun," Marguerite said drowsily from his lap and turned her head to look up at him. "I wish, though, that you would explain why he would call you a mythical figure."

Master Gryph stared at her for so long without speaking that Marguerite finally raised her eyebrows at him. "Well?"

"Marguerite," he breathed and looked away, lips pressed in a thin line.

Marguerite narrowed her eyes and sat up to face him.

"What is it that you don't want to tell me now?" she demanded.

He scanned those around them. Everyone was asleep with the exception of Kyne. "I suppose there is no point in keeping this a secret here," his eyes landed on Elhrin. "As I told Kyne, it is important that we all be able to trust one another, and they will find out eventually." He glanced at Marguerite. "My love, the So'ladiun are not mythical figures, they are very real and are scattered across all the nations of this world. Elhrin and I . . . we are the ones Solisius chose to defend Anderan."

Marguerite's face transformed into utter astonishment. Kyne made a choking sound and sat straight up. He might not believe anything she had to say, but he had shown a great deal of respect for Master Gryph, and this information she was sure Kyne believed.

"You were chosen by the God of Light? To fight his battles?" she sputtered, keeping her voice low so as to not wake those sleeping.

"I'm afraid so," Master Gryph said.

She stared at him speechless for a moment—her mouth working as if it couldn't keep up with her mind. Finally, she managed to get the two to coincide. "I guess I shouldn't be surprised. We are on our way to close a portal you say Obsudius has opened. But it never crossed my mind that you were connected directly with Solisius other than when you said he allowed you to come back here with us and wanted you to do something for him. I just thought Elhrin's powers made her the logical choice for this mission, and that was why you needed her to come," she shook her head, trying to make sense of it all. "So, is that why you generalized the details of your travels all over Anderan, and why you have those strange dreams?"

He nodded.

"I thought Goruth was sending you on those missions."

"For the most part he was. The welfare of Anderan is his responsibility and its people are the children of Solisius. The two are intertwined, and as Minister of Specialized State Defense my job officially requires me to do my part to ensure the safety of the people. Marguerite, the rulers of Anderan have always known about the So'ladiun since the days of High Lord Allurack Dwyer who united all the clans at the time into one nation. Goruth knows exactly who I am."

"He knows, but I don't?" she asked, incredulous at the revelation. "I am your wife—I wish you trusted me more." She smoothed a loose tendril of hair back, and Elhrin noticed a slight tremor in Marguerite's hand. She did not know if it was from anger or fear . . . or both.

"I told you that I do trust you. I have reasons, Marguerite. And this was something I could not tell you. I am only telling you now because of what we are about to face. That and . . . ," he hesitated, and Elhrin had the feeling he changed what he was originally going to say. "My love, I'm sorry. You deserve the truth after what you have endured for me this last year. No, make that, the last twenty years. But you must understand. I am a target. You have seen what I have had to do, to go through all these years," he clasped her hand. "Do you know what you would have done if I had told you years ago? You have a tendency to worry constantly, and would have lived every day looking over my shoulder for an assassin more so than you already do. I did not want that for you—still don't, and in the beginning I almost didn't marry you for that very reason. My life was never going to be quiet or peaceful, and you don't know how long I struggled to finally reach the decision to marry you."

"Yes, I do. It was one year, four months, and five days, from the day I followed you and Toome to Muryne," she said.

"Okay, maybe you do," he said, raising one corner of his mouth. "The point is, it wasn't an easy decision, and in the end, I just couldn't bring myself to walk away from you, so here I am, causing you a life of pain."

"Gryphon Idwyr, if I had the choice of going back and never marrying you just so I wouldn't have had to live through the countless injuries, worries, and ultimately, your death, I would not take it. I love you, and I would not trade the last twenty years for anything. I just want you to trust me more. I can handle your secrets." She gripped his hand hard. He raised her hand to his lips and kissed it.

Elhrin lowered her gaze to the glowing embers of the fire. She was in shock. What he said about being one of Solisius' So'ladiun started to sink in once and for all, and what being one meant for her future. Fighting for Solisius didn't end with this journey. It would never end, and she would spend her entire life looking over her own shoulder, assuming she survived this ordeal. She began to grow angry with frustration that her future was being taken from her without her permission. She glanced back at Master Gryph, and found him watching her.

"It's not going to be easy," he said as if he had read her mind. "You will have to make painful sacrifices that you will not want to make."

Elhrin felt something inside her snap. "Sacrifices like you had to make?" she asked as her anger escalated. "Aside from the danger to myself, now I will have a lifetime of wondering if I will ever be able to marry someone I love? Afraid all the time of what might happen to them or me? What about my happiness? Am I going to have to sacrifice the chance to have a family of my own like you?"

Master Gryph frowned and went stone still as Marguerite sucked in an audible breath of surprise.

"Possibly," he said after a moment.

"Then I don't want this," she said with heat, trying to keep from yelling at the top of her lungs. As far back as she could remember, she dreamed of a houseful of children and a solid man by her side. She didn't ask for this. She scrambled to her feet. "You tell Solisius that I don't want anything to do with being one of his chosen warriors."

"You tell him yourself," he replied calmly, his blue eyes boring into hers, daring her to look away.

"What did you say?" she asked, not sure she heard him correctly.

"I said, you tell him," he replied evenly, gesturing at the surrounding woods. "Go find a quiet place, sit down, and talk to him. He is listening."

"You're serious?" she asked, incredulously.

"What makes you think I'm joking?" he asked. "We have an hour or so before dawn. Go tell him you quit."

She stared at him, unsure of what to do. He watched her patiently, waiting for her to make the next move. *Fine,* she thought, and stalked off into the darkness without another word. She heard Marguerite ask him if she would be safe alone in the woods, but did not hear his reply.

She walked far enough into the trees until she could no longer see. The forest was an impenetrable wall of black like Bayle said. Leaning a hand against the clammy rough bark of a tree, she lowered her head and allowed tears of frustration to drip freely.

This is so unfair. I never asked for this.

She sank to the ground and hugged her knees to her chest. She was back to feeling lost again, out of control, and wondering what she was supposed to do now. She had just lashed out at the one person, besides her mother, who had mattered most in her life for so long. She rested her forehead on her knees.

He said to talk to Solisius. All right, I will, she thought. She closed her eyes, took in a deep breath, and tried to clear her scattered mind.

Solisius? Are you there? I've never been good at praying, so if I'm doing this wrong, I hope you will forgive me. I am having a hard time here. Master Gryph says that you have chosen me to fight against Obsudius. I trust him—I believe him, but I don't understand why you would choose me. I don't think I am strong enough to make the sacrifices that you will require of me. I don't know what to do.

She sat waiting for something to happen, not knowing what she was supposed to be looking for. She held her breath, listening, but only hearing the crickets and frogs that were singing in the night, and off in the distance she could faintly make out the sound of the crackling and popping of their campfire.

The next thing she knew, she was blinking against sunlight and trying to get her eyes to adjust to the unexpected change from total dark to bright light. She was no longer in the woods, but was standing next to a cascading marble fountain built into a high stone wall. The water spilled over several increasing-in-size rectangular pools as they stairstepped down into a large stream-like pond filled with orange and white spotted fish. Healthy plants and shrubs of various sizes and hues of green grew along the pond's sides as if they were growing naturally along a stream in the countryside.

Amazed and slightly afraid of what was happening, she turned around slowly. She was in a meticulously kept garden surrounded on three sides by a high rock wall. A large portion of the wall was covered in thick vines with glossy, green leaves and trumpet-shaped red flowers. A myriad of colorful butterflies and hummingbirds flitted back and forth between the blooms, drinking the sweet nectar they offered.

She stood on a wide path of red brick that meandered through the garden to a white, three-

story mansion with thick columns supporting a balcony with scrollwork iron railings. Sculpted potted plants with large blooms she did not recognize decorated the balcony and patio of the mansion. Several arched windows spanned the entire façade of the mansion, but they were dark and she could not glimpse the interior of the building. A glass double-door underneath the balcony led into the house, and as she started down the path to go see what was inside, the door opened and a man walked out.

She froze, numbed to the core of her soul by the sight of him, unable to take one step further as he stepped from the patio onto the path and made his way to meet her.

Like a beacon of supreme light, dressed entirely in white robes, he made the sun seem pale in comparison. She could hardly breathe. Never had she seen someone so beautiful—and yet, he looked familiar. Golden hair fell to his shoulders and surrounded a lean, clean-shaven face. He was of average height, but the way he carried himself—his mere presence—made him seem larger, grander than anyone who ever lived—who ever would live, and when he finally stood before her, he gazed down at her with sparkling, blue eyes and a kind smile as if he had known her all her life and was glad to visit with her once again. It was at that moment, she realized why he looked so familiar. He reminded her of the images she had seen of Obsudius. But this man's face held love and compassion instead of the malevolent hate she had seen on Obsudius' face.

"Elhrin, I have been waiting for you," he said, and the sound of his voice washed over her like a warm, soothing summer breeze.

"Solisius, My Lord," she breathed and dropped to her knees and wept, feeling so ashamed for her selfish thoughts. He knelt down beside her and pulled her into his embrace. An overwhelming sense of calm and love swept away her despair.

"Elhrin, do not cry. I know I ask a lot of you. More than you are willing to give. But you need to understand, I do not ask this of you out of personal ambitions. I ask you to do this for what is right and good, to uphold the laws that surround love and truth." He paused, resuming with a small sigh of sadness. "My brother, Obsudius, does not understand these things. Does not realize what it is that he actually seeks. He wants to turn this world into a land of despair and fear, and forces his followers to respect him whether they wish to or not. And in his jealous drive to gain dominance over me, he will never have what he desperately wants, which is dedicated, unconditional love." He shook his head. "That is something that cannot be forced, only given freely." He placed a finger under her chin and tilted her face so she would look at him. His kind smile was breathtaking. "My dear child, I need you to help me. You, and the rest of my So'ladiun, must keep the balance between peace and destruction. I know you have doubts, and you will always have doubts. It is a natural thought process, and I understand. But know this, when in doubt, all you have to do is just talk to me. I will listen."

"But am I worthy?" she asked.

"You are more than worthy."

Elhrin jerked her head up, startled by a bird singing close to her ear. It flitted off into the trees when she moved. Blinking her vision into focus, she realized she was back in the woods of the Northreach Mountains. The sun had risen, and light filtered through the canopy of the forest overhead. Smiling to herself, she could not believe that she had just met the God of Light. She knew enough now to realize what she had just experienced was no mere dream. Her heart felt lighter than air. It was no wonder Master Gryph had done what he did his entire life because she now knew that there was nothing she would not do for Solisius. She unfolded herself and stood up to stretch the cramps out of her legs. She took a deep breath. She was so ashamed of what she had said to Master Gryph and Marguerite. They had not deserved her spiteful words.

Bracing herself for the apology she had to make, she slipped through the trees back to their camp. Everyone was sitting around the fire except Master Gryph. Tomas saw her coming and stood up to meet her.

"Hey, I was worried about you. Are you all right?" he asked.

"Yes, I just needed some time to think, and now I have some apologizing to do."

She crouched down beside Marguerite. "Marguerite, can you forgive me? I am so sorry about what I said. I didn't mean to hurt you."

"I know, dear," Marguerite smiled, reassuringly. "You are under a lot of pressure. Don't worry. Everything is fine."

"Where is Master Gryph?" Elhrin asked, and started to send out her senses to locate him.

"He is behind you," Marguerite nodded.

Master Gryph walked through the trees from the same direction she had just come from.

"He followed you into the woods to keep watch," Marguerite whispered.

Elhrin stood up, feeling a little nervous, but he just smiled at her as if nothing had happened. She returned his smile.

"You good?" he asked, his eyes crinkled as he smiled wider, knowing like no other what she had just experienced.

"I'm excellent," she beamed.

He winked with a nod, and just like that, all was right again.

Chapter Twenty-One

"Shhh, we don't want to scare him. Do you have him in your sights?" Fuller whispered. "He is just beyond the bush in front of the fallen tree."

"A limb is blocking my view," Bayle whispered, his arms shaking from the strain of holding the bow string taut.

"He's moving, just wait. When you get a clear shot, just release your fingers, don't jerk the bow."

"I see him now," Bayle whispered, sighting down the long shaft of the arrow. He released the string. The arrow flew straight and true, embedding itself into the side of a tom turkey, instantly killing it.

"Woo hoo!" Bayle whooped with excitement. "I did it!"

Fuller whistled in appreciation. "You sure did. Let's go take a look."

The dead turkey lay on its side amongst the scattering of brown leaves. Fuller picked it up by its feet and judged its weight.

"He's a fat one. We'll eat well tonight," he said. "Let's get moving. We took longer than we were supposed to."

The two of them headed due east, following the discreet signs Jag left indicating the direction the rest of their group had taken after Fuller had heard the turkey sound off in the distance and wanted to see if he could find it. Marguerite had protested, but Master Gryph said he thought it was safe enough, and gave them a half-hour to find the bird before they needed to catch up with the group.

For nearly an hour, Fuller and Bayle hiked down slope, towards a valley. As they neared the bottom, they began to hear the roar of a waterfall, and Fuller found a narrow trail that woodland animals had carved into the earth. He followed the trail until it took them past the tree line and onto a rocky ridge overlooking the waterfall. A river cascaded over rock to their right and fell far below into a large clear pool with a sandy bottom before it continued on its way downward into a wide valley.

"There they are," Bayle said, pointing to where the others were resting on a sandbar by the pool.

Fuller put two fingers to his lips and produced a loud whistle. The group looked up. Bayle waved and they returned his wave.

"Come on, I think the animal track will lead us down," Fuller said.

When they reached the bottom, Marguerite was surprised by the size of the bird Fuller carried. "Will you look at that? Nice bird, boys," she said.

"Bayle shot him," he held up the turkey.

"Well, well, Bayle, you are becoming an expert huntsman," she said, smiling.

Bayle blushed at the praise, shrugging his shoulders.

"Excellent," Master Gryph said, gazing up at the afternoon sky, gauging the amount of time before dusk. "Let's camp here for the night, and get an early start tomorrow." He surveyed the wide pool of water then shot a mischievous glance at Bayle. "I bet there is a fat one in there with my name on it. It's time to teach you how a real fisherman can land a big one without cheating."

Bayle snorted, "In your dreams, old man."

"Leave it to you to grasp for a reason to fish. If we are going to stop," Marguerite looked down river, "I think I would like to wash off." She slung her pack across her shoulder and headed downstream.

"You know, she doesn't need to go off alone, and I could use a little cleaning up as well," Master Gryph said, watching Marguerite pick her way down stream. He winked at Bayle. "Your lesson will have to wait."

"I'll be here," Bayle grinned. "Of course, I don't expect you could teach me anything other than how to drown a worm."

"Is that so?" Master Gryph asked as he stooped to pick up his pack.

Bayle shrugged his shoulders.

"Well, we'll see about that won't we, boy?" Master Gryph smacked Bayle on the back when he passed. "In the meantime, I suggest you pluck the turkey in a hurry because when I get back, your lesson will begin."

Bayle groaned. He liked plucking birds just as much as he liked cleaning fish.

"Have fun," Master Gryph grinned and started to whistle a jaunty tune as he headed down river.

A short time later, Elhrin sat on the sandbar beside the pool, smelling the mouth-watering aroma coming from the chunks of turkey meat Fuller was cooking over the fire. She glanced sidelong at Tomas who was using a stick to draw circles in the sand, liking that he had shaved off his whiskers when she had taken a turn downriver to wash the dirt off her body in its frigid waters. She reached over to trail a fingertip across his jaw line. "I think I like you better without the beard," she said.

"I'll have to remember that," he said, smiling as laughter echoed from across the pool. "I tend to let it go sometimes."

Master Gryph pulled a large trout out of the water. "Ha! Beat this, boy," he called out, holding the fish up so Bayle could see from his spot further down the shoreline.

"You probably cheated," Bayle raised his voice to be heard over the waterfall.

"I did not, you impetuous imp," Master Gryph replied, grinning as he took the hook out of the fish. "Marguerite, do you want me to keep him?"

Marguerite had been half-asleep by the fire and glanced at him when she heard her name. "That depends on if you want to clean him or not," she said, standing up and dusting sand off her trousers. "I think we will have enough with the turkey."

Master Gryph nodded and released the trout back into the pool.

Elhrin sighed.

"What's that for?" Tomas asked. "Did you want him to keep it?"

"No," she grinned, and leaned back to prop herself on her hands. The sand beneath her palms was cool and soft as downy fur. "I was thinking that it's so peaceful here. I almost wish we could stay."

"That would be nice. What are you going to do when this is over? Will you go back to Glimmerdale?" Tomas asked. He picked up a smooth river stone that his stick had worked out of the sand.

"If I survive," she said, wistfully.

He grabbed her knee. "Don't do that," he frowned. "You defeat yourself before the enemy has the chance when you do that. Don't give them that power. We are going to survive this."

She smiled at him. "You sound like Master Gryph."

"Well, fighting men learn early your mental state is extremely important. If you go looking for death, it will find you."

She nodded in agreement, watching him skim the stone. It skipped five times before sinking.

"Impressive," she said, and hunted around her for a nice flat rock. She dislodged a small round rock from the sand and threw it across the water, but it thudded into the surface with a splash and sunk.

"You have to hold it like this and throw it parallel to the surface," he skimmed another stone, and she counted seven skips.

"Now I think you are showing off."

"You caught me," he grinned like a little boy. "How else am I going to impress a girl who has magic powers?"

"Hmm," she narrowed her eyes, "I can think of a way." She pointed at her lips.

Tomas' eyes widened and he shook his head as if she had lost her mind for suggesting such a thing. "No way, madam, there is one other person with magical powers nearby who frowns upon me kissing you and I happen to like living. You will have to wait."

Elhrin pursed her lips in a mock pout. "Coward."

"Yes, and I am not ashamed," he straightened his back and placed a hand over his heart, "to admit it."

Elhrin pushed him with a laugh. He fell back into the sand.

A loud whoop of laughter rolled over the pool, echoing off the cliffs rising around them. "Oh, yeah! Look at the size of this, Master Magician," Bayle yelled, pulling in a large wriggling trout. "I believe he could eat yours for breakfast."

Amused, Master Gryph stood with his improvised limb fishing pole on one hip, rolling his eyes as Bayle did a little celebratory jig.

"Enjoy it now, son. I'm not done yet," he warned.

"You might as well be, old man, because there isn't a bigger fish in this pool," Bayle taunted, unhooking the fish and holding it high in the air.

"Oh, yes, there is," Master Gryph said, and waved his right hand.

Bayle was jerked into the air by an unseen force. "Whoa!" Bayle yelped in surprise as he was thrown spread-eagle into the middle of the pool, disappearing under the surface with a splash. His fish smacked into the water near the waterfall.

"Gryph, what did you do that for?" Marguerite tried to keep a straight face as she placed her hands on her hips. "His clothes were finally dry."

"You know I don't tolerate rude behavior," he said with a grin.

Everyone was howling with laughter, even Kyne managed the first smile Elhrin had witnessed on his face. It changed him dramatically—made him almost . . . handsome? Elhrin shook herself out of that strange thought and turned her attention back to the water just as Bayle surfaced, tossing his head and sending a broad spray of water across the pool.

"I see how it is now," Bayle glared at Master Gryph, treading water. "You can't win, so you have to take out the competition."

"No, I just wanted you to get a closer look at the fish I'm about to catch," Master Gryph said, as Bayle swam back to the shore. "And you might want to reconsider the next time you want to call me an old man."

Elhrin couldn't quit laughing and had to wipe away tears that rolled down her face.

"Now, that was funny," Tomas said, trying to catch his breath. "What's it like to be able to do magic?" He reached over to clasp her hand and began to caress it with his thumb.

"Oh, I don't know, it's fun sometimes, I guess," she said, watching Bayle climb out of the water, and trying not to think about what Tomas was doing with her hand. "Then there are the times, like yesterday, that it's not. I really don't know how to describe it because I don't know what it's like to not be able to do it."

Tomas squeezed her hand. "I know the fight yesterday was hard for you. The first time I had to kill someone I couldn't sleep for a week. I still have nightmares sometimes."

"When was your . . . ?" she started to ask when a slight tingling brushed on the edge of her awareness. She felt slightly ill. Someone with strong magical energy was in the area, but not close, she thought. She grunted in frustration at her inexperience, wishing she could grasp onto the feeling better. She glanced across the pool to see Master Gryph frowning in the direction of the mountain behind her. Elhrin rose to her feet and faced the mountain, trying harder to focus on the sensation that was somehow familiar.

"Elhrin, what is it?" Tomas asked, rising to his feet.

"I don't know, yet," she tried to concentrate, but the feeling was slowly fading away from her. She couldn't hold onto it. She looked over her shoulder at Master Gryph. He dropped his gaze from the mountain and looked at her.

"It seems someone is interested in finding out where we are," he said, raising his voice to be heard over the roar of the waterfall.

"Was it Cynder?" she asked.

"That would be my guess. He is powerful enough to be felt at long distances, but you would be more familiar with the N'gethwyn's energy than me. I haven't had the pleasure of meeting him, yet," he said, flicking his line back and forth across the water before letting it settle, seeming unworried about Cynder being in the area.

"I wish I could say the same," she replied. He flashed a small smile her way.

"Gryph, do we need to leave?" Marguerite asked.

"No, we are safe for now. He was well west of us and moved off to the north back out of my range. If he is searching for us it doesn't look like he knows which direction we went, and is probably guessing we took the easier route past the mine."

"What about the fire?"

He glanced at the light trail of white smoke that swirled upward. "Leave it for now, but keep it small. The wind seems to be dissipating the smoke as it rises, and he moved away from us, so I don't think he noticed it. If he comes back, I'll know in enough time for us to move out," he said, and realized something was tugging on his line. He pulled back on the pole and set the hook. "Bayle, look out. You are going to be jealous of this one."

Chuckling to himself he pulled in his line, taking his time. Elhrin could tell he was keeping them in suspense on purpose, and when he pulled his fish out of the water everyone burst out laughing. Bayle doubled over, laughing so hard he couldn't catch his breath. Master Gryph held up a fish smaller than his hand.

"I didn't realize you fished for bait, old . . ." Bayle howled, but stopped when Master Gryph pointed at him. Bayle's eyes grew wide and he ran behind a nearby tree to hide. It was Master Gryph's turn to laugh.

"What did he do to Bayle this time?" Tomas asked Elhrin.

Bayle cautiously peeked from around the tree.

"He didn't do anything. Bayle just thought he was going to," Elhrin said, grinning. "Bayle doesn't realize the tree won't protect him if Master Gryph really wanted to do something."

"What do you mean?" he asked, grabbing her hand and guiding her down river, away from the pool.

"Sometimes we can bend the flow of energy, depending on what we are trying to do. Master Gryph could actually pick Bayle up from behind that tree if he wanted to, and move him. But he can only hold him for so long because Bayle's weight would be a strain, and after a while he would have to let the flow of energy go."

"Could he send those blue exploding things, whatever they are, around something to hit a target?" he asked, helping her step over some rocks.

"No, the energy orbs are pretty much like an arrow. We have to aim, and once they are released, we have very little control of their direction," she said, and stopped to point down the river. "Look, Tomas."

A black bear with a cub drank from the river downstream.

"I think we better not go any further, I don't want to upset the mother. She might get a little protective of her baby," he said, as they watched the bears drink, then the mother glanced their way. "Don't move," he whispered, sliding an arm around her waist.

The mother sniffed the air, testing for danger, then turned and hurried into the forest. The cub followed right on her heels.

Tomas faced Elhrin, and with a quick glance upriver to see that they were out of view of the others, he leaned down to kiss her. Elhrin wrapped her arms around him, stepping close to meld their bodies together. He held nothing back. His lips tore into hers as if he could not get close enough. He raked a hand into her hair, pushing the back of her head closer. Elhrin felt consumed, like standing blissfully inside an out of control whirlwind, her heart beating so hard she thought it would burst. She broke the kiss to catch her breath.

"I have wanted to do that for so long I thought I was going to go mad," Tomas said hoarsely.

"We can't have that happen," she panted, tilting her head back, offering herself to him.

He smiled and complied—this time with slow deliberation.

While their lips explored and tasted, she felt his hands slide down her back and tighten, pulling her closer to him. A low almost silent groan of satisfaction came from deep inside his throat and he left her mouth to caress her cheek, sliding down to nip at her neck. Chills of pleasure rippled through her, making her feel weak.

"You taste so good," he said, his voice muffled against her neck as he moved back up to suckle her earlobe.

A yearning she did not recognize set her ablaze, coherent thought left her replacing it with raw carnal need. She squeezed Tomas closer. He could not hide his desire.

She gasped when the tip of his tongue flicked across her lobe and his hands slipped to her buttocks gripping her tight to him. A burst of fire sped downward like lightning striking its mark. Desire spiraled upward. Tingling intensified.

Oh no! her mind screamed. Rational thought ripped through her mind, realizing what she was now feeling was not only her feelings for Tomas.

She tried to pull away. "Tomas," she croaked, her voice did not want to work.

"What is it? Did I hurt you?" he asked, taking her lobe once again between his lips.

Why now? She tried to push him again, but he stood firm. "No, Tomas, he's coming." She tried to back away, but he held her fast.

"Who's coming," he murmured, not comprehending what she was saying.

"Master Gryph is coming."

Tomas released her so suddenly she stumbled backward, but was glad because it put a decent distance between them as Master Gryph stepped up on a rock and pinned them both with a frigid gaze. He may not have seen, but it was obvious he knew what they had been doing.

Tomas turned slightly so his back was facing Master Gryph. Elhrin crossed her arms over her chest, trying to look as if they had been standing there innocently talking.

"It's time to eat," Master Gryph said, slow and even. He made a point of speaking directly to Tomas, and then without another word he turned to go back to the campsite.

"Whew," Tomas blew out a pent up breath. "He is going to kill me."

"No," she said, smiling at him. "He won't kill you, but you might want to consider being ready in case he decides to throw you into the pool like Bayle or hang you by your britches high in a tree."

Tomas eyed her steadily. "You aren't kidding, are you?"

"I'm afraid not," she laughed as they picked their way back upstream. "Ask Bayle how much fun hanging an entire afternoon in a tree is."

By the time they finished their meal, the sun had slipped behind the mountains, leaving a brilliant red sky dotted with purple-hued clouds. Sitting by the campfire, Elhrin had a hard time keeping her eyes open after eating more than she was accustomed to. She yawned wide, cracking her jaw in the process. Tomas chuckled when he heard her bone pop and reached over to rub her back.

"Mmm, that feels good," she sighed. "A little lower, please."

Fuller stood up and picked up his bow. "I'll go up and take a look around on this side," he pointed his bow back up the mountain above them.

"Sounds good," Jag replied, looping his quiver strap over his head. "I'll cross over and take the other side. We'll be back in a bit."

"Very good, lads," Master Gryph said as they parted in two different directions.

Elhrin followed Jag's progress as he crossed the stream a short way down, using rocks protruding out of the water. Her eyes inadvertently fell on Kyne. The socially reclusive man had placed himself just outside the circle of the fire and had his eyes closed, pretending sleep, but she knew he was not asleep. She had caught him periodically opening his eyes a mere slit to look at her as if he was afraid she would jump up and run away. Now there was a thought. She would love to run all the way to the other side of the world if she could to avoid taking one more step closer to Blackridge.

"Take that, you monster," Bayle said as he swished his sword at an unseen foe. He had jumped up immediately after eating, deciding to practice his sword skills near the base of the waterfall. "Oh, you have friends? That is nothing to Sir Bayle the Great," Bayle growled. He pivoted on his heel and swung at a bush growing out of a tumble of rocks, lopping off a dangling limb full of waxy green leaves. It plopped onto the sand, dead by his sword. "Do not challenge me, rogues," Bayle said to the bush, and whacked at another limb.

Master Gryph snorted at Bayle's running commentary of his fight. He suddenly stood up, picked up his sword from where it lay on top of his pack and crossed the sand to join Bayle.

"Do you think you could give an old man a workout without slicing me in half?" he asked.

Bayle was surprised by his request. "Um, I can try."

"You can try? I think I would rather hear you say that you could without a doubt."

"Right, sure I can, but I have never practiced with anyone who was left-handed," Bayle said, raising his sword.

"It will seem awkward, but the same principles apply. Do not leave your left side open or swing too wide. When you are ready," he said, taking a defensive stance.

Bayle swung and Master Gryph met him with the ringing of steel bouncing off the exposed rock face of the surrounding cliffs. Back and forth they traded swings, easy at first as Bayle accustomed himself to Master Gryph's style, then they became more serious. The concentration on Bayle's face was fierce, and as the match went on, it was apparent that he was surprised to find Master Gryph was no stranger to the sword, thinking he only used magic to fight opponents and the sword was for show.

They circled each other on the narrow, sandy spit of land, trading swings, until Bayle advanced with a miscalculated high swing aimed at Master Gryph's head. Master Gryph blocked it before it reached him and raised his eyebrows, questioning the move.

"Sorry," Bayle apologized breathlessly, and lowered his sword. "I need to stop."

Both of them stepped back, breathing hard from the exertion of the fight.

"Not bad," Master Gryph commented. "Who have you been practicing with?"

"Master Toome."

"I thought some of your moves seemed familiar," he said.

Kyne stood up and crossed the sand. "How do you feel about another round?"

Master Gryph shrugged out of his coat and tossed it to Bayle. "All right, but go easy on me. Bayle has nearly worn me out."

"I'll think about it," Kyne said, and without warning, drew his sword and launched at Master Gryph as if he were a sworn enemy.

The two swords rang loud as Master Gryph deftly defended himself from Kyne's attack.

"Goodness, he doesn't play around, does he?" Marguerite said, frowning.

Kyne's attack was fierce and without mercy. Elhrin leaned forward with concern. The fight did not take on the air of practice between comrades. "I don't like this," she whispered, and rose to her feet. If Kyne made one wrong move, she was going to be ready.

Tomas stood beside her. "He is good," Tomas whispered in her ear, referring to Kyne, "but the minister is better. See how he keeps Kyne off center?"

"Yes, but why is he fighting as if he means to draw blood?"

"An enemy means to draw blood. Practicing any differently would do no good. I think both of them are skilled enough to withhold a blow if one makes a mistake."

Elhrin grunted under her breath, still not liking the ferocity of the fight. It looked to her like Kyne meant to kill Master Gryph.

Kyne advanced with a swing that narrowly missed slicing Master Gryph's chest, but he bent back out of the way in time. Master Gryph then moved sideways and Kyne attacked again. Their swords locked together in a grinding hiss. The two stared at each other for a moment, sweat poured from their brows. Suddenly, Kyne pushed Master Gryph back off balance. He grimaced in pain when he planted his left foot. Kyne took advantage of the opening he had created, and swung his sword low, but Master Gryph recovered quickly and met it in another deadlock of blades. Master Gryph cocked his head, smiled, and twisted the blades. The move sent Kyne's sword flying out of his hand to land with a thud near the edge of the water.

Kyne was surprised at the move, and frowned at his sword lying in the sand for a moment then glanced at Master Gryph. He slowly smiled a genuine smile without contempt or malice. "Now that was fun."

Master Gryph nodded and clapped him on the back. "Thanks for the workout, son. I'm done," he said, wiping sweat from his brow with his sleeve. His limp was more noticeable as he walked back to the fire. "Elhrin, will you bring me your book?" he asked as he passed her and sat down with a grunt. Grimacing, he rubbed his left knee.

"Yes, sir," she said bending over to rummage through her pack, relieved that the fight was over. She shot a glare at Kyne, letting him know just what she thought about his hostile actions when he walked past her.

He snorted at her in contempt, understanding the look, but not caring about her thoughts, and returned to his spot well away from the fire.

"There was something I wanted to show you this morning, but I never had the chance," Master Gryph said, as she stood up and walked around the fire.

She handed him the book. "I'm sorry . . . about this morning," she apologized.

He gave her a brief smile. "That is done." He opened the book and flipped through its pages. "Let's see. Where are the writings of Ethelred Pentavyn? Ah, here we are," he said, stopping at a page with sketchy handwriting. He glanced up at her. "Why are you standing there? Sit down."

Elhrin settled in beside him as he reached inside his shirt and pulled out a pendant that was identical to hers, only his was a pure white, almost translucent gem with a noticeable dim glow inside.

"Where did you get that?" she asked, marveling at its perfect beauty.

"Solisius gave this to me before I left his realm," he said, turning the gem between two fingers. "A going away gift, I suppose. Or maybe it would be more accurate to say it was a coming alive gift."

She snorted at his joke.

Marguerite grunted with disgust. "Gryph, I don't think I like it when you make jokes about being dead."

"Sorry, dear," he said patting her arm. He leaned over to whisper to Elhrin. "I'm afraid Marguerite has lost her sense of humor with old age."

"I heard that," Marguerite growled. "Old man," she added after a moment.

Master Gryph and Elhrin exchanged grins. He then turned his attention back to the book. "Have you read the writings of Ethelred?"

"Was he the one who helped to stop an uprising against the crown in the city of Yradin during the reign of Vikor Muryne the Second?" she asked.

"Yes, he was."

"He disappeared without a trace not long after that, didn't he?"

"That is correct. Now, did you use your pendant with his writings?"

"No, I never got that far when I was going through the book with it," she said.

"Okay, sit where you can see."

She moved closer, and his pendant began to shine an eye-piercing, radiant white. She shielded her eyes from the glare.

"What is that?" Tomas asked.

"Just a little toy I have. Magnificent, isn't it?" Master Gryph said, moving it so it did not blind Elhrin.

"I'd say," he said.

"Elhrin, pay attention." Master Gryph nudged her with his elbow.

"I was, you weren't," she pointed out, as she watched an image focus into sharp detail on the page. It was a thick, woodsy swamp filled with moss-draped cypress trees. Their fat roots were firmly entrenched in black water on either side of a single muddy track that was barely wide enough for a wagon to use. The view changed to show a helmetless middle-aged man with close-cropped hair the color of wheat riding a roan horse. Plodding close behind him was a small group of cavalry from the King's Army. The scene felt eerie to Elhrin and the riders must have felt the same way. They looked uneasy as if expecting something to rise up out of the black water at any moment.

Abruptly, the horses began to rear and panic, and Ethelred and the soldiers worked to bring them under control. The view of the page shifted so that Elhrin now saw the road snake further into the dark swamp and the troop of men were behind her.

"Why are the horses panicking?" she asked just as a fine sliver of red appeared in midair above the road and ripped downward to the ground like a tear in a length of fabric. With a deafening roar, the line began to widen and increase to a size not much bigger than one of the soldiers on his horse, revealing a swirling mass of crackling red energy. The scene backed out so she could see Ethelred and his men and the swirling mass of energy on the page.

The men lost control of their horses. Ethelred was tossed from his saddle, landing heavily a short distance away as his terrified horse disappeared into the swamp.

"Get up, get up," Elhrin murmured, but Ethelred remained motionless.

Two more soldiers suffered the same fate. One crashed into a tree and fell lifeless into the black water. The other man dropped to the road and had to roll across the ground to avoid being trampled by his own horse.

The mass of swirling red energy roared to life, and out stepped three Do'athrim wolven equipped with bows that were already drawn. They fired immediately into the chaos, and two soldiers were ripped from their saddles, dead before they hit the ground.

The soldier on the road yanked out his sword and rushed the creatures. The middle Do'athrim calmly loaded his bow and fired, almost nonchalantly, catching the soldier in the chest and knocking him off his feet from the impact the arrow made at such close range. The remaining soldier tried desperately to retrieve his sword, but found it difficult with his horse in such a panicked state. He gave up and decided to let the horse have his head. The beast raced away from the scene tearing up the road. Sprays of wet mud flew far and wide as his hooves churned through the muck in its desperation to get away.

One of the Do'athrim laughed, and it sounded more like a maniacal growl as he raised his bow, sighted the retreating soldier and fired. The arrow caught the man in the back, throwing him forward to slump lifeless on the horse's neck as it ran out of sight.

Pleased with themselves, the Do'athrim spoke to each other in a language consisting of yips and growls, and one of them walked over to the motionless magician and grabbed him by his arm.

Ethelred moaned.

"He's alive," Elhrin whispered.

The beast dragged the man across the road like a full sack of grain and disappeared into the swirling mass of energy, followed by his companions, and as quickly as it had come, the mass of energy winked out of sight, sounding like a thunderclap.

The light within Master Gryph's pendant faded back to its original state.

"What happened to him?" she asked softly.

"I imagine Obsudius sent him to the Void," his voice was edged with a hint of sadness.

"So, that is what a Rift looks like?"

"Yes, and that is what you are going to have to look for once inside the keep." He closed the book.

"What I am going to look for? Are you not going to be with me?"

"I hope to be, but even if I am, I will not be able to help you with the Rift. That task is yours alone," he said.

Elhrin felt like her stomach had sunk to the inside of her boots. "What are you going to be doing?" she asked.

He stared into the fire and didn't answer her.

"Gryph, what are you going to be doing?" Marguerite echoed the question.

He glanced at Marguerite. "I am going to take care of Cynder. He is too powerful to ever be given the chance to come back in this world again."

"What do you mean by that?" Marguerite asked.

"Even if Elhrin closes this portal, Obsudius will be able to open another sometime down the line. If that happens, then as you know, Cynder will be able to come through again."

"He will be able to open one again? What if he does it right after I close it?" Elhrin asked.

"If all goes well he shouldn't be able to that soon," he said. "He will need some time. It takes a tremendous amount of energy for him to tear a hole between the planes of the spirit world and living world, and then maintain it. One on the scale that he has now must be an incredible strain on him, and eventually, he will have to close it himself. Even a god such as he has limits."

Elhrin had a hard time grasping the fact that a god could be restricted in capabilities. She always thought they were unlimited and all powerful. "So, what are you going to do to keep Cynder from coming out again if we manage to kill him?" she asked.

"Don't worry, I have a plan. All you have to do is close the Rift as quickly as you can," he said.

"How do I do that? You haven't told me how to close it," she said.

He touched her on her chest just below her neck with his finger, and she looked down. At first she thought he meant something profound, like for her to go with her heart, but then realized that he was touching her pendant. "My pendant?"

He lifted one side of his mouth, but the look in his eyes was unfamiliar to her. "You have the power."

"How? I thought all it could do is show me the past in the book," she said, wondering what that look was for.

"That isn't all it can do. The pendant is a gift from Solisius, and I think I told you before he instilled it with certain powers which come directly from him. Even though he and Obsudius are twin brothers, they are exact opposites, and their powers offset. If you use Solisius' magic on the Rift, it will work against Obsudius' powers to tear it apart."

"Why can't Solisius do this himself?" Tomas asked.

"Because closing the Rift has to be done from either our side, or within Do'athra, and Solisius cannot enter either place. If a god were to physically step foot on our world, his presence would destroy it. That is why he has people like Elhrin and I to carry out his wishes. Another reason he cannot enter Obsudius' realm is because of the law of separation their father, the Creator of the Universe, set down when he gave them this world to watch over. He recognized the darkness in Obsudius and the hate his son felt for Solisius, but he loves both his sons and wants them to have a place in the universe. So, in order to maintain a balance between them, he separated them into their own domains, knowing that if he allowed them direct access to each other they would fight and their powers would not only destroy each other, but the world as well."

"So how do I use the pendant to close it?" Elhrin asked.

He patted her knee. "You will know when the time comes."

"You have got to be kidding me?" she asked, stunned. "That is your answer?"

"That is my answer, and it is the best one I can give." He handed her the book. "Tomas, you and I will take over the watch when Jag and Fuller return. The rest of you should get your rest. We need to start a little earlier tomorrow if we can."

Astounded, she could not believe he had not given her a better answer, but she had to smile when she looked at Tomas' face. He was afraid of being alone with Master Gryph, and looked as if someone had just told him he was about to be executed.

Chapter Twenty-Two

After four rigorous days of hiking since leaving the peaceful setting of the waterfall, they found themselves high on a mountainside overlooking a rocky gorge that ran out of sight to the north and south and blocked their path east. Far below, a river ran through the middle of the gorge, its dark waters silent as it flowed by the craggy cliffs.

A strong wind surged around them and whipped Elhrin's hair into her eyes. She tucked the loose strands behind both ears, but it was useless. The wind jerked her hair loose once more and it flew right back across her eyes. She gave up and endured the uncontrollable torture.

"What do we do now?" Fuller asked, stepping forward to peer over the side of the cliff.

"We are going to have to go north or south. There's not a safe way to go down and then back up the other side." Jag had to raise his voice to be heard over the howl of the wind. "Minister, which direction do you wish to take?"

Master Gryph was standing off by himself, his long cloak billowing around him like a black flag as he scanned the mountains to the north. He pointed to the gorge. "How far does this run north?"

"Almost to the edge of the mountain range. Those that I know who roam this part of the mountain range never bother with the middle gorge area. They say the terrain is so rough it is not worth the bother. Personally, I have only skirted the northern and southern edges a few times. I'm not sure what we will face."

"And if we decide to go south?"

"It might be a little easier with the southern peaks being smaller, but not by much. The only problem is that it would add several days just to get to a crossing point then several more to get back there," Jag pointed directly across the gorge from them.

Master Gryph nodded. "North it is," he said.

Hours later, and many cuts, bumps, bruises, and a few choice words from every member of the party, they found themselves extremely tired and only a few miles from where they had started.

"Damn," Master Gryph muttered under his breath when he jumped down a short drop, and limped in a painful circle to walk it off. He then turned to wait on Marguerite to jump.

"Regretting your decision, Gryph?" Marguerite asked. She landed in front of him and he caught her arm to steady her.

"No, why do you ask?" He let her go and reached down to rub his left knee.

"Because you keep grumbling. Is your leg bothering you?"

"A bit," he said, and moved down the path Jag was taking, his limp definitely more noticeable.

"Do you need to stop?" she asked. "I can wrap it for you."

That brought him to a halt. He turned and gave her a look that spoke volumes as to what he was thinking. He did not want her mothering him.

She held up her hands in surrender. "Right, forget I said anything."

Without a word, he turned and limped after the others.

"Stubborn ass," Marguerite mumbled under her breath as Elhrin landed beside her. "Hurt then."

Elhrin grinned at her comment.

"Don't you tell him I said that," Marguerite said, with a little laugh.

"I won't," Elhrin promised.

The path Jag took from there zigzagged up and over craggy rock mounds and between trees that swayed dangerously back and forth from the high winds gusting up out of the gorge to their right. She kept one eye above her just in case something decided to snap and fall. They then slid down into a wide, washed out gully filled with broken shale and climbed out the other side where they faced a thick tangle of mountain laurel.

"Jag, I hate to say it, man, but could you find a harder way to go? This is too easy," Fuller huffed out of breath. He leaned over and rested his hands on his knees, spitting a glob of saliva between his boots.

Jag grunted a short laugh. "I told you it was going to be rough."

Fuller raised his head to look at the tall, dark man. "Lie next time."

"All right, men," Master Gryph breathed heavily, nodding at the next obstacle to overcome, "let's get this over with."

He led the way through the mass of gnarled limbs. When they emerged out into the open once more, they faced a worse situation. The sheer face of a rock wall loomed up ahead and blocked their way.

Jag surveyed the area as they moved closer to the cliff. They were boxed in by the cliff, the laurel, and the gorge. "It is either up or double back and head west to see if we can get around another way."

Master Gryph studied the cliff rising above them. It was nearly as tall as a three story building. He shot a questioning look at Kyne. "Son, we can do this one of two ways."

"You are not lifting me up," Kyne said quickly, understanding. "This is nothing." He removed his sword from his side and secured it on his pack, then walked along the wall until he found a spot that suited him and began to climb.

Locating hand and foot holds that Elhrin would have sworn couldn't hold him, he scaled the rock face. The wind howled around him, threatening to tear him away from his precarious hold on the slits and crevices he used to pull himself up. Halfway to the top, a sudden gust of wind pushed hard against him and his foot slipped. Elhrin held her breath as he froze, then he gingerly felt with his foot until he found another place that would hold him. He inched his way over to an angled split in the rock and used it to work his way up to a narrow ledge not far from the top. Scanning the remaining rock between him and the ridge, he tested a sapling pine growing out of a crevice for strength. Satisfied that it would hold him, he hauled himself up to the next handhold and strained to reach a ledge near the top. Grasping it with what looked like the tips of his fingers, he managed to reach up with his other hand and start to haul his body upwards. His boots slipped and scraped the side of the cliff as he tried to use his feet to help push him up. At first she thought he was losing his grip, but then he made one last surge upward. His foot caught on something solid and he used it to push his upper body over the top. He lifted his legs and rolled out of sight.

Elhrin let out the breath she had been unaware she had been holding, surprised to find that she had been concerned for his safety.

A few minutes later, a rope sailed over the side and snaked downward to dangle from where Kyne had secured it above. He peered over the edge. "Anytime you are ready," he called.

"Elhrin, you go first," Master Gryph said, grasping the bottom of the rope and holding it steady. "Unless, you want me to lift you."

"No, I'll try it," she said, knowing he didn't need to waste his magical energy if there was another way. She wrapped both hands around the rope high above her head. "But catch me if I fall."

"You can bet on it," he replied.

She pulled her weight off the ground and planted her boots against the hard surface of the cliff. Slowly, she inched up the wall. Halfway to the top she felt a tug on the rope below and looked down to see Tomas start up behind her, his weight pulling the rope taut.

"I know it's pulling, but keep going," he said, looking up.

She continued up the wall, her arms screaming for relief. It felt like forever and a day before she finally made it to the top and Kyne reached down to haul her to safety. She rolled away from the edge lying on her back as her lungs heaved to bring in life-giving air.

Tomas clambered over the side and climbed to his feet, waiting on the next person up the rope. "Nothing to it," he breathed with a smile.

"If you say so," she wiped the trails of sweat off her brow and sat up.

Marguerite was next. Tomas and Kyne grabbed her arms to haul her up, standing her on her feet. Then Fuller and Jag clambered over the edge one right after the other.

"Look out!" Kyne yelled.

Elhrin's heart leapt into her throat as she heard Bayle cry out in pain. She scrambled on hands and knees to look over the side as Jag and Fuller ripped their bows off their backs and jerked arrows out of their quivers.

Midway down the rope, Master Gryph had a firm grip on Bayle's leg, straining to hang onto the young boy as he dangled helplessly upside down with an arrow lodged in one of his forearms. The rope swung erratically back and forth, making it difficult for Master Gryph to steady the both of them with his legs.

Yips and growls came out of the trees below. Several Do'athrim flitted from tree to tree, stopping only long enough to take aim and fire at Master Gryph and Bayle.

"Bayle!" she screamed as the arrows sped through the air and pinged off the rock face, narrowly missing Master Gryph. Jag and Fuller returned fire at the attackers, but the wind gusting up the cliff face worked against them. The arrows flew in a drunken spin, missing their targets.

"How in the world did he catch up with us this fast?" Marguerite spat out.

Elhrin caught sight of a huge black wolf using a tree for cover. *Damn him!* She fired a flaming ball of energy at him. The tree trunk exploded in a spray of bark and splinters. The beast ducked and rolled, moving to another trunk. Another volley of arrows shot out of the trees. Elhrin quickly created a shield. The arrows pinged harmlessly away. Jag and Fuller returned fire, making adjustments for the strong wind currents. One Do'athrim made the mistake of stepping from his cover. Fuller's arrow lodged deep into his chest.

"Elhrin, a little help," Master Gryph yelled, "I can't hold him much longer."

"Master Gryph, I can't feel my arm," Bayle cried.

"Hang on, Bayle. Elhrin, did you hear me?" He looked up, his face red from the strain. "You pull and I'll push. I won't be able to do much from here. You'll have to take most of his weight."

Elhrin sent her energy down to envelope Bayle, hoping Jag and Fuller could protect them while she helped bring him to safety. When she felt she had him securely, she pulled upward with her magic, as if she were hauling him up by an invisible rope, and immediately felt the strain of his weight. Grasping and holding someone with magical strands took a huge amount of energy and concentration. She closed her eyes and gritted her teeth, concentrating on not dropping him and trying to block out the dangers coming from the steady volley of arrows being fired up the cliff. Bayle's weight lightened, and she breathed inwardly with relief as the strain lessened, knowing that Master Gryph was using his energy to push from below.

She opened her eyes. Kyne and Tomas had placed themselves beside her, protecting her from danger while she hauled Bayle up the cliff.

"Look out," Kyne jerked sideways deflecting an arrow with his sword—a movement so fast she would have questioned that he actually had done it if Tomas hadn't whistled in appreciation.

She pulled hard on Bayle. She had to get him up the cliff.

"Gryph, hurry," Marguerite yelled.

The beasts were edging closer, braving the danger to get a clearer shot. An arrow shattered beside Master Gryph's head.

Elhrin felt him forcefully push on Bayle, sending him upward rapidly. She had a hard time keeping up.

Arrows zoomed upward and Tomas had to duck just as Bayle reached the precipice. Tomas grabbed Bayle's arm and pack and hauled him over the side to safety. "We got him, Elhrin."

She let him go so that he and Marguerite could drag Bayle away from the edge. She then fired at the first Do'athrim she spotted just as an earsplitting detonation boomed over the mountain. A tree snapped in two, its top fell into the swaying boughs of nearby trees. The Do'athrim, Gryzzl, rolled across the ground and back to his feet, notching another arrow and letting it fly at Master Gryph who was still suspended on the rope below. Master Gryph blocked it magically with a flick of his hand.

Elhrin's flaming mass of energy tore into the side of a tree sending chunks of wood into a Do'athrim's face. He howled in pain, stepping away from protective cover. She shot a comet of fire at him. It hit him in the shoulder, tearing his arm from his body. Screaming, he fell to the ground writhing in pain.

Jag and Fuller's bows twanged simultaneously. An arrow lodged in a tree trunk, the other found its mark as a Do'athrim popped from cover to fire. It sunk deep into the beast's face. He dropped like a stone.

Two remained.

One sidled behind a boulder as Gryzzl slunk through brush to hide behind a fat northern pine. Frenzied growls and yips zipped back and forth between the two. They were not happy.

Elhrin fired on the one behind the rock. Her ball of energy exploded near his head. Chunks of granite flew in all directions. The beast howled in fright, but was not hurt. He ran. Jag and Fuller sighted him in and fired. Despite the erratic flight of their arrows, both hit the beast as he vaulted over a fallen tree—one in the leg, the other in the back of the head, killing him.

Gryzzl was now alone. He shot at Master Gryph, who had been trying to reach the top of the cliff. It thudded into his back and knocked him off balance. He lost his footing and slipped down the rope.

"No," she screamed.

Master Gryph caught himself from falling, but he swung out of control. Another arrow popped into the cliff dangerously close to him. "Kill him!" he roared, trying to regain control of the rope.

Elhrin fired a succession of flaming balls of energy at the beast. One after the other boomed into the tree and ground around him. He couldn't take the pressure. He darted from cover, running for the boulder. Elhrin flung a comet of blue flame at him. It nailed the beast full in the back, exploding in a flash of light. Blood and chunks of flesh sprayed outward like a geyser of red liquid and black fur, obliterating his top half. Only his legs remained.

Elhrin looked over the edge of the cliff. Master Gryph had steadied himself and was slowly climbing up.

"Are you all right?" she called.

"Yes," he grunted. Hauling his large body up the rope after all that strain was difficult.

She saw the arrow had lodged in his pack. Its tip stuck out the other side. She let out a shaky sigh of relief.

"Give me a hand," Kyne yelled at Jag and Fuller. He grasped the rope to pull Master Gryph up.

"Bayle, swallow more," Marguerite said. Her voice shook, unable to hide how scared she was.

Elhrin left the men and hurried to her brother's side. What she saw sent absolute terror into her soul. His face was beyond pale, almost blue, and his teeth chattered as if he were in below freezing temperatures. The arrow had penetrated completely through his left forearm, and Marguerite had tied a strip of cloth tight around his arm above the elbow.

Bayle's eyes, wild with fear, searched around until he saw her beside him. "Elhrin, I can't feel anything," he whimpered. Tears streamed out of the corners of his eyes, trailing downward into his sweat-dampened hair.

"Hold on, Bayle, it's going to be okay," she said, glancing at Marguerite, hoping to have her confirm it.

"I don't know. We have never used the antidote before," she whispered.

Never used it before? Elhrin bit back a scream of frustration.

"The wounded one is hidden. I can't get him with my bow," Jag called out.

"I'll take care of him in a moment. He isn't going anywhere," Master Gryph said as he and the boys joined them. He jerked off his pack and tossed it down in anger. He knelt beside Marguerite. "Did you give it to him?"

Marguerite nodded.

"Jag, you and the boys search the area. We are going to need a place out of the open," he said, picking up Bayle's injured arm. "Son, I am going to take the arrow out of your arm."

Elhrin had to close her eyes when he snapped the arrow in two and pulled it out of Bayle's arm, afraid she might faint.

Marguerite went to work dressing the wound as Elhrin held Bayle's other hand. He was so cold to the touch.

Please, Solisius, don't let my brother die.

A strong gust of wind swirled around her, circling her like the embrace of a friend.

Master Gryph shot her a quick glance as if he had heard her prayer.

"Elhrin," Bayle breathed. His eyes lost focus and fluttered to a close. His breathing became shallow.

"Marguerite, what's happening?" Elhrin asked, tears springing to her eyes.

"Dear heart, it's the poison, I can only hope the antidote will take effect soon," she said as a trail of tears escaped from the corner of her eye to run down her cheek. She swiped them away with a trembling hand.

"Bayle, hang in there, son," Master Gryph said, his voice rough with emotion. He stood wearily, returning to the cliff's edge to take care of the injured

Do'athrim. A moment later, an eerie howl sounded from the direction of the gorge. It faded in the distance.

"Survive that, you bastard," Elhrin heard Master Gryph say.

Marguerite finished with cleansing and bandaging Bayle's arm and pulled her bedroll from her pack. She draped a blanket over Bayle, then reached across to squeeze Elhrin's arm. She said nothing. Bayle's life was out of her control and in the hands of fate.

A short time later, Tomas and Kyne jogged back from their search. "Minister, we found a niche in a rockslide just below here we think is safe. Jag and Fuller are making the entrance easier to crawl through."

Master Gryph nodded. "You and Kyne carry Bayle."

They didn't have to go far. The mountain rose sharply above them on the left, and a large chunk of its side had broken away to form a large pile at the bottom. Jag and Fuller were standing among the rubble several feet up and scrambled down to help Kyne and Tomas. Elhrin and Marguerite hurried ahead, ducking into the narrow opening. Inside was a small space under a gigantic boulder with barely enough room for all of them to fit.

She and Marguerite quickly cleared a space on a narrow ledge and spread out a blanket. Kyne and Tomas gingerly laid him down. His breathing had become so shallow that Elhrin was terrified he had died, but then she saw his chest rise a fraction. Weak with relief, she sunk to the ground beside him to wait, willing his chest to move, and holding her breath every time it didn't. All she could think about was she had just lost her mother, and the thought of losing him too, was too much. She put her hand over her eyes and let go of her feelings, weeping like a newborn baby.

Tomas sat down behind her and put his arms around her. "Elhrin, he's strong, he'll make it through," he whispered into her ear.

She nodded, blinking back her tears, trying to calm down. She picked up Bayle's cold hand and rubbed it between hers. "I knew this was going to be too dangerous. I should have found some way to leave him behind," she whispered. "This is my destiny, not his."

"Elhrin," Master Gryph called her name gently. He was crouched just outside the entrance. The wind whipped the short tufts of his close-cropped hair to one side. "If Bayle was meant to be elsewhere, no force on earth could change that path. He is here for a purpose."

"Then what is the purpose for this?" she hissed, angrily.

"I don't know," he sighed, shaking his head sadly. "I wish I did." He glanced at Tomas. "I need to talk to you and the boys." He stood up and picked his way back down the jumble of rocks.

Tomas squeezed Elhrin's shoulder as he crawled out of the hole and left her and Marguerite alone with Bayle. Near dusk he returned to tell them they would remain outside and to call if they needed anything. They were all going to stand watch and make sure no other bands of Do'athrim were on the heels of those they had killed.

Elhrin never moved from Bayle's side throughout the night. She firmly held onto his hand as if she could will life into him through her hand like she could will her powers out of it. She frowned at the thought, staring sightlessly at her hand curled around his. She had all this power to kill or maim, but no power to heal or cure someone hurt or sick. Why? Why was that not a possibility?

She lifted her eyes to Marguerite, realizing the woman had spoken. "What did you say?" she asked.

"I said, Bayle's breathing is getting stronger."

She was right. Bayle's chest rose and fell steadily, his breathing deep and even, and some of his color had returned.

"I think it is working," Marguerite said with a tired smile.

Relief flooded every fiber of her body. "He's going to be all right?"

"I don't know. We'll just have to wait and see."

They heard someone climbing up the pile of rubble outside. Looking to see who was coming, she noticed the first touch of dawn was beginning to lighten the sky. Master Gryph bent to look into the opening, his face haggard and drawn. "How's Bayle?"

"I think the antidote is working. His breathing is stronger. Did you see anything?" Marguerite asked.

"No, it's been quiet," he yawned, "but I am betting that by now, your perpetual friend and his companions have given away our location to Cynder. I have no doubt he will be heading our way soon."

"What are we going to do? We can't move Bayle," she said.

"I know. I sent Jag and Fuller to cut branches to hide the opening. I am counting on Bayle's observation of Cynder not being able to feel my or Elhrin's energy to be correct. If not, we are in for a bit of trouble sooner than I would like."

"What do you want me to do?" Elhrin asked, wearily.

"Just be ready. But no matter what happens you have to remain focused on your task. The most important thing is closing the Rift, and you must do whatever it takes to reach Blackridge Keep. Killing Cynder is not the primary goal, do you understand?"

She nodded, thinking she had heard him say that before, then it dawned on her that what he just said was very similar to his note for her in the *Book of Tolman*.

"Master Gryph, why do you keep telling me this? Is something going to happen?" she asked.

"What are you talking about?" he yawned loudly, scrubbing his fingertips over his eyes. "What is it that I keep telling you?"

"A note you wrote in the book mysteriously appeared saying that I need to stay focused on my task and not to hesitate no matter what happens."

"Hmm, sounds like good advice to me, don't you think?"

"You wrote that note when I was just a little girl."

"Yes, I did."

"How would you know then I would need that advice now? Is something going to happen that you aren't telling me?"

"Elhrin, if I recall correctly, I put that in there as a precaution after I had a particular dream for the umpteenth time. The blasted thing will not leave me alone." He dropped his eyes to look at Bayle. "I don't know if the dream will play out as I see it, but if it does, then my advice to you remains the same because it is important."

"What is your dream?" she asked.

"That is not for you to know," he said, glancing at Marguerite. "I am going to see if the boys need help."

"Gryph, I would like to know what your dream is, too," Marguerite said, concern etched on her face.

"It wouldn't change anything, and there is no sense in worrying you. I told you, it may not turn out the way I see it." He backed out of the shelter and was gone.

"His not worrying me, worries me," Marguerite grunted in exasperation.

A few hours later, when the sun reached its zenith, the same nauseating tingling sensation that she had felt at the waterfall intruded in on her awareness. She had no doubt the powerful and vile feeling magical aura was Cynder and he was fast approaching from the north. She heard Master Gryph warn the others outside. One by one, they ducked through the brush they had used to conceal the entrance of the cave. Crouching near the entrance, they readied their weapons.

"Where's Gryph?" Marguerite asked, just as he stuck his head through the brush.

"Listen up. Remember, Cynder is a shape-changer and he can change into something that will allow him to enter this cave should he choose to, but you are to do nothing unless he finds you and you are forced into a fight. Remain as silent as possible."

"If he is a shape-changer, could he not change into something that could hunt us down like the Do'athrim wolf?" Fuller asked.

"He can change shape only. It does not alter his original senses. If he isn't capable of following a scent in his true form, then he won't be able to if he changes his shape into something that normally could," he said.

"What is his original form?" Kyne asked.

"I haven't a clue," he said, and started to back out.

"And just where are you going to be?" Marguerite asked.

"I am going to be out here just in case he needs a welcoming committee."

"Then I am coming with you," she said.

"No," he said, forcefully. "You need to stay with Bayle."

"Fine," she agreed, reluctantly.

He backed out of the brush and was gone.

Gryph chose a place to conceal himself not far from where they had climbed up the cliff. He did not want to be anywhere near the cave in case it came to a fight, which he needed to avoid if possible. Cynder was strong and the possibility of losing a fight with him was high. He could not afford to fail Solisius, or the So'ladiun by dying before his mission was accomplished. Once again, he wondered if he had made a mistake by meeting up with Elhrin instead of going ahead alone, but he knew it was no use wondering, he never could have left her to face this without him—it was his fault she was unprepared, and she was so young, still a little girl in his eyes.

He sighed in disgust.

That was what he got for thinking he had more time. He, of all people, knew time was precious and never should be wasted. Then there was Marguerite, the love of his life—his weakness. To be in this world and not see her, touch her, love her one more time—no matter how hard he tried, he couldn't bring himself to walk in the other direction when he reached the mine road and felt Elhrin's energy source brush against his awareness like a soft feather. Marguerite, Elhrin, and Bayle, they were his life and he could not turn his back on them for any reason.

He glanced at the entrance to the cave and hoped the shrubbery would fool Cynder. The branches looked natural enough from a distance, like the real bushes that had sprouted up among the rocks, but he did not think it would fool anyone who looked closely.

His senses told him Cynder was almost here, flying swiftly from the north, and it wasn't long when a dot appeared in the sky flying directly towards him. The beast was fast—faster than Gryph expected, and as he neared, he dipped low to zoom just above the treetops, swooping up and down the valleys between mountainsides then made the long ascent to where Gryph hid.

"Damn it!" Gryph swore under his breath. Cynder was carrying Gryzzl in his talons—the damn wolf would not go away.

Cynder flew directly over the cave, his great wings created a forceful downdraft of wind that whipped the brush around violently, but luck was on their side, the brush held and the cave remained hidden. Gryzzl pointed in Gryph's direction and Cynder veered to zoom past Gryph's hiding spot under a stand of mountain laurel. The limbs around him parted, but neither beast saw him lying flat on the ground, covered by his long black cloak. Bayle had been right. Cynder couldn't feel his or Elhrin's magical energy or he would have attacked him right away.

Cynder circled around and came back to the cliff where they almost lost Bayle and dropped Gryzzl neatly to the ground. Cynder then lowered himself, changing into the form of a man, cloaked and hooded, just as his feet touched the earth.

"This is where you saw them last?" Cynder asked. Gryph had a hard time understanding him. The beast's speech was thick with a strange, rasping dialect as if he did not possess lips to form words clearly.

"Yes," Gryzzl said, pointing to the edge, "they climbed up here."

"And you are not sure if you killed the So'ladiun?" Cynder strolled across the ridge, searching the area. He edged closer to Gryph and halted, staring directly at the stand of bushes where Gryph was hidden. Gryph itched to use magic for protection, but he dared not unless there was no choice. He would need every last ounce of energy if he was to fight this beast. Cynder resonated a force of power—feeling black and diseased—pure evil. There was no doubt he was a child of Obsudius.

"No, Master, I hit a boy and the old man, but they were not dead when I last saw them." Gryzzl squatted on the exact spot where Bayle had lain and sniffed. He trailed a gloved finger through the dirt then flicked a long pink tongue across it, tasting. "Blood—human, tainted with my poison. One of them is dead."

"I see no grave, dog. If one of them died they would not carry him," Cynder turned to look at the wolf. "My patience with you has about evaporated, Gryzzl. The only reason I have not sent you to the Void is that Obsudius favored you with your special senses and are able to find them quickly. I do not want to have to pull Grom away from the fight again. Take care of them once and for all, do you understand me?"

Gryzzl bowed his head respectfully then stood.

"I don't have time for chasing after Solisius' vermin. Obsudius needs my full attention on the war. I have taken care of most of the troops south of the mountains marching into the pass, but I need to return to root out that pest holed up in the mountains on the north side. He thinks he has outsmarted us, but I will correct that as soon as this is finished," he walked a few steps in the direction of the hidden shelter, scanning the layout of the area. "The So'ladiun have had nearly a day's start, but could not have gone far if they have to compensate for injuries." He jerked his cowl-covered head northward. "That is the only way they could have gone from here. I am going to search ahead from above. You locate their trail and follow it. Let's get this over with so I can fly west. Grom and Morg are too stupid to accomplish the task of killing the King of Anderan alone."

Cynder shimmered and changed back into the muscular black reptilian dragon beast he favored. He launched himself skyward and sailed down the mountain out of sight.

Gryph watched Gryzzl circle the area then turn his head to look at the rockslide. Gryzzl narrowed his eyes, then nodded to himself. Gryph quickly made sure Cynder was out of the immediate area, finding he had flown far down the mountain and was moving away from him. He had time. Gryph sent his energy speeding towards the Do'athrim, catching him around the throat in a grip like a vice just as Gryzzl started towards the shelter. The Do'athrim tried to howl, clawing at his throat trying to free himself from the unseen force. Gryph tightened his magical grip, choking the beast, but not enough to kill him. Gryph rose to his feet and limped out of his hiding place—the old injury to his leg burned like fire, but as always, he ignored the pain.

"Hello, Gryzzl, is it?" he asked, calmly stopping just out of the beast's reach.

Gryzzl narrowed hate-filled eyes at Gryph, trying to lunge for the man, but found his neck was held firmly in place.

"You are one persistent fellow, aren't you? But I must say I have had just about enough of you."

The Do'athrim continued to claw at his throat, desperately trying to breathe as he watched Gryph pull the pendant out from under his shirt.

"Let me ask you something. Have you heard of Solisius?" he asked.

Gryzzl froze at the mention of the God of Light. A glimmer of fear entered the beast's eyes.

"I see you understand me. Let me tell you a secret. I spoke with him last night and told him all about you—how dedicated you were to his brother's cause. Do you know he was so impressed by you he wanted to meet you personally? Would you like to meet the God of Light?"

A small whine managed to escape from his muzzle. He then made a frenzied attempt to break free of Gryph's hold. He was strong, but Gryph held tight.

"I take it you don't. That's too bad because you really don't have a choice. I can no longer allow you to plague us, and since you don't have the good sense to stay away, Solisius has agreed that the world and the universe could do without you," he said through clenched teeth, pulling his pendant up and over his head. It burst into a piercing white light. He wrapped the gold chain securely around his hand, allowing the pendant to dangle in his palm. He held it up for the beast to see.

Gryzzl froze in terror, unable to take his eyes off the burning gem.

"This is for attacking my wife, and nearly killing a boy I think of as a son. Oh, and for calling me old. I hate it when someone calls me old," he said with a smile he did not feel. He lunged at the beast and smacked the pendant to Gryzzl's forehead before the beast knew what hit him. A surge of magnificent power washed through Gryph's body as a brilliant flash of light winked briefly from his palm. Gryzzl disappeared.

Gryph put the pendant back over his head and scanned the area for Cynder. He felt the beast's energy search the area below. He leaned against a tree to wait. A short time later, Cynder started to fly back up the mountain. Gryph limped to his hiding place in the stand of laurel bushes and crawled into the small space underneath the foliage. Cynder flapped into view, his large head constantly roving back and forth, scanning the ground for signs of passage, then he pulled up to hover in place, puzzled.

Gryph smiled to himself. The beast was looking for his pet, but little did Cynder know, he wouldn't have to worry about his threat to send Gryzzl to the Void for his failures, Solisius would take care of that for him.

Gryph held his magical energy in check, primed to fire if needed.

Cynder returned to the spot where he had dropped the Do'athrim off then slipped dangerously close to the cave, rattling the brush covering the entrance with powerful downdrafts created from his leathery wings. Gryph watched anxiously as a branch broke free and hit the ground. Cynder whipped around at the movement, trying to see what had moved.

Gryph barely contained the force of power he wanted to use to blast the beast into oblivion. But he couldn't, not here—not now, if it could be avoided.

Cynder did not find anything out of place. He flapped in circles carefully studying the area. Out of frustration he raised his head and trumpeted a fierce roar that echoed over the valley. He then jerked his scaly bulk around and zigzagged down slope, searching. After several hours of flying in the area, he came back to the spot where he had dropped Gryzzl off. He lowered himself to the ridge, once again shimmering into the form of a robed human figure. Growling under his breath, he walked to the spot where he last saw the Do'athrim, scrutinizing the ground closely. He turned in a slow circle, searching the ground and the nearby area. He then walked towards the pile of rubble, scanning the mound.

Gryph made the decision to fire if he mounted one rock, but Cynder stopped before he reached the base of the pile, closely scanning the entire façade. He then turned to look downhill. Striding across to a stand of low growing bushes thick with tiny round leaves, he reached out a green-tinged, three-fingered hand to touch a limb.

Gryph clamped his lips firmly together. Fuller had chopped branches from that area, and he wasn't sure if Cynder would see the cuts that were low to the ground. Slowly, Gryph pushed himself up to his hands and knees. The odds were not good.

Cynder took three long strides away from the bushes. He shimmered and reformed back into the shape of a dragon, bunched his muscular legs under him and launched himself off the ground, beating his wings with great force to raise his bulk high in the air. He skimmed down the mountain then made a wide circle to fly back up—straight for the rockslide.

Gryph pulled his feet up under him, ignoring the pain when his knee protested against the position and steadied himself at a crouch. The limbs of the bush dug into his hip and shoulder, but he ignored them, too. He was ready to fight.

A breeze shifted around him, and he took in a calming breath. He was not alone.

Cynder zoomed over the top of the jumble of rock. He opened his gigantic maw and spewed a plume of fire over its entire surface. The sporadic clumps of plant life between the stones instantly ignited. Several chunks of rock dislodged and tumbled down the pile. Gryph stepped out of his hiding place just as Cynder zoomed past the cliff and out over the gorge behind him. Cynder banked in a wide circle.

Gryph spared a quick glance at the rock mound, watching the stones tumble down and dislodge more in their wake. The brush the boys had put in front of the entrance was burning furiously, but he thought they were safe for the moment. He could feel Elhrin's energy source pulsing strong from the cave as he watched one of the rocks drop onto the boulder over their heads and roll directly off onto the burning brush, effectively stamping it out and completely covering the gaping hole. Amazed at the piece of good fortune fate had just handed them, he had to bite back a howl of laughter.

The drumming of wing beats flapped closer. Cynder was on his way back. Gryph dove for the cover of the laurel but could not conceal himself in time with its foliage. He had to call on his powers to form a façade to hide him.

Cynder flew over without looking his way. The N'gethwyn made another pass at the rock pile, spewing forth more fire, burning the brush he had missed the first time. He circled around and settled to the earth at the base of the rockslide, searching for any evidence of his quarry among the rubble. Not finding what he was looking for, he hissed long and loud, sounding like an angry viper. "You may have slipped by me this time, So'ladiun, but I will find you," he hissed angrily. "I will find you."

"When the time comes, I will find you," Gryph growled under his breath.

Cynder launched himself into the air, made one final search of the area, then flew northward. A short time later, he flew out of Gryph's range and did not return.

Gryph let go of his energy, sweating furiously from the exertion of holding the magical concealment in place. His energy supply had been considerably drained, which was why he rarely used the technique. He laid his head back on the ground and relaxed for a moment, staring at the sky, letting his nerves calm down. He then hauled himself to his feet and limped down to the rockslide and clambered up the jumble of rocks. There was a narrow slit between the rock and the entrance hole. "Is everyone okay in there?"

"Yes, sir," Jag answered.

"Gryph, thank the light," Marguerite breathed.

"Move away from the rock," he said. "I'll have you out in a moment."

He heard them move to the back of the small cave as he climbed to higher ground. "Protect yourselves," he yelled. He flung a blast of energy at the rock, careful to hit it at an angle. The rock exploded outward, flinging fist-sized stone safely below the cave. A large chunk still partially covered the hole.

He picked his way back down the jumble of rock. Fuller peered at him through a craggy hole his blast had created. "I can now say that if I have the chance to return to this world as something other than human after I die, I hope it will not be as a rabbit. I do not like hiding in holes."

"You do not have to worry about that," Gryph chuckled. "You boys push on this, I'll pull." He reached down to grasp the chunk of rock covering the hole. Fuller and Jag put their weight against the backside and pushed. The rock tumbled over to one side and wedged in between two others at his feet, but the hole opened up enough to allow them to crawl out of the cave.

"That was a close one," Jag said when he crawled out.

"Yes, it was," Gryph agreed, grasping Elhrin's hand and helping her out of the hole. "I'm glad you all remained calm. It couldn't have been easy to do."

"I'm not so sure calm was the norm," Fuller laughed. "The son of a bitch would have fried us if this young lady hadn't used her magic to protect us from the heat."

Gryph shot a quick smile at Elhrin, proud of the brave young lady she was becoming. He clasped Marguerite's hand and helped her through the hole.

"How did he know we were there?" Elhrin asked.

"He didn't, really," he said, as Marguerite wrapped her arms around his waist and squeezed the breath out of him. "He found where we cut the brush to cover the hole, and guessed that we may have been hiding up here, but the rock falling over the entrance saved you from being discovered."

"What now?" Kyne asked. "He knows we are in the area. It's just going to be a matter of time before he finds us."

"We stay alert as we have been doing," Gryph answered, "and it might be a good idea to make Cynder believe we have left the area if he comes back. Fuller, you and I are going to go on a short journey."

"You aren't going to leave us, are you?" Marguerite asked in concern.

"Just for the day," he said, giving her a reassuring squeeze. "We'll hike out a few hours and set up a mock camp as if we are moving in a westerly direction away from the gorge." He pointed a little left of the direction Cynder flew, sure that he had flown towards Blackridge Keep. "When we do get to leave, I want to return to our original plan to find a point to cross the river running through the gorge."

"We are going to wait on the boy?" Kyne asked as if surprised. "I thought we were in a hurry to close this damn Rift thing."

Gryph leveled his gaze on the young man. Elene's rigid, impatient temperament ran deep in her son. "We are in a hurry, but I am not going to split us up if it isn't necessary."

"We aren't splitting up," Marguerite hissed.

Gryph said nothing, but Kyne was right. If it came down to it, he was going to have to make an extremely tough decision. "Fuller and I will go as I said. We will talk more about this when we return. In the meantime, I want you boys to remain vigilant. If I feel Cynder returning, I will draw him away." He glanced at Elhrin. Pale and exhausted, she looked on the verge of collapse. "If that happens, you must leave immediately and continue to Blackridge."

"Don't do this," she pleaded.

He reached out and patted her shoulder. "All will be well." He gave Marguerite one last squeeze. "Come Fuller, we will try to return before morning." He started down the pile of rocks. "Oh, by the way," he said, stopping to look back at them, "Cynder had a short discussion with Gryzzl up by the cliff. According to him, Goruth still stands in Kilmyn pass and Obsudius' army has not made it south. Also, Marguerite, your wolf friend will no longer hound your trail."

"That is outstanding news," she breathed, crossing her arms over her chest. "What happened?"

"Cynder dropped him off up by the ridge and I took care of him, once and for all."

"How?" Elhrin asked.

"Magic," he said, wiggling his fingers in an imitation of Bayle.

"Gryph, I hate it when you don't answer with a straight answer," Marguerite frowned. "What did you do?"

Smiling, he wagged a finger at his wife, once again climbing down the pile of rocks. "Marguerite, you are one nosey woman. You don't have to know everything, do you?" he teased, anticipating the spark of fire that he knew was coming. She did not disappoint him.

"Gryph, I swear, you are the most frustrating man," she snapped, but was interrupted from continuing her tirade against him when a weak voice drifted through the hole beside her.

"Hello, is anyone here?"

Elhrin's eyes widened. "Bayle!"

Gryph closed his eyes briefly, offering a silent prayer of thanks to Solisius. He glanced back at Fuller when the man stopped to look back. "Are you coming?" he asked.

"Sorry, sir, I just thought you would want to go back up."

He shook his head. "No, the boy is in good hands," he said, sparing one last look back. Elhrin and Marguerite had disappeared into the hole.

Chapter Twenty-Three

Master Gryph and Fuller returned by midmorning the next day, telling them that they had set up the mock camp by a tiny stream slightly northwest of their position. He had gone so far as to cut his arm and soak a strip of cloth with his own blood and left it partially burnt in the ashes of a cold fire they had covered with dirt as if trying to conceal their passage. He wanted the beast to think they would be slowed by injuries, hoping he would concentrate his search in a smaller circle for a bit. It seemed to have worked. Cynder found his camp the next afternoon and dedicated his search west and north. He did not return to their hideout again.

To Elhrin's profound relief, the antidote combined with Bayle's youth and good health allowed him to recover at an amazing rate. The poison was purged from his body, taking away the paralysis, but it left him extremely weak. Even so, he declared he was ready to travel a day and a half later, so Marguerite made a sling for his arm to keep it protected while they continued on their journey.

Near nightfall of the third day since leaving the rock shelter, they finally found a point near the end of the gorge where they could reach the river that ran through it and cross a shallow ford to the other side. Deciding to stop before dark completely fell, they set up camp by the river, and Fuller and Jag disappeared into the wood in opposite directions to patrol the immediate area for enemies.

Elhrin spread out Bayle's bedroll for him and he flopped down exhausted, complaining that his arm hurt. Marguerite plundered through her pack, pulling out a small bottle of dark liquid.

"Take a sip of this," she said, offering him the bottle.

Bayle screwed up his face in disgust. "I don't want to do this again, it reeks and tastes like dirty socks."

"Yes, meaning it is effective. Drink," she demanded.

"No, thank you." He pushed it away.

Marguerite squatted beside him. "I do not have the patience or a stick of candy to coddle you like I did when you were small, Bayle. I suggest you take this like a big boy or I will force it down your throat," she said with a hint of steel.

Bayle eyed her with apprehension, knowing Marguerite wasn't kidding. "Uh, yes, ma'am." He gagged the concoction down, then sputtered and heaved as if he would vomit the liquid back out.

Marguerite rolled her eyes at his obvious overly dramatic act, taking the vial back with a shake of her head. "Unnecessary, young man, unnecessary."

Bayle grinned wide at Elhrin when Marguerite turned her back on him.

Meanwhile, Master Gryph stood at the river's edge, magically seining the river for trout. He whistled a tune as he worked, and when Bayle heard the song, he decided to join in. His voice, a vibrant tenor, matched the pitch of the song Master Gryph was whistling, perfectly.

"Tap the barrel and set 'em down, that man there's buyin' this round,
This is his wedding day," he sang, leaning back on one elbow.
"One month ago, his girl, she was pregnant and startin' to show,
And her papa was not pleased.
He snatched up his sword and headed out the door,
A debt was going to be paid.
Oh, papa wait, the girl had to beg," Bayle changed his voice to mimic a girl's squeaky, high-pitched voice, making them all laugh. Master Gryph nearly lost his tune. "I love him this is true,
Please put down your sword, and come indoors,
You are making me so afraid.
Papa said, child, go back inside,
This is something I must do.
I know what's best, to get you out of this mess,
There's going to be a wedding day.
At the point of papa's sword the boy fell to his knees, and plead, sir, don't kill me please, I didn't know, I swear.
That the sweet love she gave, would result in a babe,
If I could take it back I would.
Papa said, no use to grovel son, your single days are done,
I have no doubt you will agree.
Because if you say no, your cod sack will have to go,
Tomorrow's your wedding day.
Yes, that's right, son, you better not run,
Tomorrow's your wedding day."

The men burst out laughing when Bayle finished the song, and Elhrin had to shake her head and smile because she knew what was coming.

"Bayle, where on earth did you learn that song?" Marguerite asked, frowning.

Bayle looked embarrassed and cut his eyes at the tall man by the river who had found a slick, spotted fish resting under a rock ledge. He twisted his hand with a quick jerk. The fish was wrenched out of the water and landed at his feet with a splat, immediately flopping back and forth in a frenzied panic to reach the safety of the water.

"Gryph, I should have known," she said, placing her hands on her hips.

"What?" he grinned innocently, as he toed the fish away from the water with his boot. "There's nothing wrong with the song."

"That's a song only fit for a taproom and you know it. Why are you teaching it to a boy?"

"Bayle's not a boy any longer, Marguerite. He's grown into a fine young man. Besides, I didn't just teach it to him, he asked me for the words to that tune long ago."

"And did it ever occur to you that he might not need to sing such things?" Marguerite asked. "It's about, well . . . it's just not a subject fit to sing about at any age."

Master Gryph shrugged his shoulders, knowing anything he said would be wrong. He winked at Bayle as he turned back to the river.

"Humph," Marguerite huffed. "Fine example you set, Minister," she said low under her breath.

Elhrin glanced at Bayle. He was beaming. Hearing Master Gryph considered him a man had just made his day.

An hour or so later, Fuller burst out of the dark forest at a run. "Where's Minister Idwyr?" he asked Marguerite.

"I'm right here. What is it?" Master Gryph called out.

He was crouched across from Elhrin and had been showing her how to cook the fish he caught with magic. They had wedge a thin flat rock over two others near the river's edge and placed the strips of flesh on its top. He had then heated the rock to a level where it tinged white and the fish had started to sizzle, an effective way to cook something small without building a fire and they could toss the rock into the river when they were done to minimize signs of their passage.

"There are Do'athrim camped about a league down river."

"Cynder must have sent out another search party." He rinsed his hands off in the river and stood. "They didn't see you, did they?"

"No, sir, there's a small ridge above their camp where I was able to watch without being seen. I counted five beasts and stayed for awhile to make sure there were no others."

"Right, show me. Tomas, you and Elhrin will join us. Jag, I want you to patrol the area around the camp again, just to make sure none slipped by Fuller," he said, strapping on his sword. "Kyne, you and Marguerite stay with Bayle."

Elhrin followed them into the woods. Luckily, the moon was now half-full and gave off enough light through the trees for them to see where they were going. Fuller led them downriver until he reached a place where the water cascaded over rocks, creating frothy white rapids. He then turned to climb uphill, parallel to the river, and wound his way around mountain laurel and hemlock trees until he reached a rocky outcrop.

"The ridge is just beyond those rocks further down the slope," he whispered, pointing towards the river to a stand of boulders that were outlined from the light of a fire on the other side.

Silently, they moved down the slope, crouching low. Elhrin cringed when she stepped on a stick and it snapped. Fuller looked back and put his finger to his lips, gesturing for her to be quiet. She nodded. They waited for a moment to make sure they had not been heard, then crept quietly around the boulders. Elhrin could see the ridge. Flickering light illuminated the area from below, casting dancing shadows among the surrounding trees. Fuller made a gesture for them to go down. They eased to their hands and knees, then inched closer to a stand of shrubs along the ridge. The beast's camp was a short drop below them.

Just as Fuller said, five Do'athrim were sitting around a fire, talking in the guttural language she recognized from the book. Two of them had the features of a large brown bear, while the other three were Do'athrim wolven.

"What are we going to do?" Tomas whispered.

"I don't want to kill them if we can get out of it. We don't need them to tell Cynder our location when they return to Do'athra," Master Gryph replied.

"We can't let them go," Fuller whispered.

"No, we can't," he said, studying the scene below.

The creatures were eating something raw and bloody, and then two of them started arguing over what appeared to be a hind leg of a deer with the brown fur still on the flesh.

"Solisius, what do you think?" Master Gryph whispered, under his breath.

Surprised, Elhrin furrowed her brow at Master Gryph, wondering why he spoke to Solisius as if he were right beside him.

A slight breeze stirred and whispered through the trees to ruffle her hair, and like a sigh barely heard, a soft voice drifted around them.

"Send them to me."

Elhrin's eyes went wide and she felt her jaw drop. She looked at Tomas and Fuller, but they were intent on the Do'athrim and made no indication they heard the voice. She glanced back at Master Gryph. He was watching her with amusement.

"I take it you haven't spoken with Solisius since the other night?" he whispered, and she shook her head no. "That's too bad. He wants you to talk to him." He turned his attention back to the creatures below. "Are you sure, My Lord?"

The voice came again on the breeze, touching her with its soft embrace, and her heart swelled with an unexpected joy from its sound.

"Gryphon, they are better off in the Void than spending an eternity of misery in my brother's realm."

"As you wish," he said, glancing at Elhrin, smiling at the look of wonder on her face. "Amazing, isn't it?"

Elhrin nodded, unable to speak.

"Okay, this is what we need to do," he whispered to Fuller and Tomas. "Like I said, I don't want any of them killed if we can help it. Fuller, do you think you can disable one of the bears from here?"

He glanced around, checking his position. "I'll have to move a bit. I don't have a clear shot, but I should be able to," he replied.

"Whatever it takes. Elhrin, I'll need you to hold one of them immobile. Can you do it?"

She nodded, hoping her strength would be enough to hold one. Gryzzl had been tough to manage back in Glimmerdale.

"Take the one closest to us. I just need you to hold him long enough for me to get to him. Tomas, you and I are going to move down to the edge of their camp. If they spot us, Fuller, go ahead with your shot. Otherwise, wait on my signal," he said, and they all nodded their understanding of what he wanted them to do. "Let's go, Tomas."

Fuller scooted silently to a position that gave him a clear shot and waited with his bow ready. Elhrin tucked her knees under her, waiting for his signal, not knowing what it was going to be. She became antsy when the minutes dragged by and nothing happened.

When a gigantic boom suddenly detonated below her, she nearly jumped from cover. The flames of the beast's fire roared upwards, scorching the high tree branches overhead. The beasts were thrown backwards away from the fire. Hot embers shot out in all directions and ignited the trousers of one of the Do'athrim bears. He roared in pain and rolled across the dirt to try and smother the flames. The others clambered to their feet in confusion, and Fuller fired his arrow into the leg of his designated beast. He bellowed in pain and dropped to the ground, pulling at the arrow in his leg.

Elhrin sat up on her knees and sent magic speeding down to her Do'athrim and wrapped it around him like a rope and pulled tight. The creature struggled against her, trying to free himself. She gritted her teeth against the strain he put on her hold. His strength was enormous.

Tomas rushed into the camp at one of the remaining beasts. The wolf saw him coming and drew his sword to meet Tomas in a ringing clash. The wolf attacked with a mindless frenzy, and Tomas kept stepping back from his blows, giving ground and taking a more defensive posture until he found an opening that would allow him to take advantage over the beast without delivering a killing strike.

Master Gryph followed Tomas into the camp, his sword in his left hand, his right hand raised, and Elhrin realized the remaining Do'athrim was also immobile and struggling to free himself from an unseen captor. The bear beast that had caught fire, managed to get the flames extinguished and jumped up to rush at Master Gryph, pulling his sword as he ran.

"Damn! I can't get a shot," Fuller swore, trying to get a bead on the beast rushing Master Gryph. "The minister's in the way."

Master Gryph ducked under the creature's swing, narrowly escaping the top of his head being removed, and jerked the hand holding his magic. The immobile wolven he was holding fell to the ground with a crash, but found that he could move again, and struggled back to his feet. Fuller sighted him in, and fired, catching him in the groin. The beast screamed and fell back to the ground writhing in agony, holding his crotch.

"Ooh, sorry about that, my friend," Fuller muttered, sounding as if he was pained by the sight himself, and Elhrin had to smile in spite of the fact she was struggling to contain her Do'athrim. The beast was relentless in trying to free itself.

Master Gryph met the back-handed swing of the bear Do'athrim he was fighting, the sword's metallic clashes mingled with those of Tomas and his adversary. The beast growled and followed through, slashing at Master Gryph's head, making him have to step back from the blade as it arced downward and ripped through his shirt. A dark stain seeped into the fabric around the edges of the tear. Grimacing, Master Gryph used his magic to pick up the beast and slammed him hard to the ground. Reversing his hold on his sword, he drove it completely through the beast's leg, impaling him to the ground. The creature howled and tried to free the pinned leg with one hand while swinging its sword wildly at Master Gryph with the other.

The first beast Fuller shot jerked the arrow out of his leg with a roar and rose unsteadily to his feet. Fuller calmly notched another arrow and shot the bear in his uninjured leg. He threw his huge head back and roared in pain, but he did not fall. Instead, he ripped out the new arrow and wildly searched for his attacker. Spying Fuller on the ridge above, he grabbed a bow propped nearby, but Fuller didn't give him the chance to load it, and fired another arrow. It lodged into the beast's belly.

"Damn, he moved. I hope that doesn't kill him," Fuller said angrily, as they watched the beast grab the arrow in his stomach and fall slowly to the ground.

Winded, Master Gryph rendered the flailing beast he had impaled to the ground immobile, and reached into the collar of his shirt and pulled his pendant up and over his head so that he held it freely in his hand. A brilliant white light erupted from the gem as he bent over the creature lying on the ground and touched the pendant to the beast's head. A flash of light winked blindingly over the camp. The beast vanished, leaving Master Gryph's sword standing upright in the dirt as if marking his spot.

Elhrin had to shake her head in amazement. "Wow," she whispered.

Master Gryph jerked his sword out of the ground and limped to the beast Fuller had shot in the groin. When Master Gryph saw the injury, he shot Fuller a questioning look. Fuller shrugged his shoulders. Master Gryph grunted with amusement then his eyes trailed to hers. He realized the strain she was under.

"Hold on, Elhrin, I'm coming," he called out. The beast tried to writhe away from him, but he kicked him in the stomach. The beast doubled up, allowing him the opportunity to slap the pendant on the Do'athrim's forehead. Again, another brilliant flash of light and the beast was gone.

Master Gryph hurried to the beast Elhrin held and sent it to Solisius. Relief flooded through her when she was able to relax, but the ringing of steel caught her attention and she saw that Tomas was being pushed back into the trees by the Do'athrim he was fighting. She gathered her magic and sent it down to wrap up the beast like she had done the other one. The beast's eyes widened in surprise when he started to swing his sword and found himself incapable of moving. Tomas hesitated, unsure at first of what had happened, then looked up at her questioningly. She managed a tight grin as another brilliant flash of light illuminated the camp. Tomas bashed the side of the Do'athrim's head with the hilt of his sword. The beast fell unconscious and Elhrin allowed his body to crumple to the ground.

Master Gryph stood over the spot where Fuller's bear had been. "Nice work, team," he panted, then limped to Tomas' beast and quickly sent him to Solisius.

"Let's go," Fuller said to Elhrin. They clambered down the short drop to the camp.

"What did you do, Minister?" Tomas huffed out of breath, swiping the sweat off his brow.

"I made sure they did not return to Do'athra or anywhere for that matter, again," Master Gryph slipped his pendant over his head and dropped it inside his shirt then grimaced as the movement of his shirt brushed the cut on his chest. He pulled aside the torn fabric to assess the damage.

"Are you okay?" Elhrin reached out to examine the wound, but he caught her hand before she touched him.

"I'm fine. It's just a scratch," he squeezed her hand, reassuringly.

"Fuller, what are you doing?" Tomas asked.

Fuller kicked one of the beast's packs to the side, searching.

"Just a minute. Ah, here we go," he stooped over to pick up a quiver of arrows. "Jag and I could use these. Our supplies are getting low."

Master Gryph slipped his sword back into its scabbard. "Let's head back and make sure the others are safe."

They met Jag in the woods on their way back to camp and he reported that he could find no other Do'athrim, but he would continue to look for a little while longer, just in case. When they emerged through the trees, Marguerite jumped up to greet them, then frowned when she noticed Master Gryph had been wounded.

"What happened?" she asked, pulling aside the torn fabric to look at his wound.

"I got a little too close," he replied.

"I can see that. Come sit and take off your shirt so I can get a better look. I'll need light," she said, leading him to a piece of rotted tree trunk wedged between the rocks near Bayle's bedroll. "Actually, what I meant was, what happened with the Do'athrim?" she asked as he lowered himself to the log and conjured a small light sphere for her. It popped into the air over her head and hovered close by.

Tomas related the tale of the fight, while Marguerite tended Master Gryph's wound. He had a shallow cut just under his collarbone and Marguerite dabbed at the wound with a damp cloth, trying to stem the blood that oozed out of the wound and slid down through the hairs on his chest. The dimly lit pendant he wore around his neck pulsed softly as if matching his heartbeat.

"Would you like to hold it?" Master Gryph asked.

"Can I?" she asked, embarrassed he had caught her staring.

"You can," he said, removing it from his neck and handing it to her.

The pendant glowed softly in her hand and she could feel the energy pulsing through it. Turning it over in her hand, she marveled at its perfect natural cut. Like her pendant, it was oblong in shape with a pointed tip.

This is unbelievable, she thought, *he actually sent those Do'athrim to Ts'aura. A link to Solisius, a . . . .*

And it dawned on her what that kind of power the pendant possessed.

"NO!" she cried, standing abruptly to her feet.

Everyone in the camp turned to look at her.

"What is it?" Marguerite asked, stunned by Elhrin's sudden outburst.

Master Gryph calmly held out his hand. "I wondered how long it would take you to figure it out."

Her hand shook as she placed the pendant in his palm.

"Why?" she asked.

"Just in case it is needed," he draped the pendant around his neck.

"What are you two talking about?" Marguerite asked, looking from one to the other.

"The pendant has the power to send someone to Ts'aura," he replied. "Even its owner."

Marguerite's face paled. "Why would you need a way back?" she asked.

"Like I said, just in case it is needed. You two quit worrying. I don't plan on using it," he glanced at his wound. "Are you finished with this?"

"No, I'm not! You know you infuriate me when you dismiss us like this," she said, angrily.

"Marguerite, I did not dismiss you. You just do not need to worry about something that hasn't happened, yet. I cannot change destiny anymore than I can change your mind when you have it dead set on something," he said, as Marguerite narrowed her eyes at him. "Let's focus on what we have to do right here, right now, and not get sidetracked with what may or may not happen. Can we do that?"

Without a word, Marguerite went back to work dressing his wound.

"Ow! Not so hard, woman," Master Gryph growled when she slapped salve onto his cut.

"When I finish with this, Minister Idwyr, you and I are going to have to have a private discussion," she said in a low, even voice.

He looked up to the moonlit heavens with a sigh, and then dropped his gaze to look over Marguerite at Elhrin. "Guess I'm in trouble again. She always uses my title when that happens."

Marguerite snatched his shirt from the ground and threw it at him. It hit him across the chest and shoulder, a sleeve draped across his face. Marguerite then strode off towards the river and disappeared into the night.

Sighing, he pulled the shirt from his shoulder and held it up to inspect the damage to it.

"Master Gryph, please tell me there is another reason you have that pendant and you aren't going to need it to return to the Realm of Light," Elhrin said, as he grimaced at the bloodstained hole in his shirt.

"Elhrin, the pendant was given to me for a purpose, and I can make you no promises as to what I may have to do with it," he pointed at his pack sitting near her feet. "Will you hand me that?"

She tossed him his pack and he searched through it until he found a dusky gray tunic. He stood to put it on. When his head popped through the top of the shirt he saw that she was not ready to give up the discussion. "Elhrin, like I said before, don't worry about what I have to do. You need to focus on what you have to do."

She slapped her leg in frustration, completely understanding how Marguerite must be feeling. "I am focusing on what I have to do. It's all I can think about, and the closer we get to the keep, the more my stomach ties up in knots. I don't know how to use the pendant to close the Rift," she stepped closer, pointing a finger at him. "And don't tell me not to worry about you. You weren't the one who had to endure the immense grief we all went through this past year. We don't want to go through it again."

He reached out and gripped both her arms.

"Elhrin, all I can say is, I'm sorry. Sorry, I can't be more help to you with the Rift. Sorry, I can't do it for you. But most of all, I'm sorry for the pain I have caused all of you and I wish I could erase the past and make all of it go away, but I cannot. I don't know what is going to happen. I can only hope for the best."

"I thought your dream has shown you what is going to happen," she said.

"The dream you speak of certainly could happen. Elhrin, maybe I didn't explain the dream concept to you properly. Certain dreams you have are important and need to be paid special attention to. You will know these dreams because they will differ from the others. But the events of the dream are not necessarily permanent. There is the possibility of change."

"I see," she said, and another question popped into her mind. "Did you really know you were going to die last year?"

"What? Where in the world did you get that idea?" he asked, incredulously.

"Marguerite said that you had a dream of Glimmerdale years ago being attacked by Do'athrim, and that we were in the dream being attacked too, and you couldn't help us. She said that when she asked you about it, the only reason you couldn't help us was you knew you wouldn't be there, that you would already be dead. You said yes, and that was why you hid the *Book of Tolman.*"

Stunned into silence he stared at her for a moment, then his face broke into a huge grin and he laughed.

His laughter confused her. "What is so funny?"

"Nothing is funny, really, it's just Marguerite has a rampant imagination. No wonder the woman worries herself to death. Part of that is true. I did have the dream of you being attacked, but I had no idea why I was not in the dream to help you. I did not see my death. I think it would be a hard thing to take, to know the exact day you were going to die, don't you? As for hiding the book, I did know that the Do'athrim were coming soon because the dream had shown me what you looked like at this age, and there you were, looking as beautiful as the young lady in my dream. Solisius felt it was best to hide it somewhere safe, so Toome and I built the room in the cave to hide it in just to make sure it would be available for you when the time came."

"But what would have happened to the book if you and Marguerite were not there to get it for me? I had no idea it existed."

"Elhrin, the book has a way of finding its way into the right hands at the right time. Such is the magic within its composition if there is no one at the time to place it into the hands of the rightful owner. That being said, Marguerite wasn't the only one that knew you were to have that book and where I had put it. Toome knew, as well as King Goruth."

"King Goruth, why him?" she asked.

"My dear, I told you before the So'ladiun are tied to the Kings of Anderan. He has known who you are since the day I had to explain to him the reason I had to leave Muryne and live in Glimmerdale."

"You have got to be kidding me? He knew who I was all this time and never spoke to me about it? Why?"

"He didn't know if you knew, and he wasn't allowed to reveal that to you, Elhrin. Goruth knows that destiny has a way of finding you, and I'm sure he was waiting for you to tell him. He must have realized you knew who you were and ready to face the fact even though you did not talk to him because he would not have let you come on this journey if he had thought otherwise," he said, glancing over her head. "I better go find Marguerite. It seems the time has come to explain some things I have put off. We will talk more, later."

After he left, she sat down beside Tomas, who was pulling bones out of a piece of the fish that Marguerite had left for them. She could not believe that the king had known who she was all along. Now she understood why he had pinned her with his gray eyes every time she was in his presence.

She smiled at Tomas, remembering the king telling her to meet with him after this was all over. If she survived, her destiny may be tied to Muryne after all.

"Not that I'm complaining, but what is that smile for?" he asked.

"No reason. I just felt like smiling," she said, and kissed him on the cheek.

Chapter Twenty-Four

Marguerite and Master Gryph stayed away from camp throughout the entire night, worrying Elhrin, and when Marguerite walked into the camp early the next morning alone to join them for breakfast, Elhrin could tell something was wrong.

"Marguerite, are you okay?" she asked.

Marguerite settled on the rotted log next to Elhrin. She looked exhausted. Her face was pale and drawn, and her bloodshot eyes were puffy and swollen.

"I'm fine, dear, my stomach is not feeling the best and I'm so, so tired," she said, taking a hunk of stale cheese that Elhrin offered.

"Where is Master Gryph?"

"He will be here shortly," she yawned, then propped her elbows on her knees and put her face in her hand.

"Are you sure you are okay?" Elhrin asked. "Please tell me what's wrong?"

Marguerite sighed and dropped her hand from her forehead, frowning at the hunk of cheese in the other. "I found out last night that there are some things in this world a person is better off not knowing." She broke the piece of cheese in two.

"Like what?" Elhrin asked.

"No, dear, this is something I can't share," she said, and took a tentative bite of the cheese, wrinkling her nose as if the taste was unsatisfying.

Master Gryph strode through the trees, limping noticeably like a wounded man carrying a load that was almost too heavy to bear. He sat down beside Marguerite with a groan. "We must be going to get some rain out of those clouds," he frowned at the overcast sky and rubbed his leg. "My leg aches worse than a bad tooth."

Fuller settled on a nearby rock and unwrapped a parchment pack of salt-dried meat. "Minister, if you don't mind my asking, how did you injure your leg?" he asked, selecting a sliver of the meat and tearing off a bite with his teeth. He leaned over to offer Master Gryph the parchment of meat.

Master Gryph picked out a fat piece. "Years ago someone shot me at close range with a crossbow and it damaged my knee. It never healed properly."

"That is because you wouldn't let it heal," Marguerite mumbled.

He glanced at her, but said nothing.

"Who shot you?" Kyne asked.

"A member of the Brothers of M'gelidia. They have wanted me dead for a long, long time and caught me alone at the docks in Muryne early one morning."

"The man must have been a lousy shot if he missed that badly," Fuller commented.

"Well, he did not want me dead at that point. He did not miss his aim."

"Weren't they worried about you using your magic against them?" Fuller asked.

"No, they weren't too concerned."

"Why not?" Kyne asked.

"Because they poisoned me."

"Was that when you were poisoned with the same poison I had?" Bayle asked, holding up his bandaged arm.

"As a matter of fact it was, and that was why they felt confident enough to only wound me. They knew the poison would put me down quickly. I only had time to take out the bowman and one other before it took hold."

"But why the poison?" Bayle asked. "It could kill you, or did they have the antidote?"

"No, they did not want to save me. They had other plans, and knew if they worked fast enough, they would be able to do what they wanted to do," Master Gryph looked directly at Elhrin as he bit off a piece of the meat.

"They were going to pull you through a Rift, weren't they?" she whispered.

Silently chewing, he nodded.

Damn Obsudius! she fumed silently, knowing the god meant to send him to the Void.

"What happened? How did you get away?" Bayle asked.

"My son saved me."

"You have a son?" Kyne asked, raising his eyebrows.

"I do. He lives in Pago Duhn. I didn't even know he existed until two days before that incident happened. He came to find me after his mother died, and on that day I was lucky he and his shipmates were nearby and heard the fight. They were able to kill some of my attackers, but the rest ran off and were never found."

"Does he have powers like you?" Bayle asked.

"No, he did not get the gift," Master Gryph replied.

"Wait a minute," Elhrin said. "Marguerite, I thought you said you hadn't used the antidote before and wasn't sure if it would work."

"I haven't," she replied.

Elhrin glanced at Master Gryph, "Then how did you survive?"

"I owe that to my son's quick thinking and the king's physician's expertise," he yawned. "When Griffyn saw what was happening, he knew it had to be poison and put a tourniquet around my leg to slow the spread of the poison even though it had already entered my system. It was enough to get me back to the palace where the physician could work on me. He is from the south where the poison originates, which is why he recognized it, having seen similar cases before in his hometown. He knew a few tricks that helped. He told me later I was lucky the poison entered my system far from my heart and owed my life to my son's quick thinking. Very few have survived the poison. After the incident with me, he and a fellow physician out of Yradin decided to look for a cure. It took years for them to come up with the antidote that saved Bayle."

"That is definitely one more experience added to the list," Marguerite whispered.

"What list?" Bayle asked.

"My list of memories I wish I could forget," she replied.

A few hours into their trek through a dense forest of deep green ferns and moss covered tree trunks, Master Gryph's prediction of rain came true. Starting out as a fine mist, it quickly developed into a soft pattering of fat raindrops, intensifying the musky, earthy smell permeating the air. Elhrin pulled the hood of her cloak low over her eyes to keep rivulets of water from trickling across her face.

"Jag, it would be nice to know just how much further we have to go before we get to this keep," Kyne muttered.

"Kyne, did you not hear me earlier? We are going due north now, and I have not traveled past the gorge but a few times, so we are just going to have to go on what little I can remember," Jag said, not bothering to hide his aggravation at having to repeat himself. "I vaguely remember that there might be an old hunter's cabin in a valley up ahead. We might be able to reach it today, but I'm not really certain. I was just a lad when my father and I camped there, so I am not sure if this is the right direction or even if it is still standing. If we find it, the keep should be about two days north of its location."

"So you are saying that we are going to have to rely on the distant memories of your childhood," Kyne grumbled. "You probably will lead us right past the damn keep, and we won't know it until we reach Duga Bay."

Fuller ground to halt and turned to wait on Kyne to catch up. "Do you want to lead the way?" he spat. They were all tired and the rain added to their discomfort. Moods were black and patience was non-existent.

"No, but if I knew the area, I would," Kyne tried to brush past the stout man, but Fuller blocked his way.

"Since you don't, shut up, and let Jag do what he was asked to do without your constant complaints and smartass remarks," Fuller was furious and Elhrin thought he was itching for Kyne to make a move so he could hit him.

Marguerite and Master Gryph caught up with the pair and passed them on the trail.

"Boys, knock it off," Master Gryph said calmly but with a hint of steel, which left no doubt in anyone's mind that he was in no mood for arguing.

Kyne and Fuller glared at each other, then Kyne brushed by the stout man without another word.

"Bayle, are you doing okay?" Elhrin asked because he seemed to be slowing down. Marguerite looked over her shoulder to check on him.

"Yes, I'm fine." He was tired, and she could tell he was not admitting to the fact he was hurting. He glanced to his left. "We are about to get drenched."

Elhrin heard the crescendo of a major downpour pelting the trees of the forest, growing louder as it swept over the mountain. It soaked them instantly, chilling her to the bone. She followed Bayle along the narrow ledge they were using to cross the mountain face, trudging uphill through the many tiny rivers that drained down from the slope above, across the ledge, and off the edge creating miniature waterfalls. The ground became increasingly slippery. Wet leaves, algae and moss covered rocks, and mud made it difficult for her boots to make purchase. She slipped and skidded twice, almost going down if it hadn't been for Tomas grabbing her.

"Better watch where you are walking. You don't want to fall over the side," he said.

She turned her head to smile at him as he released her, and heard a low rumble below the embankment where Bayle had just passed as something dislodged and tumbled down the mountainside. Without warning, the earth moved beneath her feet and gave way. She started to fall.

"Elhrin!" Tomas yelled, trying to grab her.

She flipped and rolled down the steep slope along with half the mountainside. Sharp pains bombarded her body as earth and rock pelted her. Desperately, she tried to grab on to anything to stop her fall, but her hands kept coming up empty. She spun over a fallen tree trunk and landed heavily on her back. Dirt piled over her as the back of her head cracked against something solid and her world shattered into nothing.

Elhrin watched as a plump orange and white fish wriggled away to join his fellow fish congregated on the far side of the fountain pool. It reminded her of the day she stood by the fountain in the central gardens of the Palace of Muryne when Master Gryph had told her that fish chattered to each other like a schoolyard full of little girls—and being nine years old at the time, she knew just what that was like back home in Glimmerdale. After he had said it, she had contemplated the clear waters, watching as the fish lazily glided back and forth, their mouths constantly opening and closing as if they were, indeed, carrying on a conversation. Curiosity was always her savior or her downfall, either way she tended to jump right into whatever caught her interest, which meant she proceeded without hesitation to dunk her head in the fountain to hear the fish talk. It was a short-lived wonder to see a fish-eye view of the

interior of the fountain because the next thing she knew Marguerite jerked her out of the water and scolded Master Gryph rather loudly for sitting there doing nothing but laugh his ass off while he watched her drown. He just howled that much louder. At the time Elhrin didn't understand he had only been teasing her, never expecting her to plunge her head in to find out. Still, he may not have been serious, but she could have sworn one of those fish had told her his name was Fyn.

"Hello, Elhrin," she heard a voice say, and her heart leapt with joy. Smiling, she turned to see Solisius sitting on a bench by the fountain. He looked as beautiful as he had the first time she met him.

"Come sit with me."

"Am I dead this time?" she asked.

"No, child, you are very much alive," he smiled brightly. "You have had a nasty fall. I wanted to talk to you again." He patted the bench beside him.

Feeling light as air and wonderfully free from stress and worry, she happily walked to the bench. "Are the others all right?"

"They are fine, but worried about you."

She sat beside him as a vibrant red and yellow butterfly flitted by her head and settled on his shoulder. She smiled, watching as it calmly opened and closed its wings and cleaned its antennae with its front legs. Everything in his realm was breathtaking. Nothing in the physical world compared to the perfect beauty she saw here, and she couldn't believe he would allow anything as foul as the Do'athrim to enter Ts'aura. "My Lord, did you truly send the Do'athrim to the Void?"

A glimmer of sadness entered his eyes. "I did. It is not something that pleases me, but the alternative was not an option. I agreed with Gryphon. They could not be allowed back into my brother's realm. Your mission is too important."

"Why did you pick me to do this—to be one of your So'ladiun?"

"Why not you?" he asked, looking at her sideways.

"I know you have already told me I'm worthy, but when I read about all those that came before me, I see a big difference between who they were and who I am."

"Ah, noticed that you were the first woman, did you?" he smiled.

Dumbstruck, she stared at him for a moment then smiled back. "Actually, that didn't occur to me. Thank you for pointing that out. No, I meant in terms of strength and confidence, not to mention experience."

"Gryphon says you beat yourself up all too often. I know he has told you more than once that you are stronger than you give yourself credit for being. My child, never compare your worth to others. Each child of mine is worthy in their own right and each has their own unique qualities and strengths. Do you think I would have given you this life's task if I felt you would not be able to handle it? Surely, you will have trouble. Just ask Gryphon. Do you think his life has been easy?"

She shook her head.

"No, no one has a perfect life. It is a journey through time, full of joy and heartache, and through those experiences you build strength and character and all the qualities that make you who you are. Elhrin, you already possess the power to overcome anything that stands in your way, you just have to acknowledge the fact and believe in yourself. I know finding out that I had chosen you was a shock. And I will expect a lot from you. It will not be easy, and

for that I am truly sorry. All of my warriors have been asked to live with a lifetime of stress and sacrifice, but I am pleased they were willing and none failed me. Sadly though, some have paid a price that I was not willing for them to pay, and that is an issue I plan to take up with Obsudius."

"What do you mean?" she asked.

"Obsudius knows the rules, and continues to break them. I want him to know I won't put up with him any longer."

"How?"

"Gryphon and I have something worked out."

"Is he coming back here?" she asked.

"Gryphon?"

"Yes, will he be coming back here?"

"Most certainly. You will too, eventually. Would that be so bad?" he asked, smiling.

"No, it wouldn't." As a matter of fact, leaving was going to be difficult.

He closed his eyes for a moment, frowned, and then opened them to look at her sadly.

"Elhrin, I have to leave you. Obsudius' army is keeping me quite busy. You may stay here for awhile if you wish, but do not linger long—the others are waiting," he said, clasping her hand and squeezing it before he stood. "Don't forget, I am listening if you need to talk to me."

The blackness was impenetrable, and Elhrin struggled to free herself from its hold. She couldn't move, she couldn't think, she drifted. Slowly, she became aware that she was being carried and something wet was splashing on her face. She wanted to wipe it off, but her arm would not respond to her wishes. Briefly, her eyes fluttered open, registering raindrops falling out of dark gray clouds and Master Gryph's face above her before the void of unconsciousness sucked her once again into its firm hold.

Drifting up out of oblivion, she felt a dull ache in the back of her head and as she became more conscious, the ache became a pounding force.

She moaned.

"Elhrin?" she heard his voice, sounding sweet to her ears, and tried to open her eyes. A warm hand held hers, and knew it was his. She weakly squeezed it.

"She squeezed my hand," Tomas said with relief. "Elhrin, can you hear me?"

It was the hardest thing she could remember ever doing, but she finally forced her eyes open and looked at him. He was a mess. A bandage ran across his forehead and one eye was bruised and swollen, small cuts slashed across his lips, but he was still able to produce that beautiful lopsided grin.

"What happened to you? Looks like you lost a fight," her voice cracked, barely coming out in a whisper, and she immediately regretted speaking. The pounding in her head became thunderous. She shut her eyes tightly against the monotonous thudding, willing it to stop before she became sick.

"Shh, don't talk if it hurts too much," Marguerite said.

Elhrin opened her eyes to find Marguerite on her other side. Elhrin could tell she was worn out and worried. Elhrin tried to give her an assuring smile, but didn't think she succeeded.

Bayle crawled over by Marguerite. "Hey, sis."

"Hey, you," she said hoarsely, closing her eyes briefly against the pain. "Where are we?"

"Jag found the hunter's cabin. It's not much, but at least it's dry," Tomas rubbed her hand softly between his.

"Master Gryph?" she started to ask.

"He and the boys are patrolling the area. He'll be relieved to know you are awake. We've all been worried about you," Marguerite said. "Do you think you could drink something that will help the pain a little?"

Elhrin nodded, and wished she hadn't.

She drank the foul tasting liquid that Marguerite gave her. "Bayle's right. It does taste like nasty socks," she murmured and closed her eyes, unable to stay awake.

"See?" she heard Bayle say before she drifted back into the comfort of sleep.

Elhrin opened her eyes to an almost pitch dark room and for a moment had a hard time figuring out where she was, but then remembered Tomas telling her they were in a hunter's cabin. She turned her head carefully toward the only light source and found Master Gryph leaning against the wall next to her, staring into the flames of a small fire built in a ragged stone fireplace. Those not on watch were fast asleep around her.

"Young lady, don't you ever scare me like that again," he said quietly.

"I love you, too," she whispered, thankful that the pounding in her head didn't increase.

He smiled and winked at her. "How do you feel?"

"Like someone is beating me in the back of the head with a boat oar."

"That good, huh? Do you hurt anywhere else?"

"Probably, but I'm too scared to move and find out. What happened?"

"You and Tomas were caught up in a landslide."

Now she knew why he looked so horrible. She tried to recall the incident, but all she remembered was walking in the rain.

"Do you want anything?" he asked.

"I could use a drink of water." She felt as if she had a mouthful of sheep's wool, it was so dry.

He scooted over and helped her raise up enough to sip out of a waterskin.

"I understand you finally talked with Solisius," he said, while she drank.

"I did. How did you know?"

"I talk with him every day, and while he did not discuss what you two said, he did tell me you and he visited. Do you want more?"

"No."

He gently helped her lay back down.

"It is so beautiful there, and peaceful. It was hard to leave. I don't see how you were able to leave and return to this—to all the hurts and worries?"

"I'm not going to say it was not hard because it was, but then I think about what I came back for, and who I came back to, and that makes it all worth the pains I have in my leg or my chest," he paused briefly. "Solisius gave me a second chance. I hope to resolve a few things that I've left undone before I leave this world again."

"Like what?"

"Hmm, let's see. I've been meaning to teach Bayle the Ballad of the Ball-Busting Whore just to irritate Marguerite."

Elhrin couldn't help herself and laughed, the pounding in her head slammed against the side of her skull and she put her hands on her head against the pain.

"Don't make me laugh. It hurts too much," she groaned with a smile.

"Sorry, my love," he apologized.

"You aren't going to tell me, are you?" she asked.

"Nope."

"That figures," she said. "Sometimes, I think it would be easier to row a boat across the sands of the Hai Desert than get an answer from you." She slipped a finger around to the back of her head and gingerly touched the bandage Marguerite had wrapped over her wound. She didn't know how bad it was, but she did know it hurt, considerably.

"Do you need something for pain?" He picked up a small bottle by his side. "Marguerite said to give you this if you needed it."

"Yes, I think I do," she said.

He gave her a tiny sip of the horrible black liquid. "Try to rest," he said, scooting back to lean against the wall.

She sleepily watched tiny blue and gold flames dance across the embers of the fire. "Master Gryph?" she whispered, remembering something he mentioned.

"Hmm?"

"What is wrong with your chest?"

"Every now and then I have a little pain and trouble breathing because of the injury I received last fall."

"You mean it is not healed?" she shifted her head to look at him.

"It is, but I don't think things are exactly as they were before the injury."

"Couldn't Solisius have healed you so you wouldn't have any more trouble?"

"He could have, but the laws of nature are not to be ignored or broken, even for a So'ladiun. That being said, I was healed somewhat—at least, the hole is no longer there, and I am not wheezing out of my chest."

"There is always a bright side, isn't there?" she mumbled.

"Absolutely."

Chapter Twenty-Five

Elhrin woke to an empty cabin and a monster of a headache. She turned her head to relieve the pressure on the injury to the back of her skull and saw that the cabin's door had been left open. Sunlight spilled through the opening, revealing miniscule dust motes that drifted and swirled along unseen air currents. Hearing the rise and fall of male laughter outside, she gingerly pushed herself up, wincing when the pounding in her head took on the cadence of a march.

A shadow broke the stream of sunlight and Marguerite stepped through the door. "Hello there, sweetheart," she beamed, seeing that Elhrin was awake. "How do you feel?"

"Like a herd of cows took turns to dance all over my head and body."

Marguerite smiled. "Is that better or worse than being smacked in the head with boat oars?"

"I take it Master Gryph told you I said that," she said with a small smile.

"He might have mentioned it when he told me you woke during the night," Marguerite squatted beside her. "Are you hungry?"

"No, just a little thirsty. Where is everyone?"

"Jag and Kyne are on patrol. The others behind the cabin, telling outrageous stories." She leaned over to pick up a nearby waterskin and pulled out the stopper. "Fuller killed a deer this morning and it has sparked a debate on the subject of hunting wild game. I think Gryph is making up animals that don't exist," she laughed. "Are you sure you are fine? You look pale."

"I'm okay," Elhrin said, taking the waterskin, "but I really want to go outside. The cabin smells." She didn't want to tell Marguerite the smell combined with the pounding in her head was making her sick to her stomach.

Marguerite grunted in agreement. "Yes, it does. Hunters weren't the only ones that used it for shelter. We had to evict a family of raccoon. Are you sure you can make it outside?"

"I would like to try."

Another shadow filled the doorway. "Now there's a beautiful sight."

"Why thank you, Tomas," Marguerite looked over her shoulder.

"I, uh, well," he stammered, flushing red.

Marguerite laughed. "Don't get tied up in knots, dear. I knew you were talking to Elhrin."

"Yes, madam," he breathed, coming inside.

"Since you are here, would you be kind enough to escort her outside."

"I would be honored," he stooped to help Elhrin to her feet.

Elhrin had to wait for a wave of dizziness and the thunder of drums pounding in her head to reside before she was able to move.

Tomas and Marguerite both gave her looks of doubt.

"I'm fine," she assured them, taking Tomas by the hand and confidently heading for sunshine. She wasn't about to let them know she felt weak as a newborn kitten. She needed fresh air.

"Tomas, keep an eye on her. I'm going to change out of these muddy clothes. Let me know if you need me."

"Yes, madam," he said.

The warped and half-rotted door of the cabin scraped closed behind them. Elhrin knew how Marguerite hated to be dirty and inspected her own skin and clothing, grunting to herself without surprise, finding that Marguerite had washed her and changed her clothes while she had been unconscious.

Tomas led Elhrin to an old, hand-hewn log bench in the shade of a sprawling oak. Gingerly, Elhrin sat down to view their surroundings. Tomas was right when he said the cabin wasn't much. She was amazed it was still standing. The whole cabin, made out of rough timber logs, leaned to the left, and the sagging roof was covered in a dense, bright-green moss. It had only one window opening, which was concealed by a tattered skin of an animal and the chimney was fashioned from rocks, some of which had long ago fallen, leaving the top jagged, and with the lazy tendril of white smoke from the simmering coals left over from their fire wafting out its hole, it reminded her of an old man she once saw blow tobacco smoke between a gap in the only two teeth he owned.

"Do you want anything?" Tomas asked.

"If you could find me a new body that doesn't hurt, that would be great," she said, with a smile.

"I wish that was possible. I would get myself one," he smiled, then winced when the cuts on his lips cracked. He touched them to make sure they didn't bleed.

"We are lucky to be alive, aren't we?" she sighed. The bruises on his face were a deep purple and ugly.

"Yes, we are." Tomas straddled the bench beside her. "But you are not fooling me, stubborn. I can tell you feel rotten. Here, lean back on me."

She did as she was told and snuggled happily into his arms.

"Better?"

"Much better," she said, looking past a row of fat pines to a broad, rolling meadow beyond. The cabin was settled in a small valley cove, surrounded by tall mountains. A hawk swooped down on something far out in the middle of the valley and vanished into the high grass. "Has anything happened while I was sleeping?"

"No, it's been quiet," he draped an arm low around her waist. She entwined her fingers with his. "We have been taking turns patrolling the area. So far, there are no signs of the enemy, and Minister Idwyr has not detected Cynder again since yesterday. The beast seems to be staying to the west."

Elhrin sent her senses out as far as possible and found nothing. "He won't stay away for long. We should go."

"The minister said we would do whatever was necessary for you. Don't push yourself too hard, Elhrin. I know we are in a hurry, but it won't do any good if you are hurt."

"I know, but we are running out of time. Cynder is not going to leave us alone and he will come back or send more beasts after us. I am certainly not in any hurry to get to Blackridge, and I'm scared out of my mind, but King Goruth will not be able to hold Obsudius' army off forever—assuming he has not already fallen."

"He hasn't fallen. I know he is at a disadvantage, but he is cunning, and has the best military minds around him. It would take a lot to bring him down."

"I hope you are right."

The hawk in the meadow lifted off the ground, holding something small and furry in its talons, and flew off into the forest.

They heard the cabin door being wrestled open, and Marguerite came out carrying an armful of muddy clothes, looking tired, but clean. She had changed into the only extra clothing she had packed, a tan tunic and brown trousers.

"Elhrin, I am going to wash out our clothes. Let me know if you need anything."

"Thank you, I will," she said, watching Marguerite make her way to the little stream that meandered through the trees a short distance away from the cabin. "Tomas, do you notice anything different about Marguerite?"

"No," he shook his head, "not really. She looks tired, but don't we all?"

"Yes, but this is different—I know she is worried about something she won't tell me about, but I can't shake the feeling there is something more."

"She has a right to be worried," Tomas leaned down to kiss the side of her head, "and worry can take a lot out of a person."

"Tell me about it," she said, then hesitated. His tone was off. "Are you worried about something, Tomas?"

"You bet I am."

"What are you worried about?" she asked, carefully tilting her head back so she could see his face.

His eyes lost focus as he gazed out over the meadow. "Elhrin, when they pulled you out of the mud—you looked dead," he stopped long enough to gather his next thought. "I couldn't breathe. It scared me more than anything I have ever experienced." His blue eyes fell back on her, intense with something she wasn't expecting. "I have never felt this way about anyone, Elhrin, no one. I want the chance to get to know you better, and I don't want anything to prevent that from happening."

Is it possible he loves me, too? she wondered silently, amazed at the possibility that two people could fall in love in such a short period of time. Or, was it not love, but their circumstances throwing them together, knowing that they could die on this journey? Either way, it didn't matter. She decided to live in the moment, and reached up to touch his face. "I want to get to know you better, too."

He lowered his head and kissed her softly, shifting her in his arms so he could reach her better. She moved her hand into his hair and down to the back of his neck, pulling him closer, and felt him wince against her.

"Did I hurt you?" she whispered, against his lips.

"No," he whispered back, and kissed her again, effectively washing away any thoughts of pain or discomfort.

Later, after Jag and Kyne returned from a patrol of the area, they all gathered behind the cabin to eat.

"Does anyone want more?" Fuller asked, carving a slice of meat off one of the deer roasts.

"I do," Bayle said, reaching for the piece Fuller offered.

Master Gryph rose from the log he and Marguerite had been sharing and stretched. "I've had enough. I'll take the next watch. Marguerite, do you want to join me?"

"I will in a bit," she said with a yawn, standing. "I think I would just like to lie down for a minute."

He scrutinized her face. "Is something wrong?"

"No, I'm just tired. Go. I need a short nap. I'll find you in a half-hour," she said, heading for the cabin. "Fuller, don't forget to bury what we can't carry."

"I won't, madam," Fuller replied.

Master Gryph stared after Marguerite until she disappeared around the front of the cabin, then without a word, he set off for the meadow.

Elhrin leaned over to Tomas and whispered, "See, Master Gryph didn't like what just happened. Something is off."

"Really?" he asked. "Nothing seemed wrong to me. She is just tired. We all are."

"You don't know Marguerite. I have seen that lady exhaust herself to where she could no longer stand but would keep going if something needed to be done. Standing watch is not a duty she would shirk. There is too much at risk," she bit her lower lip in thought. "She acts more than tired—almost as if she is sick, but doesn't want us to know."

"She doesn't act sick. I think you are trying to see something that is not there because she wouldn't tell you what the minister said yesterday."

"Maybe."

"Jag, Fuller said you killed a bear when you were a boy, is that true?" Bayle asked, stuffing meat in his mouth.

"It is."

"How did you do it?" Bayle asked with his mouth full.

"Out of a little sheer luck and a whole lot of scared," Jag chuckled. "A black bear wandered into our farm one day. My little sister was playing by herself near our barn, and it attacked her. I had been splitting firewood on the other side of our cabin when I heard her scream. Then I heard my mother scream. I didn't know what was going on. When I got to the front yard, my mother was trying to get the bear to let go of my sister with her broom. It did and turned to attack my mother. I threw the axe and killed it."

"Was your sister okay?"

"She lived, but the bear had mauled her arm beyond repair and they couldn't save it."

"A boy throwing an axe at a full size bear and killing it?" Kyne snorted with contempt. "Really?"

Jag gave Kyne an icy stare. "Are you calling me a liar?"

Kyne shrugged his shoulders. "Maybe you are not lying, but maybe you are embellishing a tale for better entertainment." Kyne slipped his knife from its sheath and proceeded to dig dirt out from under his fingernails.

Jag stiffened. Elhrin thought if Kyne said one more word, Jag would go after him.

"Kyne, you fancy yourself a weapons expert, don't you?" Jag growled.

"Somewhat," Kyne said, inspecting his fingernails. "Why?"

"Back home we have a harvest festival every fall. One of the things we do during the festival is hold an axe throwing competition. Have you ever seen one, or are those in the upper class too high and mighty for such backwoods simpleton games?"

"Oh, the high and mighty," he sneered, "will occasionally delve in the lower class's boring games. I have not only seen the competitions, but have competed a time or two over the years."

"Is that right? Would you care to play right now?"

"I suppose," he said, sounding bored, "but I don't think anyone is carrying an axe."

"We have hatchets. Can you handle that?"

"Of course."

Elhrin slowly rose to her feet, grimacing and holding in a groan from the thudding in her head as she stretched her sore back out.

"Where are you going?" Tomas asked.

"I think I'll join Master Gryph. I'm not interested in watching this. It could get ugly."

"Do you want me to go with you?" he asked, but she could tell he really wanted to stay and watch the competition.

"Why don't you stay here? I'm not going to go far. I just want to see if I can walk out some of this soreness."

"If you are sure," he said, taking her hand and giving it a little squeeze.

"I'm sure," she reassured him and walked out of the shade into golden light, noticing that it wouldn't be much longer before the sun would slide behind the mountains and send the valley into deep shadows. There was no sign of Master Gryph, but she could feel his energy across the expansive meadow where a large oak stood alone in the thick grass and sporadic patches of blackberry briars. She trudged through the shin high carpet of green to the tree but did not see him underneath the canopy of limbs.

"Did you need something, Elhrin?" he asked.

She moved to the other side and stopped just outside the reaches of the lower branches high above her head. He rested back against the tree with his arms crossed over his chest and boots crossed at the ankle. He watched the woods on the far side of the meadow and did not bother to look at her.

"No, I just thought to work out the soreness in my legs."

Irritated when he failed to look at her, she traced his line of sight to find nothing but trees and meadow and a fat bee zooming straight as an arrow to a patch of orange blossoms on a rogue azalea bush among the blackberry. She moved to stand in his line of sight, forcing him to focus on her.

"Actually, yes, there is something I want to know. Is something wrong between you and Marguerite?"

His brow shot up, surprised by her question. "No, nothing is wrong between us. Why do you ask?"

"Because something seems off with Marguerite besides," she waved a hand at herself, "worrying about all of this. Is she sick?"

"Ah, I see. No, she is weary and has a lot on her mind right now and needs a little time to process it. Don't worry, she'll be herself again soon," he said, then added under his breath, "I hope."

"What do you mean?"

"I told her something before," he waved a hand, mimicking her," all that happened, and she is finding what I had to say a little hard to take."

"I know you aren't going to tell me, but I'm going to ask anyway. What have you told her?"

"You are right. I'm not going to tell you."

"You know, one of these days, when it comes time for you to want me to tell you something you want to know, I'm going to refuse."

"I look forward to it," he said.

She rolled her eyes at his indifference. Just once, she wished she could get him to do something she wanted.

"How's your head?" he asked.

"Better," she was not going to admit it pounded incessantly. "I think I could make it if we wanted to leave in the morning."

"We'll see." He gave her a look that said she had not fooled him, then he nodded at something over her shoulder. She turned to see a mother deer and her fawn timidly step out of the woods, sniffing cautiously for danger, then dropping her head to snatch quick bits of grass.

Seeing the mother and the baby reminded Elhrin of her own situation and her future. "Master Gryph, can I ask you something personal?"

"Depends on how personal you are going to get."

"Did Solisius require you not to have a family?"

He grunted and shook his head slightly. "You and Marguerite are not going to let this go, are you?" He looked straight into her eyes, "No, Elhrin, it was not a requirement. It was a choice I made long before I met Marguerite. Why do you want to know?"

"Because I wanted to know if this was something I had to do, too."

"You will make your own choices when you get a better idea of what Solisius wants you to do, and I'm not talking about the Rift, but beyond, when this is all over."

Her stomach jumped a little. He was speaking as if their mission would be successful. A glimmer of optimism wedge its way into her heart.

"What made you decide?"

He looked out over the meadow, his eyes following the deer as they made their way to the other side. Sighing he glanced at her, and she knew that Marguerite had been correct.

"It was because of me, wasn't it?" she asked.

"Elhrin, I was fairly young when I realized what Solisius needed me to do, and I resolved then to remain single and childless. Solisius and Goruth were already dominating most of my time, not to mention the danger I constantly faced, and then I was going to have to be around for you, too. I figured it wouldn't be fair to bring a wife and child into that kind of situation. I knew you were going to need as much of my attention as I was able to give, so I made the decision to focus on that."

"But what about Marguerite? You married her."

"Now that is a different story. She is one woman who can be very persuasive," his face spread into a grin, "and gave me no choice but to change my mind on the matter of marriage and made it very difficult to keep my decision to not have children, especially, before I met you and your brother because I wanted nothing more than to make her happy. But after I became involved in your lives, it was easier for me. I do regret the fact Marguerite had to live with it. She deserved much more than what I had to offer."

"It is amazing to me that you knew about me before I was born. Did Solisius tell you or did you dream about me?"

"In a way it was both. Solisius showed me a baby girl with a mop of brown curls, running headlong into my arms in a dream." His eyes lost focus as he recalled the memory—a smile on his lips. "I did not know your name, but I knew you were going to be a central part of my life. Not long after that dream a second dream revealed you in various stages of growing up and that you would have the gift of magic. I knew then that you would be So'ladiun, and it was imperative that I train you."

"Solisius didn't tell you more about me?" she asked, wondering why, if the god could speak to them directly.

"No, Solisius does not reveal every aspect of our lives nor will he tell us everything that we need to know. He may give us hints—signs, if you will, but it is up to us to guide our own destinies."

"Then if you knew I was to be So'ladiun, why didn't you tell me years ago?"

"You are full of questions today, aren't you? Is it a result of that bump on your head?"

"Ha, funny," she said, and crossed her arms, waiting on him to answer.

"Elhrin," he gave her a pained look, "the truth is I was selfish. I kept telling myself you needed more time, you were too young—that you needed to be old enough to make the decision on your own."

"Until I was old enough—how old was I supposed to be before you felt I could make this decision?" she asked frustrated, realizing an instant later what she had just said. "Wait a minute, I had a choice? You made it sound as if this is what I had to do."

"I know I did. For that, I am sorry, but realize, I had made a mistake and waited too late to tell you, and it was necessary for you to make this journey. Even so, you could have flat out refused me or ignored me altogether when I told you to come, but you did not, you came anyway. What does that tell you? Elhrin, you did have a choice, still do, but Solisius chooses his warriors wisely, and none have refused him. The other night, when you wanted to quit, he would have accepted. Do you want to quit on him?"

She thought about it for a moment and was surprised at the only answer she could give him. "No, as scared as I am, I don't."

"I didn't think you did," he grinned, and held out his hand.

She closed the space between them and clasped it. He gently pulled her close and hugged her lightly.

"You have a long hard road ahead of you," he said as if he regretted she had been chosen.

"But you are going to be with me on that road, aren't you?"

"I will be for now, but I won't always be. Yet, I am not worried about that, you are ready to stand on your own."

"What does that mean?" Scared, she looked up at him.

He smiled down at her. "No one lives forever. Trust me in this. I am experienced at dying."

"I swear, if there is a joke to be made, you will make it," she squeezed him tight then stepped back out of his arms. "So is this it then? Certainly you aren't through with me."

"Define what you mean by 'through with you,'" he said.

"You said I was ready and I assumed you meant I am no longer your apprentice."

"I have taught you most everything I can think of to teach you, but don't make the mistake of thinking that is all there is to know. Things are always changing and evolving. Learning never ends, even for an old man like me. Is there something in particular you think I might have missed?"

"How did you create that sphere by the river last fall?"

He nodded and pushed himself away from the tree. "Ah, yes. Come with me."

They walked out into the middle of the meadow, and he made sure that they were well away from anything that might get in the way.

"This was something I had been saving for when we had the chance to go far away from the village, but I never seemed to find the time." He shrugged his shoulders. "Do you want me to just show you, or do you want to try it yourself?"

"I think I would like to try it."

He narrowed his eyes. "I don't know. You are still pretty weak."

"I can handle it," she said, confidently.

He stared at her for a moment, clearly at odds with allowing her to try this under her weakened condition. He finally nodded. "All right, but you have to be extremely careful. Because of its power, it takes a tremendous amount of your energy just to build a tiny sphere, and once you have it set, you must make sure that when it is released, the direction of its force goes away from you, or you will end your own life."

She nodded, wondering if maybe she had made a mistake in asking him how to do this. She did feel terrible, and it sounded dangerous to do in a weakened state.

"Okay, do you see the large briar patch with the sapling dogwood?" he asked, pointing to a tangle of brush with a baby tree stuck in its midst far out in the meadow.

"Yes."

"High above it is where I want you to place your sphere."

"Isn't that too far away?"

"If I thought you could place one further away, I would want you to do it," he said.

"Are you telling me you don't trust me to get this right?" she asked, narrowing her eyes.

"No, I'm saying you have a head injury, and as much as you would like me to think you are fine, you are not. If you want to continue with this, it is not going to help the pain one bit," he said. "Do you wish to continue?"

"I do."

"Very well, don't say I didn't warn you," he spread his hands in front of him looking as if he were waiting to catch something. A small orb of soft white light popped into midair between his palms. "I am not going to build the real thing, but you would create it much like this ordinary light sphere, only you are going to intensify the energy contained inside to a combustible force well beyond that of the fireball you like to use. As you increase the energy, its size will expand, and when you are ready to release it, force the energy away from you through the other side."

His little white sphere expanded and then bowed outward away from him to burst with a tiny popping sound.

"Okay, I think I've got it," she said, facing the briar patch.

"Elhrin, don't make it any bigger than the one I just did," he warned.

She nodded as she took in a deep breath and slowly let it out, then reached for her magical energy. The pounding in her head increased slightly, but she ignored it. Spreading her arms, she followed his instructions and created the sphere over the briar patch. Beginning with the size of a small stone, she increased the intensity of the flow, and instantly realized she was weaker than she thought and her energy source was not as strong as she was used to. Ignoring this, too, she willed more energy into the sphere, and it expanded slowly. She could feel the raw power barely contained inside the sphere as she increased the intensity. It was far different holding onto a growing force of energy than the small bursts she was used to firing away from her. A low, sizzling hum drifted over the quiet meadow. She now knew how he had managed such a level of destruction on the river the day he died.

"That's big enough," he said. "We do not want to blow up the meadow."

The pulsing orb was no bigger than a water bucket. She pushed the energy away from her and forced it through the other side of the sphere. The sound of the explosion rivaled that of a thunderclap breaking directly overhead. Elhrin slammed her eyes closed and clapped both hands on her head as pain from the back of her head seared blindingly throughout her skull. He grabbed her and turned her to face him.

"Elhrin?"

She opened one eye to see him grinning from ear to ear, trying not to laugh. "I forgot about the sound. Why didn't you warn me?" she accused.

"I did warn you," he said, not able to contain a chuckle.

"Not good enough. You should have been more specific," she grinned in spite of the pain. Mercifully, it began to subside to a dull thud. "Here come the boys."

He turned to watch them run across the grass. "Let me tell you this before they get here and pelt us with questions. It takes too much time to build and will leave you vulnerable in the midst of a fight, as I found out all too well. Be careful in choosing when to use it."

"I'm not so sure I want to do it at all," she said, feeling totally drained and thinking maybe she should not have tried it before she regained her strength. "It really does take it out of you."

"Yes, it does. As a matter of fact, the last time I used it, it took the life right out of me," he smiled.

"Another dead joke?"

"Marguerite isn't here, is she?" he asked, knowing Marguerite had warned him more than once for him to stop making jokes about his death.

"Lucky for you, no."

"What happened?" Bayle called out as he and the others halted protectively around them, hatchets readied for a fight.

"You boys missed a spectacular magical demonstration from Elhrin," Master Gryph said, and a puzzled look crossed his face when he noticed what they were carrying. "Hatchets?"

"Oh, well, we were having a little competition when we heard the explosion," Jag relaxed his stance. "Hatchet throwing."

"Is that right? Who was winning?" Master Gryph asked, and Fuller coughed behind his hand, slightly shaking his head no.

"What's that supposed to mean, Fuller?" Kyne asked, frowning. "I was winning and you know it."

"How could you have been winning? The fourth throw was questionable on points and the last throw fell out. It did not count. Right, Tomas?" Jag asked.

"Leave me out of this. I don't know the rules," Tomas said holding up both hands.

"Big help you are." Jag said, frowning. "Fuller, am I right?"

Kyne didn't allow Fuller to answer. "Jag, you are just stalling the inevitable. You had no points at all on your second throw. My questionable throw is only questionable by you. I have more points even with my last one falling out. I won." Kyne said with a knowing smirk on his thin face. "Hand over the knife you owe me."

"I'm not giving you my knife. You did not win," Jag said, voice rising. He was growing angrier by the minute.

"I should have known you wouldn't own up to your end of the bet when you lost," Kyne balled his fists at his side. "Backwoods hill folk are never good at their word."

Jag started for Kyne, but Fuller managed to grab his arm and hold him back.

"That's enough, boys," Master Gryph growled a warning.

Jag ignored him, jerking his arm out of Fuller's grasp. "Backwoods hill folk are known for keeping their word. It's the spoiled offspring of royalty or their extended family who never have to struggle a day in their life that you have to worry about. *Your kind*," he sneered the words as if they were diseased, "just takes anything you want—like now. You did NOT earn my knife."

"I said ENOUGH!" Master Gryph roared.

Jag took a step back. Elhrin bit back a smile. Master Gryph was more than a bit scary when he was angry.

"No one is going to give anyone anything," he barked. "Since you boys seem to have energy to spend, get back to the cabin and work on hiding signs of our stay here. I don't want to hear anymore arguing out of anyone. Do I make myself clear?"

"Yes, sir," Jag and Kyne answered, giving each other one last glare.

"Why are you all still standing here? Move!" he ordered.

Everyone but Tomas and Elhrin hustled away, and they no sooner took five steps before Jag and Kyne continued their argument.

"Your day is coming, you bastard," Jag hissed. "No one talks about my people."

"It is not a wise idea to threaten me," Kyne growled. "I could slit your throat right before your eyes and you wouldn't know it until the blood flowed freely down your neck."

"You think highly of your abilities, don't you?" Fuller scoffed. "Man, you don't know who you are dealing with."

"It is you who does not know whom you are dealing with," Kyne seethed.

"I've had about enough of this," Master Gryph growled. "I am going to have a private word with each of them." He glanced at Elhrin. "Do you need me for anything else?"

"No, I think I'm going to find a place to sit down and see if I can get my head to not fall off." He frowned at her answer. "But I'm fine," she quickly added, "to leave tomorrow, I mean."

"Right," he said, not believing her, but left without pressing the issue.

Tomas lifted an eyebrow at Elhrin. "I am so glad that I am not the one having a private word with him this time. It is not a pleasant experience."

Elhrin laughed. During his and Master Gryph's first watch alone together, Tomas had been forced for hours to listen to Master Gryph's stories, all of which had been designed to get one single point across—don't hurt his little girl in any way, shape, or form, or he would regret it, immensely.

Chapter Twenty-Six

Elhrin woke with a start. Immediately, an overwhelming sense of suffocating fear and deep dread engulfed her—threatened to make her sick. Instantly alert by the vile and repulsive energy intruding on the edge of her awareness, she rolled out of her blankets. Her body protested the sudden movement and the dull throb in the back of her head made her dizzy. She closed her eyes and waited a moment for it to clear, focusing on the foreign energy source sending an alarm throughout her system. Cynder was on his way—he was far to the west, but his energy source was steadily increasing in strength.

She opened her eyes to the dark of night. The fireplace was now cold. Someone had put it out. She rose to her feet and made her way to the open door of the cabin, careful to not step on the sleeping forms on the floor. Master Gryph was not one of them. His energy source was in the direction of the meadow. She stepped outside and nearly screamed when a dark form materialized beside her.

"Kyne, don't do that," she spat, squeezing her booming head between her hands, trying to quell the pain. She vowed to hurt him if he startled her one more time.

"Do what?" he asked. "I was already here when you came out."

"Never mind," she fumed. "Are you and Master Gryph the only ones up?"

"No, he and Jag are out patrolling. I was told to stay and watch the cabin."

Her senses told her he was in the meadow, coming back towards the cabin. "Cynder's on the way. Wake everyone. I'll be right back." She pushed past him and hurried to the edge of the meadow.

Master Gryph was running as fast as his limp would allow across the thick grass. Bow drawn and arrow at the ready, Jag ran beside him. "Elhrin, gather your things," he yelled, waving for her to go.

"You think he will find us here?"

"He knows where we are." He slowed and grabbed her arm, pulling her along with him.

"He does?" She stumbled, trying to match his long stride. Her head thundered in pain at the sudden movement.

A small white sphere popped into view as soon as he stepped through the cabin door.

"Thank you," Marguerite said, glancing up from where she had been trying to roll up her blanket, "what's going on?"

"Cynder's found us," he growled, out of breath. "Jag and I ran into a band of Do'athrim on the other side of the meadow. Had to kill a few, but left the rest wishing they were dead." He stopped to breath. "No doubt they soon will be."

"You didn't send them to Solisius?" Bayle asked.

"No time," he breathed, stuffing a blanket into his pack. "I managed to get one of the wolves to talk before we left them. He told me Cynder led them to our mock camp. They followed our scent back to the rockslide and discovered our true trail. He no sooner said that Cynder had to answer a summons to return to Blackridge but was expected to find them this morning, when the N'gethwyn's energy source entered my range of awareness."

"Why can't the son of a bitch just drop dead," Marguerite hissed, slapping her blanket onto her pack and securing it with leather straps. She seemed to be on the verge of crying.

Master Gryph reached over and clasped one of Marguerite's hands. "That is already assured," he said with a hint of steel.

Marguerite clamped her lips into a thin line. Staring into his eyes, she slowly shook her head.

"All will be well," he said, softly.

"I wish I could believe you," she replied.

"Come, everyone." He tugged her up. "We need to move."

Elhrin longed to ask Marguerite what was wrong, but knew she wouldn't tell her. She picked up her pack and rushed out the door. The clear night sky glistened with a million stars. The moon was edging its way down on the western horizon, and Cynder was under it somewhere heading their way.

"Jag, we will need to try and stay in areas with as much overhead cover as possible," Master Gryph said, heading towards the northern edge of the meadow.

"Yes, sir," he replied, falling in step with the older man.

"The Do'athrim you said were still alive won't follow us?" Bayle asked, nervously eyeing the western side of the meadow.

"Not without legs they won't," Jag growled.

As the night slipped towards dawn, Cynder's magical energy drifted closer. He didn't seem to be in a hurry which gave them time to move further away from the cabin.

Jag led them on a northwest direction, moving closer to the northern edge of the mountain range so he could gauge their proximity to the keep in territory that was more familiar to him, keeping to the woodsy stream beds and valley areas, but when the sky above started to lighten, they found themselves surrounded by the mountains and the only option was to climb up and over.

Cynder was now behind them, and when the beast's energy stopped in one place, she knew he had found his Do'athrim and the cabin. Master Gryph halted, turning to look back the way they had come. The others looked puzzled when he offered no explanation as to why he stopped.

"I think Cynder has found the cabin," she said.

"Do you think he will pick up our trail?" Bayle asked quietly.

"I do not know," Master Gryph answered him, staring at the sky. "It's possible, if he brought more of his friends."

Cynder stayed in the area around the cabin for several minutes then she felt him on the move again, heading northeast of their location.

"Interesting," he mused, indicating for Jag to move along. "He's not moving straight at us. He must be alone for now."

Pushing their way upward through thick undergrowth and over rocky outcrops, exposed roots, and washed out ravines, they kept a steady pace. It didn't take long for the constant uphill exertion to wreak havoc on Elhrin's condition. The pounding in her head rose to a thunderous, stomach churning level.

She swiped a cold sweat from her brow.

"Elhrin, are you all right?" Tomas asked, as he offered her a hand up a steep embankment. "Your face is pale."

"Yes," she managed to croak as she clambered up, "I'm fine."

"You don't look fine," Tomas said.

"Elhrin, do you need something for pain?" Marguerite asked.

She wanted to say no, but she knew it was no use. She nodded.

"Gryph, hold up," Marguerite called out as she retrieved a bottle from her pouch and gave it to Elhrin. "Just a small sip, it makes you sleepy, and we don't want you falling. Next time, don't wait to ask me for help."

"I won't," she said, grimacing at the foul taste of the liquid.

Over the next hour, the sun drifted above the mountain tops. Cynder was still searching the area to the east, but had drifted a little closer. It seemed he knew that they had just left the cabin and was thoroughly searching the area close to it. She wished he would just go away. The pain in her head made it difficult to concentrate and keep track of where he was with her senses. The serum Marguerite had given her had eased the pain in her head to a more manageable level but did not make it go away, and as Marguerite had warned, it was making her sleepy. Elhrin didn't know which was worse, fighting the pain or fighting sleep. She couldn't have her mind fuzzy. It needed to be clear if they were forced to face Cynder.

Higher they hiked across the face of the mountain, stopping only once to catch their breath before they needed to move again. Cynder drifted closer.

"This is not good," Jag commented.

"What isn't?" Bayle asked.

Jag pointed to where signs of a fire had scorched tree trunks and burned patches of ground. "There's been a fire here recently. This looks like where it ended."

They crunched over the dry and blackened earth, leaving the canopy of living trees and entering a world of desolation. The entire pinnacle of the mountain above them had been decimated by the fire. Hundreds of tall and blackened tree trunks sprouted from the charred earth like sharp spikes. Very little living vegetation remained.

"Not good at all," Master Gryph reiterated. He turned his head to look in the direction of Cynder's energy source, gauging the distance. He looked back to the group. "Are you kids ready? Let's see if we can get over the peak before we are found."

They quickly made their way up. Black and gray ash puffed up in little clouds with each step, and as they moved closer to the top and far from the cover of the trees below, fate handed them one more blow. Cynder's energy veered to the west—straight towards their location. He was not taking his time any longer.

Master Gryph swore loudly.

"What is it?" Marguerite asked.

"We need a place to hide. Right now," he said, scanning the mountainside.

"There's a stand of saplings along the crest," Fuller pointed above them. A small copse of scraggly pines had been spared major damage from the fire by an exposed rock plateau surrounding them.

"It'll have to do. Go," Master Gryph ordered, grabbing Marguerite's arm and propelling her forward.

Tomas seized Elhrin's hand and pulled her up the slope behind him. Cynder was closing in fast. Elhrin kept glancing at the horizon as they scrambled up the mountain. She expected Cynder to be somewhere over the eastern mountaintops, but couldn't find him anywhere.

Lungs burning from the exertion, they reached the crest of the mountain and raced for the trees. The rocky terrain made running difficult, and Marguerite stumbled and fell. Without breaking stride, Master Gryph and Jag grabbed Marguerite's arms and jerked her back to her feet. The three of them sprinted across the crest ahead of Elhrin and had to skirt a huge boulder to reach the trees. Master Gryph stopped and waited on Elhrin and the rest of the boys while Marguerite and Jag disappeared into the foliage.

"Elhrin, hurry," Bayle yelled. He, Fuller, and Kyne were right on her and Tomas' heels.

"I'm trying," she shouted. The effort to run was tremendous. Her pounding head felt like it was going to explode. She tripped and almost went down, but Tomas caught her arm before she fell. Master Gryph was waving for them to hurry. Rushing around the boulder, they ran past him and crashed through the prickly branches of the small pines. The boys came bursting through behind them.

"Everyone, lie flat and cover up anything that might attract his attention," Master Gryph ordered, making sure everyone was behind him when he flattened himself to the ground and used his cloak for cover. Elhrin wasn't sure the bristly needles of the young pines were going to be enough to hide them from Cynder.

The beast was somewhere nearby. The intensity of his magical energy at such close range was almost more than she could bear on top of the pounding force in her head. She tried to find him through the branches of the trees, but he was nowhere to be found. She couldn't seem to get her rattled mind to focus on pinpointing his exact location.

Where is he? she screamed in her mind.

Master Gryph looked back over his shoulder. "No one is to do anything unless we are forced into a fight," he said quietly, and just as he was turning his head back around, Cynder zoomed straight up from the mountainside below, directly over their hiding place.

Elhrin almost screamed. The force of the wind from his passing made the small trees whip back and forth violently. Bayle made a small whining sound and shifted as if he wanted to jump up and run. How could she not have known the beast had been flying low, almost following the same path as they had coming up the mountain?

Cynder circled around behind them, and Master Gryph flipped on his back.

"Stay still!" he ordered, and Elhrin felt Master Gryph's energy intensify dramatically. She hadn't realized before now that she could actually feel when he reached for his magical energy. She followed his lead. The pain in her head was enormous, making it hard to keep focus and hold on to her magic.

Without taking his eyes off the sky, he said, "Elhrin, do nothing. Cynder is my fight."

"No," she said. He glanced sharply at her. "This fight belongs to all of us."

"Your fight is at Blackridge Keep. I told you the Rift is your primary goal," he growled, shifting his gaze back to the sky to follow Cynder's progress. "If it comes to a fight, Kyne, I need you to make sure to get her out of here safely, understood?"

"Yes, sir," he replied.

Why Kyne? Elhrin frowned at Kyne. He met her stare with a look of stone. She had no doubt he would use force if he had to, to obey that command.

"I will keep her safe, sir," Tomas said.

"Yes, Tomas, all of you should go if we are attacked."

"Gryph," Marguerite whispered.

"All of you," he ordered, demanding to be obeyed even by her. He raised a hand, urging them to be still. Cynder was coming back.

The beast flew up to the ridgeline, not far from their hiding place, and settled to the ground. She could not see him from her point of view, the boulder was in the way, but she could hear him draw deep huffs of air into his gigantic lungs. Without warning, he released a long, deafening roar. Elhrin clenched her eyes shut, fighting the overwhelming urge to scream. Cynder let his roar go and huffed in huge breaths as if he was testing the air for a scent. Growling, he started running along the ridgeline straight for them. Instinctively, Elhrin raised a hand, prepared to fire on the beast. Master Gryph closed his fist at her, warning her to do nothing. Cynder jumped up on the boulder that had hidden him from Elhrin's view. Huge red eyes scrutinized their hiding place. Again, he sniffed the air, scaly nostrils expanded and contracted. A low rumble slipped from his huge, toothy maw. He lowered his head to peer underneath the foliage of the pines.

Elhrin bit back a cry and the strong desire to throw a blasting force of energy at Cynder, wondering why Master Gryph was waiting. The beast was going to see them, yet the man lay there with his hands in the air not doing anything. She couldn't take it—a tiny flash of light winked from the direction of the mountain opposite them as if sunlight glinted off something metallic. Cynder jerked his serpentine head around. He scrambled across the rock and launched himself into the air, speeding towards the flash of light.

Tears escaped from the corner of Elhrin's eyes, and she rested her head face-down on her arms. She felt like a stampede of cattle was raging through her skull.

No one moved. They waited to see what Cynder was going to do next.

"How did he not see us?" Bayle whimpered, sounding as if he was on the verge of crying.

"Bayle, be still," Master Gryph ordered.

Elhrin used her senses to follow Cynder. The beast flew back and forth across the face of the opposite mountain for what felt like an eternity, periodically trumpeting loud bellows of frustration. Finally, he gave up and flew off to the west.

"Well, well," Master Gryph breathed. "I think Cynder's dragon form is not his true form. With a nose that big he should have smelled us. Bayle alone puts a skunk to shame."

"What?" Bayle whimpered, still scared, and Master Gryph's attempt to break the tension for him did not work.

Furrowing his brow in concentration, Master Gryph said, "And I do believe the old boy is going to be useful."

Elhrin had been following Cynder's flight just as he had. The beast moved northwest until he was barely on her edge of awareness, but before he dropped out of her range, he stopped to stay in one place.

"Why?" Marguerite asked.

"Because if I am not mistaken, he has just taken himself to Blackridge Keep, and as long as he stays there, Elhrin and I can find it."

Elhrin raised her head. Master Gryph was drenched in sweat, looking as if he had dunked himself into a lake.

"Master Gryph," Bayle said, shakily raising himself to his elbows, "why didn't he see us?"

"This old man has a few tricks up his sleeve," Master Gryph wiped sweat from his face, then smiled. "Watch this."

He held up both palms, winked at Marguerite, and then disappeared.

Elhrin gaped, "What the . . . ?"

He then popped back into view, still sitting in the same place as before.

"How did you do that?" she demanded.

"It is a gift I have. I can hide myself from view by simulating my surroundings," he said, and slowly got to his feet. "In this case I had to hide all of us which takes an extensive amount of energy to hold on to."

"Simulating your surroundings? How does that hide you?"

"When someone looks at me they will only see what I want them to see. I made it look as if the trees were empty to Cynder."

"I thought you weren't doing anything," she complained.

"You wouldn't have known. From your or my point of view, nothing changes."

"Why haven't you shown me this before?"

"I have shown it to you before—many times. Have you not watched me make objects disappear? I did it all the time for you children."

"Yes, then why didn't you teach me how to do it?"

"I cannot teach it to you."

"Why not?"

"Because, as hard as this will be to understand, there are certain gifts or talents unique to individuals that cannot be taught—this is one of them. I have no way of showing you how to do it. It is a part of who I am. Did I ever tell you my predecessor, Hiram, could communicate with birds?"

"Yes," she said.

"That is the kind of gift I am talking about. I can't understand them no matter how hard I have tried," he grinned. "There were times I was extremely jealous of his gift. He had a hawk named Flick that would scout for him. A bird's-eye view can be useful when you can't see your enemies."

"I wish I had a something like it," she mumbled.

"It is possible that you do have an extraordinary talent no one else has— maybe even more than one. Sometimes you just have to stumble across them," he said, giving her a strange look she could not interpret. "If we have time one day, I will tell you how I stumbled upon mine. Jag, come with me so I can show you the direction of the keep."

"I wonder what caused the flash of light on the mountain across the way," Kyne mused aloud.

Master Gryph raised a corner of his mouth, "Why don't you ask Elhrin."

"I had to do something," she said, massaging her temples, wishing the pounding would go away. "I thought you weren't going to do anything."

"Elhrin, I don't want you to get in the habit of disobeying a direct order, but just so you know, I'm glad you did . . . this time."

He motioned for Jag to follow him.

"What did you do, Elhrin?" Tomas asked.

"I made a light sphere flash. It wasn't really on the mountain. I made it so small it looked as if it came from a distance," she said. "I had to get his attention away from us, or I was going to scream."

Elhrin laid her head back down and closed her eyes. She wished she had time to take a nap.

"You know, as a man, it is hard to admit when I'm scared," Fuller said, "but I have to say, I think I almost shit myself when that oversized lizard jumped up on that rock."

"Me, too," Tomas chuckled, and placed a hand on Elhrin's back. "Elhrin, do you need anything?"

"I just need a minute to rest," she said, and allowed herself to drift. Vaguely, she thought she heard her name called, but she was too tired to move. Moments later, someone squatted beside her.

"Elhrin," Bayle said, startling her from a light slumber she hadn't realized she had been in.

"Not now, Bayle," she moaned, irritated he had taken her from a brief respite from the pain.

"I'm sorry, but Master Gryph wants you to come see this."

"See what?"

"Blackridge Keep. You can see it from here."

She raised her head to find she was alone with him. Everyone else had left the trees. She slowly rose to her feet with Bayle's help and joined the others. Off in the hazy distance and partially blocked by the mountains that surrounded it was the top of a black structure, and Cynder's energy was coming from its direction.

"If we are able to continue until nightfall, I think we will be able to reach it sometime tomorrow," Jag said to Master Gryph.

"What do you think, Elhrin?" Master Gryph asked, not bothering to turn around to face her, and for some irrational reason it annoyed her that he didn't feel the need to look at her when he spoke.

"Why are you asking me? You are the one making the decisions," she snapped. She knew she was wrong for lashing out at him, but she was miserable and wasn't thinking clearly.

He bothered to look at her then, raising his brow at her tone. "I'm asking you because this is your decision, too. You are the one with the head injury and only you can know if you are going to be able to handle a hike for the rest of the day."

Looking at the distance to the keep made her want to cry. All she wanted to do was lie down and sleep for a week, and walking for the rest of the day was going to be difficult, but she knew she had no choice. The king's army was at stake, Anderan was at stake, and the Rift needed to be closed. They had already been delayed on this trek far too long.

"We had better get started," she said tiredly, and turned to go get her pack.

Marguerite caught up with her. "Elhrin, you are going to have to drink and eat something."

"I don't know if my stomach can handle anything right now."

"You need to try, anyway," she said, and opened Elhrin's pack, pulling out some of the rations she carried. "Here, try a piece of the flatbread. It might help settle your stomach."

Elhrin sat down, took the bread and the waterskin Marguerite offered, and tentatively took a bite. Marguerite sat down next to her, pulling her own pack closer.

"Marguerite, thank you," she said, trying to swallow the dry piece of bread, and thought she might as well eat her sleeve. It would probably taste better.

"For what, dear?"

"For everything. For allowing me to invade your home nearly every day for the last fifteen years, for standing by my side and believing in me, just for everything that you have done for me," she said, as Marguerite stared at her in surprise. "If it hadn't been for you after mother was killed, I don't know where Bayle and I would be right now."

"Elhrin, I have done nothing special. There was never a question as to where I was going to be, except with you and Bayle. You two are my babies," she smiled, and rubbed Elhrin on the back. "You don't have to thank me for something that comes naturally to me. What has brought this on?"

"I don't know," Elhrin said with a sigh. "I guess because we are almost there, and I don't know what is going to happen, and it hit me that I owe you so much. I thought I might not get the opportunity to say anything later, and I just wanted you to know that I appreciate you."

"It's always nice to hear when one is appreciated, but let me tell you one thing, you owe me nothing. When you love someone like I do you and Bayle, payment is not required. Now, stop talking as if you are not going to make it through this," she said, putting her arms around Elhrin's shoulders and hugging her.

Elhrin put her head on Marguerite's shoulder and closed her eyes, comforted by her touch. "Marguerite, I am so tired, and my head is killing me."

"I know. We don't have to go as far as Jag suggested today, but I do think we need to get off the top of this mountain," she said.

Elhrin felt Master Gryph come into the trees. She opened her eyes as he squatted down beside them, and the boys filtered in behind him to pick up their packs.

"Do you think you can make it long enough to find a place to stop?" he asked, and seeing the concern in his eyes made her sorry for snapping at him earlier.

"I want to try and get as far as we can," she said, pulling away from Marguerite.

He held her eyes for a moment then glanced at Marguerite. "We'll see."

Tomas and Bayle hovered close by her side like mother hens the entire afternoon, both in not much better condition than herself, but stoically offering her their support without complaint. Master Gryph stopped often to allow them to rest, and once, when they had found a decent place to camp, he was going to halt for the day, but she wouldn't let him even though she was more than ready to stop. He didn't like it, but he didn't argue with her and they continued on.

Sometime during their trek down into a washed out narrow cleft of rock and dirt, she felt Cynder leave the keep. She hesitated before crossing a rivulet to monitor his direction of flight.

"What's wrong?" Tomas asked.

"Cynder left the keep," she said. The N'gethwyn dropped out of her range, and did not come back. "He's flying west." She stepped over the tiny trickle of clear water and followed Bayle down the steep ravine that was just as strenuous on her body going down as it had been going up the mountain earlier. By the time they reached the bottom where it leveled out, she was sure she was done, but she resolved to keep going.

Marguerite looked her over. "This is ridiculous, young lady. You need rest," she said.

"Just let me get my breath," she huffed, catching herself in time before she reached up to squeeze her pounding head between her hands.

"Gryph," Marguerite called.

Master Gryph and Jag were well ahead, leading the way. He stopped to look back.

"She needs to stop."

"No, we can keep going," Elhrin protested.

He said something to Jag and made a circular gesture with his hand. Jag, Fuller, and Kyne disappeared into the woods. Master Gryph came back to where they stood. "I sent the boys to look for a better place to camp," Master Gryph said, crunching through dry leaves as he approached. "We are too close to the keep to be sitting out in the open like this."

Elhrin eased to the ground and lay back in the thick carpet of dead leaves. She crossed her arms over her aching head, willing it to stop.

"Do you think he has sent out more Do'athrim to look for us?" Bayle asked.

"More than likely, which means we are going to have to be more cunning to avoid them," Master Gryph said.

"What about . . . ?" Marguerite nodded at Elhrin.

"We'll rest for tonight," he said. "Tomorrow we'll see if we can move on."

"I can make it," Elhrin mumbled, closing her eyes. She seized the opportunity to relax, to drift away from the conversation, knowing that for a brief moment she was safe to give in to her fatigue, but it was short-lived. The next thing she knew, she was being picked up, and opened her eyes to find that Master Gryph held her.

"What are you doing?" she croaked, and cleared her throat. "I can walk."

"Are you sure?" he asked, and she nodded.

He lowered her feet to the ground, and as soon as he let go, her knees buckled. He caught her.

"Are you sure, you're sure?" he asked.

No, she didn't. Why did she have to feel so weak? "Yes," she told him.

He grunted, doubtfully. "All right, Jag, lead the way."

Jag and Fuller turned and made their way into the woods. Master Gryph, Marguerite, and Bayle followed. Kyne gave her one last look, his eyes trailed to

Tomas beside her, and she could have sworn he grimaced in distaste before he stalked after the others.

She briefly wondered what that look meant, but then dismissed it as him hating people in general. She glanced at Tomas. "It didn't take long to find a place. They just left."

"No, they have been gone for a while," Tomas grinned at her. "Do you know you snore?"

"I wasn't asleep," she protested. "And I don't snore."

"If you say so," he replied. "Come." He took her hand.

They traveled down an easy slope, crossed over a deep gully, and started uphill once again. Lagging behind, she eventually lost sight of Jag and Fuller, who ranged far out ahead.

"Where are we going?" she asked, out of breathe once again.

"Jag found a cave," Tomas said. "Are you going to make it?"

"Of course," she answered, and was never so glad to prove it when they caught up with Jag on the other side of a rise in the mountainside standing next to a hemlock tree with fat roots wedged between large rocks. Behind him, the mouth of a cave yawned against the mountainside.

"Are you sure nothing lives in there?" Marguerite asked, peering into the darkness of the cave.

"Not totally," Jag said, "it goes back pretty far, and without a torch I could only see a short distance in."

"Yes, a torch would have been useful on several occasions," Kyne murmured under his breath.

"Kyne," Fuller hissed, stepping closer to the wiry man, "if I had a torch, I would stick it up your ass."

"You could try," Kyne said, low and deadly, "but you would die for your efforts."

"You aren't that good," Fuller scoffed.

Master Gryph pointedly fixated his gaze on the two. "I believe we had an agreement, did we not?"

"Yes, sir," Fuller bowed his head, respectfully.

Kyne kept quiet. Lips clamped firmly shut.

Master Gryph pushed past them and walked into the cave, conjuring a tiny light sphere to light his way. Jag and Bayle followed him in.

As soon as Master Gryph was out of sight, Kyne and Fuller exchanged glares and separated. Kyne mumbled something about being right back, then disappeared into the laurel. Fuller dropped his pack to the ground, and taking only his bow and quiver, announced he was going to patrol the surrounding area.

Marguerite dropped her pack to the ground and reached into her pouch for the bottle of pain serum.

Elhrin grimaced in distaste when she saw the bottle. She did not want to drink the foul stuff at the moment. She needed her wits about her, not a mind clouded by sleep.

"Here, Elhrin," Marguerite said, giving her the bottle, "I want you to take a little more than you did earlier."

"Marguerite," she protested, "I can't take that much. It makes me too sleepy."

"I know, but you need the rest."

"But if I'm sleepy, I won't be able to think clearly if something happens. What if Cynder comes back or another pack of Do'athrim shows up?"

"We'll have to take the chance, Elhrin. Don't fight with me on this. If you don't get some decent rest, you won't be able to do anything, anyway."

"Can I just wait and see what Master Gryph thinks?"

Tilting her head to one side, she put her hands on her hips. "Do you think he is going to disagree with me, young lady?" she asked.

Elhrin knew she was always on the losing end of any disagreement with Marguerite, but she wasn't going to back down this time. "Probably not," she said, "but I want to wait and see what we are going to do."

"Did he teach you to be stubborn because you certainly act like him, or did you learn that all on your own?" she asked, then turned to look into the cave when she heard someone shout. The sound echoed hollowly out of the black hole. She shot a puzzled look at them then stepped closer to the entrance. "Gryph?" she called into the black abyss.

A strange whirring sound answered her. Faint at first, the sound grew steadily louder.

Marguerite backed away from the entrance. Tomas drew his sword and stepped forward, protectively. Suddenly, Marguerite yelped and ducked as hundreds of small bats came pouring out of the cave and swirled up through the tree tops. Every last one vanished into the red-tinged sky.

"Tomas, I don't think they are coming back to attack," Elhrin said.

He lowered the sword he had raised when the bats had swept out of the cave. "You never know," he grinned, and slid it into his leather scabbard.

"This is going to be interesting," Marguerite said. Her face alight with a humor Elhrin had not seen in a long while.

"What is?" Tomas asked.

"Just wait," she said, grinning wider when they heard laughter bouncing out of the cave entrance and getting louder. "Ah, here we go."

Bayle and Jag stumbled out of the cave. Both were bent over double howling with laughter. They were followed by Master Gryph's light sphere which winked out of existence near the entrance as he emerged. He was not laughing, but seemed to be making an effort not to smile.

"Elhrin," Bayle tried to talk, but couldn't stop laughing. His laughter was infectious, causing her to smile even though she did not know what was so funny. "You should have seen it," he breathed.

"What is it?" she asked, looking from Bayle to Master Gryph, who shrugged.

"I never thought I would see the day," Bayle wheezed, trying to catch his breath.

"Bayle, you do realize I can make your life difficult," Master Gryph warned.

"I don't care. This is too funny," Bayle pointed at Master Gryph. "He screamed like a little girl. The bats, they flew off the walls when his light went by, and two of them landed on his head."

He stopped to laugh, leaning on Jag who was wiping his eyes from the tears that rolled down his face.

"He jumped around, slapping at his head, yelling for us to get them off. The bats had already flown off, yet he was still smacking his head," Bayle snickered, finally able to get himself under control. He glanced at Master Gryph. "I have never seen anyone hit himself so hard."

"Bats," he grimaced, running a hand over his hair as if their touch revolted him, "you know how I hate bats?" he asked Marguerite.

A hand over her mouth to cover a grin, she nodded without a word.

"I take it we won't be staying in the cave?" Tomas asked, with a laugh.

Tomas earned a look of annoyance. "No, it does not mean we aren't staying in the cave," Master Gryph mocked. "I can handle the bats."

Jag and Bayle chuckled, and it was their turn to receive a level stare that dared them to say anything further. Bayle held up his hands to let him know he was done.

"There is a space inside with a high ceiling that I think is safe enough to build a small fire for light. It felt like it had enough air circulation so we wouldn't have to worry about the smoke," Master Gryph said, and glanced at Marguerite. "Are you done laughing at me yet?"

Marguerite lowered her hand, but kept the smile. "Since you are here, O Brave One, could you please convince your apprentice to take the medicine for her head so that she can sleep tonight?"

"Why don't you want to take it?" he asked.

"It's not that I don't want to take it. I just don't want to be so drugged that I can't function if I need to. What if Cynder comes back, or the Do'athrim find us again? What if we need to leave and I can't get up?"

"Elhrin, what we need is for you to rest. Cynder may come back, but let me worry about him and everything else tonight. After that, I'll let you worry about anything you want," he said, then pointed at the bottle she was holding. "Take it."

He began to pick up the packs sitting near the entrance, not noticing that she had not moved. Unwilling to take the medicine, she sat there frustrated that he didn't see her point of view.

"You taught her well," Marguerite mumbled to herself.

"What?" he asked.

"Nothing," she said, and nodded her head in Elhrin's direction.

Master Gryph saw she hadn't taken the medicine and scowled, shouldering his and Elhrin's pack.

"Um, I'm just going to gather firewood," Jag said, uncomfortable with the situation. "Bayle, you want to give me a hand?"

"Yes, I believe I do," he said, following Jag into the woods.

"Come on, Elhrin, it'll be all right. You need to do this. You can't continue to go on the way you are right now," Tomas said.

"Tomas, you don't understand," she said.

"Yes, I do. You feel helpless and you don't like it."

"Well, I don't."

"All right, Elhrin, you win. Get up and help Marguerite with the packs. I can help Jag and Bayle with the firewood," Master Gryph said, dropping the packs to the ground.

"Gryph, what are you . . . ?" Marguerite began, but he cut her off with an impatient gesture of his hand.

"She knows what she can do better than we do, Marguerite, and I'm done arguing. But before I go, answer me this, Elhrin. If you had to, could you close the Rift right now?"

She stared at him, frowning. He knew she couldn't. She didn't have the energy, nor did she think she could concentrate long enough. Slowly, she shook her head. "But I don't have to right now."

"No, you don't. But if you reach the keep in the same shape you are in right now, what difference is it going to make? Either you rest now, while you have the chance, or make it difficult for the rest of us when we have to carry you to the keep and find that you aren't going to be able to help us at all."

No longer able to meet his gaze, Elhrin glanced away, knowing he was right.

"Take it," he ordered.

Sighing, she opened the bottle and swallowed. "Happy?" she asked, cringing at the bitter taste of the black liquid.

"Ecstatic," he responded. "Marguerite, help me get the packs inside."

Elhrin walked through the back door of their cottage, and her mother was sitting in her chair by the fire, sewing the hem on a wedding gown. Glancing over her shoulder when she heard Elhrin enter the room, she smiled. "What do you think?" she asked, holding up the gown made out of a fine, ivory fabric trimmed with gold stitching that Elhrin knew was hard to find in Glimmerdale.

"It is beautiful. Where did you get the material?" she asked, picking up a corner and rubbing it between her fingers to feel the silky texture.

"The King sent it to me. It is Chyrzinian silk," she smiled. "Wasn't it good of His Majesty to think of us?"

"Why would the king send this to you? Who is the gown for?" she asked, dropping the material.

Her mother stared at her in puzzlement. "What is wrong with you?" she asked. "The gown is for you."

"For me? I'm not getting married," Elhrin laughed just as a spark from the fire popped out onto the gown, instantly setting it aflame as if it had been immersed in lamp oil.

Her mother cried out and jumped up to stomp out the flames, but they spread quickly, heedless of her effort to extinguish them. Elhrin ran to the kitchen to get the bucket of water they kept for cleaning, but found it empty. Her mother screamed. Elhrin whirled around to see that the flames had ignited the hem of her mother's dress.

"NO!" Elhrin screamed. She knocked over a chair in her effort to reach her mother, and tried to beat out the flames with her bare hands. Her mother grabbed her and pushed her away.

"Do not worry, my beautiful girl, I'm fine," she said.

Her mother stood without fear as she became a human inferno.

"No!" Elhrin screamed.

Do'athrim were firing arrows across the river as their cohorts slogged through the current and were already halfway across. Master Gryph created a large sphere of energy, his face a mask of determination, as he stepped closer to the river's edge. A lone arrow sped across the water toward Master Gryph from upriver. With a sickening thud, it hit him in the chest. He jerked back from the impact and grimaced in pain, but did not let go of his magic. Instead, he ignored the arrow sticking out of him. A moment later, his eyes widened in surprise and his arms dropped like he could no longer support them. The sphere exploded in a blinding flash.

A young girl cowered in the corner of a darkened bedroom, the only light coming from dying embers in a large stone fireplace. The noises of a battle outside the closed windows had ceased and it was quiet. Eerily quiet. She heard someone come down the hall and stop outside the locked door of the bedroom, and she whimpered. Surely, he was not coming back now. Tears began to stream down her face. Hearing the lock being released she covered her head with her arms, and tried to make herself as small as she could. She could not endure anymore. It was too much. Peering through her arms, she saw a man enter the room, but it was not who she had expected. This man was slight in build with a seemingly kind face, instead of the bulky monster who thrived on her suffering. Peering into the darkness, he searched the room. A small globe of white appeared in the air and illuminated the room with a soft glow. Inadvertently, she drew in a sharp breath at the unexpected sight and it caught his attention. Seeing her cower in the corner, he squatted before her and smiled with compassion. "Do not be afraid, child. It is over. Worelin is dead."

Giggling, the child, Elhrin, clung to Master Gryph's leg as he tried to walk down the walkway outside of Marguerite's apothecary shop, her tiny bottom balanced on top of his boot, her arms and legs wrapped securely around his calf. When he reached the doorway Marguerite had open because of the warm summer day, he stuck his head around the doorjamb.

"Marguerite, I was wondering if you had something in there that could help me with a little problem I have," he said to his wife.

She looked up from her sweeping. "Did you hurt yourself again?" she frowned, leaning on the broom and placing a hand on her hip.

"No," he smiled, "but I seem to have something unusual growing on my leg."

He moved into the doorway, and when Marguerite saw Elhrin stuck on his leg, she burst into laughter.

"Let me think about this," she said, tapping a finger to her lips as she scanned the wares on her shelves. "You know, I do believe I have something that will cure that." She wagged her finger at him and walked to a nearby jar on the back counter. She pulled out a hardened piece of mint candy.

"Why don't we try this," she said, holding it out for Elhrin to see.

Elhrin let go of his leg, scrambled to her feet, and ran to Marguerite.

"Can I have one, too?" she asked, and Marguerite stooped to her eye level.

"You can have this one," she smiled, and gave Elhrin a hug.

"What do you know," Master Gryph said, testing his leg, "it worked."

Elhrin and Marguerite exchanged girlish giggles as Elhrin put the candy in her mouth. Happy, she felt tingly all over.

Master Gryph frowned, "Marguerite, you two stay in here."

"What is it?"

Without answering he hurried into the street, waiting. Moments later a group of rugged riders galloped down the dusty street. They stopped in front of the Glimmerdale Inn.

Ducking back beneath the covered walkway, Master Gryph disappeared a few doors down into Maye and Master Toome's shop.

"Gryphon, what a pleasant surprise. How are . . . ?" Maye Toome started to ask, but stopped in surprise when he jerked a sword from a nearby display.

"Maye, I need to borrow this," he said, and rushed back out into the street.

She followed him out the door, curious to see why he needed to take one of her weapons. Marguerite and Elhrin joined her, ignoring his order for them to stay inside.

One of the riders, a large man with long black, greasy hair and a wide streak of gray along one side, was waiting on Master Gryph in the middle of the street. He lazily swung his sword back and forth as if he was warming up for a practice match with a friend instead of a forthcoming battle with an enemy. The men that accompanied him stood silently behind him, armed and more than ready for a fight. Pedestrians along the street gathered at a discreet distance to watch, whispering and pointing in subdued excitement, sensing a fight was imminent.

"Hello, Idwyr," the greasy-haired man said, revealing gleaming, metallic pointed teeth, "had I known you would be here to welcome me, I would have brought you a gift. Oh, wait. I do have something for you."

Lifting his wicked looking sword, he pointed it at Master Gryph, and laughed. "My lord bade me to give you his best wishes," he said. A beam of red light shot out of the tip of his sword at Master Gryph.

Master Gryph raised his free hand. The beam hit an invisible barrier and sizzled to a stop in mid-air. Master Gryph advanced slowly. The beam shortened as he closed the distance between them.

"Grom," he said with deadly intent, "I am amazed you showed up here knowing I have been looking for you."

Grom released the beam and smiled. "I have no fear of you, Idwyr." He then launched himself at Master Gryph. Their swords met with a resounding crash just as Master Toome rode up the street in his wagon. Seeing what was happening, he halted his team of horses and grabbed a sword from underneath the driver's bench. He jumped from his wagon, yelling at the nearby men of Glimmerdale to follow him. Quickly arming themselves from Maye's shop, they ran up the street to where Grom's cohorts stood watching the fight between their leader and Master Gryph. One of the men noticed Master Toome and the others coming at them, and alerted his companions. They met the onslaught, even though they were outnumbered two to one. The brawl didn't last long. All but one of Grom's companions fell to Glimmerdale blades, dead. The only survivor had been disarmed and was slammed into unconsciousness by the hilt of Master Toome's sword.

Meanwhile, Master Gryph and Grom circled each other in the center of the street, furiously exchanging blows. Master Gryph held out his free hand as he blocked Grom's swing. Grom's eyes widened as he gasped for air and, trying to free the chokehold Master Gryph had on him with his magic, he kicked Master Gryph in the stomach. Master Gryph doubled over, nearly going to his knees, but regained his balance in time to block a downward swing that would have severed his head from his body.

Grom raised his hand, and streams of red, blazing energy flew out of the tips of his fingers quickly encircling Master Gryph and covering his entire body. An inferno of flames roared to life.

The child Elhrin screamed. Marguerite dropped to her knees and drew Elhrin into her arms, holding her tight. "It is okay, sweetheart," she reassured the child, but Elhrin could hear the fear in her voice.

A thunderous boom shook the ground. The flames that engulfed Master Gryph exploded outward, extinguishing themselves. Master Gryph stood rock-solid in the street sweating, yet unscathed. He was furious.

Grom took a step back, readying himself for an attack. Sword raised and free hand facing palm out, which told the onlooker Elhrin that he had a shield in place to protect himself. Master Gryph lowered his sword to his side. He then walked steadily toward Grom as if he was no longer a threat and merely wanted to talk to the N'gethwyn.

Grom did not attack, curiosity at this turn of events had him wondering what the So'ladiun was up to. "You giving up, Idwyr?"

Master Gryph did not reply, nor did he stop until he was an arm's length away from the villain.

Grom did not like the close proximity or the lack of response from Master Gryph. He dropped his shield and lunged. Master Gryph deflected Grom's attack with a backhand sweep of his sword, but the defensive move was not enough to prevent Grom's blade from entering his side.

A horrified intake of breath from the shocked onlookers, swept up and down the street as they watched Master Gryph, surprisingly, remain standing—and calm, as if he had planned the event.

"You have just made a mistake, Grom," Master Gryph growled hoarsely.

Grom's eyes went wide as a crackling noise emanated from the sword in Master Gryph's side. He looked in horror at the weapon in his hand and saw strands of fiery white light sparking along the length of the blade. Grom began to convulse. He could not release the weapon. Shaking wildly, his knees buckled, causing him to crash to the ground. Master Gryph shouted in pain as the sword was jerked out of his body. He staggered, but remained standing.

Convulsions continued to rack Grom's body. Arms and legs slapped the hard packed dirt violently. Master Gryph raised his sword above Grom with both hands and drove it through the man's chest, abruptly ending the convulsions.

Master Gryph let go of his sword. He lurched to the side, managing to turn and face Marguerite and Elhrin. Blood poured from his wound and soaked his shirt and the top of his pants. His face was deathly white. "I'm sorry," he tried to say, but no sound left his lips. He then dropped to his knees and fell face down into the dirt.

"No," Marguerite cried. She jumped up and ran to his side, pushing her way through the

crowd who had rushed in when he fell.

Tomas smiled at Elhrin and her heart soared. *He is so handsome wearing his dress uniform,* she thought, as he held her hand and bowed, bringing her hand to his lips. Straightening, he pulled her closer and placed her other hand in his, and began moving their bodies to the rhythm of the string ensemble playing in the balcony above them. It was then she noticed the other dancers in the magnificent hall of the palace, the women in resplendent gowns, and the men dressed in their utmost finery. Looking down, she frowned in dismay at her own state of dress. She was in an old green tunic, unwashed brown trousers, and her knee-high, mud-caked work boots.

"Tomas, I need to change," she whispered to him.

He just shook his head and smiled. "Please don't ever do that, Elhrin. I love you just the way you are." And he twirled her into the sea of magnificent dresses, unheeding of her pleas.

She found herself alone in a darkened stone-clad corridor, lit only by the occasional smoking torch spaced at long distances from each other. Looking behind her, she could see a yawning doorway leading out into a sunlit courtyard. Turning to face the other direction, she could see the hallway had several openings indicating doorways or corridors branching from its path. At its end was an open archway. A red glow emanated from the opening, pulsing as if it was alive. She could almost feel her heartbeat match the tempo of the rise and fall of illumination.

As if she were in a trance, she walked toward the red glow, wanting to turn around and run the other way, but her feet betrayed her and she continued down the hall until she reached the opening. Swallowing hard in fear, she peered around the stone archway into a large room and saw the source of the pulsing glow came from a swirling mass of energy along one wall of the room. Realizing where she was, Elhrin imagined the room would have to be the grand hall of Blackridge Keep and the Rift had completely consumed one of its walls. Amazed, she slowly entered the room and studied the Rift. No wonder Obsudius was able to move as many souls out of his Realm into the living world. As big as it was, at the very least, twenty men could pass through side by side and still have room to spare. Her pulse raced.

How? How was she going to close this?

She jumped as a door slammed shut in the corridor. Hearing footsteps come her way, she knew she was in trouble. No one in the keep would be a friend. Looking for a way out or a place to hide, she noticed another large opening on the other side of the room and ran for it. The footsteps entered the grand hall and ran after her. She entered a stone corridor that matched the one on the other side of the hall except she could not see the end as it disappeared into darkness.

Running as fast as she could, she heard the pounding of feet draw closer. Suddenly, Marguerite appeared in front of her. "Elhrin, where are you going? You have to close the Rift."

Elhrin stopped, looking back the way she came. The corridor was empty.

"Marguerite, someone was after me," she said, but when she looked back, Marguerite had disappeared as well.

Unexpectedly, concussions from a magical battle shook the keep. She whirled around just in time to see the bright sizzle of a blue sphere pass by the open archway and explode inside the rift hall. She approached the archway. Master Gryph was fighting an enormous black, reptilian creature who filled the huge room. Cynder!

Elhrin tried to run into the room to help, but Master Gryph faced her, anger lining his *face.*

"No!" he yelled, taking his attention from Cynder. "You must close the Rift."

Cynder grabbed Master Gryph in one of his huge talons and threw him across the room toward the Rift. Master Gryph sent out his magic and grasped Cynder in an invisible hold just as he disappeared into the swirling mass of red energy. His magic pulled Cynder through with him.

"No!" she screamed, as both man and beast entered the Realm of Darkness.

"Elhrin, wake up," someone shook her. She jerked awake. Marguerite was hovering over her.

"Marguerite," she said, her heart still beating wildly from her dreams, "where is Master Gryph?"

"Outside with the boys," Marguerite said.

They were alone in the cave. The light of a small fire cast eerie, distorted shadows along the cave's rough walls. Elhrin rolled over and pushed up off the floor. Without a word of explanation, she ran down the tunnel that led outside, conjuring a tiny white sphere to light her way. She emerged from the cave at a run and saw him standing with Jag. His back was turned to her and he held a bow as he listened to Jag, who was pointing at something in the trees. Not slowing down, she barely heard Bayle's exclamation of surprise at her sudden appearance, and ran into Master Gryph's back throwing her arms around him and nearly knocking him down.

"Oof!" he grunted.

"Please, don't do it," she cried.

"I was only going to shoot at the tree, but if it bothers you this much, I won't do it," he said, disengaging her arms from him so he could turn and see her.

"Not that. Cynder, don't fight Cynder."

His smile faded and he handed the bow to Jag. "Elhrin, what is wrong?"

"Twice I have had a dream of you and Cynder, and both times you have ended up in Do'athra. Please, don't do it," she pleaded.

"Ah, I see. Elhrin, you know what I have to do," he said. "Don't worry about your dream."

"But you were the one who said to pay attention to dreams that stand out in my mind," she said. "Are you saying this one wasn't important?"

"No, I didn't say it wasn't important, I just said don't worry about it. What you have seen may or may not happen."

"Why chance it? Don't fight him."

"I don't think I have a choice, young lady."

"Yes, you do."

"I do?" he asked, amused.

"Let me do it."

He chuckled. "You must feel better if you are willing to take on Cynder and close the Rift."

Startled, she realized she did feel better and the pounding in her head was gone. She cautiously reached up to touch the healing cut on the back of her head, wincing when she touched it. It was still tender. Furrowing her brow, she took in her surroundings—the sun in the sky was low. It would only be a few hours before nightfall.

"How long have I been asleep?" she asked.

"Since yesterday evening," he said, looking over her head at Marguerite who stood at the cave entrance extinguishing a fire brand she had used as a torch.

"Did anything happen while I slept?"

"No, it's been quiet."

"What about Cynder?" She couldn't feel the beast's energy.

"He has been spending most of his time in the west. Goruth must be giving him more trouble than he expected to occupy so much of his attention. With us so close to the keep I assumed he would be hunting us down."

"Should we try to reach the keep before he returns?"

"Oh, he is already back."

"But I don't feel his energy." She sent her senses ranging out again—nothing.

"That is because he is in Do'athra."

"How do you know?"

"His energy source disappeared shortly after he returned from his flight west. I can only assume he entered the Rift."

"Why would he go back through the Rift?" Bayle asked.

"Well, his boss is in Do'athra, and I expect they are formulating their plans for Anderan's demise."

"They are just wasting their time because it's not going to happen," Elhrin said.

Master Gryph smiled at her. "That's my girl," he said as he patted her on the back.

Chapter Twenty-Seven

Elhrin crouched between Tomas and Bayle along the edge of a cliff. Hidden behind a jumble of rock and scrub grass, they overlooked the backside of Blackridge Keep where it sat in a valley cove surrounded on three sides by dismal rock-sided mountains. In the far distance, situated outside the mouth of the valley, was Shimmerfin Lake. The late afternoon sun glinted off the lake's smooth surface, giving it the color of molten gold, a shining contrast to the horrific sight that lay on Shimmerfin's shores. The entire town of Blackridge had been decimated and burned to the ground. Only broken and blackened pieces of buildings remained to indicate a town had ever existed.

"Ugly, isn't it?" Fuller murmured, keeping his voice low.

"And armed to the teeth," Tomas replied.

"At least, we don't have to worry about Cynder," Bayle said. The N'gethwyn had flown west before dawn and had not returned.

"At least, not yet," Elhrin whispered, studying the decaying structure built into the side of the mountain. Reminding her of Obsudius' keep in the *Book of Tolman*, it was a single box tower rising five stories from ground level. The top floor had partially caved in, and gaping holes dotted the exterior walls. Its notorious black paint had long ago eroded, exposing the raw granite rock underneath. Surrounding three sides of the tower and the smaller exterior buildings and grounds were thick, protective stone walls with tall square turrets on every corner, and they were crawling with Do'athrim. The fourth side of the tower was protected by the sheer rock face of the mountain.

"It's going to be interesting getting inside," Marguerite observed with a sigh. Master Gryph reached over to rub her shoulder. She grabbed his hand and squeezed.

The entrance, an arched gateway in the western wall was open, but that was not going to be an option for them to get into the keep. Do'athrim and human soldiers were camped outside its walls—on every side. Getting inside without being killed seemed impossible.

Please, Solisius. Let us make it through this, she prayed, silently.

A soft breeze blew across the ridge to caress her cheeks, and as it passed she heard the God of Light whisper, *"Do not forget, I am here for you."*

Hearing Solisius, Master Gryph cut his eyes at her. A corner of his mouth lifted slightly.

"How are we going to get down from here and into the keep without anyone spotting us?" Bayle asked, inching forward. He wanted to peer over the edge of the cliff.

Elhrin grabbed the back of his shirt and pulled. "Get back before someone sees you, bone head."

"They can't see us up this high, can they?" he asked. They were on the uppermost peak. A mounded mountaintop eroded smooth by time.

"Better not take the chance," Jag said. "You never know when eyes are looking your way."

"I don't see any way down from anywhere in the valley," Tomas said. "Nothing but steep cliffs and almost no tree cover to hide us going down if we could."

"What now?" Marguerite asked.

Master Gryph studied the valley in silence.

"If we could get to the bottom, maybe Master Gryph could hide us with his magic long enough to get through that hole in the wall and into the keep," Bayle murmured. There was a spot near the rear turret where the top half of the wall was missing.

Master Gryph grunted with a small chuckle. "I should have remembered that." He looked at Bayle. "Thank you for reminding me."

"About . . . ?" Bayle asked.

"About an important piece of history," he said, easing away from the cliff. "Elhrin, come with me. The rest of you sit tight. We will be right back."

Elhrin followed him well away from the others and down into a gully.

"This should be good enough," he said, crouching low. "Let me see the book."

She slipped off her pack and sat it on the ground. "What are you looking for?" she asked as she unbuckled the pack's leather strap and flipped the top flap back. She rummaged under spare clothes and ration packs, and pulled out the small leather satchel where she kept the book.

"One of our predecessors, Lleiff Halite, was here many moons ago during the siege that ousted the keep's final owner. I am interested to see if the book will reveal how that siege was ended and if it will help us to find a way in."

"I read about him, and strangely, I think I dreamt about him the other night," she said, slipping the book from her satchel and handing it to him. "He found a girl hidden in the lord's bedchamber."

He pursed his lips and nodded. "That is a good sign if you dreamt of him. Maybe we are on the right track," he said as he pulled his pendant from his shirt. The light within the crystal instantly brightened as soon as he touched it. "Excellent," he murmured, as the book was going to reveal something and the words on the open page started to blur and distort, whirling into a moving image. When the scene sharpened into focus, they could see a man with a slight build and wavy brown hair, wearing a grape colored coat trimmed in gold cording, and white trousers stuffed in knee-high glossy, black boots. He walked through the encampment of a large armed force spread far and wide across an expanse of down-trodden grass and black mud.

"It was him," she breathed. "I don't remember the uniform, though. Is that what you wear when you are in Muryne?"

He grimaced at the notion. "Absolutely not. Queen Egeria tried over the years to saddle me with hideous uniforms, but gave up after I showed up to a court function wearing one inside out."

She stared at him open mouthed. "Didn't that make her mad?"

"Oh, indeed it did, but I told her that if she continued to try and force me to dress like one of her fancy peacocks in the gardens, the next time I would show up with nothing on at all."

Elhrin laughed softly. She loved her mentor's adventurous sense of humor. "Wouldn't that land you in jail?"

"Probably, but it would have been worth it to see her face," he turned his attention back to the scene unraveling in the book. "Look here."

A catapult slammed forward, throwing a load of head-size stones high into the air and over the walls of the keep to rain down on whatever, or whoever, happened to be in the way. Archers along the ramparts popped up from behind the walls to fire a volley of arrows down at a mass of soldiers carrying long ladders toward the wall. Scores of men fell from the deadly rain and officers yelled for more soldiers to fill the vacant spots. Archers from the King of Anderan's army returned fire, and the men along the ramparts ducked behind the safety of the walls. Screams could be heard from those not lucky enough to be missed. The keep's archers stood back up and fired another round down at the king's soldiers moving the ladders. The intensity of the barrage was too great, and the soldiers on the ground had to give up, dropping the ladders and running back out of the range of the bows.

The scene shifted back to Lleiff who was now standing by a tall, barrel-chested man encased in polished steel armor. Fiery red hair sprayed across his shoulders from under his crown-encased helmet, and a thick, wiry beard hung well below his chin, almost touching the golden lion stamped on his purple tabard. This was the King of Anderan, a great-something grandfather to King Goruth, and there was a slight resemblance to the current king in the man's gruff features.

"Worelin has to be growing weary by now, Your Majesty," Lleiff said.

"You would think so. I know I grow tired of trying to oust the rat out of his hole. This place feels evil."

"That could be it, My Lord," Lleiff said.

"What are you prattling on about?" the king asked.

"Holes. There is a mine underneath the keep in the mountain, is there not?" he pointed high over the tower. "Wouldn't that mean they would have made air shafts?"

The king surveyed the area where Lleiff pointed. "Not necessarily if there is enough air filtering in naturally," he said.

The page shifted and swirled, and the words written by Lleiff appeared as he had written them. Master Gryph snapped the book shut and handed it back to her.

"What?" Elhrin said. "Why did it end there?" She stuffed it back into her satchel.

"It gave us all the information we needed to know," he said, turning to climb up out of the gully.

"So we need to look for air shafts?" she asked, quickly stuffing the satchel in her pack and shouldering it.

"Or something similar."

She crawled out of the gully and followed him back to the ridge where the others waited. Crouching down beside Tomas she clasped the hand that he offered.

"Did you find out anything?" he asked.

"Yes, we think there may be a way into the keep through the mountain. We just need to find the entrance," she said, searching the mountainside above the keep.

Kyne and Jag were a short distance away on their stomachs, cautiously peering over the edge of the precipice, looking for a way down.

"Kyne," Master Gryph called quietly.

Kyne did not hear him. Suddenly, he jerked and flipped onto his side to look in their direction.

Master Gryph waved him over.

The two eased back from the edge and crawled back. "Did you have to do that?" Kyne asked Master Gryph.

"You automatically assume I did something," Master Gryph said, raising his eyebrows.

"Well, yes," he said, and shifted his eyes to Elhrin.

She gave him a little wave of her fingers.

"Did you have to pinch me so hard?" he asked her.

"Sorry, we needed you over here. I guess I got a little carried away," she shrugged. She did not reveal just how good that had felt.

"All right, young people, your eyesight is better than mine. I am looking for anything that might suggest an opening into the mountain above or around the keep. Long ago, this place was built over an iron mine. They may have built ventilation shafts through the exterior of the mountain."

"Why would anyone build a keep over a mine?" Fuller asked.

"Protection," Master Gryph answered. "Rumor had it that there was more than iron in the mine at the time, possibly gold. If there was, no one has been able to prove it since, and more than a few have died trying to find out in the old decaying mines."

"What about there?" Bayle asked, pointing to a place where the rock face of the cliff had split away from the mountain, creating a gap, but no opening could be seen.

"It's a bit high, but would be as good a starting point as any," Master Gryph said. "Let's get a closer look."

They backed away from the ridge and wound their way around scrub brush and jagged outcrops of rock that made up the crest of the mountain. Elhrin had noticed that, oddly, not too many trees grew along the mountainsides facing the valley where the keep sat, but there was an abundance of trees on the opposite sides.

They reached the area where they thought Bayle's spot was located nearly two hours later. Once again, they crouched low to move silently towards the ridgeline. Kyne led the way, and when he got closer to the edge he held up his hand for everyone to stop. He then dropped to his stomach, slowly inching his way forward to the precipice to peer over the edge. He ducked back down in a hurry.

"There is a path to a fissure on the other side of this hill. Something rattled a bush down there. I couldn't tell if it was man or beast."

Master Gryph inched up to join him and peered over the edge. Long, tense minutes dragged by before he finally slid back away from the edge.

"I did not see anything," he whispered and moved past them. "I am going around for a closer look. Jag you are with me. Everyone else stay here. Kyne, keep watch. If you see something let Elhrin know," he glanced at her. "Send me a warning if he does."

She nodded.

Anxiously they waited after he disappeared around the hill, and every fiber of her being screamed for her to go after him. What if it was a trap? It had been too easy to get to this point. Minutes dragged by. No one moved. Elhrin forced herself to remember to breathe, keeping a sharp eye on Kyne in case she needed to move in a hurry.

Bayle couldn't take the wait any longer. "Kyne, see anything?" he whispered.

Kyne scowled down at him and jerked his head no. Turning his head back to watch below, he stiffened. Elhrin held her breath, fearing something was wrong, but then he relaxed and scooted back away from the edge.

"The minister signaled it was all clear," he whispered. "He wants us to join them."

They followed Kyne around the hill and back up between two rises. Staying low, they slipped to the top of the rise where Master Gryph and Jag waited. A short drop below was a narrow ledge along the rock face of the mountain.

"I don't know what you saw, Kyne, but there is no one here. Whoever it was may have left in another direction or gone this way," he pointed to the ledge. There was a well worn path in the dirt, but no distinctive prints could be seen. "Someone or something is using this ledge for passage, and I have a feeling it is going to be useful for us, as well. There is a space where the rock has pulled away from the mountain and created a cleft." He pointed to the right, but Elhrin couldn't see the cleft from her vantage point. "The trail leads into it. Fuller, you and Jag scout around us in the immediate area just to make sure we don't have company behind us," he shielded his eyes from the setting sun. "We won't go until the sun sinks below the top of the mountain range across the way and no longer casts light on this mountain. The shadows should shield us from being seen from below."

Elhrin glanced down at the valley floor. Already, the silent advance of the opposite mountain's deep shadow touched the hard stone of the battlements, making the campfires scattered among the tents and makeshift shelters outside the keep's walls shine a bright orange, looking like hundreds of tiny suns in the bleak and bilious world of Blackridge's guardians.

Jag and Fuller slipped back down the rise to scout the area. Master Gryph and Kyne kept one eye on the ledge for movement and the other on the army below. Marguerite and Elhrin settled down nearby. Tomas and Bayle drew their swords and moved down to keep watch on the mountain behind them.

"Elhrin, how is your head?" Marguerite asked, quietly.

"It's fine." She reached up to gingerly touch the raised lump under her hair. She had removed the irritating sweaty bandage before they left the cave that morning. "The cut is sore and itches, but I haven't had any more pounding headaches, just a dull throb every once in a while."

"That is good to hear." Marguerite yawned and rubbed her eyes. "Sounds like your injury is not as severe as I feared."

"More men are marching out of the keep—about fifty to seventy-five." Kyne tilted his head sideways to get a better look. "I thought this place would be overrun, but there are only a few hundred or so around the keep. If you had an endless supply that could stream out of the realm of the dead, shouldn't there be more?"

"Maybe Obsudius has about exhausted his realm of souls to send through the Rift," Marguerite replied through another yawn. "I wish I would quit yawning." She blinked her eyes wide as she unplugged the cork in her waterskin and wet a small cloth. She then dabbed her face and eyes.

"I imagine those not needed to defend Blackridge have been sent along west to join the battle against Goruth and Lakeshore Glen," Master Gryph said. He stroked his beard thoughtfully. "But if Goruth is still standing, I have to wonder why Obsudius is not utilizing his resources. If he was sending everyone out of his realm there would be a steady stream." He turned to look at Elhrin. "Why would the entire north not be filled from mountain to shore with his men?"

"Are you asking me?" Elhrin pointed to herself.

"That, I am."

"I don't know," she answered. How was she supposed to guess the mind of a god? "Maybe all of the men and the Do'athrim hybrids that he has here are only from those souls that have died in Anderan over the years." She shrugged her shoulders. "Or maybe he sent everyone else to the Void."

Master Gryph lifted a corner of his mouth and nodded, apparently satisfied with her answer. "He might be sending some to the Void, knowing how impatient he is with those that displease him, but I don't think that is the answer. I do think you are correct about the ones we are seeing here being only those that have died on Anderan's soil, and by the looks of it, maybe only those that once lived here in the north."

"Why would he do that?" Kyne asked.

"Obsudius and Solisius are subject to logistics even within their own realms. Do'athra and Ts'aura were designed by the Creator to mimic the physical features of this world, so when an individual dies, their spirit ends up in the realm of the dead in the exact same spot where they died. Obsudius would have to expend extra energy to collect and transport those in other areas across his realm to here or await their arrival from his summons." He turned to look back down at the keep. "He would have had the time to get them here before he opened the Rift, but it seems like he did not bother with them. Like I said, he is not utilizing his resources or the time he has while the Rift . . ." He cut himself off. "Something is off about this invasion."

"I thought he wanted to conquer the world," Kyne said. "Why would he hold himself back?"

Master Gryph flicked a quick glance at Kyne. "Why, indeed?" he muttered. "Elhrin, when all of this is done, you will need to be extra vigilant." The look he gave her sent a trickle of unexplained fear down her spine.

A branch snapped below. She reached for her magic as everyone around her prepared for a fight.

A moment later the low, almost inaudible call of an owl hooted in the brush. "It's us," Jag whispered, hoarsely, carefully easing into view. "The area is clear."

Elhrin expelled a pent up breathe.

"Just in time," Master Gryph said. The sun had sunk behind the far peaks and the light was fading fast. "I think we had better go before it gets too dark."

"I'll go first," Kyne offered, and Master Gryph motioned for him to lead the way.

Elhrin allowed the others to go ahead then slipped down to the narrow ledge behind Bayle. Flattening her back against the mountainside, she sidestepped her way to the cleft where there was a wider expanse of jumbled rock that allowed them all to huddle close and remain hidden from view from below. A narrow, jagged opening yawned black against the rough rock of the mountainside, having been revealed when the split from the mountain had occurred.

"Are we going in there?" Bayle asked.

"Do you have another idea?" Master Gryph asked, peering into the dark hole.

"Uh, no," he said.

"It's going to be a tight squeeze for you and Jag," Marguerite said to Master Gryph, keeping her voice low. "Are you sure this is the way?"

"No, but instinct tells me that we give it a try."

"Who's first?" Bayle asked.

"I'll go," Fuller said.

"No," Master Gryph said, removing his pack, "I'll go and make sure it's safe."

Elhrin understood his logic. Weapons would be useless in such a tight place if it came to a fight. He, however, did not need room to use his magic.

"Aren't you afraid there might be bats?" Bayle asked, grinning.

Master Gryph gave him a level look then crouched down to get a closer look.

"Guess not," Bayle murmured.

"Bayle, you have just won the privilege to carry my pack through this hole."

"Lucky me."

Master Gryph conjured a tiny sphere of light that resembled a firefly, causing it to wink on and off as if it were the real insect, and sent it into the narrow opening. The glow was just enough to reveal the details of the narrow cave.

"It looks like it widens out a bit further in," he whispered, glancing up at Marguerite. "Wish me luck."

Marguerite kissed him on the forehead. "Don't get stuck."

He grinned. "Not exactly what I was hoping you'd say, but it'll do."

He stuck his head and shoulders in, using his hands for leverage, he wriggled sideways into the narrow opening until they no longer saw him. Occasionally, a low expletive drifted out of the opening.

"Gryph," Marguerite whispered into the darkness, "you do know we can hear you?"

The expletives stopped, and for the next few minutes they listened to his struggles go further away from them then abruptly stop. No one moved. Elhrin strained to hear any movement in the darkness, but it was quiet as a tomb.

"I don't like this," Marguerite whispered. "Gryph?" she called quietly into the opening.

Still they heard nothing.

"Gryph, are you there?" she called again, worry creeping into her voice.

Finally, they saw a glow in the darkness, and his little sphere of light came into view, only it had morphed into the shape of a tiny figure with arms and legs. It stopped short of the opening to beckon them inside, its light changing from the soft glow of green into a deep blue, then purple, and back to the green.

Elhrin and Bayle let out a quiet burst of laughter.

"Thank the light," Marguerite breathed with relief.

"What is that?" Kyne asked, staring in confusion at the glowing figure.

"That is Shiner. Master Gryph used to entertain us with him when we were little," Bayle said. "The changing of the colors means he is happy."

The little light man crossed his arms and began tapping his foot impatiently.

"It has been far too long since I have seen him," Marguerite said, smiling fondly at the little light. "I guess we better go. Jag, since you are going to have as much trouble getting through as he did, why don't you go next?"

Jag nodded and removed his pack.

"I'll carry your gear," Kyne offered.

Elhrin shot him a look of surprise. That was the first time he had offered to help anyone besides Master Gryph. He rewarded her look with one of his own. The snide smirk she found extremely irritating.

At first the narrow tunnel was difficult to navigate with her pack strapped on. Elhrin stripped it off and carried it in her hand, dragging it through until the craggy walls widened out to where she had more room to move. She slipped it back onto her shoulders and clambered over one last rocky barrier to reach the others who waited in a scooped out cavern bowl that abruptly doglegged to the left and declined down into the unknown abyss of the mountain's interior.

Stooped over because of the low ceiling, Master Gryph waited until Tomas and Kyne, who struggled through behind Elhrin, joined them before he spoke. "I investigated the tunnel a short way down. It leads into a larger cavern and continues on. I did not find any evidence of human or Do'athrim passage, but I did see signs of animal passage. If Kyne saw an enemy, he must have gone in another direction. We must remain alert. This may not be the only entrance into these tunnels," Master Gryph said. He morphed the little light man into a simple orb of white and lowered it so they could see the cavern floor. The path was worn and there were droppings here and there from some small animal.

Jag squatted for a closer look. "You are right. Looks like rodents, but," he pointed at a large scuff mark in the dirt, "there are also some tracks of a larger animal."

"What kind of larger animal?" Marguerite asked.

"I'm not sure, madam, the tracks aren't clear."

"It doesn't matter. We all must be ready for anything," Master Gryph said, pulling on the pack that Bayle handed him. "Let's move on."

An unexpected surge of emotion overwhelmed Elhrin. Maybe it had to do with the appearance of Shiner reminding her how long and how rock-solid his commitment as a friend, a teacher . . . a father . . . he had been over the years for her and Bayle. Or maybe it was the fear that she would lose him again— whatever it was, it didn't matter. She could not go one step further without showing him how much she loved him. She placed a hand on his shoulder, stood on her tiptoes, and kissed him on the cheek.

"What was that for?" he asked, surprised at the gesture.

"No reason. Just felt like it," she said, conjuring her own light sphere, and for the first time on their journey, led the way. When she reached the opening into the larger cavern, she sent her light in to inspect the area. The cave floor was a short drop below her, and two tunnels on either side of the cave led off into darkness.

Tomas halted behind her. "Do you want me to go first?" he asked, peering over her shoulder.

"Be my guest," she said, and stepped to the side to let him by.

He jumped down and held up his arms, waiting for her. She jumped into his arms, but he did not let her go. Instead, he let her slowly slide down his body until her feet touched the floor.

"I think I'm going to be sick," Bayle said, from the ledge.

"Shut up, Bayle," she said, and gave Tomas a quick kiss on the lips before moving out of his arms.

Bayle jumped down, stumbled, then fell face first into the thin layer of dirt that covered the rock floor. He grabbed his injured arm.

"Are you all right?" she asked as she and Tomas helped him up.

"Yes, I just banged my arm a bit," he said, face scrunched tight in pain. He jerked off the sling and tossed it away. "This thing hinders me."

Jag and Kyne jumped down, followed by Fuller.

"Which way do you think?" Fuller asked, walking over to one of the two openings as Marguerite and Master Gryph appeared above them on the ledge.

A low growl and an angry hiss drifted out of the dark hole.

Fuller backed away from the tunnel opening. "Something is in there," he warned, reaching for his sword.

Elhrin readied for a fight. The men around her jerked their swords from scabbards.

"Marguerite, let me by," Master Gryph said, and jumped down from the ledge, wincing in pain when the impact jarred the old injury in his leg. He sent his sphere of light into the hole. Two reflections of light stared at them from deep in the tunnel.

"Looks like a cat," Kyne said just as the animal issued a terrifying warning with an angry roar. The cry was deafening as the sound bounced off the hard surfaces of the cave.

"It's a big cat," Bayle commented, backing up a step.

"That's a Duga panther," Jag said quietly. "Probably a mama and we have invaded her den, but it is strange for her to be here. I have never seen one this far south. They usually stick to their homeland in the hills around Duga Bay."

The cat snarled and hissed. She sounded primed for attack and eased closer, stepping into the light cast from Master Gryph's magical orb.

"Dear god," Marguerite breathed.

The cat was a gigantic vessel of dangerous muscle and sharp teeth with fur the color of honey except for her soot black paws and her black tail that whipped back and forth in agitation. She was a magnificent but terrifying sight. Hackles raised along her back, the fibers of her fur brushed the ceiling of her tunnel.

"Good kitty. Stay right where you are," Fuller murmured.

"Elhrin, block her," Master Gryph ordered. "Marguerite, jump down," he held his arms up for her.

Elhrin created a shield to block the cave, incorporating light into her flows so that the others could physically see the shield, but left it translucent so they could see the cat on the other side. The sudden appearance of a glowing wall startled the cat. She jumped back hissing and spitting. She couldn't take the pressure of danger from the unusual intrusion on her home and nervously backed out of sight into the shadows of her cave. Low, feral growls continued to rumble from the dark.

"Everyone back out through the other tunnel," Master Gryph said.

Not taking their eyes off the cat, they filtered into the tunnel, following it until they couldn't see that part of the cave any longer. Elhrin let go of the shield and turned around, reforming her light sphere and sending it ahead of them. They quickly followed the twists and turns of the tunnel until they were sure they had put a safe distance between them and the cat.

"Stop," Jag ordered.

Everyone halted dead in their tracks.

"What is it?" Tomas asked.

"Elhrin, can you shine the light at the ground."

Puzzled, Elhrin lowered the light as Jag eased ahead of her scrutinizing the ground.

He turned to look at Master Gryph who had positioned himself protectively in the back of the line. "Sir, there are no prints of any kind in the dirt. Nothing living has passed this way in a long time, if ever."

"So we are going the wrong way?" Kyne didn't bother to hide his displeasure.

"Are you eager to get inside the keep and meet your future eternal companions, Kyne?" Fuller asked.

"Shut up," Kyne spat, "I wasn't talking to you."

Marguerite grunted in annoyance, tired of their constant verbal jabs at each other.

"Quiet," Master Gryph ordered, staring at the floor, thinking about the situation. He turned to stare into the black abyss from which they came, then nodded to himself as if agreeing with his thoughts. "We continue on."

"But, sir, there are no signs of passage. This couldn't possibly be the way," Kyne protested.

"You are assuming that someone besides us and the cat knows about this passage. She has no reason to venture this way, and from the looks of it, no other living being needs to be down here, either. That does not mean this will not lead us to where we need to go."

"Still . . . ," Kyne started to argue.

"Kyne, do you presume to think I would waste precious time leading us astray on purpose?"

"No, sir, I didn't say you would lead us the wrong way on purpose. I'm just wondering how you could be so sure you are right."

"Instinct, my boy, and years of experience. Do you have any better ideas?"

Kyne clamped his lips into a thin line, then shook his head no.

"Good, now that we have that settled, let's get moving."

The tunnel they were following wound downward, and every so often they were forced to jump or climb down drop-offs. On one occasion they came upon a place where the path branched off into another tunnel, and randomly choosing one of the openings, found that the one they chose led to a dead end and they had to backtrack to take the other tunnel. Kyne mumbled something about instinct the whole way back under his breath until Elhrin rounded on him, giving him a fierce glare. No words were said, but surprisingly, he stopped grumbling.

It felt like days to Elhrin, but she knew that it only had been a few hours since they had first entered the cave. Dread began to build inside her. Instinct told her Master Gryph was right. The tunnel had to be the way into the keep. And as if fate deemed she have an answer to her questions, they came to the end of the natural tunnels and entered an old, man-made tunnel with thick wooden shaft supports.

"Looks like we found the mine," Jag commented, stepping out into the shaft. "It hasn't been used in some time."

She could see just as he did that the dirt and rubble on the floor was undisturbed.

"Still think we are going the wrong way, Kyne?" Fuller asked.

"Shut up," Kyne hissed.

"Stop," Elhrin raised a hand in warning. A vile, nauseous feeling touched on the edge of her awareness. "Cynder's coming back to the keep." She glanced at Master Gryph. His face was set in a mask of grim resignation. "Why does his energy feel strange?"

"His energy is mixing with the energy of someone else. He is bringing Grom back to the keep."

"That is not good."

"No, it's not."

"Why? You killed him before. Can't you do it again?" Bayle asked.

"Killing him is not what I'm worried about, Bayle. The fact that he can locate me and Elhrin concerns me quite a bit."

"What are we going to do?" Marguerite asked.

"We are going to have to hurry and get into the keep," he said, sending his light down the mineshaft and taking the lead. "After that, we will need to split up and divide his attention."

"No!" Elhrin protested.

"No?" he asked.

"No. I don't want to split up."

"I don't think we will have a choice."

Cynder was drawing nearer to the keep as they jogged down the mineshaft. The passageway ended into another shaft which led to their left and right. Without hesitating, Master Gryph turned to the left. The new tunnel spiraled downward, curving gradually, until it opened up into a carved out grotto.

"Elhrin, extinguish your light," Master Gryph said, letting his own sphere of light wink out. The grotto was thrown into darkness. When her eyes adjusted to the loss of immediate light, she could see a dim glow emanating from an opening in one wall. Master Gryph silently moved to the opening and cautiously peered outside.

"Come, but be quiet," he said, softly.

They followed a short passageway until it opened into another tunnel lit by smoking torches spaced along the walls of the mineshaft. Master Gryph carefully peered around the corner, and not seeing any danger, moved silently into the other passageway, waving for them to follow. They could hear the distant ringing of hammers on steel.

Master Gryph stopped and quietly pulled his sword from his scabbard. The men followed his lead. He motioned for Tomas and Kyne to come with him, indicating for the rest of them to hang back until he assessed the situation.

Hugging the walls, Master Gryph, Tomas, and Kyne moved slowly down the passageway and disappeared from view when they rounded a curve. Anxiously, Elhrin followed his progress with her senses. With agonizing slowness, he moved down the passageway away from her. Elhrin checked on the progress of Cynder. She stifled a groan. It wouldn't be long before he reached the keep.

Elhrin returned her attention to Master Gryph's energy. He was coming back, and when he rounded the curve, he motioned for them to move back down the passageway until they were a safe distance from the enemy.

"There is a weapons forge set up in a cavern up ahead. Miners are pulling ore out of another mine shaft and dumping it for them to melt down," he said quietly. "There is no way to get by them without being seen. We are going to have to fight our way through. Elhrin, I want you to collapse the tunnel the miners are using. It will be the one to the right of this shaft."

"Okay."

"Fuller, you and Jag are up first. There are several Do'athrim working around the smelting furnaces and I saw two blacksmiths at the forge. Take out as many as you can with your bows, then make your way to the tunnel to the left and keep anyone from coming out of it. The rest of us will manage those remaining inside."

Jag and Fuller put away their swords and removed their bows. Quietly, they all followed the two bowmen back down the passageway. Jag worked his way down one side while Fuller worked his way down the opposite wall until they could see the Do'athrim in the grotto. There were fewer than Elhrin expected.

Sighting in two of the beasts, Jag and Fuller released their arrows. Instantly, the Do'athrim dropped to the ground. At the same time, Master Gryph released a blazing ball of magical energy that exploded into one of the furnaces, turning it into a spectacular spray of white-hot molten fire. The unlucky ones who had been standing near the furnace were bombarded with chunks of stone and searing sparks that burned deep into their flesh. Several fell dead while the others dropped screaming and writhing to the ground.

Tomas and Kyne charged into the grotto, engaging nearby Do'athrim who had recovered from the surprise attack and had picked up weapons to defend themselves. Elhrin stepped out of the way of her companions and located the mine shaft Master Gryph asked her to collapse. She decided to use the sphere of energy he had taught her in the valley. Spreading her arms, she placed the sphere just inside the opening of the mine and increased her energy. Knowing how powerful this particular magical sphere could be, she decided to make it comparable in size to the one she had built in the meadow. She did not want to take the chance the entire cavern would collapse if she made one larger. When it reached the size she wanted, she began to put pressure on it from below, forcing the energy out the top. It exploded upward with a deafening boom. The tunnel collapsed immediately with a roar, killing Do'athrim caught up in the blast of debris spewing from the hole. The floor of the cavern shook and the mountain groaned as if it were going to fall, too. Rocks and dirt rained from the shadow encased ceiling above, but the mountain remained intact and after one last protest, shuddered to a standstill. Elhrin turned her attention to the fight. All of her companions were engaged by the remaining enemy.

Kyne was directly in front of her, fighting a Do'athrim in the form of a large, striped cat. Growling, the cat tried to swipe at Kyne with razor sharp claws. Elhrin hurled a blue sphere at the cat. Its head exploded in a shower of blood. Kyne threw up a hand to protect his face from the explosion.

"I'm not afraid anymore," she growled when he glanced at her in surprise.

"Good to know," he replied then turned to help Bayle and Tomas. The two men were hard pressed with three enemies against them.

Elhrin looked around the cave to see who needed her most. Jag and Fuller had moved across the length of the cave. There was another tunnel entrance at the top of a carved ramp in the cavern floor and they were firing a volley of arrows into its opening.

Marguerite was near the other ore furnace and impaled a man who had tried to take her head off with an axe. She did not know there was a blacksmith charging her from behind. Elhrin started to throw a fireball across the cave at the man, but a blue ball of energy sped from the other side hitting him solidly in his back. The blacksmith's body exploded in half.

Elhrin wondered how Master Gryph had managed to send the ball across the room. He was in the middle of a fight with a strange, human-looking Do'athrim twice his size. The beast had amazingly long horns coming out of his head and dagger-like claws on his hands, replacing all of his fingers. He swiped at Master Gryph with both hands. Saving his magical energy, Master Gryph retaliated with a fierce swing of his blade. The beast jumped backwards and picked up a nearby wooden cask. He threw it at the magician. Master Gryph used his magic to catch the cask, and like he wielded an invisible slingshot, whipped it back at the monster. It crashed into the beast and shattered. A cloud of black powder covered him. Master Gryph smiled and waved his hand negligently. Flames appeared along the beast's body, the powder ignited and exploded. The beast's body blew apart, showering the area with gore.

"Jag, they're coming fast," Fuller yelled, notching his bow with two arrows instead of one. "I'm almost out."

Elhrin ran across the cave to help the two bowmen. The passageway was filled with Do'athrim who had massed behind their brothers holding a wall of shields in place. The whole mob advanced steadily against Jag and Fuller's barrage of missiles. A Do'athrim behind one shield made the mistake of exposing his snarling muzzle to them. One of Jag's arrows popped him in the eye and sunk deep into his skull. His fall broke the seamless wall of wood and steel, momentarily. A bulky black beast with a shield of his own immediately closed the gap and resealed the wall.

"Let's see how well those shields stand up to this," she muttered, and sent a flaming ball of energy exploding against the shields. The force of her attack splintered the shields and knocked the beasts back into the ones behind them. Blood curdling screams and howls echoed out of the tunnel as her flames singed hair and flesh. Jag and Fuller took advantage of the chaos and fired arrows into exposed bodies. At the same time, Elhrin hurled two more spheres of blazing energy down the passageway. One slammed through the head of a beast, ripping bone and flesh from one side of his face. The other sphere blasted into more upraised shields decimating them and their holders.

Unexpectedly, a large white sphere of intense energy sizzled by Elhrin's ear from behind, she instinctively ducked. The sphere grew in size as it zoomed towards the beasts, consuming the entire passageway from ceiling to floor. They tried to run, pushing and shoving those behind them. Howls of fear roared loud just as it slammed into the packed mass of bodies. It detonated in a horrendous flash of light. Body parts flew wide. Blood soaked the walls and floor. Only two Do'athrim managed to escape harm. They clawed their way back down the passageway to seek safety. Jag and Fuller fired before the beasts could escape. The beasts dropped to the ground like stones. One tried to rise again, but Elhrin used her magic to slam him hard against the stone wall. His head cracked audibly against the hard surface. He fell and did not rise again.

It was then she realized that no sound came from the forge behind her. Scared of what she would see, she turned to look. She breathed a heavy sigh of relief. They were all safe. Tired, scraped, and bruised, but safe.

"Did you have to get so close to me?" she asked Master Gryph. "What if I had stepped in front of that?"

"You were in no danger. Cynder has arrived. We need to go."

He was right. Cynder's energy combined with Grom's was close by. Master Gryph rushed down the passageway. She and the others ran after him, jumping over the dead bodies littering the tunnel.

The mineshaft twisted and turned, and occasionally intersected with other passageways. They had just passed one of the intersections when they heard someone coming their way. Master Gryph ground to a halt and had them hurry back and cut down a side passage. When they were out of view of the main corridor, they stopped and waited. A troop of men ran past in the direction of the cave. Master Gryph gave the men a moment to get further down the tunnel. He then eased up to the main corridor and peered around the corner to make sure it was clear. Motioning for Elhrin and the others to join him, he disappeared around the corner.

They followed him down the tunnel at a dead run. When they rounded a bend in the tunnel, they found that they were finally at their destination. The mineshaft opened up into a well lit, stacked stone wall room that had to be part of the keep's foundations. Master Gryph held up a hand and slowed to a halt. Listening for sounds of movement, he eased into the room.

"It's clear," he said, motioning for them to join him. He then slid the heavy door to the mineshaft in place and barred it against any enemy left in the mine.

The room was a storage arsenal filled with weaponry of all kinds. Seeing an ample supply of arrows, Jag and Fuller replenished their quivers.

From here, Cynder's energy was strong. He was above them somewhere in the keep. Grom's energy source now had a distinct location. He had separated from Cynder and seemed to be moving down into the keep. Cynder was moving across the top of them, but his energy did not appear to be coming closer.

"This is where we must part," Master Gryph said. He dropped his pack and reached for Marguerite to give her a hug.

"What are you doing? I'm going with you," Marguerite protested.

He shook his head. "No, I am going alone. Elhrin needs you, remember?"

She nodded, reluctantly, as she stepped into the circle of his arms.

He glanced back at the rest of them. "Don't be fooled by the bulk of Blackridge's guardians being outside. I have no doubt that Grom has raised an alarm that we are here. I am going to try for the main entrance and see what I can do to keep as many outside as I can. We all know the uppermost floors have caved in by what we saw on the ridge, so the lower floors should be well occupied. It will take you all to ensure that Elhrin reaches the Rift," his gaze swept the men. "Hopefully, Grom's hate for me will draw him away from you. Stay to the rear of the building if you can and, Elhrin, avoid Cynder if at all possible. Do you know where to find the Rift?"

"It is in the main hall. If I can trust my dream," she said hoarsely, working hard against the desire to plead and beg for him not to go. She was terrified.

"You can trust it," he said, and looked down at Marguerite. "Stay safe."

"Let me go with you," she pleaded.

"You can't. Don't forget what I told you," he said, then kissed her softly.

"As if I could forget what you told me," she whispered. "Gryph, please, this is too hard. Don't go. I can't live . . . ."

He placed a finger on her lips, stopping her from what she was about to say. "My love, we can't change what must be," he said softly. "I love you."

"I love you, too," she said. Tears filled her eyes, but she did not let them fall.

Hugging her one last time, he then faced Elhrin.

"This is it, young lady. You save as much energy as you can. You will need it for the Rift, okay?" she nodded at him, unable to speak. He hugged her hard, then let her go.

"Bayle, take care, son," he squeezed Bayle's shoulder and headed for a massive door across the room. There were two other exits in the room besides the mine shaft. One was through the door he chose. The other was up a stairway along the wall to her right.

"Boys, my girls are in your hands. Keep them safe," Master Gryph said as he disappeared through the door, and was gone. She could feel his energy recede down a corridor on the other side.

Jag dropped his pack to the floor, removing items from it that he thought he would need, and everyone decided to do the same, freeing themselves from the extra weight. Elhrin pulled out the small satchel where she kept the *Book of Tolman*, then slung it over her shoulder so that it hung out of the way behind her.

"Those men might come back. The door won't hold them long. Let's get out of here," she said. Elhrin was halfway up the stairs before she realized Marguerite had not moved, and was staring at the door Master Gryph had used.

"Marguerite, we need to go," Elhrin said.

Marguerite nodded slowly. "I know," she whispered, and with one last look at the door, mounted the stairs.

The hallway above the stairs ran into a dim, torch-lit corridor that led in opposite directions to their left and right.

"Which way?" Bayle asked.

"I'm not sure. My dream put me in a corridor from the courtyard entrance to the main hall. Which way do you think that would be?" Elhrin asked.

"We need to go up. We are still too far down," Marguerite said hoarsely, pointing to an arched opening to their left. "There are the stairs."

The stairway led both up and down. Jag and Tomas mounted the stairs.

"Hey, where's Kyne?" Bayle asked.

Kyne was nowhere in sight.

"Where could he possibly be?" Elhrin asked, fuming that he would leave them without a word. Wasn't he supposed to be her bodyguard?

"He'll have to catch up," Marguerite said, and started up the stairs.

With one last look down the hall, Elhrin followed. As they ascended, she sent out her senses and found Master Gryph above them and to their right. Grom had been drawn to his energy and she could tell he was closing in on him. Cynder was also above them somewhere in the center of the keep. Elhrin groaned out loud.

"What is it?" Bayle asked, looking over his shoulder.

"Master Gryph has drawn Grom's attention, but I don't think he would ignore us. I'm sure we have company coming. Also, I am almost positive Cynder has positioned himself in the main hall with the Rift."

Marguerite let out an explosive burst of air. "Let's try to keep quiet, but let's move quickly. We don't want to give those outside time for them all to come in."

They reached the next floor. The corridor outside the stairwell was in total darkness. Tomas checked for enemies.

"There is nothing there," he said, quietly.

"We are still too far down," Elhrin said, certain now that Cynder was in the main hall. "We need to go up about two more flights."

He and Jag started up the next flight of stairs.

They were approaching the next floor when Jag grunted in pain and fell back into Marguerite, knocking her into the wall as she caught him. They both went down. An arrow protruded from Jag's shoulder.

Elhrin looked up. A bowman stood on the landing, notching another arrow. Tomas charged up the stairs. Elhrin shot a flaming ball of energy past Tomas. It exploded into the bowman's chest. He bounced off the wall beside him and landed face down at the top of the stairs. Tomas didn't stop. He reached the top of the stair and ran into the hallway. They heard him yell when he clashed with another enemy. Fuller and Bayle rushed up after him.

Elhrin quickly glanced at Marguerite and Jag. Marguerite was in the process of ripping off Jag's sleeve, but glanced up when she noticed Elhrin was still beside her.

"Go!" Marguerite ordered. "They need you."

Elhrin ran up the stairs. She grimaced when she jumped over the dead man. Her fireball had blown away half his torso. Blood poured from him like a river and flowed down the stairs.

The boys were outnumbered in the hallway. Using her magic, Elhrin threw one of the attackers hard against a wall. His head cracked against the stone, and he dropped to the floor, but she knew he was not dead. She drew her sword for the first time. Swallowing hard against what she was about to do, she plunged it deep into his chest. Her stomach roiled. She quickly withdrew the sword and backed away, fighting a wave of nausea. Physically killing him with a weapon had been much harder than she thought. A small bolt pinged against the wall dangerously close to her head. She whipped around, and fired at a man who stood down the hall cocking the string of a crossbow. He threw himself to the side wall. Her ball of energy passed him by and exploded at the end of the hall, blasting a hole into another room. She fired again. This time he was too slow to get out of the way. Her attack slammed into him and exploded. His body ripped in two and both halves were flung violently in different directions.

Meanwhile, Bayle backed away from a narrow miss when his burly adversary tried to cut him in two with an axe. Bayle struck back and managed to nick the man's face with his sword tip. Furious, the man heaved his axe sideways at Bayle. Bayle ducked under the swing and lunged, full force. He drove his sword deep into the man's stomach and used his momentum to throw a shoulder against him at the same time. Both crashed to the ground.

On the other side of the hall, Tomas kicked the man he was fighting in the stomach, sending him crashing into the stone wall. Amazingly, the man remained on his feet, and Tomas attacked. Swinging in a downward arc, he intended to severe the man's neck, but the man rolled out of the way. Tomas' sword clanged against the wall, sending a shower of sparks cascading down its stones. The man retaliated with a backhand swing and Tomas jumped to the side. The blade clipped his shirt, but did not connect with flesh. Tomas squared himself against the man. The man glared at him, then lunged. Tomas backed away, knocking the man's sword to the side at the last moment. Yelling at the top of his lungs, the man mounted a raging assault. Tomas gritted his teeth. The force of the blows was tremendous, and Tomas had to grip his sword with both hands to keep from losing it. Fortunately for Tomas, the man finally made a mistake and left one side unprotected. Tomas cleaved a deep gash into the man's side. Blood spewed down Tomas' blade like a fountain. The man tried to swing again, but couldn't. Tomas placed a boot on him and kicked the man away. His sword, slick with blood, slid out of the man's body.

On the opposite side of the hall, Fuller jumped to his feet and felt his bloody eye with his free hand where his attacker had sucker punched him to the floor. The man gave him an evil grin, and swung his sword, barely giving Fuller time to block it and back away. Blood poured into Fuller's eye, rendering it useless. Quickly, he tried to wipe it away with his sleeve. The man swung again, and Fuller caught the glint of the blade in time to block it before it hit him. The force of the blow knocked his sword to the floor and made him stumble into the wall. The man grinned, knowing he had Fuller, and reared back, ready for the kill. Fuller couldn't see out of his eye at all, and in the dim torchlight, he couldn't tell where the man was going to swing. He readied himself to move. The man started to plunge his sword into Fuller's gut, but was surprised to find he couldn't move. Then he began to gasp for air. His eyes bulged and his face turned a deep shade of crimson. Unable to breathe, his eyes rolled back into his head and his body went slack. Fuller heard a slight snapping noise come from the man's neck. The man's sword clanged to the floor, and for a moment he stood upright, then abruptly, he crumpled lifeless to the floor. Fuller reached up to wipe the blood out of his eye.

"Are you hurt, Fuller?" Elhrin asked.

"No, just couldn't see there for a minute," he said, bending down to get his sword. "Thanks for the help."

"Any time," she said as Bayle and Tomas joined them. "Are you two okay?"

"Never better," Tomas grunted.

Bayle wiped sweat from his brow, using the bandage on his left arm, and Elhrin noticed that blood covered the bandage.

"Bayle, are you bleeding?" she asked.

"I don't think so," he said, checking himself over.

They heard footsteps scrape in the stairway. To their relief, Marguerite walked out with Jag. His face was grim, lacking its normal color. Sweat poured down his forehead as if he had been running on a hot summer's day. He held a cloth to the wound on his shoulder. Marguerite had removed the arrow, thankfully, it had been poison free.

"Are you going to make it?" Fuller asked him.

"Yes," Jag grunted, and noticed Fuller's bloody face. "What happened to you?"

"I tried to hit his fist with my eye," he said, nodding to the dead man at his feet. "I don't recommend it, though. It's not very effective—landed me on my ass."

Despite the major danger they were in, they had to smile at Fuller's attempt at humor. Elhrin breathed in heavily, taking advantage of the short break to send out her senses in search of Master Gryph. She nearly panicked when she could only pick up one energy source other than Cynder above them, but then relaxed when she realized it was his energy source and not Grom's. She scanned around, but still could not pick up Grom anywhere.

"I think Master Gryph has killed Grom. I can't find him," she said, glancing at Marguerite.

"Where is he?" Marguerite asked.

"Above us. On the same level as Cynder."

Marguerite turned and ran up the stairs.

"Marguerite, wait," she yelled, but the lady did not slow down. Elhrin ran after her, calling to the boys over her shoulder. "Let's go."

Somewhere above them a thunderous boom shook the entire keep. Elhrin grasped at the craggy stones of the wall to keep from being thrown to the ground. Her senses told her Cynder was moving towards Master Gryph.

"What was that?" Fuller asked. He and the others had braced themselves against the stair's sudden shift below her.

"I'm not sure, but I think Master Gryph and Cynder are about to find each other. Let's move," she turned and raced up the stairs, relieved to see Marguerite was safe and waiting for them on the landing of the next floor.

"Is this it?" Marguerite asked.

"Yes, this way."

She raced down the hall, but before she reached its end, a corridor to her right caught her attention. She skidded to a halt. Here was the hallway of her dreams. It was long and partially lit by torches placed periodically along the walls. Several openings along either side indicated where doorways or hallways led off in other directions. At the end was an arched doorway, an eerie red glow pulsed through its opening like a visible heartbeat. She was confused. She thought this corridor led from the hall to the keep's courtyard, but they were on the opposite side of the keep, in the back.

"We've got company coming," Fuller warned.

Boots pounded down a nearby hallway to their left. A group of human soldiers appeared around the corner.

"There they are," one yelled. He was a giant of a man, and pointed a deadly, serrated-tipped sword at them.

"We'll try to hold them, Elhrin. Go!" Tomas ordered, running to meet the attackers.

Elhrin flung a ball of energy past Tomas. It zoomed over the heads of the advancing men and exploded into the ceiling. Rock and timber fell in a billow of dust behind the enemy and partially blocked the corridor. She hoped it would be enough to slow down any others from that direction.

"Come!" Marguerite grabbed Elhrin's arm and propelled her down the corridor toward the pulsing light. Somewhere on the other side of the main hall an explosion went off and a flash of light winked through the arched opening. As they neared the doorway, they could see part of the main hall. Across the room was a matching doorway, and most likely the hall that led to the courtyard she remembered from her dream.

Suddenly, the wall beside that doorway exploded. Cynder, stone, mortar, and a billow of dust rolled across the floor of the hall. Growling fiercely, Cynder scrambled up on all four feet. Raising a scaly claw, he hurled a fiery green orb back through the destroyed doorway. It exploded in a flash of light somewhere down the hall's length. Cynder started for the door, but an unseen force slammed into him. He flew backwards out of her view into the nearby wall with a thunderous crash. Dust sifted from the ceiling, creating a dense cloud. She couldn't see. Elhrin started forward, but Marguerite grabbed her arm and held her fast.

"I need to help him," she whispered, but Marguerite shook her head firmly. "Why not?"

"He told me to keep you out of this fight," Marguerite said.

"What? Why?"

"Elhrin, he told you to focus on the Rift. Do it!"

"How can I close the Rift with Cynder here?" she hissed, trying to move into the hall.

Marguerite's grip dug painfully into her arm and pulled her against the wall. "Don't you argue with me, girl. Gryph has his reasons. He has told you to avoid Cynder more than once. Obey his orders."

"What are his reasons?" she asked. This was ridiculous.

"You will see," Marguerite choked out the words. She let Elhrin go.

Frustrated by the lack of valid logic, Elhrin craned her neck to see inside the room. She could not see Cynder, but she could hear stones clattering across the floor as he heaved his huge body up. Across the room, Master Gryph limped through the opposite door, warily watching Cynder's movements. Behind him was the silhouette of a wiry figure.

"There's Kyne," Elhrin gasped, pointing to the broken archway across the hall. "He followed Master Gryph."

The sound of steel against steel clanged in the hall behind her. She and Marguerite whirled around, ready for a fight. Bayle, fighting a soldier twice his size backed into the hallway. Soon he would be cornered against the wall where he wouldn't be able to maneuver. She sent an invisible stream of energy speeding down the hall. She wrapped it around the enemy's neck and jerked back hard on the flows as if she had just roped a runaway bull. The unsuspecting soldier was jerked sideways and crashed to the floor. Bayle didn't hesitate and plunged his sword into the offender then jerked it back out. He saluted her with the bloody blade before disappearing back into the fray in the other corridor.

"Well, So'ladiun, you are much stronger than the ones I have had the pleasure to kill before. I like it. It gives me more of a challenge," Cynder growled behind her. He limped through the rubble into Elhrin's view.

"Glad to accommodate you," Master Gryph said, and launched two beams of fluorescent green light into Cynder, burning a hole through one leg and the tip of a folded wing.

Cynder trumpeted in pain. The sound was so loud Elhrin and Marguerite had to clap their hands over their ears. Cynder was furious. He retaliated with crackling strands of violent energy. Master Gryph formed a shield to deflect the intensity of the attack. Seeing the direct attack was not working, Cynder diverted the strands into the wall beside Master Gryph. It exploded in a spray of shattered rock behind Master Gryph's shield and knocked him to the floor.

"No," Marguerite gasped.

Her voice had been low, but Cynder heard her. He whipped his serpentine head around and bared his fangs in what Elhrin suspected was the closest thing he could get to a smile. "Look who we have here. I was beginning to wonder where you were, So'ladiun. I hope you have brought me a present."

He limped towards them. Elhrin's heart began to slam against her chest. She readied herself for an attack.

Cynder drew in a huge breath, and Elhrin knew what he was about to do. She created a shield and jumped in front of Marguerite. Cynder spewed flames from his mouth. The force of his fire slammed into Elhrin's shield and drove her back into Marguerite. Arms immediately wrapped around Elhrin's waist and kept both of them from falling. The heat from Cynder's intense flames surrounded them, and Elhrin had a hard time keeping her shield intact. The beast's power was immense and the heat unbearable.

Without warning, his fire was cut off as something exploded into his back. The beast was thrown across the hall, tearing up flagstones as he slid across the floor. His tail clipped a huge stone pillar, causing it to shift out of place and dislodge stones from the ceiling. They rained down and covered him in a mound of rock.

"Master Gryph," Elhrin whispered helplessly. Her mentor sat hunched on his knees. His face was covered in blood, and he was coughing furiously.

Growling in absolute fury, Cynder burst out of the mound of rock and faced Master Gryph. Master Gryph rose unsteadily to his feet and waited on Cynder's next move. It was all Elhrin could do to not rush in and help him as she watched him try to catch his breath between hard fits of coughing. Without thinking, she took a step forward, but Master Gryph held up a hand, "Elhrin, stay where you are!"

"Yes, Elhrin, stay where you are," Cynder mocked. The beast limped toward Master Gryph. "I'll deal with you in a moment." He barked a laugh as he addressed Master Gryph, "That was one I have never seen before, So'ladiun, I'll have to remember it for the future."

"There is no future for you," Master Gryph rasped then spat out a stream of red fluid to the floor.

"I should say the same for you," Cynder growled, and sent a fiery green orb at Master Gryph, who launched himself sideways to the floor and rolled. Cynder quickly closed the distance between them and grabbed Master Gryph into his huge claw and squeezed. Master Gryph shouted out in pain.

"Oh, god," Marguerite moaned under her breath, "this is too hard."

"Obsudius is waiting for you, So'ladi—," he growled, but couldn't finish. Blue strands of energy shot from Master Gryph's hands and wrapped around Cynder's neck, choking him. Cynder's visage flickered and blurred briefly into the triangular form of a giant insect similar to a mantis, but then he managed to return his form to the powerful dragon.

Master Gryph set the magical strands on fire. Cynder raised his head towards the ceiling. Opening his maw in silent agony, he thrashed his head about in a frenzy trying to break the hold searing into his scaly flesh. Not able to free himself from his captor, Cynder reared back and threw Master Gryph across the hall. He landed hard and rolled towards the Rift, but he did not release his fiery hold on Cynder. He painfully pushed up to his knees, holding tight to the magical strands that threatened to break from his grasp. He shot a quick look at Marguerite—a look that broke Elhrin's heart because there was no disguising the love and regret so apparent in his eyes. He set his mouth in a tight line and wrenched the strands of his magic over his head as if he was setting the hook on a fishing pole. The force of Master Gryph's magical pull caught Cynder off guard and jerked him across the hall. The beast crashed into Master Gryph. Both man and beast rolled in a tangle of limbs and magic straight into the Rift. They disappeared into the realm of Do'athra in a thunderous flash of red light.

"No!" Elhrin screamed. Her body went numb. She couldn't believe her dreams had just come to pass. "He did that on purpose," she whispered.

"Yes," Marguerite said, her voice heavy with anguish. "Elhrin, hurry, you must close it."

"But Master Gryph . . . ."

"Close it!" Marguerite yelled.

Elhrin would not argue, even though every fiber of her being wanted to jump into the swirling mass of energy and save him, not cut him off from this side if he could get back. "Kyne, help the others," she shouted.

He rushed full force towards the fight in the back hallway without a word. From the intense sounds of the fray, more of the enemy had joined the fight.

She picked her way through the stone debris until she was in the middle of the room. She could not bring herself to get any closer to the gigantic angry mass of swirling energy that encompassed the entire back wall of the hall. A rumbling hum rose and fell with the pulsing of the energy, and she could feel vibrations in the stones beneath her feet mimicking the deep sound. It, indeed, felt like the pulse of a slow methodic heartbeat.

Marguerite stumbled into the room behind her. Wiping a river of tears from her cheeks with the back of her hand, she planted herself behind Elhrin, ready for any attack.

"Marguerite, are you sure?" she asked one last time.

Pale as death, Marguerite nodded for Elhrin to proceed.

Elhrin faced the Rift. Taking the pendant from around her neck, she grabbed her magic. Instantly, the pendant burst into a bright green light. What was she supposed to do now?

She studied the swirling mass, rotating slowly as water would when it seeped down a partially blocked sink drain. An unlikely idea formed in her mind. Could it be as simple as trying to halt the flows of energy within the Rift? Would that change or reverse the magic within it? Surely not, but she did not have time to debate the unknown, nor did she have a better idea for closing the portal. With nothing to lose, she sent a strand of energy from her palm directly into the pendant. The pendant erupted into a brilliance that chased all shadows from the hall.

"Oh!" she gasped. A power like she had never experienced coursed through her body—strange, powerful, yet familiar and right.

Elhrin raised her hand and directed a fine beam of green light towards the Rift. The beam latched onto the edge of the swirling mass like a key fitting into a lock. Maybe she was on the right course. She sent strand after strand of raw power out of the gem until the entire perimeter of the Rift was encircled in a conical web connected to her hand. She poured more energy through the pendant and directed the flows of the beams in a circular pattern, counter to the direction of the swirl inside the Rift. It felt like she was trying to halt the current of a raging river. Gritting her teeth, she pushed on the flows, and felt the force of the Rift grind against her will.

"Oh, no you don't," Elhrin heard Marguerite yell behind her and then a resounding clang of steel reverberated throughout the room. Daring a quick glance over her shoulder, she saw Marguerite swing her weapon with two hands and knock a Do'athrim's axe wide. She then pivoted and kicked him square in the stomach. The Do'athrim doubled over. In a furious rage Elhrin was sure had to do with Master Gryph's passage into Do'athra, Marguerite drove her sword downward through the beast's back with the force of a mighty warrior.

Elhrin felt her focus wavering and returned her attention back to the Rift, pouring more of her energy through the pendant. Slowly, the beams of green light started to move, but it was as if the energy within the Rift recognized the threat. An unexpected build up of power roared through its mass. The Rift turned a bright, ugly red and flooded Elhrin's beams with a massive amount of energy. Using the beams as a conduit, the backlash of energy hit the pendant. Malicious power slammed into her system. Fiery sparks flew far and wide and she was hurled into one of the hall's massive pillars.

"Elhrin!" she heard Marguerite scream.

It sounded like the woman called her from a distance. She couldn't see or breathe. Her entire body felt like it had been set on fire and the muscles in her arms and legs were wracked with spasms.

Marguerite fell to her knees beside Elhrin and grasped her face between her hands. "Can you hear me, sweetheart?"

With an extreme effort, Elhrin sucked in a lung full of precious air. Coughing and gasping to catch her breath, she groaned, "I now know what it feels like to be hit by lightning." She tried to get up. Her entire system felt like it had been fried. "Oh, god," she breathed.

"Come on. You need to hurry. It sounds like the fighting is coming our way," Marguerite said.

Grasping her arm, Marguerite helped her to her feet. Trembling like a baby foal standing for the first time, she turned to face the Rift again, then realized to her horror, that she had dropped the pendant. Frantically, she scanned the floor for the gem.

"Elhrin, what are you doing? You must hurry!" Marguerite said, as the sound of battle was definitely getting closer. Elhrin realized the boys must be in trouble.

"Marguerite, I've lost the pendant!" she cried.

"There's the bitch," a deep voice growled.

"Damn it!" Marguerite cursed, turning to face a new threat.

A pack of Do'athrim streamed out of the main corridor through the doorway Cynder had destroyed. Despite the weakness she felt, Elhrin launched fireballs into the snarling beasts. The explosions sent sprays of blood and gore in all directions as the beasts in the lead blew apart, but that did not deter their companions. Howls rose loud and frantic from the remaining Do'athrim. As one, they jumped over the dead and injured bodies of their companions and raced towards the two women.

Chapter Twenty-Eight

Gryph and Cynder rolled across the freezing cold surface of hard paving stones, entangled limbs separated and Gryph kicked the beast away. Somehow the N'gethwyn's form had changed during their crossover into Do'athra. He now possessed the form of a mantis and skittered across the floor on the hard shell of his elongated back, six spindly legs flailed desperately for purchase to right himself.

Gryph painfully tried to breathe. The crossing through the Rift had been excruciating. His body had felt like it was being ripped apart by the seams, and now, in the foul and hostile environment of Do'athra, he was in agony. A living child of Ts'aura was not supposed to be here. He was alive, but it wouldn't be for long. His body had started to die the second he landed in Obsudius' realm.

"My Lord," he heard Cynder rasp.

With a groan, Gryph rolled to his side. He and Cynder were not alone in the room that was an exact duplicate of the hall they had just left. A hooded figure dressed in deep crimson robes stood mere paces from him. Pale hands reached up to withdraw the covering that hid his face in shadow, revealing a man whose features were almost exact copies of Solisius', but not quite. The exceptions being defined not only by physical features, a deathly gray pallor, raven hair that brushed the rumples of his cowl, eyes blacker than a starless night, but also by the abysmal hate and the dark and foul supernatural power that resonated from his being—this was Obsudius, this was the God of Darkness.

"Well, So'ladiun, it seems you made it to my keep contrary to my orders," his voice rang deep with the air of someone bored.

The sound invoked a trickle of unwanted fear in Gryph, even though Gryph had long ago accepted this path that was his destiny. Fear could not be allowed to consume his thoughts. His mind was already clouded by the intense pain that was being inflicted on his body. He had to stamp everything down and discard it. He had to focus.

"How is it that he made it here, Cynder?" Obsudius continued without looking at the beast behind him who had morphed into the human-like form Gryph had seen on the mountain.

"My Lord, Grom and Morg failed," Cynder rasped.

"And you, did you not fail?" Obsudius asked.

"My Lord, I . . . ."

"Shut up! I will discuss this with you later." He glared at Gryph. "I thought my brother had finally gone mad, designating a weakling girl child as one of his warriors and sending her here to face certain death. But then Cynder informed me you were back in the world and on your way here with her, which made more sense, but I must say I almost did not believe him. Unlike me, my proper, play-by-the-rules brother does not like to disobey our father. The pressure of my impending triumph must have him desperate to allow you to walk among the living again. How is Solisius faring," a malicious smile revealed a row of perfect white fangs, "with my little war?"

"He fares well. He sends you his regards," Gryph choked out the words. His throat was extremely dry, making speech nearly impossible. He rubbed his chest. It felt like an elephant was sitting on him. Solisius had told him to expect the painful effects on his body as soon as he entered Do'athra. Each internal organ would begin to deteriorate until they all failed, and he would feel every single event in excruciating detail until he was dead. Then there would be the matter of his soul being trapped in this realm if he could not escape before he died. Here, the pain would not end for him like it had in Ts'aura. Here, he would be in endless agony and he would be powerless to stop it. The only option to end the suffering would be for Obsudius to send him to the Void, and that he would welcome with relish. Not because of the pain inflicted by Obsudius, no there was a pain far worse than any the dark god could inflict and that was the insurmountable pain of spending an eternity without the love of his life.

"I seriously doubt my brother would send me his regards," Obsudius snorted in contempt.

Behind the dark god, a regiment of soldiers started to file through an arched doorway. Obsudius turned his hate filled gaze on Cynder.

"Not now!" Cynder roared at those entering the hall, understanding his master explicitly. The men froze where they stood and waited.

Taking advantage of the diversion, Gryph reached inside his shirt and clasped his pendant. He wrapped the chain around his palm and pulled until he felt it snap. Keeping the pendant hidden in his fist, he slowly pushed himself to his knees. This had to be quick.

Obsudius tilted his head back and contemplated Gryph, unconcerned by his movements. "What does my brother seek to gain by sending you here, I wonder?" he mused, almost to himself. "Well?" he asked when Gryph did not offer an immediate answer.

Gryph tried to produce moisture in his throat, but it was useless. "He is tired of you causing the untimely deaths of his children." Talking set his throat on fire.

"But it suits my purpose to stamp out every So'ladiun and every human who loves Solisius. Actually, the entire human race will be gone by the time I am finished. All this," he nodded at the Rift behind Gryph, "is just the beginning. Solisius thinks he has a hold on this world, but my brother does not know or see everything. When my plan is complete, Solisius will have no one to love him. This world will be full of my children, and Solisius will not exist to them." Obsudius swept a hand toward the Do'athrim waiting behind him. "Aren't my children beautiful?"

"You will not succeed," Gryph gasped for air. It was getting harder and harder to breathe. Soon his lungs would collapse. "Solisius will never allow you to get that far."

"Allow me?" Obsudius laughed. "There isn't anything he can do or is willing to do to stop me."

"What makes you so sure?"

"It is obvious, So'ladiun. With you here, there is no one else remotely capable of standing against me. My army will eliminate your king and his pitiful army, and finish the task I have for them long before Solisius will be able to come up with any kind of defense, and even if he did, I'm afraid he is already too late. My plan is in motion."

"What plan is that?" Gryph tried to gulp in air. He had to make a move soon, but he hoped Obsudius would give him more information before he did.

Obsudius stared hatefully at Gryph, saying nothing. He narrowed his eyes. "You think to escape me, don't you?" he finally asked. "My brother is a fool. Your destiny lies within the Void."

"My destiny doesn't matter," Gryph gasped.

Obsudius stilled, contemplating his words. He started to laugh. A hollow hideous sound that should have invoked unimaginable fear, but it didn't. Determination was the only thing on Gryph's mind now—to live long enough to finish his mission.

"Is that so? Then who will save poor Anderan? The girl? I thought my brother was smarter than this. Even you, his strongest fighter, do not possess the power to stand against me. Why would he send a weak female?" he scoffed. "Oh no, her destiny is just as assured as yours."

And that was one thing that Gryph could not allow. He hauled himself to his feet. The effort nearly made him pass out. His vision blurred, making the figures of Obsudius and Cynder splinter in two then merge back together.

"I did not give you permission to rise," Obsudius barked.

"I did not ask for permission," Gryph hissed. He blinked, trying to clear his vision. He couldn't wait any longer. Hiding the hand holding his pendant from Obsudius' view, Gryph seized his energy.

"So'ladiun, you have made a serious error," Obsudius said. "No one has ever reached for their powers in my presence. You . . . ." He raised a hand.

Gryph had to stop him before he used his power to send him to the Void. "I have a message from Solisius," Gryph coughed.

"Never interrupt me!" Obsudius snapped.

Obsudius immobilized Gryph in a cocoon of traumatic pain. He felt like he had just been stabbed by thousands of sharp knives. Gryph tried to use his power to break free, but it wouldn't respond.

"You see? Your magic offers you no protection against me," Obsudius sneered. He intensified the pain.

Gryph yelled. The pain was almost more than he could bear.

Laughing, Obsudius let him go.

Gryph staggered and doubled over. Heaving furiously, he tried to catch his breath. It was by sheer force of will that he managed to remain standing. Obsudius' magic still rampaged through his dying body, and he had a hard time concentrating, but years of managing and ignoring pain had trained him to fight through it.

"Do you feel it, Cynder?" Obsudius spread his arms wide and breathed deeply in pleasure. "I should have done this with the others. The suffering—his pain is different from an ordinary human. So invigorating," he gasped as if in ecstasy.

"Yes, My Lord," Cynder laughed in agreement.

Obsudius held up a hand and cut off Cynder's laughter. "Tell me Solisius' message, So'ladiun, be quick about it," he barked the order.

"Solisius . . . is tired of you killing his children . . . and sending them to the Void," Gryph rasped. "Never again . . . will you be able to pull a Child of Light . . . into your realm."

"Is that so?"

"Yes," Gryph lifted his head and smiled through his pain at Obsudius, "from now on . . . you can be assured Solisius will fight you any way . . . he can . . . beginning with the girl. Do you actually believe . . . she is like any other So'ladiun?"

As if on cue, the Rift flared behind Gryph and a thunderous roar filled the room. His smile widened. Elhrin had figured out how to close it.

"Cynder, get the girl and bring her to me!" Obsudius ordered. Raising both hands, he directed his power at the Rift. The maelstrom behind Gryph erupted, turning the room blood red. Cynder started for the portal.

"NO!" Gryph yelled.

Raising his pendant, Gryph poured a massive amount of power into the crystal. A shaft of brilliant, white light shot out of his fist and seared into Obsudius' face. Obsudius blocked the beam with his own power. Gryph diverted his beam to Cynder, changing the magic to do what was necessary to eliminate the N'gethwyn. White light wrapped around the beast like a second skin and exploded. Cynder was gone—obliterated into non-existence within the Void.

The light within the pendant died. Gryph dropped to his knees. His strength was spent. Do'athra's hostile environment and Obsudius had taken their tolls on his body. The magic he had invoked against the dark god and Cynder had depleted the majority of his magical energy. He tried to call upon the magic in the pendant that would take him back to Ts'aura, but he failed. Darkness was coming for him.

"Damn you to the Void," Obsudius roared in furious pain, his hand covered his right cheek where the pendant had burned him. Rays of pure light glistened through the god's fingers, shining like the first touches of dawn on a clear morning. Solisius' magic had burned his insignia into Obsudius' flesh. Within its mark was a power that would forever protect future So'ladiun from being drawn into the realm of darkness against their will.

Gryph braced for Obsudius' retaliation. "I love you, Marguerite," he said out loud, even though he knew she would not hear him.

"You will pay for this!" Obsudius raged. He flicked his hand in Gryph's direction.

Gryph instinctively built a shield for protection, but in his weakened state it was no match for Obsudius' power. The god ripped through it as if it were nothing more than paper. Gryph felt an unimaginable force slam him in the chest and bones broke. Sparks flew wide from Gryph's hand as his pendant flared bright without his help. Two powers collided. His body was jerked off the floor by an unseen force. A force filled with love and light.

Chapter Twenty-Nine

Elhrin quickly built a shield and sent it slamming into the attacking Do'athrim. Sprawling bodies disrupted their momentum, temporarily stunning the ones who managed to escape the shield to a standstill. Marguerite slashed into the nearest beast struggling on the floor just as a knife flew across the room and embedded itself into the neck of a beast trying to regain his feet. Kyne ran into the fray.

Elhrin started to launch a volley of fireballs when the Rift roared to life and something crashed into her back, knocking her to the rock hard floor. Fearing that more Do'athrim had come through the Rift, she flipped over ready to fire, but found she was face to face with Master Gryph.

"Elhrin . . . I don't know what you are doing, girl," he said through gritted teeth as he curled in agony holding his chest, "but there is a whole regiment . . . about to come through that Rift . . . it needs to be closed."

Elhrin's heart dropped. "Master Gryph," she whispered, "I lost the pendant."

"Elhrin, look out!" she heard Tomas yell, just as a loud clang deafened her. She covered her head. Peering through her arms, she saw Tomas engaged with a beast over her body. She slammed a fist into the beast's leg. It was enough of a distraction to allow Tomas an opening. He drove his sword into its belly.

"Elhrin!" Master Gryph barked.

Elhrin jerked her head around to look at him.

"Listen . . . to me!" he coughed. "You don't need it. You can close . . . the Rift without the pendant."

Elhrin stared at him in horror. "What are you talking about?"

"Just trust me! You can close it . . . get up! You don't . . . you don't have time . . . to lie there! Go!" Master Gryph ordered with a groan.

Elhrin scrambled to her feet. The entire room was in chaotic battle. Relying on her companions to keep danger away from her, she faced the Rift.

"You have got to be mad," she said under her breath. "There is no way I am going to be able to do this without the pendant."

Raising a trembling hand towards the Rift, she summoned her energy. The Rift roared to life and several Do'athrim jumped through it into the hall.

"NO!" she yelled.

She swept the first two beasts to the side with her magic, slamming them with bone cracking force against the far wall. A fiery ball zoomed past her and slammed into the others in an explosion of sparks, causing the Rift to flare a bright red and give off a thunderous boom. The entire hall shook. The Do'athrim had been thrust back through. Only a single boot remained on the floor beneath the swirling mass.

"Now!" Master Gryph shouted

Hoping she was weaving the flows of energy right, she recreated the beams that had come from the pendant. Amazingly, the bright green shafts shot from her hand to encircle the perimeter of the Rift.

How is this possible? Amazed, she forced her flows of energy against the Rift's rotation.

The Rift's swirl slowed, and Elhrin felt the retaliatory increase of energy building inside its mass. This time she was ready for it. Before it could push back into her, she sent a massive flow of her own energy against it. The two forces slammed into each other with a deafening roar. The floor of the keep shook violently. Chunks of stone and wood rained down from above. An old rusty steel chandelier broke free from the ceiling and crashed to the floor. Blood-freezing screams filled the hall. She planted her feet wide against the lurching of the floor and pushed with all her strength. Her flow of energy ground against the Rift's current. Increasing in volume, the Rift howled in protest. Strands of white hot fire flared sporadically from the mass' surface. Muscles straining, sheer will holding her steady against the tremendous flow of power, she pushed harder. Finally, she felt something within its maelstrom give way as if it had broken and the swirl of the Rift came to an abrupt halt, but its surface continued to shimmer violently, crackling and popping like a lightning storm of red energy. Its roar escalated to a deafening pitch. Her ears felt like they were going burst.

Something exploded dangerously close behind her.

"Focus," she growled to herself. She was not through. She had to reverse it.

Forcing the flow of the Rift in the opposite direction, she could feel it start to weaken. The roar coming from its mass grew louder. The keep felt like it was coming apart. Thunderous crashes of stone fell everywhere. Part of the wall to her left fell outward, leaving a black gaping hole. She dropped to her knees to steady herself. The Rift's edges started to fray. Patches of solid rock started to appear through the holes that were forming in its mass.

The keep swayed to the side. "Please give me enough time to close it," she growled, planting her knees further apart to keep from falling over.

She pushed with her energy again. She felt a shift in the energy of the Rift, but this time it was against her. Its strength began to increase again. She steeled herself against the force that was strengthening the Rift, but it was too strong. What was left of her energy started to deteriorate rapidly. The Rift started to swirl back in its normal direction.

"Solisius, what is happening? I can't do this!" she yelled, feeling her resolve start to waver.

"Obsudius is testing you. Before, he had not needed to focus his energies on his portal—its maintenance was on his subconscious level. Now he knows he has made a mistake in thinking you unequal to this task and will have to address you directly. Elhrin, you must hurry before he decides to commit himself fully. You can do this. You have the power."

An unseen touch brushed lightly across the top of her head, and a sense of calm washed through her, taking away her doubts.

Damn it! She would close it!

Bracing herself against the tremendous force of Obsudius, she poured everything she had into her magic. The two forces slammed against each other. Yelling at the top of her lungs, Elhrin pushed against Obsudius' power. Something inside her shattered. A massive amount of power she did not know she possessed flooded her being and poured through her hands into the beams rotating against the Rift. Her beams turned from a bright green to a deep blue and increased in speed, kicking up a wind throughout the hall. Spinning ferociously against Obsudius' force, her beams created a solid funnel from her hands to the Rift. The winds in the hall screamed around her. She felt Obsudius' force push against her then ease off. Solisius was right. He was testing her and not putting his full attention on keeping the Rift open. He wanted to see just how strong or weak she really was, but she wasn't about to give him the chance to find out.

He pushed against her again. This time, she eased off. Her beams slowed dramatically. She could almost envision the dark god laughing at her weak female strength, thinking she was ignorant and unworthy to come up against his supernatural power. He started to rebuild his force within the maelstrom. She latched onto his power and used its momentum against him. With a twist of magnificent force that far surpassed anything she ever imagined, light and dark powers clashed and ripped apart. The Rift exploded.

Elhrin protected her head with her arms, but nothing touched her. The winds stilled and the shuddering of the keep stopped immediately. All around her clangs of steel hitting stone filled the hall.

"My god," she heard Marguerite whisper, quietly crying with relief.

She peeked through her arms at the wall where the Rift had been. Staring back at her was an age-old fireplace large enough to roast a cow. It was as if the Rift had never existed. She couldn't believe it. She had actually battled against Obsudius and won. Where had that extra force of power come from?

"It was always there, my child. You just had to find it. Well done," Solisius whispered, and was gone.

"I wonder if Solisius would consider letting me retire," Master Gryph gasped behind her. "I'm too old . . . for all this."

Marguerite laughed through her tears. Elhrin turned in time to see her kiss Master Gryph's blood drenched face. Tired but jubilant faces were beaming at her. Everyone was safe, but they were now alone. Not one Do'athrim body was anywhere to be seen amongst the rubble of the hall.

Tomas picked his way through the broken stone and grabbed her into a bone-crushing hug. "You did it," he whispered, then gave her a sound kiss on the lips.

Bayle crushed her from behind and wrapped his arms around both of them. "Way to go, sis!"

Elhrin laughed against Tomas' lips. "You two let me go before I suffocate. What happened to the Do'athrim?"

"They turned to dust as soon as you closed the Rift," Tomas said.

"They did?" Elhrin asked, wondering why that happened, but was glad it did. She was too tired to fight any more.

"A sight to behold," Fuller grinned from ear to ear. "We owe you our sincere thanks." He bowed dramatically.

"You owe her thanks," Kyne said, leaning at ease on his sword. "I was in no danger of having my throat slit."

"Shut up, Kyne," Jag said.

"Elhrin," Master Gryph tried to speak, but Marguerite was wiping blood from his mouth. He pushed her hand away. "It's fine," he growled.

She gave him a look that told him she was in no mood for any argument. With a resigned sigh, he dropped his hand to let her do what she wanted. She dribbled water onto a piece of her shirt she had ripped from her hem and dabbed at his forehead.

"Elhrin," Master Gryph repeated, but was interrupted by a fit of coughing. He groaned, clenching his eyes shut and holding his chest with both arms. Elhrin knelt at his side and reached for his hand. Rough and bloody fingers squeezed her tight.

He took a deep, shuddering breath, "Young lady . . . don't ever let me hear you say . . . you can't do anything again."

"I won't," she placed a kiss on his cheek, "I promise."

He tried to smile. "I will hold you . . . to that promise."

"I don't understand what just happened. I thought I needed the pendant," she said.

"You are not any ordinary . . . So'ladiun . . . sweetheart," grimacing, he coughed. He was having a hard time catching his breath. "Solisius has given you . . . an extraordinary gift . . . he has given no other. You have . . . some of his own powers in you."

"What?" she said in disbelief.

"Can we discuss this later?" Marguerite asked. "I want to get out of this foul place."

"Good idea," Master Gryph said, raising a hand. "Help me up."

Tomas and Bayle helped him to his feet. Groaning, he immediately hunched over. "It's going to be . . . a long walk . . . back to Glimmerdale," he grumbled.

Marguerite bent where he could see her face. "At least you get to go back to Glimmerdale, for which I am grateful."

He smiled at her, and she kissed him again. "I love you, Minister Idwyr."

"I love you . . . Madam Idwyr."

Elhrin scanned the hall. "What about the pendant?"

"You need . . . to get it."

"I lost it when I hit a pillar," Elhrin said, moving to the spot where she landed, searching. Bayle, Tomas, and Fuller joined her search.

"Elhrin," Master Gryph coughed.

She turned to look at him.

"I would rather not wait . . . for you to search . . . the entire hall. Call for it," he said, lifting a corner of his mouth. He was enjoying playing with her, even though he was hurting and having a hard time breathing.

"Just once, I wish you would come right out and tell me what I need to do instead of making me guess. What are you talking about?"

"The pendant . . . will recognize . . . you. Use your powers . . . to find it."

She frowned at him. He could be so frustrating.

She swept over the area with her powers. Astonishingly, a burst of green light erupted from a crevice in the floor not far from where she had crashed into the pillar. She glanced at him in wonder.

"See?" he asked.

"When we have the chance, you and I need to sit down and talk for a long, long time," she growled as she dug her pendant out of the crevice.

"That we do," he coughed, and leaning heavily on Kyne and Marguerite they walked into the corridor that led to the courtyard.

"Uh, how are we supposed to get out?" Bayle asked.

The hallway near the keep's entrance had caved in and was blocking the way out.

"It's a good thing you closed the Rift when you did, Elhrin. This old keep couldn't take much more," Fuller said.

"She didn't do this," Kyne nodded at Master Gryph, "he did."

"You blocked the army outside for us," Marguerite said, placing a loving hand upon his cheek.

"There was already . . . enough inside," Master Gryph said.

"So, how do we get out?" Tomas asked.

"The wall at the end of the hall to our left . . . is an exterior wall. It should hold if we blow a hole through it," he coughed.

"I've got it," Elhrin said. She flung a small white sphere down the corridor. It exploded into the rock with a boom. When the dust cleared, the dim glow of dawn filtered through a man-sized opening. "What do you know? It's morning."

Chapter Thirty

It had been unnerving to walk into a valley filled with the trappings of a full army complete with standing tents and burning fires, but not a living soul to be found. It was eerily quiet. No birds sang. No insects buzzed. The air was still as if Obsudius' army of living dead had swept the land free of life with its passing. The valley felt . . . repulsive. Everyone agreed to keep moving until they were at the mouth of the valley and the end of the army's tent line. Marguerite then called a halt, only because they were all beyond exhaustion and she didn't think Master Gryph could walk any further in the state he was in. As horrific as it felt to stay anywhere near the keep, the decision was made to clear out some of the empty tents near the mouth of the valley and rest before they traveled on to Lakeshore Glen.

Grateful to have the chance to be alone where she could think, Elhrin lay staring at the patterns in the cloth that made up her ramshackle tent. She grimaced when she realized what she was looking at—the cloth was probably someone's bed covering stolen from the village of Blackridge. Yawning, she closed her eyes against the sight. Immediately, the events of the night replayed in her mind. It was unbelievable that they had made it through alive and that she had closed the Rift without the pendant. The unexpected power that had coursed through her had been immense. She could still feel it pulsing inside, waiting for her to call on it.

"Why did you give me this gift, Solisius?" she whispered.

She expected a reply from Solisius, but instead, heard someone walk by and crawl into the tent next to hers. Tomas, she smiled sleepily. Earlier, he had helped her clear out the mess left behind from Obsudius' soldiers, and had taken advantage of the private moment to kiss her like he was afraid he would never get to kiss her again. Then, frustratingly, Kyne had interrupted them when he squatted at the open entrance to ask Tomas for help in a search for water where they could replenish their supply. She was positive Kyne had interrupted them on purpose because he could have asked any of the others to go with him. Well, Kyne may have interrupted, but she knew one thing for certain. She was going to finish that kiss as soon as she could if she had any say in the matter. And with that last thought, she fell into an exhausted, dreamless sleep.

Elhrin woke to the sounds of laughter. Night had fallen, and the glow of a fire flickered against the sides of her tent. Still tired, she wrapped her cloak tight around her and decided to go back to sleep. They could wake her if they needed her.

"Tell Bayle about the Plow and Plunder," she heard Tomas say with a laugh.

"Delightful girls, but a bit pricey," Fuller replied. "It's cheaper near the waterfront. The Drifter is a good place. Cleaner than most, and there is a show every night if you know what I mean." The men whooped with laughter.

"That big, huh?" Bayle laughed. "I must see that."

See what? She frowned. Afraid they were trying to corrupt her brother, she crawled to the entrance and pushed aside the tent flap. The boys were huddled around a blazing fire, carrying on about things they shouldn't. She crawled out into the cool night air and stood to stretch her back until she felt it pop.

"Good evening," Kyne hissed unnervingly close to her ear.

She jumped. "Damn it, Kyne," she turned on him, hand raised threateningly. She wanted to slap him so hard his teeth would fall out. "If you ever scare me like that again I will not restrain from smacking you."

"Don't flatter yourself into thinking you could, lady," he said calmly. "And just to clear matters further, I did nothing wrong. I was merely returning from a patrol of the area. You are the jumpy one," he smirked then sauntered away to join the others by the fire.

"I hate him," she hissed under her breath. "I really, really hate him." She crunched across the dry grass behind him. The boys stopped talking when they saw her coming. "What were you talking about?" she asked. Pretending she had not heard their topic of conversation, she circled the group until she came to Tomas. Bayle guiltily ducked his head and looked away.

Tomas pulled her down beside him and hugged her close. "Nothing much," he grinned. "Bayle was curious about Muryne, so Fuller was telling him about a few good taverns where . . . ."

"They have the best food," Fuller finished Tomas' sentence.

She gave Fuller a long, level look. "I am sure they do, but I don't think Bayle should be trying the Plow and Plunder or The Drifter's fare anytime soon."

Fuller had the decency to flush crimson for being caught, but he howled with laughter right along with the rest of them, except Bayle, Bayle gave her a horrified look.

"We were just talking," he sputtered.

Elhrin raised her eyebrows and shook her head, but then flashed him a reassuring smile. She had made him a promise to let him find his way, and she intended to keep it . . . within reason.

"Kyne, could you help me?" Marguerite called.

Master Gryph was leaning heavily on Marguerite as she tried to help him to the fire.

"I can get there," he grimaced.

Kyne and Tomas both jumped up to help.

"I still don't see why you insisted on coming out here," Marguerite said. "Elhrin could have come to the tent."

"I wanted to talk . . . to all of them," he said, breathlessly.

Elhrin frowned. She hated what Do'athra had done to him.

"Sit here, sir," Jag offered a camp stool he had found in one of the tents.

Gingerly, Master Gryph lowered himself to the stool. "Did everyone get rested?"

"Yes, sir," Jag answered.

"How do you feel?" Elhrin asked. His face was bruised with cuts slashing across the right side of his face, but Marguerite had managed to stop the bleeding and clean the wounds for him.

He grunted, "Like I've been . . . beat to a pulp with a boat oar."

She grinned at his reference to the statement she had used in the hunter's cabin. "I know the feeling."

He raised a corner of his mouth. "Well, everyone . . . I know you want answers about what happened . . . but first I think you need to understand . . . certain things should not be shared with anyone outside of this circle. It is imperative that you adhere to this request."

"Like?" Kyne asked.

"Like, who Elhrin and I are," he said. "And I don't think . . . the general public needs to know anything . . . we are about to discuss. You men were sworn to withhold state secrets when you joined the army. That oath holds here. Do you agree?"

Everyone nodded.

"Elhrin," he stopped to draw in a gulp of air, "I suppose you want to know . . . ."

"About these powers you say are a gift from Solisius," she finished for him.

"Right, well, Solisius has been planning . . . for you a long time. Remember when I told you . . . he gave me the task for teaching you . . . when I was a young man? Before you were born?"

She nodded.

"He knew the time had come . . . when he needed more than a talisman to hold some of his power . . . . He needed to place powers of his directly into someone. He chose you."

"Why me? Why not you? You are much stronger than me."

"Don't confuse experience . . . with strength," he fell into a fit of coughing. Grimacing, he crossed both arms over his chest until he was finally able to stop.

"Maybe this should wait," she said, concerned.

He jerked his head, no, at the suggestion. It took him a moment before he could continue. "Elhrin, you were also chosen because he needed someone . . . who would not abuse the power . . . and someone Obsudius would never suspect as a threat . . . but would also possess the courage . . . and intelligence to actually stand against him. I think you proved that today."

"It would have been nice if you or Solisius had told me about this special gift before I lost the pendant. It would have saved me from a lot of anxiety."

"I am truly sorry about that, but the fact is . . . telling you could have done more harm than help. You see . . . the powers would not manifest unless you reached inside yourself . . . and found them on your own. Similar to how I found my own gift. I told you that sometimes we have to stumble upon our hidden talents. This is what I meant. Better to find them unexpectedly . . . than to expect them . . . and not have them show up when you need them."

"So, the pendant isn't important?" she asked, still not sure his explanation was good enough.

"Of course, it is. It is still a talisman . . . from Solisius and has to be kept safe along with your book," he said. "But it was not the key to closing the Rift, you were."

Her jaw dropped.

"Nothing possessed the power to close it, but you."

"What about you?"

"Not even me."

"What if I had died?" And another horrible thought crossed her mind. "What if I had quit?" she whispered.

"Then Anderan would have had to stand as long as it could until Obsudius' energy to hold the Rift open," he paused to breathe, "diminished enough to force him to close it on his own."

She shook her head in disbelief and reached up to feel her pendant beneath her shirt, thankful she had not followed through on her anger that night in the woods. "My new powers, is that how the pendant recognized me when I searched for it?"

"Those powers have been in place since you were born, Elhrin. It should have always recognized you," he said, with a cough. He cleared his throat, turned his head and spat out a thick blob of mucus. "Did it not glow when you reached for your magic?"

Elhrin thought back to the night in Marguerite's cottage when she first saw it shine bright. It seemed like a lifetime ago. "Yes, but I never noticed it unless I was using it to look in the *Book of Tolman*."

"Where did you keep it?"

"Under my shirt," she realized the answer as soon as she said it. "I never saw it glow because it was hidden."

He winked at her with a half smile. Unexpectedly, that one gesture threatened to make her cry. She swallowed hard against her emotions. He had smiled and winked at her countless times throughout the years, and the fact that he had come back—was still with them and able to do it again, made her so happy she could burst. Lips quivering, she tried to smile back.

He saw her dilemma and gave her a moment to collect herself. "Who else has questions?" he asked.

"I was wondering why Obsudius' entire army disappeared," Bayle mused.

Master Gryph breathed in heavily through his nose. Lips clamped firmly in a tight line, he did not answer the question.

Bayle shot a questioning glance around the group. "Was that a bad question?"

"No, son, it was an excellent question," Master Gryph said. He frowned as if the answer made him angry. "I am going to have to say that Obsudius didn't think things through . . . when he put conditions of life on his Rift."

"What do you mean?" Tomas asked.

"My guess is that when he made the Rift . . . so that his soldiers would dissolve when they died . . . giving them the opportunity to come back through . . . he did not set a condition . . . where his soldiers left here would continue to live . . . when the Rift closed." He frowned at Marguerite. She placed a hand on his arm and squeezed.

"You would think a god wouldn't make mistakes," Kyne smirked.

"Obsudius is far from the perfect power-filled god you believe a god should be," Master Gryph said, almost with disgust.

Elhrin studied him, taking note of Marguerite's reassuring squeezes on his arm. "What happened in there?" she asked. What was going on? Why would answering that question bother him so much? Marguerite knew why, she was sure.

He turned ocean blue eyes her way. "I put the mark of Solisius on Obsudius."

Elhrin sat forward. "You did what?"

"What does putting a mark on Obsudius do?" Bayle asked.

"Obsudius will never be able to pull a Child of Light into his realm against their will again."

"How did you keep him from sending you to the Void?" Elhrin asked.

"He tried, but Solisius had other intentions that he did not share with me." He looked at Marguerite and his hard features softened. He placed a battered hand on top of hers. "I thought I was destined for the Void or worse, an eternity in Do'athra. The pendant's magic not only protected me from that fate, but it is truly a connection to Solisius for me even through the barriers of the spiritual realms. Through it, Solisius was able to draw me back through the Rift."

The knuckles on Marguerite's hand whitened as she squeezed his fingers and held on tight.

"So, your plan was to enter Do'athra all along," Elhrin said with a touch of anger. She knew that their paths, their lives were sacrifices for the sake of humanity, but still it was hard to take, knowing that if something had gone wrong he would have made an unimaginable sacrifice.

"It was, and I wanted to make sure . . . Cynder went with me. That's why I told Marguerite . . . to keep you out of my fight with him. I needed to send him to the Void . . . and can only do that if I am in the Realm of the Dead with him."

"Why couldn't you have sent him to Solisius like you did the Do'athrim?" Tomas asked.

"It is too dangerous for an N'gethwyn to be in his realm," he lifted the corner of his mouth. "Obsudius found that out . . . with a So'ladiun."

"Did you send Cynder to the Void?" Bayle asked.

"I did."

Bayle burst out laughing, "I bet Obsudius is fuming that you wiped out his favorite pet."

"Oh, he is fuming all right," he said without humor. He sent Elhrin a look of regret. "He will never make the mistake of thinking you weak again. He may not be able to pull So'ladiun into Do'athra anymore, but he will be able to send others after us."

She nodded her understanding. The both of them had angered the god and there was no doubt that they would be the focus of his revenge against Solisius. "Are you sure he won't open another portal here?"

A soft breeze shifted her hair. "*I will answer this one,*" Solisius said.

Elhrin smiled. Hearing his voice was soothing. It took away the anxiety she had been unaware she had been feeling.

"*Elhrin, Obsudius was not expecting your ploy of weakness there at the end, and when he finally realized what you were doing, he tried to pull the force of his energy back into place to counter you. So when the two powers ripped the Rift apart, he inadvertently drew the force of its destruction into Do'athra. That is why nothing touched you in the hall when it exploded.*"

"Okay, how does that answer my question?" she asked.

"Who are you talking to?" Bayle asked, puzzled. "No one answered you."

She held up a hand for him to be silent, listening as Solisius continued his explanation.

"*Obsudius and I may be gods, but we are not omnipotent like our father. We can be injured. He was already hurt and in a frenzied state of mind from what Gryph and I did to him. I have no doubt that the backlash of his own power did additional damage to him and he will need time to recover. For now, you all are safe, and it will be long after your deaths before he will have the strength to open another portal of the size you just closed. Still, once he begins to recover, he will be able to open a small one if he so desires and send more of his minions out.*"

"And we will have to be vigilant," Master Gryph said to her.

"Am I missing something?" Bayle asked, looking from one to another.

"Bayle, they are So'ladiun," Marguerite explained, patiently. "They can hear the voice of Solisius. I'm thinking he is talking to them."

Bayle's eyes went big as teacup saucers. "I had no idea," he murmured in awe. "What is he saying?"

Elhrin smiled at her brother, glad that he could still sound as innocent as a child after all that they had been through. "He says we are safe from Obsudius for now."

Marguerite breathed out a sigh of relief. "Good news, at last."

Kyne slipped a blade from his boot. "By the way, Jag, here's your knife." He flipped it once and neatly caught the blade end, offering Jag the hilt.

"My knife?" he glared at Kyne, patting his side where his blade should have been. His sheath was empty. "You thief," he growled and jerked to his feet, ready for a fight. "It's past time someone taught you a lesson."

"Jag, enough," Master Gryph coughed. "He is trying to give it back. That knife saved me . . . from wasting my energy on Grom."

"Kyne killed Grom?" Elhrin asked.

"Yes, and helped me with dispatching his men, as well."

"Why didn't Grom come back through?"

"I'm not sure where he went. He did not show up in the Rift hall while I was in Do'athra." He put a hand on Marguerite's shoulder. "That is enough for tonight . . . I think I will rest. We will speak more tomorrow."

By Marguerite's orders, they spent far longer than intended in the valley because Master Gryph had not been able to sleep until almost dawn and she wanted him to get some rest before moving on. Around mid-afternoon she announced he was awake and they could go, asking Jag to help her get him on his feet.

Bayle jogged back from his perch on a nearby boulder where he had been keeping watch of the road. "There are riders coming," he announced.

Elhrin shielded her eyes from the sun. Dust billowed from the dry roadbed as an entire regiment of men galloped their way.

Fuller crawled out of a tent and joined them. "Who is it?"

"I believe it is the king," Kyne said, right behind Elhrin.

She jumped from his unexpected voice, and whirled to slap him.

He caught her hand in a grip hard as steel. Slowly, his lips slid into the familiar hated smirk. "I told you not to flatter yourself."

"Let me go," she growled, "before I break my rule to not seal your lips together."

He opened his fingers and she jerked her arm away. He brushed past her as if nothing had transpired. "It is the king or someone from his party. That's his standard flapping in the lead."

Elhrin straightened her shirt and glanced at Tomas. He frowned at Kyne, not liking what had happened, but said nothing to the wiry man.

The riders drew closer, and Elhrin forgot all about Kyne. "It is the king," she grinned with relief, "and Master Toome is with him."

Their horses rumbled up the road and had no sooner skidded to a halt when Master Toome flung himself from his mount and ran over to grab Elhrin in a huge hug, pulling her up off the ground.

"You don't know how glad I am to see you are safe," he grinned at her, his voice gravelly with emotion.

"I'm glad to see you are safe, too," she beamed. He let her back down to the ground and reached out to shake Bayle's hand, pulling him into a bone-cracking hug, as well.

"Maye will be so pleased."

"Miss Caddoch, you did it," King Goruth strode up. Pulling black leather gloves from his hands, he tucked them into his sword belt. "I suppose we owe you an apology for doubting your story concerning the Rift. I am assuming your closing it is the reason we no longer have an enemy to fight."

"That is correct, Your Majesty, the army vanished as soon as it was gone," she replied with a slight bow.

He acknowledged her bow with a nod of his head. "You will have to explain why that is to me. I have many uneasy men trying to rationalize an enemy disappearing before their eyes. What do I tell them that would not cause widespread panic among our people?"

Elhrin tucked her bottom lip in her teeth. Their disappearance was going to be hard to explain. It would not be good at all if the public knew a god could open a portal and allow a host of monsters out into the countryside on a whim. "I'm not sure, Your Majesty, I . . . ," hold on, she smiled. She had a better idea. "I am still trying to come to terms with it myself. Perhaps you should speak to someone who could explain it all better."

The king looked puzzled by her statement. "Who would that be?"

"Elhrin, where is Marguerite?" Master Toome interjected before she could answer. His eyes swept the area almost in a panic.

"I am right here," Marguerite called out. She and Jag were helping Master Gryph through the maze of tents and shelters.

The air audibly whooshed out of Master Toome's lungs as if someone had punched him in his stomach. "My god," he breathed, pale as death.

"Son of a bitch," King Goruth choked.

Master Gryph chuckled at their reaction. "It seems I am an unexpected guest, Marguerite."

"Seems so," she agreed.

Master Toome and King Goruth warily closed the distance.

"I thought you were dead," Master Toome whispered, his voice cracked.

"I was," Master Gryph said simply. He undraped his arm from Marguerite's shoulders and smiled slightly at King Goruth. "I would bow, but this is as far as I can go."

King Goruth shook his head in disbelief. "I don't need it. I am confused. How in god's name are you here?"

"Solisius can create a portal just as well as Obsudius."

"Ah, I see," he drawled slowly as the answer dawned on him. He smiled wide. "Welcome home, my friend." He offered a hand and Master Gryph took it. King Goruth clasped it between both of his hands and leaned closer. "You look like shit."

Master Gryph burst out laughing, and instantly realized it was a mistake. "Oh," he groaned, and jerked his hand free from the king's grasp. He gripped his broken rib cage.

"What happened?" Master Toome asked. A trail of moisture spilled from his eyes, but he was now smiling.

"Long story . . . we will tell you about it later," Master Gryph grimaced, rubbing his chest. "Right now, I would love to go home."

"That can be arranged," King Goruth said. He turned and whistled between two fingers. A man broke away from the regiment and hurried over.

Tomas bent low and whispered in Elhrin's ear. "Will you come with me?"

Curious, she let him lead her between the tents a short distance away.

"What is so important that you needed privacy?" she smiled, thinking she knew the answer.

He pulled her into his arms. "I seem to recall a conversation near a dilapidated cabin where a certain green-eyed, gorgeous lady said she would like to know me better. Do you know what I'm talking about?" He leaned down and nipped at her lower lip.

"Sounds familiar," she murmured, allowing him to roam at will. Her thoughts skittered to the wind.

After a moment of lips melding, exploring, tasting, he pulled his head back. "Well?"

Confused, she raised her eyebrows. "Well, what?"

"Do you want to get to know me better or not?"

"Of course I do, but if you insist on wasting our time alone talking and not kissing me, I may reconsider."

"I can't let that happen," he grinned wide and hugged her tight, crushing his lips on hers.

Elhrin heard someone walk by the tents behind her. "I think I'm going to lose my breakfast," Bayle groaned.

"Shut up, Bayle," Elhrin giggled against Tomas' lips.

Epilogue

Elhrin pulled out a stack of small wooden boxes with no tops, filled with various bits of clutter he had stashed away over the years. She and Marguerite had never touched these boxes when they had searched his study, and Master Gryph had asked her to glance through them to see if they held anything of interest before taking them out of the room. She was thankful this was the last stack crammed underneath the table below the double window overlooking part of Marguerite's garden. Rifling through the top box, she found old papers, notes he had written to himself, broken pens, empty ink bottles, and other pieces of junk he should have thrown out long ago. Shaking her head, she slid the box to the side and looked to see what was in the next one, and laughed.

"What is it?" Master Gryph asked. He stood behind his desk, shuffling through the papers Marguerite had tried to organize weeks ago.

"Were you saving this for any particular reason?" she asked, and picked up a plate that held something shriveled and no longer recognizable, but was clearly an uneaten dinner from long ago.

"Hmm. Wonder how that got there?" he smiled.

"Well, I know this couldn't be yours because I have never seen you pass up anything to eat if it is set within arm's reach," she said, and set the plate on the table. "I wonder what it was?"

"No telling," he answered, distracted by something he was reading.

Looking through the contents of the other boxes and not finding anything of interest, she stacked them back.

"Do you want me to put these with the others or throw them on the burn pile?"

He glanced over to see what she was talking about. "Just put them with the rest. I'll go through them . . . when I get a chance."

"You know, you don't have to move everything out. It won't be long before I'll be going to Muryne, and Bayle doesn't need the whole room."

"I know, but right now this will give you two a little more privacy than sleeping on the floor beside the fireplace. It's only temporary until the renovations are complete."

"Why don't you just build somewhere else or tear the cottage down and start over?" She smiled. "By the time you finish, it's going to be the biggest building in Glimmerdale. What happened to your theory of not attracting attention?"

"Well, my aim is not to attract attention. We will need the room, and Marguerite deserves a nicer place to live. Besides, I'm not getting any younger, might as well," he hesitated, taking a deep breath as he glanced at the door, "enjoy the third chance I've been given."

Elhrin hated that he still had to stop every once in a while to catch his breath. He had told her that being in the Realm of Darkness and being touched by Obsudius' magic did irreversible damage and he did not think he would totally heal. She refused to believe him. Surely with more time he would heal. She picked up the boxes from the floor, and realized what he meant by that last statement. "Third chance? Not a very good dead joke."

"Yes, I should work on those, but with the door open, I was afraid Marguerite might hear me and decided to be a little vague." Smiling, he winked at her.

She loved that gesture more and more each time he used it. "Wise decision," she agreed, and carried the boxes out into the hall. It was already filled along one side with the things they had removed from his office, and she couldn't find a place among the mess on the floor to put the boxes. She decided to place them in his desk chair sitting by the door. Looking at all the things, she guessed it would take him at least a month to go through everything. That is, if Marguerite would actually let him leave all of it out here, and knowing Marguerite, it was highly unlikely.

She went back inside his office to survey their work, noting that aside from the larger furniture and the clutter on his desk, they were almost through. Master Toome could deliver the beds he and Bayle were making as soon as they finished.

She didn't know how long she was going to stay before she decided to go to Muryne. King Goruth had told her to rest, and when she was ready, to come meet with him. Thinking about it, she decided she was in no hurry to begin the next chapter of her life. Besides, Tomas was in Glimmerdale. He had asked the king for permission to stay, and his request had been granted. Elhrin thought back to the day, just a little over two weeks ago, when they were on their way back to Glimmerdale. They had just said their goodbyes to Kyne, Jag, and Fuller, who had to rejoin their regiments, when the King had requested Tomas and Elhrin's presence. He surprised Tomas by promoting him to the rank of captain, and then had put him in charge of a new patrol regiment that was to cover the South and West roads, along with keeping the peace in Glimmerdale and surrounding communities. She smiled. That should be easy—aside from the Do'athrim attacks, the only thing that ever happened out of the ordinary in the village was when Doogan's cows escaped their pastures and ran up and down the streets, remembering a time when a bull walked through the open door of Triva's shop, sending the short woman screaming out the back door.

Thinking about Triva reminded her of the unexpected joyous homecoming they had received when they had entered the village of Glimmerdale. It all had to do with a rumor purposely spread that Master Gryph was alive and well, obscurely hinting that his death had been faked and he had been sent on a secret mission and ended up saving Anderan from the flying dragon. This idea had been spawned when Master Toome had asked how they were supposed to explain Master Gryph's sudden resurrection from the dead. Master Gryph had thought about it for a minute then smiled and said Bayle had the solution, explaining that Bayle had thought he had faked his death in order to carry out a secret mission for the king. The king latched onto the idea and had sent a runner ahead to spread the word from Greystone to Muryne and all outlying farms in between that Master Gryph was alive. So when the people of Glimmerdale had learned they were almost home, they had gathered along the main street to wait on them to arrive. She would never forget the look of sheer annoyance on Master Gryph's face when they heard the thunderous roar of cheering long before they crossed the stone bridge spanning the Green River. He had grumbled under his breath all the way into town until they were forced to stop at the Glimmerdale Inn by the crowd, complaining that there were more important things for people to do than to make a fuss over their arrival. This still brought a smile to her face, thinking it funny that a man of his stature was so uncomfortable with being the center of attention and thought of as a hero. No one was ever told about the Rift, or that it was she who was responsible for the end of the war, and she wanted it to remain that way. She was quite content to let the people think that the destruction of the magical creature Cynder was directly related to the disappearance of his magically constructed army of Do'athrim. Besides, the story was a good one and was quickly becoming a favorite bar and hearthside tale, and Elhrin had no doubt before all was said and done, it would be passed on to future generations, portraying Master Gryph as an all powerful dragon-slaying giant.

The rustling of paper broke her train of thought, and something crossed her mind she had been meaning to ask him. "Are you going to Muryne with me?" she asked, as he opened a piece of correspondence he had found among the stack of papers.

"I said I would, didn't I?" he said, then began to read his letter.

"You said that before you and Marguerite decided to redo your house. I didn't know if you had changed your mind."

"Haven't changed my mind," he mumbled, more interested in what he was reading than having a conversation with her, so she gave up and started to move the table in front of the window when Marguerite came in looking anxious and worn out.

"Marguerite, is something wrong?" she asked. "You look pale."

"No. I don't know. I'll find out in a minute," she said, stopping in front of his desk and waiting patiently while he read his letter.

He was so engrossed in the letter, he was unaware Marguerite was now in the room. Elhrin cleared her throat loudly to get his attention, wondering why

Marguerite hadn't spoken herself.

He glanced up, and seeing Marguerite, he held up the letter. "When did this arrive from Griffyn? There is no date."

"Sometime around the beginning of the year," she said, crossing her arms over her chest.

He furrowed his brow. "Why didn't you . . . tell me he married and has a child on the way?"

"I honestly forgot. I guess I had other things on my mind," she said, flicking a hand in the air, impatiently. "You of all people should know firsthand about not telling somebody something important," she added with a little heat.

"Point taken," he said, puzzled by her behavior. "Is there something else on your mind?" He lowered the letter to the desk.

"Yes, there is." She fiddled with a button on her blouse. "Gryph, I," she had to stop to clear her throat. It was obvious she was nervous about what she had to say. "I'm pregnant."

"Woo hoo!" Elhrin shouted. "Marguerite, that's wonderful." She wrapped her arms around Marguerite, giving her a huge hug. She then realized she was the only one in the room who had moved or spoken.

She glanced at Master Gryph. The blood had drained completely from his face as he stared at Marguerite in shock. He slowly started to sit down. Not realizing his chair was out in the hall, he fell heavily to the floor with a thud, going completely out of sight behind his desk. "Oof."

"Gryph!" Marguerite exclaimed.

She and Elhrin peered over the desk to see him lying flat on his back with both hands covering his face, convulsing silently, and Elhrin didn't know if he was laughing or crying.

Marguerite hurried around the desk. "Gryph, are you hurt? Your ribs . . . ."

He pulled his hands away from his face, revealing that he had been laughing. "Oh, Solisius has played . . . a fine trick . . . on me. I bet he is enjoying . . . it too," he said with a boyish grin spread across his face.

He reached up to Marguerite and she grabbed his hand to help him stand, but he had another idea. He pulled her gently down to him, grunting in pain as she accidentally pressed on his injuries.

"Your ribs," Marguerite protested, trying to get up, but he wouldn't let her move.

"They are fine," he said, and kissed her briefly. "Are you sure you're with child?"

"I'm sure," she smiled down at him, and he startled her when he rolled her to the floor so that he was lying over her.

He kissed her soundly on the lips, then raised his head to study her eyes. "Are you positive?"

"There is no doubt, whatsoever," she whispered.

He covered her lips with his, muffling something she was trying to say.

"What did you say?" he mumbled.

"I said, Elhrin is still in the room."

"Elhrin is old enough to have the good sense to know when to leave."

Smiling, Elhrin took her cue to go, and closed the door behind her. Spying her satchel hanging on the back of his chair, she hooked the strap with her thumb and slipped it over her shoulder. She decided now was as good a time as any, and Harper's Stream was where she wanted to be. She quietly escaped the cottage and crossed the lawn to the riverbank.

She felt truly free and full of life for the first time since the day Master Gryph was killed by the Green River. They were home, safe for now. She knew her mother resided with Solisius in a magnificent realm and was happy. Master Gryph was on the mend. Marguerite was pregnant, and knowing how much they had both wanted children, she couldn't think of a more appropriate gift.

"You did this, didn't you?" she asked quietly, as she settled on the same rock she had sat on weeks ago. This time there was no snow.

Feeling a small breeze drift along the stream and lightly shift her hair, she heard Solisius' voice. *"No, Gryphon did it, I just made sure he did it right."*

Hearing the humor in his voice, she laughed. The breeze picked up again, caressing her cheeks. *"Elhrin, it's long past time."*

"I know."

"Then I'll leave you to it." With that, she knew he was gone.

She reached into her satchel to pull out the *Book of Tolman* along with a pen and a bottle of ink. Opening the front cover of the book, she dipped her pen in the ink, and scanned the names written inside. She then placed the pen's tip underneath Master Gryph's and scratched her name across the space.

Elhrin Caddoch

ACKNOWLEDGMENTS

I would like to thank all my family and friends who support me not only in my writing endeavors, but through life's journey as a whole—to my laughing buddies, shoulders to cry on, cheerleaders, and spiritual guidance counselors, I send all my love and a huge hug of gratitude.

To Ellen Johnson, for showing me the errors of my ways—without your guidance and honest input, I would still be floundering like a fish out of water. Thank you for kicking me back in the river.

To Laura Capell, I have to say a special thank you for two things you said to me during a selfish bout of whining—there are many brands of one product sitting on the store shelves, and God is coming for you. Yes and yes. Thank you.

To my sister, Cheryl Youngblood, there are not enough words to express how grateful I am that you are in my life. A creative genius, you are, and our talks, thoughts, musings, and plain old far-fetched ideas have helped to stretch my imaginative horizons. One day we are going to sit down and write that comedy we have been dreaming up.

To my parents, Ray and Rachel Youngblood, you two are rock solid, a heart of gold, a true friend—you are home to me, and you are loved beyond measure. Thank you for your unending support and love. You are, by far, the best role models a child could ever be blessed with in a parent.

To the two men in my life, my son and my husband, you guys are my world. Optimistic and funny, you bring a deep and uninhibited love and a flood of joy into our home each and every day, and your dedicated support throughout the years has simply been amazing. I love you both so, so much!

Last, but certainly not least, to my daughter, a young lady wise beyond her years. This journey has taken long, agonizing years to bring into fruition, and throughout it all, you have been by my side. You were my first reader and the one who said the story should be published (even though that had not been the plan at the time), and the one who wanted a sequel (encouraging a weary soul forward). All of the hard work is because of you, and for that I am grateful. However this turns out, whether a single shot fired in the dark or an explosion of goodness, I am a better person for plowing through the process and I owe it all to you—YOU, who lead by example, inspire me. I love you, baby girl, beyond the edges of an infinite and ever growing universe.

ABOUT THE AUTHOR

Laurie Y. Elrod, an artist of varying talents, wallows in creativity every chance she gets. While she does possess a Bachelors Degree in Business and has held a myriad of jobs throughout the years, she is a true believer that one is never too old to start anew and follow a dream. So, stepping out on that ever swaying but sturdy branch of faith, she dove head first into the waters of the writing world and is swimming hard, come what may. A South Carolina native, Laurie is surrounded by her loving husband, two children, two dogs, two goats, a cat, and a horse.